Unplanned
Sarah Biglow

For information contact; www.sarah-biglow.com
Cover Design by Ana Grigoriu

ISBN: 978-1512347517

Originally Published by Musa Publishing: December 2012
2nd Edition Published by Sarah Biglow: June 2015

10 9 8 7 6 5 4 3 2

CONTENTS

In loving memory of Sharon Vassilopoulos (1951-2012)
Auntie, I know you would have been proud

Chapter One

August 7th

SHANNON ATWATER TRAIPSED THROUGH THE FRONT door after her son and daughter, her neck stiff from sun exposure. The stirrings of a headache thrummed at the base of her skull. Giddy shrieks echoed off the walls as Christian kicked off flip-flops and dropped a towel by the door. Meghan followed suit, light brown hair matted to her face as she took off after him.

"Christian, Meghan. You need to change before you get the furniture wet," Shannon called.

Tanner clung to her chest. His small arms wreathed her neck, making it difficult to move as she tried to set down the bag of damp towels. Sandals thudded softly as her youngest reluctantly climbed from her arms. He started to pull his bathing suit down, when she stopped him.

"Here, sweetie. Let Mommy help you."

She led him down the hallway and into a room cluttered with toy cars and action figures. A big bear sat atop a multi-colored racecar blanket. She rooted through drawers and pulled out fresh underwear and shorts. After a few minutes of struggling, he was dressed in clean clothes.

"Can I play now, Mama?"

"Sure. Why don't you bring your toys into the living room?"

He scooped up an armful of figurines and cars and marched after her. She returned to the front hallway and dragged the bag down a flight of stairs to the laundry. Hastily, she dumped the bag's contents into the dryer. She shut the door and gripped the edge as her vision swam. Shannon sucked in a breath as the feeling passed. Part of her wanted to believe she'd just spent too long in the sun. Her neck and back certainly ached from the exposure at the pool. But the headache and nausea weren't new symptoms. She'd had them before. But not in years.

"Don't be ridiculous."

Shannon went back to starting the dryer. She pulled a dryer sheet from the box on the shelf above the washer and tossed it in before setting the time for an hour. Not two seconds after the machine began jostling the contents around, a loud shriek echoed from above. Instinct sparked maternal worry deep in Shannon's gut, and she raced back to the first floor. She rounded into the living room to find Tanner surrounded by his action figures. Megan huddled by the couch, nursing a bruised arm. A car sat at her feet.

"What happened?" Shannon demanded.

"Tanner threw a car at me."

"Did not," Tanner replied, sticking his tongue out.

Before Shannon could respond, Christian's voice echoed from the next room.

"Mom, something's on the computer."

"Not now, Christian."

She bent down to look at Meghan's arm. A spot, bright red and splotchy, marred her skin.

"Run some cold water over it."

"Can I have a Band-Aid, too?" Meghan asked between sniffles.

"Yes."

Meghan got to her feet and glared at her brother before disappearing in the direction of the bathroom. Shannon stood as well and dragged Tanner to his feet. He immediately started screaming.

"You are going to sit in time out for that."

"No, Mama. I don't want to."

"Mom," Christian called again.

The headache continued to thrum in the background, sending shooting pain up and down her neck as Christian's voice reverberated off the walls. Tanner kicked as she picked him up around the middle and hauled him into the dining room. Christian sat at the desk in the corner with a message flashing in green on the computer screen.

"Give me a minute, Chris."

"But I think the computer's broken."

She pulled a chair out at the table on the other side of the room, plopped Tanner down, and set the egg timer for five minutes.

"You're going to sit here until the timer goes off. And then you're going to tell Meghan you're sorry."

Tanner sniffled and rubbed his nose but didn't move. One crisis averted, she turned her attention to Christian.

"What's wrong with the computer?"

"I don't know. I wanted to go online, but this thing keeps blinking." He clicked the flashing screen, and a message popped up.

"Damn." She immediately gave Christian an apologetic look.

"What is it?"

"I have a phone call in—" she checked the time "—two minutes."

"Aw. I can't play a game?"

"Not right now. I need you to watch your brother and sister for me."

Christian pouted but got up from the chair. "Okay."

She gave him a quick kiss on the cheek and watched him wander away. Shannon donned a wireless headset and launched a chat program. The program beeped twice, signaling the connection was strong. With the click of a button, it placed a call to her client.

"Hello?" a voice said from the other end.

"Hi. This is Shannon Atwater."

"Shannon. Thanks for calling. We were hoping for an update on the project."

Shannon clicked through a mess of folders on her desktop to pull up her notes.

"I've been working with your content editor this week to get all the site's information correct. I should be able to have a preliminary design to you by Monday."

"Sounds great. We're actually hoping you could add a few more pages worth of material. We'll send you what we need."

"Of course. But I'll need to run them by the editor before submitting anything."

"Absolutely."

Behind Shannon, the timer dinged, and Tanner jumped out of the chair. She turned to catch him before he could run off.

"You need to apologize to your sister," she reminded him with a stern look.

"Excuse me?" her client asked.

"I'm sorry. I was talking to my son."

"Well, do you have any questions about the timeline we're working with?"

"No, sir. I think having a workable site design by the end of the month should be fine."

"Great. I'll let you get back to work."

"Thanks. Have a great afternoon."

"You, too. Goodbye."

Shannon ended the call and removed her headset. She exhaled slowly, trying to keep calm. It would be so much easier to do her job once Christian and Meghan were back in school and Tanner was spending time at day care. Shannon sifted through a backlog of e-mail messages from clients, sorting them into appropriate folders before shutting down her other programs. She'd worry about work tomorrow.

"Christian, you can play on the computer for an hour."

He raced into the room and opened a game.

"One hour," she repeated.

"Okay, Mom."

Afternoon quickly turned to evening. By the time Shannon's husband, Mike, pulled into the driveway, the kids sat in front of the TV, watching a Disney movie. Chicken baked in the oven, and salad waited on the table.

"How was work, honey?" She kissed him on the cheek once his briefcase was deposited in its usual spot.

"Good. I have a few court dates next week I need to prepare for. How about you? Make your conference call on time?"

"Yeah. Just barely. We got back from the pool a little later than expected."

Meghan nearly bowled Shannon over as she tried to hug her dad around the legs.

"Hey, baby girl," Mike greeted, picking her up and swinging her around.

"Hi, Daddy."

"Did you have a fun day today?"

"Yeah. We went swimming at the pool and had lunch at the park."

"Sounds like a lot of fun."

Behind them, the microwave timer beeped, and Shannon maneuvered around Mike to pull the chicken out of the oven. She set it on the stove and stopped. A wave of nausea hit her, and black spots popped in front of her eyes. Shannon pulled herself together before Mike noticed. He'd ask too many questions or say she was working too hard.

"Honey, can you cut the chicken?"

"Sure."

She walked into the upstairs bathroom and patted a cool cloth on her forehead and neck. Something was off. This wasn't the first time she'd felt uneasy. She took a breath, in and out.

What if she was pregnant? No, that couldn't be right. Could it? She was late by at least a week. That wasn't much, but after three kids, anything was possible. She opened the cabinet and searched until she found the right box. Her hands shook as she pulled out the remaining test and sat down on the toilet, praying it would come up negative. She washed her hands and waited, pacing back and forth.

"Mom, dinner's ready," Christian called from downstairs.

"I'll be right down."

The clock on the wall ticked the seconds by in agonizing slowness. She picked up the test and stared at the small pink plus sign. There was nothing ambiguous about it.

Positive.

Her knees buckled, and she slumped to the floor. She blinked twice, but the tiny plus sign wasn't going anywhere. Tears blurred her vision. A wave of panic lanced through her chest and down to the pit of her stomach. The feeling settled like a rock, and numbness took over. *But we're done having children. Three is all we wanted.* Shannon dried the tears on her cheeks and wrapped the test in a tissue before tossing it in the trash. When she finally got her legs to move past the threshold, she headed down to join her family for dinner.

"Tanner, chew with your mouth closed, please," she chided.

His cheeks puffed out as he closed his mouth and continued to chew. The meal passed quickly enough, and Shannon set Christian to clearing the table.

"Mike, I need to talk to you for a minute."

"What's up, Shan?"

She led Mike into the living room, moving some dolls and action figures off the couch. She toyed with the hem of her blouse, keeping her back turned.

"Shannon? What's going on?"

"I'm pregnant."

"What? You're kidding."

She shook her head. "I wish I was. I've been feeling off lately. I tried to put it off as too much sun, but I was just trying to convince myself it wasn't true. And I'm late."

"That's happened before."

"I'm telling you, I'm pregnant. I just took a test."

Mike leaned back on the arm of the couch and stared at Shannon. She tried to guess what he was thinking—and then realized she didn't want to know. Shannon listened to the kids squabbling in the other room over who was going to get the TV next, and the numb feeling from before returned. Her world tilted on its axis, and all she could do was hold on for dear life.

Chapter Two

August 14th

THE SUN SANK LOW OVER THE SKYLINE AS LISBETH Marquez sat next to her partner, Candace, on the couch.

The light reflected off the tops of buildings, coloring the carpet a vibrant orange. No sound came as the day ended. Candace stretched and stood.

"You want anything while I'm up?"

Lisbeth shook her head. "I'm fine. Thanks."

"You sure? Because you know the doctor said not to move around a lot."

"Candace, I'm okay. We've been through this before."

"If you say so, Lissie. I just want to make sure nothing goes wrong."

"You're cute when you're annoyed," Lisbeth called as Candace disappeared from view.

The TV remote sat within reach of Lisbeth on the table. She picked it up and flipped through channels. Nothing of interest. The sounds from the kitchen drew her focus.

"What are you doing in there?"

"Dishes, silly. And no, you can't help."

"You've been waiting on me for days. I'm not sick."

"Consider yourself lucky."

"Hurry up. I'm getting lonely in here."

Lisbeth smiled as Candace's laughter filled the apartment. Seven years together, four of them married, and Candace still managed to make her smile in all the right ways. Finally, the water turned off, and Candace reappeared, a towel in her hands.

"Let's do something," Lisbeth said.

"Like what?"

"I don't know. Go for a walk or something. I need to get out of here for a while."

"The doctor said—"

"The *doctor* is going to make me crazy."

"Maybe a short walk. We are almost out of milk."

Lisbeth got to her feet and slipped into her shoes. Candace snagged the keys from the hook by the front door, and they left the cool air of their apartment. As they waited for the elevator, Lisbeth checked herself in the small mirror.

"You look beautiful."

"You're just saying that." She tugged on her hair to make it look less frizzy.

"As your wife, it is my duty to comment on your sexy factor."

"Shut up," Lisbeth said and shoved her playfully.

The elevator arrived with a loud *ding!* and interrupted their flirtation. They stepped inside and stayed quiet on the ride down. The summer heat hit them, and sweat accumulated on their skin the instant they stepped outside.

"Who knew it could be this hot so late at night?" Lisbeth linked arms with her wife.

"You've been cooped up in the nice air conditioning," Candace said. They paused at the corner to wait for the walk signal.

"I'm thinking a really short walk."

They wandered up the street to the edge of the Common, and the screech of the T below them punctuated the air. People rushed by on both sides of the sidewalk as they entered the grassy park. A band somewhere down the way, maybe near the pavilion, played loud jazz music. Kids raced around, chasing after each other and the occasional ball or Frisbee.

"It's a gorgeous night," Candace said, squeezing Lisbeth's hand.

"It is," Lisbeth agreed as a beach ball flew in their direction.

Lisbeth caught it and tossed it back to the group of boys who'd been chasing it.

"You sure you don't want me to stay home with you tomorrow?" Candace asked.

"No. I'll be fine. I've got a bunch of movies to keep me company. And there is some laundry that needs to be done."

Candace gave her a concerned look.

"It's a light load."

"I just don't want to mess this up. We've waited so long. And you know we haven't been lucky so far."

Lisbeth glanced at the ground. "I know. And it's our last chance. I promise I won't do anything too stressful."

They exchanged a brief kiss under a low-hanging branch as the music swelled and the band ended their set. It felt like a perfect moment.

"I'm worried," Candace said.

Lisbeth gripped her hand tight. She understood Candace's concern. Their chances were slim, and they'd had more than their share of failed cycles. Her hand moved to her stomach, and a shiver ran the length of her spine. Her chest tightened, and she inhaled shakily, barely able to force air into her lungs.

"I am, too."

"I know I should be thinking positively, but—"

"It's been so rocky to this point, you can't help but assume it's going to fail," Lisbeth finished.

"Exactly."

They sat in silence a moment, and Lisbeth watched the musicians at a distance.

"Come on, let's head back," Candace said, tugging on Lisbeth's arm.

"Not just yet. I want to listen awhile."

They settled on a bench with the band in sight now. The trumpet player waved to the crowd before counting off a four count. The band plunged headlong into an improv number. Lisbeth tapped along to the beat for a while before her head began to droop.

"It's time to get back."

Lisbeth didn't argue. They walked back up the Common and across the street. A few minutes later, the elevator deposited them on the seventh floor.

"I hate that the meds make me so tired." Lisbeth yawned.

"Only a few more days."

"If all goes well, we'll never sleep again." Lisbeth attempted to sound positive.

"Don't say that." Candace batted Lisbeth's shoulder.

Back in the coolness of their apartment, Lisbeth made a beeline to their bedroom and stripped off her sweat-soaked shorts and T-shirt, exchanging them for night clothes.

"You coming to bed?"

"In a little while," Candace answered.

"You know where to find me."

Lisbeth lay atop the covers for a while, letting the air cool her skin. The next thing she knew, the bed shifted beside her, and Candace appeared.

"What time is it?" Lisbeth slurred.

"Around ten."

Lisbeth burrowed beneath the layer of blanket and sheet, snuggling against Candace's shoulder.

"What time are we supposed to get the call tomorrow?" Lisbeth asked.

"Around two or three. Don't worry about it. You'll drive yourself nuts."

"Good thing I've got a masseuse."

"Physical therapist. There's a difference."

"I know that. You still give the best massages in the whole city."

Lisbeth rolled onto her side and felt Candace's hands move over her neck and shoulders. She sighed as the muscles began to relax. The less tense her shoulders became, the more painful her lower back ached. She pulled away.

"What's wrong?"

"The site hurts is all."

One of Candace's hands dislodged from Lisbeth's shoulder and moved to her lower back. The tips of Candace's fingers moved over the sore spot.

"Yeah, right there."

"I can put some ice on it, if you want. It might help."

"Yeah. That might be good."

Their lips touched, and Candace climbed out of bed, returning moments later with an icepack. Lisbeth pressed it against the ache in her lower back and side. She hoped the pain was nerves and not something related to the procedure. They curled side by side until Lisbeth drifted to sleep. The cold on her back eased the discomfort, but she woke with her nightshirt wet.

"Damn," she mumbled, still half asleep.

She pulled the wet cloth from beneath her to reveal a big damp patch on the sheet. Disoriented, Lisbeth fumbled her way to the kitchen. Tossing the cloth in the sink, she stumbled back to her room for a dry shirt. Lisbeth saw a dim reflection of herself in the mirror as she stripped the other material from her body.

Running her hands over the muscles of her smooth, taut belly, she shivered. If they were lucky this time, her body would be in for a change. She glanced over her shoulder at Candace's sleeping form, but instead of climbing back into bed, Lisbeth grabbed a blanket from the linen closet and headed for the couch.

"SWEETIE, ARE YOU OKAY?" CANDACE'S VOICE SOUNDED miles away as Lisbeth awoke.

"You're out on the couch," Candace said.

Lisbeth sat up and rubbed at her face.

"I know that. I didn't sleepwalk out here."

"Then what are you doing out here?"

"The ice melted, and the sheet got wet."

"Oh."

Lisbeth ran a hand through Candace's hair, so silky and different from her own. Candace sat down beside her and squeezed her hand.

"Now, you're absolutely sure you don't want me here with you?"

"I'm sure, Mom."

"Because I can do a half day."

"You have people to see. Besides, one of us needs to work if we have any hope of paying the bills. Even if this doesn't work."

Candace held up her hands up in defeat. "Okay, you win. And try to stay positive."

Lisbeth threw aside the blanket and stood up. She wandered into the kitchen and set the coffee to percolate.

"You aren't supposed to have coffee," Candace reminded her.

"And you're unbearable without your daily dose."

They moved around each other as if they'd been doing it all their lives. Arms and hands crossed without a falter. The toaster popped, sending a bagel flying across the room before Candace caught it. She set it on the table with a glass of juice. Lisbeth joined her with a plate of eggs, bacon, and a cup of coffee. They swapped seats and enjoyed a quiet breakfast together.

"How many patients do you have today?" Lisbeth asked around a bite of bagel.

"I think four. And maybe a few referrals when I get in."

"Sounds good. I might go for a walk down by the Common. Read a book in the shade for a bit to get out."

"Sounds like a good plan. Getting some fresh air is never a bad thing."

Candace downed her coffee and set the dishes in the sink. She grabbed a briefcase from a nearby chair and kissed Lisbeth goodbye.

"I'll see you tonight."

"Do you want me to call when I hear?"

"Surprise me when I get home."

"Your self-control is overwhelming."

"Have a good day."

With that, she left Lisbeth to finish her bagel and juice. Lisbeth sat at the table, listening to the quiet of the apartment. She looked at the DVR clock—six hours at least before she got any news. Plenty of time to do a few loads of laundry and get out for some exercise. No going stir crazy with anticipation. She finished her meal and did the dishes, setting them out to dry. Stretching her arms behind her back, she went in search of a book. She walked past the second bedroom and stopped.

It was mostly empty, save an antique rocking chair by the window. She walked in and sat in the chair, tucking her legs beneath her. Lisbeth leaned back and let the gentle rocking soothe her nerves. She could picture the items that would fill the room if they were successful.

Subconsciously, her hands drifted to her lap. She'd waited so long for this. Sure, there were other options open to them, but it wouldn't be the same. As the possibilities filled her thoughts and images danced in her head, sadness invaded her heart, constricting her lungs. She fought for breath until the feeling passed.

"Get up and do something, Lissie."

A moment later, she dragged herself to her feet and continued her search for a book. She finally found one with a bookmark a third of the way through sitting on Candace's nightstand.

Down on the Common, she found a shady place to sit. The Starbucks across the street called to her. It begged her to go in and get a venti-iced coffee. Lisbeth shook her head and turned her back. *No coffee today.* She tried to focus on the book, but the people around her were distracting. An older couple wandered out of the outbound Boylston stop and toward the grass. A couple of college-age kids loitered just outside the inbound stop. She loved Boston, being right in the thick of it. She could be herself in the city.

A half hour later, she got to her feet, legs stiff from sitting cross-legged for too long, and headed back inside. She relished the cold air as she made a frozen meal. Candace would have scolded her for all the processed fats, but she wanted the little bit of comfort the junk food afforded her. Tossing the fork in the sink and the carton in the trash, Lisbeth gathered up a load of dirty clothes and headed down the hall to the laundry room. She got there just as one of the other tenants moved his load to the dryer.

"Washer's all yours," he said as she dumped her clothes on top of the machine.

"Thanks."

By the time she got back from swapping the load into the dryer, her phone buzzed. It skidded along the coffee table toward the edge before she caught it. Her fingers fumbled as she tried to answer the call. Her nerves were back in full force. Finally, on the sixth ring, she managed to hit talk.

"Hello?"

"Miss Marquez?"

"Yes."

"This is Maureen from New England Medical."

"Hi." Lisbeth immediately began to pace.

"We have your results."

"And? What do they say? Did it work?" Her heart thumped against her ribs as an inkling of hope bubbled to the surface.

"You're pregnant."

Lisbeth let out a whoop of excitement. "Thank you, so much. You have no idea how long we've been waiting for this."

"Congratulations. We need to set up your next appointment."

Lisbeth waited while they set up her next check-up, ended the call, and fell onto the couch with the phone clutched to her chest. Another yelp escaped before she could stop herself. She was having a baby. *They* were having a baby.

Her good mood faltered a moment later. They'd had one good round before, but it had ended in miscarriage.

The next three and a half hours were torture as she waited for Candace to get home. To help them celebrate, she'd gone to the store and picked up a champagne substitute, even if it was still cautious optimism. At six fifteen, she greeted Candace with champagne flutes.

"We're going to be mothers!"

Candace's smile turned into a Cheshire-Cat-sized grin, and they exchanged fevered kisses before Lisbeth shoved the glass into Candace's hands.

"You shouldn't be drinking."

"It's sparkling cider."

"You think of everything, don't you?"

"Today, yes."

They toasted their good fortune and ended up curled together in the rocking chair in what would become the nursery.

"I still can't believe it worked," Lisbeth said.

"I think there's someone watching over us. But we just have to be careful."

Lisbeth nodded. "I know. I'm terrified, but I've got you, so whatever happens, we're going through it together."

Chapter Three

August 18th

RENEE BLACKWELL WALKED OUT OF THE EMPLOYEE bathroom. The aquarium swarmed with tourists and families trying to get a last visit in for the summer. She checked the time and headed for the entrance, where one of the tours awaited her. A small group of girls dressed in brown met her just beyond the ticket takers. *Girl Scouts. Cute.*

"Hi, everyone."

"Hi," a chorus of voices replied.

"Has anyone been to the aquarium before?"

Standard question to ask a new group. Inevitably, someone's always been before. One little girl in the back with bushy blonde hair raised her hand.

"It's pretty cool, right?" Renee asked, flashing a smile.

"Yeah."

"Well, it may look a little different right now because we're doing some construction. But how about we get started?"

She led them into the air-conditioned interior of the aquarium, taking them by the empty penguin tank. The girls stopped briefly to peer at the bluish water and sparse rocks.

"Where are the penguins?" the blonde asked.

"Well, right now, the aquarium is making changes to some of the habitats, and we had to move the penguins so we didn't disturb them. But when we go outside, we can see blue penguins all the way from Australia."

The promise of exotic birds urged them onward around to the Tropical Gallery. They stopped and crowded around the Dangerous Species exhibits.

"You wouldn't want to meet these guys out in the ocean."

Gasps and squeals bubbled over as a pair of lionfish darted among the coral, peering at the group before disappearing again.

They marched up the ramp, gawking at the Giant Ocean Dive Tank. Myrtle, the aquarium's resident sea turtle, lounged just beneath a rock.

"Anybody know how long Myrtle has been at The New England Aquarium?"

Blank expressions waited for her to answer her own question.

"She's been here since 1970. I bet some of your parents remember seeing her when they were your age."

The troop leaders smiled amongst themselves. Apparently, they could relate. The ramp up to the next level continued, and they paused to get different views of the tank, pointing as enormous fish swam along. Just as they rounded to the back half of the second level, she spotted one of their largest stingrays.

"Hey, everyone, take a look down there."

"Oh wow."

"How does it swim like that?" one of the girls asked.

"See how it ripples along the edges. It uses its body like fins."

"Can we touch one?"

"When we get to the touch tank upstairs."

Next on the agenda...the sea dragons. Before coming to work here, she'd never seen any. One of the critters popped into view, earning excited *oohs* from the tour.

"What are they?"

"They're called sea dragons. There are only two types in the world, and we are lucky enough to have both of them. See if you can spot them in there. They like to hide to keep from getting eaten."

"Is it like a seahorse?" the blonde said.

"Sort of. They definitely look like they are related."

Once satisfied they'd spotted as many dragons as possible, they rounded the last ramp up to the Edge of the Sea exhibit. The touch tank covered the length of the back wall, and three or four of her colleagues stood ready to instruct the kids on how to properly interact with the animals on display.

"How come there aren't any big starfish?" one girl asked as she peered down at a couple of tiny stars lounging in the left-most part of the tank.

"Starfish are really sensitive. So we keep them in the glass tanks. You can look, but touching them will hurt them, okay?"

The Scouts spread out along the tank, petting horseshoe crabs and hermit crabs. Renee waited near the next exhibit, glad to let her co-workers handle the group for a little while.

"Can I touch that?" a shy brunette asked, pointing at the stingray.

"Sure. Just don't touch the tail. It might sting you."

The girl paled and started to pull her hand back. Renee gave her a reassuring smile.

"It's okay. It won't hurt you if you're gentle. Here, watch."

She stuck her hand into the tank and ran her fingers along the stingray's back.

"I think it likes it," the girl said.

"Now you try, Kelly." One of the leaders nudged the girl onward.

Kelly inched over the artificial habitat and touched the stingray.

"Everyone had their turn? Make sure you wash your hands before we move on."

One by one, the girls washed their hands. When everyone stood waiting for her to lead on, she ushered them back down to the first level and outside to the larger pens. Hanging a quick right, they squeezed into the blue penguin exhibit. Ten noses pressed against the glass as penguins waddled with cautious steps down the padded ramp to the sand pit below. Several birds paddled in the shallow pool. The heat coming in through the windows hit Renee hard as they rounded the fur seal and sea lion enclosure. She was probably coming down with something. She tried to shake off the feeling as the girls watched the sea lions stretch out on one of the platforms. As the rank smell of dead fish assaulted her senses, she faltered. By now, she was used to the smell, but it overwhelmed her today. Come to think of it, smells had been bothering her a lot.

"Can we pet those?" one of the girls asked.

Her friends giggled at her question.

"Not today." She checked her watch. "But we're just in time for the Fur Seal Training Session."

Scurrying to get front row seats, the girls took off without their chaperones. One of the leaders touched Renee on the shoulder.

"Are you all right? You look a little pale."

"I'm fine. Just spending too much time inside. The heat gets to you."

"The girls really love this. They're earning their marine life badge."

"That's great. I was a Scout when I was little. I think I made it a few years past them before I stopped."

"We're hoping our girls go all the way."

Renee settled in for the show. Half an hour later, they made their way to the gift shop.

"I hope everyone had a good time. You can look through the gift shop before you go. There are free brochures and post cards along that wall, so help yourselves."

"Thank you," the girls said in unison.

She waved goodbye to the group and checked her watch. Time to clock out and hit the T. If she didn't leave now, she'd be late for her appointment.

The ride seemed to take forever. The blue line was quick enough, but her transfer to the green line took entirely too long. It didn't help that Government Center was extra crowded. By the time she hopped the red line at Park Street, she had ten minutes to make her appointment. A mass exodus erupted from the train as people disembarked. Thankfully, few people got on, and she snagged a seat. She glanced up at the map of the red line. One more stop, and she'd be there.

"Come on."

The train screeched around a corner and finally came to a halt at the Charles/MGH stop. She leapt to the platform and nearly bowled over an older gentleman trying to get on.

"Sorry," she called over her shoulder as she raced through the exit and up to street level. Slowing her pace, she walked into the hospital and checked in with the clinic. Not two minutes later, a nurse appeared.

"Renee Blackwell."

Renee stood up and followed the woman into an exam room. Renee sat down in a chair and waited for the nurse to say something.

"So, Renee, what's been bothering you?"

"I've been feeling dizzy lately. Like when I go outside. I thought I was spending too much time inside at work, but I don't know if that's it. And smells have been really weird."

"Weird how?"

"Overpowering. I was at work earlier, and smells that don't normally bother me nearly made me vomit."

"Any other symptoms? Aches and pains?"

"General headache."

"Okay. Well, I'm going to run some tests, okay?"

"Sure."

The nurse took vital signs and shined a light in Renee's eyes. It didn't help the headache, but she tried not to complain. Not if it meant making her better. The nurse disappeared and returned with a cup. Renee gave a shy smile but took it and followed the woman down the hall to the bathroom.

"You can leave that in here when you're done," the nurse instructed.

"Okay."

The door shut, and Renee exhaled and glanced from the cup to the toilet and back again. No sense in putting it off, even if it made her feel uncomfortable. A frustrating ten minutes later, she returned to the exam room. Lacing her fingers together, she waited for the nurse to return. She didn't know how fast they could get results, but she hoped she could walk out with a prescription today.

A knock on the door caught her attention. She looked up as a man with thinning gray hair walked in. He gave Renee a calming look and took a seat in the vacant chair.

"Renee?"

"Yes."

"Hi, I'm Dr. Fillmore."

She gave him a nod.

"How are you doing?"

"Um...not great."

"Well, hopefully we've got some good news for you."

"The tests are done already?"

Dr. Fillmore nodded and leaned back in the chair. She watched him watch her, and the tiny hairs on the back of her neck prickled. *What's wrong with me?* Horrible scenarios raced through her mind as she waited for the doctor to explain her condition.

"You said you've been feeling generally dizzy the last few weeks? And smells have been bothering you?"

"Yeah. I already told the nurse that."

"With headaches and nausea?"

"Yes. What the hell's wrong with me?"

"There's nothing wrong with you. You aren't sick."

"That's ridiculous. Your tests are wrong."

Dr. Fillmore held up a hand to silence her. Renee bit the inside of her lip and hoped the nervous butterflies didn't overtake her.

"Our preliminary tests indicate you're pregnant."

It wasn't entirely out of the realm of possibility, but it had to be something else. She wasn't ready to have a baby.

"Are you sure? I mean, it's a preliminary test, right?"

"Yes, it's preliminary, but it's conclusive. From what you've been describing, it sounds like you're still early in the first trimester."

Renee sank in her seat. She could feel the color drain from her face as his words took hold in her head. She was pregnant. No question about it. All of her fears of horrible symptoms and diseases were replaced by a cascade of other worries.

"Renee?" Dr. Fillmore's voice sounded miles away.

"Huh?"

"I asked if you'd like me to refer you to an obstetrician."

"No...I have my own...I'm really pregnant?"

"I'd recommend getting blood work done to determine how far along you are."

"Okay. Uh, thanks for everything. I pay out front, right?"

Dr. Fillmore stood and offered his hand. She took it and allowed him to pull her to her feet. He seemed nice enough and escorted her out to the waiting area. She paid for the visit and walked out into the sweltering, summer afternoon heat. Luckily, the sun had begun to set. Renee wandered the streets outside the T stop to clear her head before she started home. Unfortunately, her phone interrupted alone time. Groaning at the display, she let it ring twice more before mustering up the courage to answer it.

"Hey."

"Hey, babe," a male voice responded.

"What's up?" Renee asked, moving out of the flow of pedestrians heading for the T.

"Nothing. Just getting ready for work. Where are you?"

"Uh…just heading to the T. I should be home soon."

"Okay. I'm heading out in probably forty minutes, so I'll catch you before I leave."

"All right. I love you. Bye."

Renee ended the call and willed away the urge to vomit. A part of her—a pretty big part, in fact—hoped her path didn't cross with Bryce's tonight. She wasn't ready to dump this on him. Still, she knew it was the mature thing to do. So, pulling her Charlie Card from her purse, she bounded down the stairs and hopped the red line to Braintree.

Stepping off the train at Park Street, she bounded upstairs to the green line platform. There, she scanned the trains pulling in to the station: Cleveland Circle and Heath Street. She'd have to wait. Renee rested against one the supports on the platform as more people funneled up from the red line. Just as the mass of people started to make her feel overwhelmed and claustrophobic, a train approached heading to Riverside. It stopped, and she climbed aboard, counting the stops in her head as it left the center of the city.

"I'm home," she called as she walked through the front door of their apartment some twenty minutes later.

Footsteps echoed in the kitchen, and Bryce appeared. He was dressed in a red jacket and black pants—standard valet fare.

"Hey."

They shared a brief kiss before Renee headed for the fridge. She pulled out a bottle of water and downed half in one gulp. Maybe not the best idea, given how easily her stomach did somersaults these days.

"Whoah, take it easy, Nee."

"Sorry. It's hot out there. I was thirsty."

The less she had to talk right now, the better. She wouldn't spill the beans about her doctor's visit that way. She only hoped he hadn't seen the note on the calendar. He glanced in the direction of the calendar, and she winced.

"You had a doctor's appointment today?"

Busted.

"Yeah. I've been feeling a little off the last few days. Thought maybe I was coming down with a cold or something. Kids get germs everywhere at the aquarium."

"What'd they say?"

Renee twisted the bottle cap between her fingers and searched for something, anything, to deflect his question. The time flashed at her from the microwave.

"Aren't you going to be late for work?"

Bryce shrugged and wrapped her in his arms.

"I can be a little late."

Damn him.

"They did some tests."

"Okay. Well, do you need me to pick up anything?"

"That's sweet, honey. No. I'll be okay. Now get going."

She swatted him on the butt and watched him grab his keys and leave. Slumping against the sink, she sighed with relief at barely avoiding that disaster. Renee set about making some dinner and watching the news. Nothing really kept her attention. Her thoughts constantly drifted to Dr. Fillmore's words. *You're pregnant.*

The reality was setting in fast, and she couldn't keep it to herself. She grabbed the phone and dialed her mother's number.

"Hello?"

"Max? What are you doing at Mom and Dad's place?" she asked her younger brother.

"They invited me and a couple of friends for dinner. Not going to pass up Mom's cooking."

"Is Mom there?"

"Yeah. You want me to put her on?"

Renee exhaled in annoyance. "No. I was just asking for the hell of it. Yeah, I want you to put her on."

"Don't have to get all bitchy with me."

She could hear footsteps on the other end as her brother went in search of their mom. Moments later, the sound of the phone changing hands filled Renee's ear.

"Hi, sweetheart."

"Hi, Mom. Do you have a minute to talk?"

"I just served dinner. Can I call you back in a little while?"

"It kind of can't wait."

"Of course. What's up?"

"I went to the doctor today. I'm pregnant."

Silence on the other end lasted an interminable time.

"Mom?"

"Yeah. I'm still here. Are you sure?"

"They did a test and everything."

"This is...unexpected."

"No kidding."

"Have you told Bryce?"

"No. I'm kind of scared to tell him."

"You should tell him right away. Don't wait."

"He's already at work. I...I just don't know what to do, Mom."

"You need to make an appointment with your obstetrician and go for an exam."

Renee bit the inside of her cheek to keep calm. "Okay. I can do that."

"Do you need me to come over, Renee?"

Renee weighed the options. She could use someone to stay with her for a few hours. It would save her from going stir crazy.

"Yes, please." She couldn't keep the signs of an imminent breakdown out of her voice.

"I'll be right over."

"Thanks, Mom."

They ended the call, and Renee rested her head against the couch. She had to keep it together long enough for her mom to arrive. She got to her feet and began pacing until she heard a sharp knock on the front door. She crossed the length of the apartment in three big strides and yanked open the door. Her mother stood opposite her, and Renee couldn't help but fall into her mom's arms. They ended up on the couch, curled up with a tub of ice cream between them. The best treatment for a bad day, ever.

"Did they say how far you are?" her mom asked and ran a hand through Renee's hair.

"They weren't sure but thought maybe six or seven weeks."

"You didn't notice you'd missed your period?"

"I had some spotting. I thought it was just light. God, Mom, what am I going to do?"

"That's your choice."

"I've always wanted to have kids. But...I'm not sure I'm ready now."

"You won't be in it alone. Your father and I will support you, whatever you decide to do."

"Thanks. Sorry I pulled you away from dinner."

"My baby girl needed me."

Renee gave a watery smile and yawned.

"Come on, sweetie. Let's get you into bed."

Renee didn't argue as her mother ushered her into the bedroom. Renee stripped down to her bra and underwear and crawled beneath the covers. Exhausted from all the stress and the crying, she didn't have the energy to put on night clothes.

"You want me to stay the night, Nee?" her mother asked as she perched on the edge of the bed.

"No. I'll be okay. Thanks for coming over."

"All right. You really should tell Bryce in the morning, honey."

"I will."

Renee curled up and let exhaustion take over. She didn't hear her mother leave the apartment or Bryce return at his usual time of half past two. She was only conscious of his return as the bed shifted beside her and he pressed his lips to her shoulder. Despite the heat, Renee curled up against his chest, wishing it was all just a dream. His arms wrapped tight around her stomach, and she was safe. Too bad the crushing weight of reality filled her dreams.

Chapter Four

August 21st

ERIKA LIND LAY IN BED, CHEST HEAVING FROM THE exertion while some guy she didn't quite know sighed beside her. Somewhere in the distance, music pounded, and the walls vibrated with the bass. The voices of the people beyond the bedroom were low in comparison to the booming of the rest of the surroundings.

"That was amazing," he said and kissed her shoulder.

She looked at him, his face fuzzy from her stupor.

"Yeah. Great."

She could make out a half-smile painted on his lips.

"What?" she asked.

"We could...go again."

She rolled over, and her head throbbed along with the bass in a very uncomfortable rhythm. All she wanted was for the sound to stop and to be left in peace. She needed the quiet, or she was going to explode.

"Erika?"

She moaned and stumbled out of bed. As best she could, she pulled on her skirt and top and threw herself into the din of the party beyond the bedroom. Maybe she could get people to leave early. Erika searched faces, looking for anyone remotely familiar. She finally found one. Dane. He leaned against the stereo system, a plastic cup in his hand.

"Hey, Erika. Great party."

"Make them go, please," she begged, latching on to his shoulder before she tripped over open air.

"Babe, you okay?"

"I'm just tired. I need to sleep. Can't sleep with everyone yelling."

"But it's only two o'clock."

"Please?"

"Okay, okay." He set his drink down and cut the music. "Everybody, party's over. Get gone."

Loud protests filled the room, and it was all Erika could do to block it out. She let Dane lead her to the couch and sank onto the soft cushions. What would she do without him? She had no idea how long it took to get everyone to clear out, but the next time she looked around, Dane sat on the table across from her.

"They gone now?"

"Yeah."

The bedroom opened and closed, and the guy sheepishly walked out. "She okay?"

"She's fine. Party's over. Get out."

"Okay. Jeez, don't have to be an ass about it. I had a great time, Erika."

"Bye." The one word response squeaked out. It was all she could manage.

She thought she saw Dane give the guy a withering look but everything tilted, and she curled into herself.

"You want to go to bed, babe?"

Erika shook her head. "Couch is comfy."

"Well, scoot over."

She curled up against the couch and let Dane snuggle with her, relishing his muscles and beer-scented body. Sometime later, a loud beeping filled Erika's ears. It roused her from sleep, and she stumbled off the couch in search of the noise to shut it off. The source was the alarm in her room. Seven thirty in the morning. Groaning, Erika made her way to the bathroom. She couldn't show up at work looking like crap.

The water felt amazing as it peppered her neck and shoulders. The steam wrapped its tendrils around every inch of her body until she could at least see straight. By the time she dried off and stepped out of the bathroom, Dane was sitting up on the couch.

"You're up early."

"I have work."

"You need me to drive you?"

"No. I'll catch the T."

Dane shrugged and followed her into her bedroom. She didn't bother shutting the door—he'd seen her naked plenty of times. Even if it was in the distant past. She ran a comb through her hair and donned make up. She was an expert at covering up dark circles. A couple of drops, and the redness in her eyes disappeared.

"That really was a good party last night," he said.

"Thanks."

He walked up and wrapped his arms around her waist. Always the flirt. Too bad they were over. He ran a finger down her right arm, landing on the yin yang inked on her wrist.

"You remember when you got this?"

"Eighteenth birthday. You were trashed," she said.

"So were you."

"I was not."

"Oh, come on. Admit it."

"I was a little buzzed. And besides, it wasn't like the tattoo guy even cared."

"I miss college," Dane said with a laugh.

"You could always go back."

She pushed away from the mirror and made a beeline for the kitchen with only enough time to butter some toast and run to the T before being late for work. *Again.*

"Call me if you want to hang later or something," Dane said as he walked her out of the building.

"Sure. Later."

She munched her toast as she crossed the street and ducked through the turnstile at Brookline Hills. She waited with the mass of other people on the platform for the train to arrive. She looked at all the men and women dressed in suits with briefcases. She couldn't help but laugh a little. What a bunch of uptight people. Some five minutes later, a train heading to Government Center arrived, and she climbed on, managing to snag a seat. After all, it was a good half hour to Park Street.

The rumbling of the train echoed the rumbling in her stomach as she digested the toast. At least she had food in her. By the time she stepped off the train at Park Street and walked up to street level, the sun was already beating down. She brushed sweat from her neck and walked the two blocks to the temp agency. It wasn't real work. Not like all the people with "real" degrees had. But it worked for her.

"Morning, Erika," her boss said the minute she walked in.

"Hi, Maggie."

"You're late."

Erika followed the woman back to her desk. A list of phone calls awaited her. Just what she wanted to do with a raging headache. She sat down and forced a smile.

"Have fun," Maggie said before disappearing around a corner.

"Yeah, lots of fun," Erika said under her breath before picking up the phone and dialing the first number on the list. She really hated being the one who had to do to follow-up on all the temp employees who got fired.

By lunchtime, she'd called back everyone on her list and spent a good forty minutes being berated by some woman who kept insisting Erika had the wrong number. Her arm tingled with pins and needles as feeling surged through when she finally changed position. She took a trip to a nearby Mexican place and ordered a burrito. Steak with extra sour cream and guacamole. She paid and went to eat out by the Common. Swallowing the first bite, she had to fight off the urge to vomit. Maybe this hadn't been the best food choice after a night of partying, but Erika forced it down and returned to her cubicle to make more calls. That lasted maybe five minutes before she found herself hugging a toilet in the women's bathroom. Everything came up. And the sight made her dry heave.

"Erika?" Maggie called outside the stall.

Erika continued to dry heave. Tasting tears as she got to her feet and flushed the toilet, she stepped from the stall and reached for a paper towel.

"Are you okay?"

"Bad burrito."

"You sure that was all it was?"

"I'm not sick or anything."

"You haven't been looking a hundred percent for a few days now. You can have the rest of the day off if you need to see a doctor."

"Thanks. But I'm fine. Really. The burrito just didn't agree with me."

"Take the rest of the day off anyway."

Erika opened her mouth to protest, but Maggie gave her a look that said they were done talking. So, she grabbed her purse and headed back to Brookline. A few hours of sleep might make her feel better. It would do wonders for her hangover at least.

She made it back to her apartment before she started vomiting again. It was less violent the second time but just as unpleasant. She crawled to the couch and wrapped up in a blanket with a bottle of water. If she didn't move, maybe she wouldn't get sick again. The water stayed down, and she finally felt well enough to heat some mac and cheese.

As she spooned the cheesy pasta into her mouth, she thought about Maggie's assertion that she hadn't looked well the last few days. She hadn't done anything different than she'd been doing since graduating from college. Or during college for that matter.

"I'm not sick." She tossed the empty container in the trash.

Afternoon became evening as Erika dozed on the couch. She awoke to the sound of a knock at the door. She stumbled to her feet and pulled the door open. Her landlord stood on the other side of the threshold.

"Is something wrong, Mr. Sanger?"

"I got complaints of loud music again, Erika. I'm not going to warn you again. Another complaint, and we're going to have some serious problems."

Erika just nodded and gripped the doorframe. The world began to spin.

"Did you hear me?"

"Yeah. I uh...I have to go. I promise, no more loud parties, Mr. Sanger."

She slammed the door and dove for the bathroom. This time, it was mostly dry heaving. She thought about calling Dane but knew he'd just baby her. And she had to stop turning to him every time things got rough. Sure, they were friends, but he still wanted to be more. And she had moved on. So she sat slumped against the bathroom wall and fell asleep.

She woke the next morning in a cold sweat. Erika opened one eyelid, then the other, and looked around. Even sitting down, her head throbbed with pain. Maybe Maggie was right. Maybe she *was* sick. Dragging herself to her feet, she made her way to the bedroom for a change of clothes. Donning sunglasses and a sweatshirt, she left her apartment and headed in search of a doctor.

There was a free clinic a few blocks over, but the walk was excruciating. Everything seemed too bright, too loud and even normal voices made her head scream with pain. The usual odors of the city seemed magnified a hundredfold. Weaving through people on the sidewalk as fast as she could, her stomach gurgled with a new bout of nausea. She gritted her teeth and willed the feeling to go away. Only one more block, and she'd be at the clinic.

"Watch it!" a man yelled at her as she narrowly avoided stumbling into him.

She ignored him, all of her energy focused on one task. One foot in front of the other. *Almost there,* she reminded herself. She walked into the clinic and sucked in a breath of cool air. It helped quell her shaky nerves.

"Can I help you?" the receptionist asked.

"I need to see a doctor."

The receptionist nodded and handed over a form.

"Just fill this out, and someone will see you."

Erika slid into a chair and stared at the form. Words swam, and she blinked a few times before she could read properly. Definitely too much partying. She wrote her name on the top of the form and proceeded to complete the rest of it quickly.

"That was quick," the receptionist said.

Erika shrugged and sank back into her seat. She stared around the waiting room with its bright overhead lights and beige wallpaper. Mercifully, Erika was one of only a few people in the room. A woman with two loud children sat a few seats away. The boy kept shoving the girl to the floor when she tried to stand up. Despite her churning stomach, Erika hoped they would be called soon. She dozed off and jolted awake when someone shook her arm.

"Huh?"

"Are you Erika?" A man in a white coat stood over her with a concerned expression.

Erika nodded and wiped the drool from the side of her mouth.

"Why don't you follow me?"

Erika got up and walked as fast as her legs would carry her out of the waiting area. They stopped at a door marked with a gold foil 5.

"Have a seat in there, and I'll be right in."

Erika pushed the door open. A sterile room with some chairs and a less-than-stellar-looking exam table greeted her. She felt her gag reflex kick in. Panicking, she looked around the room until she spotted a trashcan in the corner. It would have to do. She was hunkered over the basket when the doctor walked in. Erika couldn't look at him. Cheeks flushed with embarrassment, she batted away the tears with the back of her hand.

He remained quiet as he sat beside her and rubbed her back.

"How long have you been sick to your stomach?"

Erika reached for a paper towel, and he handed her several and a small cup of water. She wiped her cheeks and rinsed out her mouth before she dragged herself into the chair opposite him.

"Since lunch yesterday. I ate a bad burrito."

The doctor nodded and felt her forehead and checked her pulse. By the time he sat down again, she felt a little better.

"Do you have any other symptoms?"

"Uh...a headache. Everything is too bright and loud."

"Well, it sounds like you have a hangover."

"No shit."

"I take it this isn't your first time."

"It's never been this bad, ever. I think I got food poisoning from that damn burrito."

"You're sure it can't be anything else?"

"Like what?"

He cleared his throat and smoothed the edges of his coat. It made Erika anxious. What was he getting at?

"I need to ask you a couple of questions. They may make you uncomfortable, but I need you to answer them honestly, okay?"

"Yeah. Sure."

"When was the last time you had your period?"

"Like a month ago. I'm a few days late. But it's been kind of stressful with work and stuff. I have to work two jobs."

"Have you been sexually active in the last month?"

She stared at him. How was that his business? "Yeah."

"Is it possible that you're pregnant?"

"No. I'm not stupid. I'd know, and I'm definitely not."

"With your permission, I'd like to do a pregnancy test anyway. Just to be sure."

"Like...draw blood and stuff?"

"No, nothing intrusive. Just a urine test. Would that be all right?"

Erika fidgeted in the chair. "I guess. But...it could be food poisoning, right?"

"We'll check for everything."

She nodded and watched him walk out of the room. A shiver danced up her spine, as if the air temperature had suddenly dropped ten degrees. He returned minutes later, followed by a nurse.

"Nicolette will show you to the bathroom."

"Okay."

Erika followed the girl down the hallway. As she passed by the other exam rooms, she heard children crying and wondered if they were the same ones from the waiting room.

"Just leave it in here when you're done."

Erika took her time. She stared at herself in the small mirror above the sink for a few minutes. Bloodshot eyes. Pale skin. She looked like crap and somehow didn't care. The little cup sat on the counter next to her, taunting her. She snapped it up and settled onto the toilet. Nothing happened. Her fingers shook, trying to hold the cup steady, but still she couldn't fill it. The back of her neck burned with frustration until finally a tiny stream tinkled into the damn cup. *It won't come back positive. It can't.*

"It's food poisoning, isn't it?" Erika asked when the doctor returned, looking grim.

"No. The test came back positive. Erika, you're pregnant."

She shook her head vigorously. She didn't want to hear it. It couldn't be true. He stepped closer and put his hand on her shoulder.

"The burrito may not have sat well with you. Many women find meat disagrees with them during pregnancy."

"But...it's not..." Thoughts jumbled together in her head, and Erika couldn't think. She couldn't be pregnant. She just couldn't.

"Do you need someone to pick you up? I can have Nicolette call someone."

"No. I'll walk."

"I suggest you see an obstetrician in the next few days just to confirm." He handed her a slip of paper. "I've written down some prenatal vitamins you should take."

She took the paper without looking at it.

Panic rapidly replaced disbelief as she left the clinic. The world moved by in slow motion as she walked the three blocks home. She walked into her apartment and collapsed on the couch. Tears soaked the blanket she pulled around her shoulders. Time faded away as she cried every last tear she had in her, and fear froze her in place.

She knew in the back of her mind she needed to call her waitressing job and tell them she wasn't going in tonight, but she couldn't make her arms reach the table to pick up the phone. Eventually, sleep overtook her.

Sometime later, her phone rang loudly, jolting her from sleep. She stared at it. Dane's number flashed on the screen. She hit the ignore button and buried her head under the blanket. Nothing was going to pry her away from her cocoon on the couch. Not tonight.

Chapter Five

SHANNON SAT CURLED UP ON THE COUCH WITH A crossword puzzle propped against her knees while the kids entertained themselves. The relative quiet of the house soothed her nerves as she tried to pay attention to the words on the page in front of her. But she'd re-read the same clue for the fifth time without really reading it. She set it aside.

"Mama, I'm hungry," Tanner said from his position on the floor.

"It's a little early for lunch, sweetie. Can you wait a little while?"

He picked up a dump truck, flipped the bed up and down a few times, and nodded. "Okay."

She gave him a smile and settled against the arm of the couch to watch him play. She would miss him while he was at daycare. Her cell phone buzzed on the table, and she picked it up without looking at the screen.

"Hello?"

"Hi, honey."

"Mike, I thought you were in court today."

"The other side filed for a continuance. Anyway, I've been thinking. I think it's time we told the kids."

She stepped around Tanner and walked into the hallway, away from curious ears.

"Are you sure? I mean I'm not showing yet. We could wait until then. I like it just between us."

"Shannon, come on. It's going to be fine."

She forced a smile, even though he couldn't see it, and said, "Okay."

"I was thinking of coming home for lunch, but don't tell the kids. I want it to be a surprise."

"Okay. I'll talk to you later."

A short while later, she stood over five sizzling grilled cheese sandwiches as the kids occupied themselves with a movie. Shannon tightened her grip on the spatula as Mike entered the front door moments later.

"Hi. How are you feeling?"

"I'm fine," Shannon said and stepped away from the stove to give him a kiss on the cheek.

"Where are the kids?"

"Living room. Watching Nemo."

"Meghan's favorite."

"I'm just happy they're all getting along." She flipped the sandwiches and transferred them to plates.

"I'll let them know lunch is ready," Mike said and disappeared.

Shannon set the five plates on the table and waited the thirty seconds for the kids to thunder in. Grilled cheese always won them over. On cue, Tanner skidded to a stop in front of his chair.

"Grill cheese!" He clambered into his seat. His siblings arrived moments later.

"How come Daddy is home?" Christian asked as he sat down at his place.

"Because Daddy wanted Mommy's grilled cheese, too," Mike answered.

Shannon joined her family and watched them dig into the greasy meal. She ate her sandwich slowly, savoring each bite. Luckily, the last few weeks had been light on morning sickness. Despite going to the doctor to confirm the news, the emotional numbness and cut-off feeling continued to surface.

"Mommy makes the best grilled cheese," Meghan said, peeling off the crust of her sandwich.

"Thank you, Meg."

Shannon glanced at her husband a few times and finally caught his eye. Brushing the crumbs from his hands, he cleared his throat.

"Guys, Mommy and I want to talk to you about something."

"Are we in trouble?" Christian asked.

"No. Of course not," Shannon answered.

"We...have a surprise," Mike continued.

"A puppy?" Tanner blurted.

"No, not a puppy," Mike replied. He squeezed Shannon's hand. "Mommy is having a baby."

Shannon watched the statement begin to take hold in each of her children.

"But I want a puppy," Tanner said.

Shannon caught Christian kicking his brother under the table. "You can't get a puppy, stupid."

"Christian. Don't kick your brother."

"I want a girl baby," Meghan said.

Shannon smiled at her daughter. She always felt for Meghan. Being the only girl between two rowdy brothers couldn't be easy. Meghan's enthusiasm didn't surprise Shannon.

"Well, we'll see what we get," Mike answered.

"I want you guys to understand that things are going to change," Shannon said.

"What kind of change?" Christian asked, leaning on the table.

"You remember when I was pregnant with Tanner. Mommy got a big belly."

"I don't want baby," Tanner whined. His lower lip shook.

"I know it's going to be a big change, buddy. But once the baby comes, you'll be a big brother."

"No."

Shannon's neck and ears burned hot, and sound turned to a low buzz. She could see her family talking, but she couldn't process anything. Finally, the feeling passed. The news was going to take some time to sink in. She'd known it for a few weeks now, and it was still hard to believe.

"We can talk more about this in a while, okay? Mommy has to do some work." She headed for the dining room.

Mike looked annoyed, standing by his chair. He never had to do the dishes. She fixed him with a pleading look, but he didn't move.

"Can you please handle the dishes? I really need to get some work done."

After a minute, he relented and turned toward the sink.

"Who wants to help Daddy with the dishes?" Mike asked.

"Me!" Meghan said, waving her hand in the air.

"That's my girl."

"When you're done, why don't you all read a book for a little while? Chris, you still need to finish your summer reading project," Shannon suggested.

Christian opened his mouth to complain but stopped. Instead, he dutifully brought his dishes to the sink and led Tanner back to the living room.

"Do you want me to stay for a while?" Mike asked as Shannon sat down at the computer.

Shannon tried not to look surprised at his offer. He rarely took time from work to stay home and watch the kids. She would never admit it, but it hurt that all the childcare responsibilities fell in her lap.

"No. I'll be fine. They'll read for a while, and I can get a few hours of work in. We do need to talk about when we're starting Tanner in day care."

"When I get back."

"All right."

Shannon tried to tune out the noise in the kitchen and focus on the layout she'd been working on that week. She pulled up her notes from the content editor and skimmed the latest revisions. Shannon groaned as she got to the end and it hit her: She had another two pages worth of design and content to add to the project before the draft was complete.

"Mommy," Meghan's voice interrupted her thoughts.

"Not now, Meghan. Mommy is working."

"I don't know what to read."

"Ask Daddy to help you pick a book."

"He left."

Shannon pursed her lips, spun around in the chair, and allowed Meghan to lead her upstairs. A pile of books sat on the floor by her bed. Shannon got on her hands and knees beside her daughter and sifted through the pile until Meghan found one she hadn't read.

"You can read up here if you want so the boys don't bother you."

"Okay."

Shannon returned to the computer and managed almost an hour and a half of uninterrupted work before her attention was required in the living room. She found Tanner on the floor, crocodile tears welling up in his eyes.

"What's going on in here?"

"It's my time to watch TV, and Tanner didn't give me the remote," Christian answered.

"So you pushed him?"

Christian looked away and dug his toe into the carpet. "No."

Shannon scooped up the four-year-old and held him close, rubbing his back until he stopped crying.

"Christian, go to your room."

"But my TV show is on."

"You're going to stay there until I call you for dinner. No TV today."

"That's not fair."

"Life isn't fair. Now go."

Christian stormed out of the living room. Loud thumps punctuated his ascent on the stairs. Shannon patted Tanner's back a few more times and sat down with him on the couch.

"I want to watch TV," he said, whimpering.

"You can."

She picked up the remote and flipped to cartoons. Within seconds, Tanner sat contentedly beside her. She picked up her puzzle from before and found it easier to concentrate this time. It was a nice distraction.

"Mom?" Meghan's voice called from upstairs.

"In the living room."

Footsteps thundered down the stairs, and she appeared, book still in her hands.

"Can I read with you?"

"Sure." She looked at Tanner. "Can you make room for Meghan to sit down?"

Tanner scooted to his right, leaving enough room for his sister to join them.

"Is it a good book?" Shannon asked.

"Yes."

"Is something wrong, baby girl?"

"Chris is throwing things."

"He's what?"

"I heard him. He told me to go away."

Anger flushed her cheeks, and Shannon set her book down in her spot.

"Stay down here, please. Why don't you read to your brother?"

Meghan's voice got softer as Shannon climbed the stairs. She stopped at the top and listened. It was quiet for a moment and then something crashed. She walked the half a foot to the closed door and pushed it open. Christian sat in the middle of his room, toys strewn all over the floor, and video game cases lay cracked. He bore obvious signs of crying.

"Christian, stand up."

"No."

"Christian Patrick, stand up right now."

He hiccupped and sniffled but got to his feet and turned to face her stern look of disapproval.

"Why are you throwing toys?"

"Because I'm mad."

She bent down and picked up one of the cracked video game cases. "Was this cracked before?"

Christian shrugged.

"I want a straight answer."

He looked away, "No."

Shannon set the case down on the dresser and ran her hands through her hair. She could guess what was making him so upset. And a small part of her didn't blame him.

"Sit down, and talk to me."

She settled on the edge of his bed and waited for him to join her. He finally flopped down beside her, staring at his hands and saying nothing.

"Christian, tell me what's bothering you."

"I don't want another brother or sister."

"We don't always get what we want."

"They cry all the time, and they smell, and they're a pain."

"You've been a really good big brother with Meghan and Tanner."

Christian rubbed at his nose.

"I know babies are a big change. We're all going to have to make some sacrifices. And I think you're old enough to understand that. Whether you like it or not, your brother and sister look up to you. Your dad and I need you to act like the almost ten-year-old you are. Can you do that?"

"I guess so."

"Thank you." She wrapped him in a hug. It always hurt to see her kids upset.

"Can I come downstairs now?" Christian asked softly, his head still buried against her shoulder.

"Clean up here first. Then you can come downstairs."

"Yes, Mom."

Shannon kissed the top of his head and stood up. He slid off the bed and started gathering up toys and games.

"I love you, Mom," he said as she walked out of the room.

"I love you too, Chris."

By the time Christian joined his siblings downstairs, Shannon stood in the kitchen heating up tea and preheating the oven. Chicken potpie sat on the counter ready to be cooked. The door opened to her right, and Mike entered the kitchen.

"How was the rest of your day?" she asked.

"Not bad. I have a court date next Monday for the Petersen case."

"I thought you'd settled that case."

"There are a few issues the other side decided they wanted to argue in front of a judge."

"You'll do great."

"How was your afternoon?"

"I got a little work done. Not as much as I would have liked, though. Chris had a meltdown, but he's doing fine now."

"A meltdown?"

"Not looking forward to having another sibling."

"Kids all react differently to the news."

"I know. I just hate to see him so upset. He was throwing toys and video games upstairs."

"He didn't break anything, did he?"

"No."

"Do you want me to talk to him?"

"No. He and I talked."

"Maybe I should just so he knows we're a united front."

"Mike, he knows that. He just needs some time to adjust."

Shannon stuck the chicken in the oven and walked away. She wasn't in the mood to argue with him.

WITH THE KIDS IN BED, SHANNON SAT WITH MIKE IN THE living room. He flipped through the paper, and she waited in silence. It was almost a pleasant silence. In no time at all, they wouldn't have these moments together.

"So, you wanted to talk about putting Tanner in daycare?" Mike asked as he set down the paper.

"I talked to Alana. She can take him when Christian and Meghan start school. It would only be a few hours. Just to get him used to being away from me."

"Every day?"

"It gives me time to get work done while they're at school."

"How much is she charging?"

"Twenty-five dollars a day. Same as when Meghan went."

"Do you think we can afford that with the baby?"

"It's only a hundred dollars a week and only for the school year. I'm not due until April. And the kids will be almost done with school by then. I'm sure we'll manage."

"Well, Shan, I can't exactly charge my clients more in case we have a tight month or two."

"I didn't ask you to."

"Four hundred a month is a big expense."

"I could take on more work."

"Don't put too much strain on yourself."

"Of course."

In the back of her mind, Shannon wondered whether he would take on more clients, too. She doubted it. They fell silent for a while as the clock chimed on the mantle. Shannon toyed with the edge of her bookmark and finally broke the silence.

"I found a prenatal yoga class online. It's downtown, not far from Chinatown."

"Yoga?"

"Yeah. When I went in for my exam, the nurse mentioned that she did it when she was pregnant with her daughter and it was great. It helped during labor. She always felt refreshed, and it eased some of the discomforts of pregnancy. I remember someone mentioning it when I was pregnant with Tanner, but I just never found time."

"How often does this class meet?"

"Once a week. It's late morning to early afternoon while the kids are at school and Tanner is at day care. I did my homework, Mike. I can fit it into my schedule."

"I don't doubt you've got it all figured out Shannon. If you think it's best for the baby, then go for it."

Shannon could hear the hesitation in his voice.

"What's wrong? Are you worried about money?"

"No. I just don't want you to stress yourself out running all over town dropping the kids off, picking them up." He leaned over and kissed her cheek.

She forced a smile and patted his knee. She knew he was worried about money. They didn't live beyond their means, but with another mouth to feed in the coming months, it would be a lot tighter.

"Go have fun with yoga. I wouldn't object to a little extra flexibility." He waggled his eyebrows at her, and she swatted him on the arm with her book.

"Stop that."

He laid his hand on her stomach and leaned in close. "The baby can't hear us."

"The other kids might," she said and playfully swatted him away. Despite the early hour, exhaustion wrapped itself around her, and with a parting kiss, she headed for bed.

Chapter Six

September 2nd

LISBETH WRANGLED TWO SHRIEKING TODDLERS WHO were chasing each other through the rows of tiny plastic chairs. "James! Margaret! That's enough!"

Immediately, the pair stopped moving and gawked at their teacher. She approached, hands on her hips and shook her head.

"You know there's no running in the classroom."

James began to pout, and in short order, Margaret joined him. Lisbeth continued to give them her version of "the evil eye," but their quivering lips and watery expressions were no match for her. After corralling fifteen preschoolers all morning, she was ready to go home and relax. She knew it was a luxury to be paid full salary for half days of work. It was the one reason she'd agreed to work for a private school. She'd only been at work for two weeks, but the kids were wearing her out.

"He chased me first," Margaret finally said.

Lisbeth bent down to their eye level. "I know. Next time, you tell him to stop, okay?"

"Okay."

"Come on. Let's get you ready for your Mom."

Taking them by their hands, she led them to the rack of coats. James slipped into a sweatshirt, and Margaret put on her jacket. The rest of the class had already been picked up by their parents or departed on the few school buses that serviced the school for morning and afternoon classes. Lisbeth handed each child a packet of papers and a picture.

"Can you give these to your Mom?" she asked as they took their bundles.

"Yes," they replied in unison.

Two minutes later, a woman with dyed red hair walked in, car keys swinging from a clip on her purse.

"Mama," James squealed.

He took off at a wild sprint and wrapped his arms around her stomach.

"Hi, baby."

"Mama, look what I made," Margaret added, waving her picture at her mother.

"I see. It's beautiful, Mags."

Stepping around her children, their mother asked, "How were they today?"

"They were fine. Everyone was a little rowdy today. But it's to be expected."

"And they're getting along with the other kids?"

"They do spend a lot of time amongst themselves during play time, but they're starting to make other friends. I wouldn't worry about them, Mrs. Johnson."

"All right. Thank you. Jimmy, Mags, come on. It's time for some lunch." Mrs. Johnson led the twins out of the room.

Lisbeth watched them leave and heaved a huge sigh. She'd forgotten how tiring kindergarteners were. And how messy. Systematically, she moved through the room, righting and stacking chairs along the way. She wiped down the tables and did her best to pick up the bits of paper that had fallen on the carpet. She was so busy cleaning up, she didn't hear the knock on the door.

"Lisbeth? Are you in here?"

Lisbeth popped up from behind a cabinet. "Ellen. Hi. Yeah, I'm here." She got to her feet.

Ellen White, the afternoon kindergarten teacher, leaned in the doorway. "A bunch of us are having lunch in the cafeteria if you want to join us."

"Lunch, sure. Let me just finish up in here. I'll meet you there in five."

"See you there."

After another cursory glance, she grabbed her purse and wound her way through the halls to the cafeteria. She spotted Ellen with a group of teachers she recognized. They wouldn't have long to eat. They moved en masse to the lunch line, and Lisbeth slipped in front of Ellen.

"How are your kids this year?" Ellen asked.

"Good. A little rowdy this week."

"You have the Johnson twins, right?" Mark, one of the second grade teachers, asked from down the line.

"Yeah. James and Margaret are definitely a handful," Lisbeth said and leaned around Ellen to grab a Caesar salad. She also grabbed a bowl of clam chowder.

"I think I had a cousin of theirs last year," Ellen said.

They moved through the rest of the line, and Lisbeth snagged a bottle of water from the cooler by the cashier. Five minutes later, they took over a table in the back of the cafeteria, and Lisbeth found herself seated next to a guy she didn't recognize.

"You're one of the new first grade teachers, right?" she asked.

"Yes. Jack."

"Lisbeth. Nice to meet you."

They shook hands.

"So, what do you think of our school so far?" she asked.

"Good. The kids seem really eager to learn. I spent the last few years teaching fourth graders in public school. A lot more attitude."

"I'm not surprised." Lisbeth drizzled a quarter of the dressing packet over her salad.

"Little bland, isn't it?" Jack teased.

"I'm trying to eat healthy."

"Well, whatever you're doing, you look great."

Lisbeth nearly choked on a bite of salad as he leaned in closer.

"You okay?"

She swallowed. "Yes. It's just...I'm married."

Jack's cheeks flushed a vibrant shade of red. "I...I'm sorry. I didn't mean to."

"It's all right. You're not the first guy to do it."

"I hope your husband isn't the jealous type."

"You're very lucky because *she's* not."

His cheeks burned brighter. "I really am sorry. I'll just stop talking now."

Lisbeth gave him a sympathetic smile. "It's really all right. I'm used it."

"But I shouldn't even be hitting on you. We're colleagues."

"I won't tell if you won't," she whispered.

"So you teach kindergarten?" he asked.

"Yep. Well the morning class. I'm surprised you didn't hear us this morning. We were doing animal sounds with vowels."

"I think my classroom is down the opposite hallway. But I'm sure it was very informative."

Lisbeth swallowed a spoonful of her chowder and let it fill her up. She loved chowder. She had to thank Candace for that. She'd never had chowder before they met. The conversations soon died down as everyone focused on wolfing down lunch before heading back to teaching. Lisbeth picked at her salad and downed the bottle of water during the remainder of the meal.

"That must be some salty salad," Jack said.

"Trying to stay hydrated. Doctor's orders."

"Hey, could I maybe walk you out to your car? As an apology for...ya know?"

"You don't think you'll be late for your afternoon session?"

"No. They have gym right now, so they'll be straggling."

Lisbeth bid farewell to the other staff at the table, and she and Jack headed for the front of the school. She checked out, and Jack assured the secretary on duty he'd be right back.

"So how long have you taught kindergarten?" They crossed the front of the property to the teachers' lot.

"I was lucky enough to get hired right out of school. So I guess it's going on six years now. How about you?"

"About seven. I taught fourth for three years. Then I did a stint in fifth, and now I'm in first."

"They bounced you all around."

"Such is the existence of an elementary school teacher."

"Exactly."

"So, do you have kids?" Jack asked.

Lisbeth could tell he immediately regretted the question.

"God, I'm such an idiot today. Don't answer that."

"Give me about eight months, and I will."

"Congratulations."

"Thanks. We've been trying for a long time. We've had some less than stellar results in the past. We just got lucky that this last round worked."

"I bet you'll be a great mom."

"Well, thank you."

"My sister just had a baby in June."

"That's great."

"A little boy."

"I'm just trying to do everything my doctor says. I don't want anything to go wrong."

She looked away and wiped at her nose. She couldn't tell him about the last the time. If she thought about it too long, she'd break down, and he'd be late for class.

"Yeah. I mean...you'll do great."

"You think your sister has any suggestions?"

"I know she did like mommy yoga or something. She said it was a lot of fun."

"Yoga, huh?"

"She said it was great. Made some friends, too."

"I'll have to check that out. Thanks."

He smiled and shoved his hands in his back pockets. Lisbeth fished her keys from her purse and turned to face him as they reached her car.

"Well, here we are."

"Nice car. Oh...I'm not usually this stupid around women."

"Cut yourself some slack. You'll find the right one."

She waved goodbye and climbed into the driver seat. Glimpsing the bike rack in the rearview mirror, she smiled and wondered how long she'd be able to ride before she got too big and heavy. Her thoughts momentarily filled with images of herself blown up like a balloon, trying to ride a bike. *Time to go home and relax.*

Dinner was a quiet affair that night. Pasta and buttered Italian bread by candlelight. Lisbeth stared at Candace as the flame cast a warm glow on her face.

"You're quiet tonight," Candace said.

"Just had a long day."

"Kids tire you out?"

"Not as much as lunch."

"You do something special?"

Lisbeth smiled a little. "Not really. A few of us had lunch in the cafeteria. One of the new first grade teachers came on to me."

"Oh no."

"He felt really bad about it. And he's now possibly a little scared of you."

"You're a horrible tease. You probably made him scared of women all together."

"No. He was a sweet enough guy. Really apologetic. But he did give me a good tip for handling the pregnancy."

"What sort of tip?"

"He said his sister had a baby a few months ago, and she found doing yoga helpful while she was pregnant."

"Yoga is always good for the body. I'm sure whatever sort of poses they do help widen the hips and strengthen your core. Most likely makes labor easier."

"Labor...I'm not sure my head's in that place yet."

Candace stroked her hand. Lisbeth held tight and let the contact calm her.

"We will get there, honey."

Lisbeth nodded and leaned over to give Candace a kiss.

"So, yoga. You want to come with me?"

"I think I'd look a little out of place."

"Don't be ridiculous."

"Did you find any places nearby?"

"Yeah. I looked this afternoon. One does Wednesday afternoon classes up on Boylston. Class starts at noon."

"You're going to have to enjoy the other beautiful women without me. I don't think I could get out of work in time."

"We could always try some of the poses on our own." Lisbeth winked.

"Careful. I might just take you up on that offer."

They burst out laughing. It was an easy, comfortable laugh. Lisbeth stood up and pulled Candace to her feet.

"You are a constant amazement," she whispered.

"I try," Candace whispered back.

They shared a kiss, and the world melted away for that moment until the phone rang. Lisbeth didn't want to let go. The machine could get it, for all she cared. Candace took a few steps forward, forcing Lisbeth to back up.

"You should get that," Candace said.

"The machine can pick up."

"It's your parents' number."

Lisbeth groaned but reached for the phone. "Hello?"

"Lisbeth?"

"Hi, Mom. What's going on?"

"Can't a mother call her daughter?"

"Of course. I was just finishing dinner. About to start dishes."

"Oh. How is school?"

"The kids are great. Rowdy, but you know I love it. I've gotten to know a few new colleagues."

"Anyone nice?"

Lisbeth bit her lip to keep from groaning. Her mother was relentless about relationships. Even if Lisbeth had explained to her parents years ago about her and Candace. She watched Candace pick up the dinner plates and set them in the sink.

"Mom, please."

"And you and your roommate are still getting along."

Lisbeth had to stifle a laugh. "Yes, Mom. Don't worry so much, okay? Everything is fine."

"I just miss you when you aren't here."

"I know. But Elena is around."

"Your sister misses you, too."

"Tell her I'll call her this weekend. I have to go. Love you. Bye."

Lisbeth ended the call and tossed the phone on the couch then went to help in the kitchen.

"You should tell her she's going to be a grandmother," Candace said.

"I'm not ready, yet. They still don't acknowledge that we're married. You know she wouldn't understand. They'd stop talking to me."

"You don't know that would happen."

"Candace, I know my family. They would freak out, and then they would stop talking to me. And if they didn't freak out, they'd be devastated if anything happened. I couldn't put them through that."

Candace dried her hands on a dishtowel and placed them on Lisbeth's shoulders.

"They'll find out eventually. You can't avoid them forever. They live in the same state."

"Now isn't the right time to tell them," Lisbeth said.

"Okay. When you're ready, we'll tell them."

Chapter Seven

September 4th

RENEE SAT AT THE KITCHEN TABLE, WAITING FOR Bryce to get up, staring into a half empty cup of tea, now lukewarm and undrinkable. He didn't work on Friday nights, so the wait wouldn't be much longer. Even though she'd promised her mother to tell Bryce about the pregnancy, Renee had lied to him, claiming the test results showed she'd had a heat stroke. Bryce believed her. A part of her wondered if he really cared if she was sick or not. She heard noise down the hall, and the shower started. Only he took showers on Saturday mornings. Renee tapped her fingers absently against the mug, thinking about her doctor's appointment on Monday. She hadn't even told him about the appointment. Not yet. Ten minutes later Bryce appeared in sweat pants and a T-shirt. He went straight for the fridge and pulled out the orange juice.

"Use a glass. I don't want your nasty germs on the carton," Renee chided as he started to put the opening to his mouth.

"I'm not germy."

"Doesn't matter. You're not in college anymore. I have to drink out of it, too."

"Okay. Chill."

Renee stood and stuck her tea back in the microwave. Even with the summer heat, she was suddenly frozen.

"You okay?" Bryce asked.

His expression was *mild* concern. Renee nodded in response. At least he showed some sort of emotion. The microwave beeped, and she pulled out the mug, now hot to the touch.

"I didn't sleep very well last night," she admitted.

He nodded and sat down at the table. "I noticed."

"Sorry," she mumbled.

Bryce rummaged in the bread drawer and popped two pieces of bread in the toaster. Renee inhaled and gripped the mug of tea. *Now or never.*

"Look, I'm glad you're up. I need to talk to you about something."

"Sure. What's up, Nee?"

Renee took a sip of tea and swallowed, letting the heat slither down her chest and settle in her stomach. Maybe it would give her the strength she needed to admit the truth.

"Um...the tests the doctor did. I didn't have heat stroke."

"So he got it wrong? Do we have to sue him or something?"

"No. Bryce, just listen."

He downed the rest of his juice and set the glass back on the table. She tried to focus on anything but him when she told him.

"The tests said that I'm pregnant."

Bryce gaped at her like a fish caught on a line. She didn't blame him. His hand gripped the chair in front of him, turning his knuckles white. She cringed in anticipation that he'd somehow hulk out and smash it to pieces.

"Bryce, say something," Renee begged. She reached a hand out to touch him, but he shrank back.

"What do you want me to say?"

"I don't know. That we'll be okay."

"You're absolutely sure that you're pregnant?"

"Yes. They said I'm about seven or eight weeks now. I have a doctor's appointment Monday morning before work. I thought...maybe you could come with me."

"I work Sunday night."

"I know. But...it would only be an hour at most. I could drop you off on my way to work. Please, I want you there with me."

Bryce moved away from the toaster and paced the length of the kitchen. His hands twisted the hem of his T-shirt, and his cheeks puffed in and out. Frustration and shock radiated from him. But there was something else: hurt. Renee swallowed the lump in her throat.

"I'm sorry I didn't tell you sooner. I just...I didn't know the right time to tell you. And you had to work."

"A baby. Fuck, Nee. I don't know how to handle this."

His tone echoed a shift from hurt to anger. Renee scooted toward the table to give him space. She wasn't sure what he would do.

"You're not the only one. I know it's crazy and overwhelming. But if we stick together, we can deal. We just have to go through it together."

He finally stopped pacing, and it made Renee feel a little less anxious. He ran his hands over his face a couple times before closing the gap between them.

"I'll go with you on Monday if it will make you happy."

"It would make me very happy."

"Okay." He let go and headed for the couch.

"Hey, I am sorry I didn't tell you before."

"You were freaked. I get it."

She smiled and curled up next to him. While he scanned the sports section of the paper, she channel surfed and glanced at him every now and then but didn't make eye contact. She guessed he was still a little freaked out by the news. But at least he was trying to be cool. Most of the tension had left Bryce's body, as far as Renee could tell, by the time they went out to grab Chinese for lunch.

"You sure you're supposed to eat this stuff?" he asked as she devoured sweet and sour chicken.

"Why not? It's not like I'm shoveling cartons of ice cream down my throat."

"So, does your mom know?"

"Yeah. I told her. I guess she probably told my dad. I don't know if they told Max."

"Right. Makes sense you tell them first."

"I panicked, and I needed her. You know she and I are close since..." Renee trailed off. Even years later, talking about Alyssa was hard. But he'd known that when they got together.

"Renee, don't stress. I get it. You and your mom got close after what happened. Look, I don't mean to be such a dick. I just...I'm trying to process. It's not like we were planning any of this."

Renee leaned across the table and planted a kiss on his lips. He returned the gesture, his hands reaching out to tickle her under the table. She failed to contain a shriek of laughter.

"Don't do that. You want the other people to think we're crazy?"

"Well, maybe we are," he said.

"Funny guy all of a sudden. I like it."

"You know...it's how I roll."

She laughed at his expression, trying to look cool. Even as she enjoyed being out with him, something in the back of her mind tried to tell her that all was not well. Bryce was too chipper and calm. She wiped stray sweet and sour sauce from his lips and tried to push the thoughts away.

"Come on. Let's pay and get out of here. I need some air."

Bryce tossed the bills on the table and signaled the nearest waiter that they were done. Renee stepped outside and inhaled deeply. The air cleansed her lungs, and she smiled.

"You okay? You going to get sick or anything?"

"No. I'll be fine. I was just getting a little claustrophobic in there."

"Is that a pregnancy thing?"

"I don't know. I just needed to get some air is all."

They started walking down the street until they came to the Arlington T stop. Renee fished in her purse.

"What are you looking for?"

"My T pass. I feel like going to the mall."

"Oh no. You're not going to start buying stuff now. It's like way too soon."

"No. But Max's birthday is in a couple of weeks, and I need to get him a present."

Once Renee found her card at the very bottom of her purse, they headed down the outbound stop and waited for an E line train. The stop was unusually empty for a Saturday.

"So, what are you going to get him?" Bryce asked.

"I don't know. Maybe gift cards he can use places. Like the Game Stop or something. He and his friends love their gaming system."

"He does have a pretty sweet set up."

"I'm sure he appreciates your approval," she teased as a train to Heath Street finally arrived.

They climbed on and managed to find two seats together. Renee slid in first and watched the tunnel whiz by from the window. She zoned out as the conductor announced their arrival at Copley. Half their car disembarked. A few people climbed on before it continued to Prudential.

"Nee, we're here," Bryce said, drawing her from her thoughts.

She gathered her purse and climbed off the train. They followed the throng of people up the stairs and through the turnstiles. Thankfully, a large chunk of people took the stairs up to the main level. Renee stepped from the escalator and headed straight through the doors in front of her.

"So where to?" Bryce asked.

"Upstairs and past the Barnes & Noble a few stores," she said.

"Lead on."

They stepped onto the escalator, and Renee paused in front of the Barnes & Noble after stepping off. She could feel her body gravitating toward the entrance. She could never resist just wandering in and browsing. This time, she could probably find something useful.

"Renee, I thought we were going to the game store."

"Yeah, uh, if you keep going straight, you'll see it on the right."

"Wait, you're sending me off to shop for your brother?"

"You guys like the same games. Get him something you'd like."

"What are you going to do?"

"Just browse."

She walked in, headed down the center aisle, and then followed the left side branch towards the DVDs and children's sections. She glanced at the section full of DVDs and pulled herself away. She was here for something else. She found the women's health shelves and started to browse. Just beyond her, a group of kids crowded around a display table with picture books. She glanced over and couldn't help but smile as she thought of her own child. She moved down the shelf, still not seeing what she was looking for.

"Can I help you find something?" a woman in a Barnes & Noble shirt asked.

"Um...maybe."

"What are you looking for?"

Renee felt her cheeks flush as she looked at the woman. *What to Expect When You're Expecting,*" she said softly.

The employee gave her a broad grin. "Let's check the system to see if we have it in stock."

Renee followed the woman around the corner and waited while she typed the title into the database. She clicked through a few screens and said, "We have it. Follow me."

Back to the bookshelf. The woman reached above Renee's head and pulled out a copy of the book. Renee took the book and flipped through it.

"Can I help you find anything else, today?"

"No, I think that's it. Thanks so much," Renee answered and wandered to the other side of the store in search of the checkout line. Just as she reached the counter, she saw Bryce standing outside. She flagged him down, and he walked in.

"Do you have a Barnes & Noble membership card?" the cashier asked.

"No."

"Your total comes to fifteen dollars and eighty cents."

Renee handed over a twenty and waited for her change. She twisted the handle of the bag between her fingers while the cashier ripped off the receipt.

"Have a good day."

She took the receipt and shoved it in the bag.

"What did you get?" she asked Bryce as they stepped out of the store.

"Two gift cards and a new game for his Wii."

"Buy anything for yourself?"

"Maybe."

"Bryce?"

"Okay, no. I was good."

"Good."

"What'd you get?"

"A pregnancy book."

"Oh. Okay. So do you want to look around more or go home?"

Renee thought about it for a moment, even though she knew the logical thing was to go home and not spend any more money. And she did want to start reading the book.

"Let's go home. We have to start saving money."

"You sure? I saw this really sexy dress in one of the stores. You'd look great in it."

"I'd fit in it for like a month."

"You'd look really hot for that month."

"You saying I'm not going to look hot with a big belly?"

"I don't know...does that mean there's more of you to love?"

"Nice save."

They walked downstairs to the T and picked up the B line to Government Center, getting off at Boylston. They walked the short distance to their building and headed upstairs. Renee inspected Bryce's present choices and gave him her nod of approval before flopping down on the couch and opening her book.

"You sure you don't want to do something else?" Bryce asked as he picked up her legs and sat down.

"Nope."

"You're absolutely—"

"I'm reading."

"Fine. Don't talk to me, then."

"Go play a game or something," she said, trying to not sound irritated.

Monday morning came quickly. Thanks to her nerves, Renee was up twenty minutes before her alarm. She'd been reading the pregnancy book since Saturday and now had a million worries running through her head. Stretch marks and contractions. Breastfeeding and ultrasounds. Renee sat at the kitchen table, nibbling on a piece of toast while she waited for Bryce to get up. Checking the time every two minutes was driving her crazy, and she had to move around as a distraction. Renee was about ready to burst by the time Bryce stumbled out of the bathroom after eight o'clock.

"Come on. We have to get going," she said.

"Can I have coffee first?"

"We can stop at a Dunkin Donuts on the way."

"You're way too chipper for this early in the morning."

"I've been up since six thirty."

"Damn."

Renee pulled on her jacket and tossed Bryce the car keys. They walked downstairs and around back to the reserved parking. Bryce unlocked the car and waved to the guard on duty. Renee could barely keep still on the drive to the doctor's office. Her mood was not going to rub off on Bryce anytime soon. She jumped out of the car before Bryce could cut the engine.

"Nee, slow down."

"I'll see you inside," she called.

She made it inside and checked in with the receptionist. The waiting area was empty. She hung her coat on the wall and sat down. Two minutes later, she was up again.

"Where's the bathroom?" she asked.

The receptionist handed over a key and pointed down the hall.

"Thanks. Oh, and if a guy comes in looking kind of grumpy and confused, just tell him I'll be right back."

"Sure."

Renee returned from the bathroom with an empty bladder and found Bryce sitting in a chair. He stared straight ahead, but it was clear he wasn't focused on anything in particular. Sitting beside him, she brushed her hand against his knee to get his attention. He blinked and turned to face her.

"You okay?" he asked, his voice betraying only the faintest hint of emotion.

"Yeah. Just had to go. And you could act like a human being instead of a zombie. It's not that early," she answered.

"Just tired," he mumbled.

"Renee?" a nurse called.

"Guess we're up," Renee said and took Bryce's hand.

They followed the nurse back to the first exam room. Renee looked at the ultrasound equipment and squeezed Bryce's hand. A paper gown waited on the exam table.

"You'll need to undress from the bottom down. The doctor will be in shortly."

Renee waited until the door closed before picking up the gown. She shook it open and looked from it to the table and back again. *This isn't the kind of exam I read about in the book.* Gingerly, she pulled down her pants and underwear, folded them on the nearby chair, hoisted herself onto the exam table, and stared at the blank screen to her right. Bryce sat in the chair next to her, expressionless.

"Can you look less like a zombie when the doctor comes in please?"

"Sorry. Just had a late night."

Renee wiggled on the table, trying to get comfortable. She hoped the butterflies flapping around in her stomach didn't have any adverse effect on the ultrasound. A knock on the door lessened her anxiety for a moment. The door opened, and a woman in her late thirties walked in.

"Hi, Renee."

"Hi, Dr. Kenneth."

"So, first of all, congrats on the pregnancy."

"It wasn't something we were planning, but thanks."

"So we're going to do a transvaginal ultrasound today. It will be the first picture of your baby."

Renee looked at Bryce. "Isn't that cool?"

"Yeah."

"He's not a morning person," Renee said, not understanding his mood change.

"That's okay. Now, this is going to be a little uncomfortable," Dr. Kenneth said and pulled a tiny wand from the side of the ultrasound machine.

"What is that exactly?" Renee asked.

"Since you're so early in your pregnancy, the normal ultrasound technique of going through the abdomen isn't as accurate. This will give us a clearer picture," Dr. Kenneth answered.

"Oh. It won't hurt, will it?"

"No worse than an exam. You'll feel some pressure, though."

Renee settled back with her feet in the stirrups and tried to relax. Her hands wrapped around the edges of the gown as Dr. Kenneth inserted the wand. Renee needed a distraction.

"When am I supposed to start showing?"

"Around twelve to sixteen weeks. But some women, depending on their frame, might start showing a little sooner."

"Oh. Okay."

Renee took slow breaths as Dr. Kenneth maneuvered the wand around for a few minutes until she found what she was looking for.

"There's your baby."

Renee struggled to see the image. "What's it look like?"

"A gray blob in some other gray stuff," Bryce answered.

"I'll print it out for you so you can see it better," Dr. Kenneth said.

"Thanks."

She removed the wand and tossed the cover in the trash.

"Do you have any questions before I do that?"

"Yeah. I was reading in this book that yoga is good during pregnancy."

"Prenatal yoga, yes."

"So I should do that?"

"It can be very beneficial. Exercise is essential for preparing the body for labor. And since you're a first-time mom, it would definitely be a good idea."

"Would you recommend any place in particular?"

"Let me check my literature. I'll be right back."

"You want to spend money on yoga?" Bryce asked the second they were alone.

"If it helps with the baby, yeah," Renee answered and pulled on her underwear and pants.

"Do we have money for it?"

"I don't know. I'll handle it."

Bryce huffed and crossed his arms. She mirrored his gesture. He could be such an ass.

"I'm just trying to do the right thing, here. Make the best of the situation," she said.

"Okay. Fine."

Dr. Kenneth walked back in and handed Renee a pamphlet and a picture.

"This is for a studio up on Boylston. They have very good prices, and their classes meet once a week."

Renee looked at the brochure and stuck it in her purse. She focused her attention on the picture. Dr. Kenneth pointed out a circle in white.

"That's your baby."

"It's so small."

"It will get bigger. Why don't you schedule another appointment for twelve weeks?"

"Okay. Thanks. I guess I'll see you in a month."

Renee climbed off the table and picked up her purse. Bryce trailed after her. She made her appointment and pulled on her jacket. She said nothing to Bryce as she dropped him off and headed for the aquarium. It didn't matter if he was still grumpy. All she could think about was the baby growing inside her. She put the sonogram picture on the inside of her locker at work and went to meet the first tour group of the day.

That night when she got home, Renee found Bryce sitting at the kitchen table in the same clothes he'd worn that morning. She checked her watch. He had fifteen minutes before he needed to be at work.

"Bryce, you're still home," she said.

"I called in sick."

"You're not sick."

"I know. We need to talk Renee."

The look on his face and the tone of his voice sent shivers down her arms. Setting down her purse, Renee settled in the chair opposite him and waited. He stayed silent.

"Bryce, say something. What's going on?"

"We can't do this."

"Do what?"

"You know."

"No, I don't. So just tell me what's bothering you."

"We can't be parents. There's just no way it can happen."

Renee jumped to her feet and said, "This *is* happening, Bryce. You saw the ultrasound. We are having this baby."

"No. We need to get rid of it."

Color and heat drained from Renee's cheeks, and breaths came in shallow gasps as she stared at Bryce. *He did not just say that. He wouldn't say something so cruel. He's just joking, right?* Clammy chills peppered every inch of exposed skin, and her legs turned to JELL-O.

"What did you say?" Her voice was barely above a whisper.

"I said we need to get rid of it."

Renee gripped the table to steady herself and stared at his chin. If she looked directly at him, she might reach over and rip off his face with her bare hands.

"I am *not* going to get an abortion."

"It's not just your decision," Bryce said.

"It's my body. You can't tell me what I can and can't do with it. So don't you ever say something like that again."

"You can't want this kid, Renee. You weren't ready."

"Not being ready and not wanting it are two different things. You've known since we started dating that I wanted kids."

"That still doesn't change the fact we can't keep this baby. We make enough to support ourselves but can't handle a baby, too. There's got to be someone out there who would want it."

"No. I'm not giving this baby up."

"This isn't fair, Renee. It's my kid, too."

"Life isn't fair, Bryce. And let's face it. We're not kids anymore. It's time to be a grown up and accept what's happening."

She turned away and started for the bedroom. She needed to be alone and calm down.

"Why are you so sure you can do this, Renee?" Bryce called.

"Because I have to believe I can. For this baby's sake. Because I could never just cast it aside."

She slammed the door closed and curled up on the bed, ignoring him as he came in and pulled on his uniform. She pretended she didn't hear him slam the front door a few minutes later.

Chapter Eight

September 7th

ERIKA DRAGGED HERSELF OUT OF BED JUST BEFORE eleven. She had a shift at the restaurant that she couldn't miss because she was already in deep shit with her boss for skipping out so often in the last few weeks. Routinely drowning her sorrows in alcohol until passing out made the time since getting the news nothing but a blur. Dane probably thought she was dead. Erika just wanted to forget. Forget she had a baby growing inside her. Forget she had no idea about the father. She'd looked into getting an abortion, but she wasn't exactly conscious enough to remember what she'd found. And for all she knew, it would just go away on its own. That happened sometimes. Erika stumbled into the shower and let the warm water wash away her hangover. A loud buzzing noise filled the apartment as she wrapped herself in a towel.

"What the hell?" she mumbled.

At last, she found her phone buzzing along the table by the couch and scooped it up. Dane's number flashed on the caller ID, daring her to answer.

"Hello?"

"Erika! Jeez, where the hell have you been? I've been calling for weeks, and you don't answer."

"Sorry. I've just been really busy. And I'm kind of late for work. Can I call you tonight?"

"Yeah, sure. But you better call."

"I will. Bye."

Erika tossed the phone on the couch and headed into her room to find clothes. She slipped into her work pants and shirt and checked herself in the mirror. The reflection showed nothing different: bloodshot, red-rimmed eyes. Eyeliner and eye drops would take care of that. After running a comb through her hair, she leaned in close to get the eyeliner just right. By the time she finished, she looked normal again. Maybe a little too much blush, but she needed the color. In the living room, her phone beeped, reminding her she had twenty-five minutes to get to work. She tugged flats on and downed a cup of day-old coffee before running out the door. She danced from foot to foot while the elevator slowly climbed to the third floor.

"Come on."

"You late?" a voice asked.

"What?" Erika asked and turned to see an older guy in a track suit.

"You look like you're running late," he said.

"Oh. Sort of. I just hate how slow the elevators are in this building."

"Don't we all?"

The elevator dinged, and the doors slid open. The man held out his arm to let her get on first. She gave him a half smile and stepped on. The elevator stopped at every floor on its way down. *Why the hell is it so busy today?* Stuck in the back corner of the elevator, Erika fiddled with the Internet on her phone, skimming the search results on abortion. She gulped down fresh—or as fresh as city air can be—air as soon as she stepped outside. She checked her phone for the time.

"Damn." Twelve minutes to walk four blocks. *No time to surf the web now.*

Speed-walking down the sidewalks, Erika arrived as the lunch crowd started filtering in. She sneaked in the back, tossed her purse on a hook under some jackets, and pinned her nameplate to her shirt before her manager appeared.

"Nice of you to show up, Lind."

"I lost my phone charger, and it died, so I couldn't call."

"Just get out there. You're working tables twenty-seven through forty."

Erika bit back a comment about the huge section, grabbed a stack of place settings, and set the tables. *Just my luck.* Every old person or mom with whiny little kids in the whole damn city ended up in her section.

Perfect.

"Excuse me, miss? I asked for iced tea. This has no ice in it," a woman said, flagging Erika down. She waved the glass of tea around so vigorously, Erika was surprised its contents didn't slosh all over the floor.

"I'll get you some ice," Erika said and took the glass.

She wound her way through the tables and booths back to the kitchen. "I need some ice in this," she called. "And you might want to dump some of the tea before you do it."

Someone snatched the glass away and put it back seconds later. Ice cubes floated on top of the tea. *Good enough.* Erika returned the tea and checked on her other tables.

"Hey, Erika," Jessa, one of her coworkers called.

Erika was bent over an empty booth, trying to retrieve the shreds of napkin from the floor. As she wiggled from under the table, she saw Jessa propped against the booth.

"Yeah?"

"You've got someone waiting at table thirty-six."

"Can you handle it for me? I've got to get this ready for a family of four."

"They asked for you by name."

"You're kidding."

"Nope. If I were you, I'd take it. I'll cover you here."

Erika handed the cleaning rags to Jessa and then wiped her hands on her apron. "Thanks."

"Go get 'em," Jessa called, whipping the towel at Erika's butt.

Erika wound her way through tables twenty-six through thirty, took a left at thirty-one, and ended up at a table in the back: thirty-six. She nearly turned tail and ran. Dane sat at the table.

"What are you doing here?" she asked as she approached.

"Waiting for the waitress to tell me the special of the day and take my order."

Erika glanced around the restaurant and, once sure no one would notice, slid into the seat opposite him.

"I'm serious. Why are you here?"

"I am, too. Take my order, and we can talk."

"I'm not on break for another hour."

"Well, take my order. I'll order an appetizer and something that takes a long time to make. That way, by the time I get it, you'll be off."

"Fine." Erika stood up. "What can I get you?"

"I'll have a strawberry milkshake and an order of onion rings."

"What else?"

"I'll have one those really big hamburgers with pepper jack cheese and double bacon. Oh, and can I get extra pickles?"

"Sure. I'll be back with your shake and rings."

"I'll be waiting."

Erika stopped by the kitchen to drop off the order before tending to a couple of other tables. She ran into Jessa on her way to deliver drinks for table twenty-seven.

"So, that guy's cute, right?" Jessa whispered.

"Don't go there."

"Oh, come on. It's not like you're seeing anyone."

"I'm not seeing him, either."

"What's wrong with him?"

"He's my ex. That's what's wrong with him."

Jessa made a pained face. "Ouch. Feel the burn."

Erika shook her head and waited by the kitchen for Dane's order to come up.

"Thirty-six. Order of onion rings," the cook shouted.

Erika grabbed the plate and finished making Dane's shake. She weaved through running children and other waitresses to get to the table.

"God, why'd you pick a table all the way back here?" she complained, setting the drink and rings down.

"So people wouldn't think I'm weird, eating alone."

"Enjoy. Your burger will be out soon."

"I'll save you some," Dane said, pointing to the onion rings.

Erika's stomach grumbled louder than she expected. "Thanks."

By the time she brought out his burger, her break was five minutes in. She slid into the booth and pulled the half-eaten basket of onion rings over. She munched on them while Dane tried to take a bite of his burger.

"That thing is bigger than your mouth," she said with a laugh.

"It's a manly burger. I will conquer it."

Another giggle slipped out as she licked her fingers and pulled his shake across the table. The cold hit her too fast, and she scrunched up her face.

"There's some karma for you."

"What the hell?"

"Didn't say you could steal my shake."

She massaged her forehead until the discomfort subsided. They sat in silence for a while, Dane slowly making the burger more manageable. Erika started tearing a paper napkin to shreds.

"So, why are you here?" she asked. "Besides for lunch."

"Because you disappeared from the face of the Earth for like two weeks."

"I was busy."

"You barely work. And I came by here a few times, but they said you weren't here."

"You stalking me or something?"

"No. I just...we were supposed to hang the day after the party, and I never heard from you."

"I guess I was just kind of out of it, sorry."

"Erika, we've been friends since freshman year. I think I know by now when you're lying." He reached out and took her hands in his. "So, spill. What's really going on?"

Erika wrenched her hands away and started to finger comb her hair. *If I tell him about the baby, it'll make it real, and I'm not ready to handle that.* But Dane was persistent. He'd keep bothering her until she fessed up. *Maybe he'll be willing to help me get rid of the problem.* Unsure if she really wanted to tell him, she sat in silence.

"Erika. Come on. You can tell me anything."

"I don't know. It's just been weird between us."

"I know things haven't been great since graduation, but I'm still your friend."

Erika smoothed her apron, tugged at her hair. Anything to keep her from blurting out the ugly truth. Dane tossed some cash on the table and got up. He pulled on his coat and had it halfway zipped up when she bolted to her feet.

"Dane, wait."

"No. I get it. You don't want to tell me. It's fine." He took two steps away from the table.

She followed him and grabbed his wrist. "I...I'm pregnant."

The words just spilled out. She could feel the world spinning off its axis around her. She'd said it, it was real, and now everything was going to come crashing down. She shivered as he wrapped his arms around her. Erika clung to him. *I'll just stay here forever, nice and safe. Maybe he'll stop time for me or turn it back so this never happened.*

"You should sit down." Dane's voice was barely a whisper.

Instead of fighting him, Erika slid into the booth, still attached to Dane. He held her for what felt like hours but was only minutes.

"You're sure?" he finally asked.

"Yes."

"What can I do?"

"Make it go away. Please."

"Are you sure that's what you want?" he asked.

"Yes. I...tried to look stuff up. But I don't know what to do. Or where to go. It's all just too much."

"I'll do whatever you need me to. You know that."

"Just find someplace that will do it. And do it fast."

He squeezed her shoulder, and she bit her lip to keep from sobbing. She couldn't lose it at work. She still needed the job. She pulled a few napkins from the dispenser and wiped her cheeks. So much for not smudging her eyeliner and mascara.

"We'll get through this. I promise," Dane whispered before he stood and helped her to her feet.

"Thanks. I don't know what I'd do without you."

Chapter Nine

September 8th

SHANNON TOOK THE STAIRS TWO AT TIME, GRABBED some pathetically unused exercise clothes, threw them in a bag, and returned to the first floor. Tanner sat on the ground, tugging on his sneakers. *Thank God for Velcro.*

"Can you zip me?" Tanner asked and pointed to his jacket.

She pulled the zipper up to his chin, grabbed her jacket from a hook on the wall, and took a moment to make sure she had everything before ushering him to the car. Shannon backed out of the driveway and turned down their street. Thankfully, they didn't have far to go.

"You be a good a boy today," Shannon said and gave Tanner a kiss on the cheek when she dropped him off.

"Bye, Mama."

Shannon waved as she climbed into the car and took off. She checked the time every few minutes as she pulled on to the highway. To her surprise, the roads were relatively clear, despite the lunch hour. The thought of lunch made her stomach rumble. She promised herself a big dinner and stopped for a quick bite at Starbucks on her way to the yoga studio. Not the healthiest, but it was relatively cheap, and she didn't have to make it. She weaved through residential and industrial streets until she spotted the sign for Maternal Instincts Yoga. A small row of parking spots was available across the way, and she managed to snag one and get inside just before eleven forty-five.

"Hi, can I help you?" a young woman sitting behind a desk asked.

"I'm here for the yoga class at noon."

"Great. Just fill this out. There are changing rooms around the corner."

Shannon took the clipboard and pen from the receptionist and sat down by a young woman in her late twenties.

"This your first time, too?" the woman asked.

"Yeah. I'm Shannon."

"Lisbeth. Nice to meet you."

Shannon focused on the form, trying to do the math in her head. When had her doctor said she was due? Sometime in April? She scribbled it down and, after filling in her contact information, returned the form to the receptionist.

"I guess I'll see you in there," Shannon said, addressing Lisbeth.

"Yeah."

Shannon rounded the corner and found an empty stall that reminded her of changing rooms in clothing stores, with a mirror covering the length of the right wall. Shannon took a minute to stare at her bare belly. It was probably her mind playing tricks, but she saw the tiniest bit of bulge. Shannon pulled the T-shirt over her head and put on workout shorts. She found a clip and pulled her hair away from her face. When she stepped out, she found Lisbeth heading for the studio. By Shannon's watch, they had a good five minutes before the class began.

"So, have you done this before?" Shannon called, jogging to catch the younger woman.

Lisbeth stopped walking and turned around, water bottle strapped to her wrist.

"No. Though I hear it's supposed to be really good strength building."

"I haven't, either. I thought about it before but just didn't have the time."

Lisbeth raised an eyebrow. "Not your first?"

Shannon smiled. "No. Fourth."

"Brave woman."

Shannon bit her tongue. "Thanks. What about you?"

"First...well...second, but it didn't go well. We got really lucky this time. I'm just trying to do everything I can to make it to term."

"Congratulations. I'm sure you'll do great. I'll keep you in my thoughts."

"Thanks."

Before they could continue their conversation, a woman in bright blue spandex walked out of the studio and into the waiting area.

"Ladies, come on in."

"After you," Shannon said and allowed Lisbeth to enter the studio ahead of her.

Several other women stood around the room with foam mats and towels draped around their necks. Shannon watched some of the other women, who looked almost eight months along, stretching. Transfixed, she stared as they bent far lower than she thought possible. There was no way she could have done that with any of her previous pregnancies. Kids were just too damn big.

"That looks like it's got to be painful," Lisbeth whispered.

"I'm sure they know what they're doing."

"I can't believe they can still exercise that far along."

"I worked up until a few days before I had my third child. So I'd imagine as long as they're careful, they can continue to exercise until their due dates."

"All right, ladies. Welcome to Maternal Instincts Yoga. My name is Carolyn. I'll be your instructor. I want everyone to grab a mat. If you don't have one, we have extras along the back wall. We're going to start with some breathing drills."

Shannon and Lisbeth grabbed mats and stood in the middle of the room. Shannon tried to clear her thoughts and focus on her breathing, but it was more difficult than she'd imagined. She mapped the route from the studio to school to pick up Christian and Meghan. Then to daycare and home. She thought about the various projects that needed work done by the end of the week. Too many things jumbled in her brain for her to focus on breathing.

"Okay. Now we're going to move to some simple stretching poses. Why don't we start with the tree pose," Carolyn said, interrupting Shannon's thoughts.

Shannon refocused on the people and the room around her. Others in the class started to balance on one foot. She watched some of the women who were farther along and wondered how they didn't topple over from all of the weight.

"Bring your arms above your head and press your right foot to your left knee. If you can't reach your knee, rest your foot against your calf. I know it's tempting to just aim for your ankle but you can get higher," Carolyn said from the front of the room.

Shannon slowly lifted her arms above her head and pressed her right foot to her left knee. She drew in a breath and tried not to fall over. Her left leg began to wobble, and she slid her foot down to her calf. Her balance stabilized just in time to come out of the pose and switch legs. Shannon saw Lisbeth suck down some water before continuing with the second tree pose.

They moved on to the half moon pose next. Less fear of falling over. Definitely a stretch in her sides. Shannon inhaled deeply and tried to focus on the stretch. She counted to fifteen and switched sides. The soft music filled her ears and helped calm some of her whirring thoughts. Instead of every detail of the life waiting outside for her, she thought about the one growing within her. The baby she hadn't planned. Shannon's heart skipped a beat. She hadn't really thought of it as a new life. It had just been "the pregnancy" for weeks now. A tiny smile spread over her lips at the realization that she was creating a brand new person.

"Okay, ladies."

Shannon refocused on the room around her and saw Carolyn waving people together. Shannon took a few steps to her right and scooted next to Lisbeth.

"What's going on?"

"I'm not sure. She'll explain."

"We're going to partner up for a few thigh-strengthening exercises."

Shannon eased herself to the floor and waited for Lisbeth to join her. After watching Carolyn demonstrate the stretch, Shannon linked hands with her partner. She tugged lightly on Lisbeth's arms. The room was silent, save the music filtering through at the lowest volume possible. Shannon fought the urge to talk. She got the sense that breaking the silence was a big no-no, and she didn't want to upset anyone.

"This wasn't exactly what I was expecting," Lisbeth whispered.

Shannon nodded. "Me, either."

Shannon felt worn out as class wrapped up. Maybe it was hormones going haywire. Or it could be the workout since chasing a four-year-old and wrangling a six- and nine-year-old wasn't exactly what one would call exercise. She followed the rest of the group out of the studio and back to the changing rooms. She slipped into her other clothes and shoved the workout clothes in her bag. She pulled her hair loose from the clip and checked herself in the mirror. She stepped out of the room and nearly collided with one of the other women.

"I'm so sorry," Shannon said.

"No need to apologize. I should have watched where I was going."

Shannon glanced at the woman's belly. "When are you due?"

"Last week. My doctor thinks the yoga will help get labor started. Personally, I'm convinced she's going to stay in there forever."

"Well, I'll keep you in my thoughts," Shannon offered.

"Thanks. Good luck with your little one."

Shannon headed for the front door and caught Lisbeth before she left.

"Thanks for being my partner today."

"Anytime. I felt a little bad about talking in there," Lisbeth admitted.

Shannon stifled a laugh. "So did I."

They walked out of the building and stood in the cool September air. Other women from the class passed them by with a small nod or a wave. Shannon fished her car keys out of her purse.

"So are you coming back next week?" Shannon asked.

"I hope so. That's the plan anyway. What about you?"

"Also the plan. I didn't think I'd be so tired afterwards."

"It was kind of nice. After chasing four- and five-year-olds all morning, it was relaxing," Lisbeth said.

"Teacher?"

"Kindergarten at a private school. It's nice to be able to make full salary and only teach mornings."

"My youngest will be starting school next year," Shannon said, toying with her key ring.

"How old are your other two?"

"Christian's nine, and Meghan's six." Shannon opened her wallet and pulled the most recent picture she had of all three kids.

"And Tanner is four," she said.

"They're adorable."

Shannon smiled. "Thank you."

Her phone beeped an obnoxious ringtone. One of the kids must have gotten hold of the phone while she wasn't looking. Rooting around in her purse, she finally found it at the bottom and pulled it out. She jumped at the time.

"Sorry to just run, but I have to get home and finish some things before I pick them up from school."

"Not a problem. I'll see you next week."

Shannon waved to Lisbeth while jogging across the street. She climbed into the driver's seat, drove into the traffic, and had to go around the block to get back the way she had come. Downtown Boston streets were always so complicated with one-way streets never going the direction she needed. Shannon eyed the clock every two minutes as she pressed down on the gas. The car whizzed along the highway back to Cambridge, and she pulled into the driveway with forty minutes to spare before the elementary school let out. Leaving her workout clothes in the back of the car, Shannon rushed through the front door, settled at the computer, and scanned her to-do list on the desk.

By the time quarter of three rolled around, she'd ticked two things off the list. It would have to do. By three, she'd pulled into the school parking lot and joined the line of parents waiting to pick up their kids. After about ten minutes, she spotted Christian and Meghan. She honked the horn and rolled down the front passenger window.

"Hi, guys," she said as they climbed in.

"Hi, Mom," Christian said.

"Hi, Mama."

"Did you have a good day at school?" she asked and pulled out of the parking lot.

"I made a picture for you, Mama," Meghan said, kicking the back of Christian's seat.

Through the rearview mirror, Shannon watched as Meghan started to open her backpack.

"Why don't you show me when we get home, okay? I can't look at it while I'm driving."

"Okay, Mama."

"Chris, what's wrong?"

"Nothing. I just don't want to talk about school."

"Did something happen?"

"No."

"Christian, if something happened, you need to tell me."

"I saw a girl kiss Christian. Like a Mama and Daddy kiss," Meghan said in a singsong voice.

"Shut up, Meg," Christian said.

"Christian, do not tell your sister to shut up."

Christian crossed his arms over his chest and stared out the window. Shannon pursed her lips, trying to figure out what to say.

"Is it true?"

"I don't want to talk about it."

"Fine." She eased off the gas as she took the turn onto their street. "I want you to go straight to doing homework."

"Yes, Mom," he said.

Shannon pulled into the driveway and watched as Christian trudged up to the front door. She'd have to talk with him after dinner. Shannon grabbed her workout clothes from the back seat and headed inside.

"I'll be back in a few minutes, Chris. I have to pick up your brother," she said as she walked into the kitchen, Meghan trailing behind her.

"Okay."

"Do you want to come?"

"No."

"I'm going to lock the door when we go. Don't open it."

"I know, Mom."

"And get right to homework."

"I know."

Shannon led Meghan back to the car and got her buckled in.

"So did you do anything special at school today?" Shannon asked.

"We learned about numbers."

"You did?"

Meghan nodded. "I can make big numbers."

"Show me."

She watched her daughter's forehead wrinkle with concentration. "Like um...you put the two and the three together, and it makes five."

"Very good."

Shannon pulled the car into a driveway and turned off the engine.

"Stay here. I'll be right back."

"Okay, Mama."

Shannon walked up to the front door and rang the bell, shifting her weight while she waited for someone to answer.

"Hi, Shannon," Alana said.

"Hi. Is Tanner ready?"

She turned around and called, "Tanner, your mom is here."

Footsteps thundered on the hardwood floor, and Tanner came into view.

"How was he today?" Shannon asked as one of the older kids helped Tanner with his shoes.

"Fine. As always."

"Great. Thanks so much, and we'll see you tomorrow."

"Bye, Tanner," Alana said.

"Bye, bye."

Shannon hoisted Tanner onto her hip and carried him to the car. She got him settled in his car seat before climbing behind the wheel.

"Tanner, sweetie. Take your finger out of your mouth."

"I got a tooth, Mama."

"Well, leave it alone until we get home, please."

Ten minutes later, she escorted Meghan and Tanner inside. "Chris, we're back," she called and shut the front door.

"Mama. Look at my picture now," Meghan said, tugging on her hand.

"Just a minute, honey." She helped Tanner out of his coat. "Come into the light so I can see your tooth."

He opened his mouth and stuck his finger in. She tilted his head back, peered in, and moved his finger so she could get a proper look.

"You're right. You do have a tooth coming in."

He giggled.

"Does it hurt?"

"No."

"Good. Why don't you go play?"

Tanner scurried off into the living room, leaving her and Meghan standing in the hallway. Shannon followed Meghan into the kitchen. Meghan pulled out a picture and handed it over.

"That's Daddy. And Christian and me and Tanner. And that's you."

Shannon looked at the figure with the big belly.

"And that's the baby."

A little stick figure fit neatly inside the big belly circle.

"It's very nice. Why don't we put it on the fridge, and you can show Daddy when he comes home."

Meghan stuck the drawing to the fridge with two cartoon magnets.

"Let me know if you need help with your homework," Shannon said as Meghan picked up her backpack.

"I can do it, Mama."

"I know you can. But I'm here if you need me."

Shannon watched her disappear around a corner and clomp up the stairs. She moved to the dining room and checked her e-mail for the fiftieth time that day, rubbing her temples as the screen blurred out of focus. *Yoga took more out of me than I realized.* The screen came back into focus, and she managed to answer a few e-mails before footfalls descended the stairs. She didn't turn around until a voice spoke.

"Mom?"

Shannon turned around. "Yeah, Chris?"

"I need help with my math homework."

He held his math book and a sheet of paper against his chest. Shannon rolled the computer chair over to the table and let him sit beside her.

"What's giving you trouble?"

"I don't get these problems."

He pointed to three long divisions problems that hadn't been touched.

"Did you try them?"

He nodded slowly but didn't make eye contact.

"Christian."

"No."

"Well, try them first, and then if you still don't understand, let me know."

Shannon returned to the computer and fiddled with layout designs she'd been coding the previous day. She listened as Tanner made car noises in the living room.

"Can you check them?" Christian asked.

"Let me see."

He handed over the paper, and she glanced at the numbers. She held her hand out for his pencil, and he passed it to her. She circled the second problem.

"Look at this one again."

Christian whined but took the paper back and madly erased the work he'd done. She watched him work, noting the hunch of his shoulders and how tightly he gripped the pencil.

"Is it right now?" he asked and thrust the paper back toward her.

She looked at the paper and shook her head. Shannon rolled the chair back to the table and erased the answer and the work. Color tinged his cheeks, and his eyes shone with tears. Chris hunched his shoulders and looked away from the problem.

"Get me a piece of scrap paper," she said and pointed to the printer.

He pulled a sheet out of the tray and handed it over. She copied the problem and read aloud, "Okay. One hundred-sixty-five divided by six."

Christian tapped the pencil against his hand and stared at the problem.

"How many times can six go into sixteen?"

"One."

"No. I think it can go in more."

"Two?"

"Is six times two the closest to sixteen?"

"Yes."

"Okay."

He wrote a two above the six in sixteen and then wrote twelve beneath it. He looked at it for minute and then carefully wrote a four beneath the equal line.

"Good. So now what do you do?" Shannon asked.

"Bring the five down to the four."

He did so and looked at the number forty-five. Shannon brushed a few eraser crumbs from where he'd erased before.

"How many times can six go into forty-five?"

"I don't know."

"Yes you do."

"Eight?"

"What's six times eight?"

"Um...forty-eight."

"Can you subtract forty-eight from forty-five?"

"No."

"So what's the next smallest number?"

"Seven."

"Okay. Try that."

He wrote seven next to the two in his answer and then forty-two below the forty-five. He wrote three below the equal line.

"You can't do six into three," he said.

"So what do you have to do with the three?"

He wrote a small r3 after twenty-seven. She nodded.

"See, you could do it."

He copied the answer and work to his homework page and shut his book. She waited for him to stand up, but he didn't move.

"You okay, sweetheart?"

"Meghan told the truth. A girl kissed me at recess."

Shannon tried to hide a smile. "She did? What girl?"

"Jenny Hammond."

"Is that the girl that you wanted to invite to your birthday but she couldn't come?"

"Yes."

"She sounds like a nice girl."

"She's not. She's mean and picks on me."

"Then why'd you want to invite her?"

"I thought she liked me."

"Oh, Chris. Well, she kissed you. Maybe that's her way of showing you that she likes you."

"I heard her laughing with her friends before science. They said it was a dare. She doesn't like me."

Shannon wrapped him in her arms and planted a kiss on the top of his head. "I'm sorry, sweetie. Things have been pretty rough the last few weeks, huh?"

"Why would she do that?"

"Because sometimes, girls can be mean. And sometimes, when someone picks on you, it's their way of trying to tell you that they like you."

"Well, I don't like her anymore."

"That's okay. You don't have to like her."

"Thanks, Mom."

"It's what I'm here for. Do you have any other homework to do?"

"Reading."

"Get to it."

Christian took his book and pushed the chair in. He wandered through the living room and back upstairs. Shannon sat at the table and laid her head in her arms. *I am so not ready to raise a pre-adolescent and a newborn at the same time.*

Chapter Ten

September 12th

L ISBETH CURLED UP BENEATH THE BLANKETS AND sighed. She had nowhere to be today, and sleeping in past nine a.m. sounded like a really good idea. In fact, she could stay in bed all day. Maybe she would. Too bad the tantalizing smell of breakfast roused her senses. She rolled over and saw Candace carrying a tray.

"You made me breakfast."

"I'm not allowed?" Candace asked.

Lisbeth gave her a sleepy smile. "Thank you."

She sat up against her pillow and let Candace set the tray down. She surveyed the plate, and her stomach rumbled loudly. They laughed, and Candace perched on the edge of the bed.

"Eat up, missy."

Lisbeth picked up the fork and scooped up scrambled eggs. She could taste the little bit of ketchup and hot sauce mixed in. Just the way she liked them. Lisbeth smiled as she ate.

"Perfect."

She washed it down with a swig of orange juice while Candace scooted over to sit beside her at the head of the bed.

"So what do you want to do today?" Candace asked.

"Nothing. Today feels like one of those days that you just stay in your pajamas and do nothing."

"I think we can handle that," Candace replied.

Lisbeth enjoyed her breakfast, even though the bacon was a little greasy. Candace took the tray away, and Lisbeth lounged in bed until ten. She finally emerged and made it to the couch, lying so she spanned the entire surface. She lifted up her top to stare at her stomach. From this angle, she could see a slight bump.

"Candace, come here," she called in excitement.

"What is it?"

"Look. I have a baby bump already."

Candace laughed and bent down to examine Lisbeth's stomach. She ran her fingers over the exposed skin, leaving tiny quivers in their wake.

"I don't see it."

"You're not looking from the right angle," Lisbeth said.

Candace moved to the other end of the couch and resumed her squat.

"Now I see it. Right there," she said. She leaned up and kissed just above Lisbeth's belly button.

Lisbeth pushed herself to a sitting position, and their lips touched. "Careful. The doctor said no strenuous activity," she teased.

"Are you sure about that?" Candace asked with a wink.

Lisbeth laughed and wrapped her arms around Candace's neck. "You're too good for me."

"Oh, stop it."

"So do you think we'll get a boy or a girl?" Lisbeth asked.

"I don't know. I'll be happy with either."

"I know. I almost feel bad thinking about it so early. After everything that happened last time."

"Sweetie, we're doing everything the doctor told us. Sometimes, things just happen. But I have to believe this time will be different. Someone was watching over us."

"I want to be positive. I'm just scared we'll lose this one, too."

Candace squeezed Lisbeth's shoulders. "Whatever happens, I'm here. You know that won't ever change."

"I love you."

They sat in silence, curled up against each other.

"We're going to have to start decorating the nursery in a few months," Candace said.

"Sometimes, when I come home after work, I just sit in the rocking chair and think about holding our little baby in my arms, rocking them to sleep. Those are the times I feel most at peace and confident we'll make it through," Lisbeth admitted.

Candace kissed Lisbeth on the cheek and brushed a stray piece of hair back into place. "You're going to be a wonderful mother."

"So will you."

"I've been thinking. What are we going to do for last name?" Candace said.

"I think we have time to figure that out."

Around mid-afternoon, the phone rang, and Lisbeth reached for it from her spot on the couch. She looked at the caller ID but didn't recognize the number.

"Hello?"

"May I please speak with Ms. Marquez?"

"This is she."

"Hi. I'm calling from your gynecologist's office to remind you about your appointment Monday afternoon at one thirty."

"Right. Thanks so much. I'll see you at one thirty."

"Have a good day."

"Who was that?" Candace called from the kitchen.

"Doctor's office reminding me about my appointment on Monday."

"Do you want me to take off work early and pick you up?"

"Yes."

Candace appeared with a tray of assorted crackers and cheeses.

"You're spoiling me, woman. And those are hard cheeses, right?" Lisbeth said as she bit into a Triscuit.

"Yes. And no, you can't steal the Pepper Jack. It's all mine," Candace said, nudging Lisbeth in the arm.

"You're no fun," Lisbeth said and bit into a cracker.

"So, you never told me about yoga on Wednesday."

"Yes, I did."

"You said you went and that it was a relaxing workout. But did you meet anyone?"

"One woman. Her name's Shannon. She's having her fourth child. She's really nice. I'm looking forward to seeing her this week."

"Not too happy to see her, I hope."

"Oh hush. She's married, silly. And so am I."

"Yes, you are." Candace reached over and took Lisbeth's left hand in her own.

Lisbeth rested her head on the pillow behind her and stared out the window across the room. Her life was good right now. She was happily married to her soul mate, and they were going to have a baby. Now if only her family could accept her.

"What are you thinking about?" Candace asked.

"Just how happy and lucky I am to be where I am."

Monday morning arrived, and as Lisbeth escorted James and Margaret out to meet their mother, Jack flagged her down. She waved at him as she pointed out the twins' mother. Jack joined her as she headed back inside.

"Have a good weekend?" he asked.

"Yes, thank you. How about you?"

"Yeah. I was wondering if I could ask you something."

"Okay. I'm heading out shortly."

They walked back into her room, and she began reorganizing the craft table. She could feel his gaze on the back of her head.

"I've got a younger brother. He's heading off to college next fall, and I think he could use someone to talk to."

"Isn't that what big brothers are for?"

Jack scratched his neck. "Well...he told me he thinks he might be in love for the first time, and I guess that's more a woman's department."

"He can't talk to your parents about it?"

"Not really."

Lisbeth set the glue stick down on the table and turned to face Jack. She saw the redness in his cheeks as it crept up to the tips of his ears.

"Oh. *That* kind of first love."

"I couldn't think of anyone else I could talk to or ask for advice. I mean...you don't have to talk to him. I can do it. I just need...some pointers."

Lisbeth raised an eyebrow. "Pointers?"

"Like...do I tell him it's okay? That what he's feeling is normal? Because I don't know."

"You don't have a problem if he is gay, do you?"

"He's my baby brother. I just want him to be happy. I just don't want to give him the wrong idea. I don't want to see him get hurt."

"You tell him that his feelings are normal and acceptable. And not to be afraid of them. But he doesn't have to tell everyone right away if he finds his feelings are genuine. Just be there for him, Jack. Trust me; it's hard to come out to family sometimes. My parents still blissfully ignore the fact that I'm married."

"So he shouldn't tell people how he feels?"

"Admitting the truth is hard for a lot of people. It was for me. But I found the most wonderful person that I plan to spend the rest of my life with and raise my child with. Just remind him that his happiness is what should come first."

"Thanks," he said.

"I know it's hard. But you'll both get through it."

"Can I walk you out?"

"Sure. Don't push him to talk about it, either. He may not be ready," she added.

"Okay. And uh...sorry for being an idiot...again."

"You weren't being an idiot. Really, you weren't."

"Then why are you running like I've got three heads?"

"Sorry if I seem a little distracted. We've got a doctor's appointment this afternoon. It's kind of a big deal."

"Oh." He blushed some more. "Good luck."

"Thanks. Good luck to you, too."

Lisbeth grabbed her purse, and they walked out to the lobby. She signed out and waved goodbye to Jack. She watched him turn back toward the upper-grade hallway and shook her head. She wasn't used to being the resident gay expert. Lisbeth climbed into the car and pulled out of the lot. An hour later, she and Candace sat in the waiting room of her OBGYN, hands clasped together to help defray the nerves. There were a few other women in the waiting area in various stages of pregnancy.

"Lisbeth Marquez," a nurse called.

"We're up," Lisbeth said and held Candace's hand all the way back to the exam room.

A paper gown waited on the bed. The nurse instructed her to put it on and wait for Dr. Ellison. Candace sat in the chair by the bed and waited. Lisbeth stripped down to her underwear and pulled the gown around her body. She slid her panties down her legs and stepped out of them.

"They said it's not the usual ultrasound," Lisbeth said when Candace gave her a confused look.

Lisbeth got comfortable on the table and rested her hands on her stomach. The room had the faint smell of disinfectant and rubber gloves. Not the most pleasant combination.

"Are you nervous?" Candace asked.

"A little bit. We're close to where we lost the baby last time. I know we have each other, but I'm honestly not sure if I'd be able to handle not making it past this point."

A knock sounded on the door, and Dr. Ellison walked in, followed by a nurse. The nurse turned on the ultrasound machine. The tiny cylindrical probe made goose bumps break out over her exposed arms. The last time she'd seen that instrument, she'd been given the devastating news that she'd miscarried.

"How are you feeling?" Dr. Ellison asked.

"Good. Just general nerves. You know our track record."

"I do. And just to be sure, there's been no spotting or bleeding of any kind? No abdominal discomfort?"

"None. We've been following all of your directions."

"That's good to hear. We'll get the exam started. You're going to feel a little discomfort, but it shouldn't be painful."

Lisbeth reached for Candace's hand regardless and squeezed tight as she felt pressure between her legs. She watched the screen next to her for the image to appear, and pinpricks danced along her arms as it began to take shape. He leaned in close. Lisbeth held her breath and searched every pixel on the screen to differentiate the shades of gray. Was the child still within her growing?

"That blob right there. That's your baby," he said.

Lisbeth exhaled and loosened her grip on Candace's hand. Lisbeth squinted and could just make out the light gray blob on the screen in contrast the rest of the dark gray around it.

"And it looks healthy?" Lisbeth asked.

"Your fetus is perfectly healthy."

Lisbeth and Candace exchanged elated grins. The doctor moved the wand, and Lisbeth winced. A new image appeared on the screen.

"Where'd the baby go?" Lisbeth asked.

Dr. Ellison examined the image again.

"Right there. It appears to have moved a little."

"Is it supposed to do that? Move this early?"

"Let me get a better look here," he said.

He moved the wand around until there were two clear gray blobs on the screen. Both pulsed with what Lisbeth guessed were heartbeats.

"Is that what I think it is?" Candace asked.

"If you're thinking multiple embryos, yes. It appears we've got twins."

"There's more than one?" Lisbeth asked, and the sound barely passed her parched throat.

He scanned some more in silence, nodded to himself, and then hit a button on the machine twice. The nurse disappeared from the room. The doctor pulled the wand out from between Lisbeth's legs.

"You've definitely got twins."

"You're sure about that?"

"Yes. It's not uncommon with IVF pregnancies to have multiples. We discussed the possibility at the outset, if you recall."

Lisbeth licked her lips and swallowed. "Right. Of course. I guess I've been so focused on getting past this point with one baby. A second didn't even occur to me."

"Is there anything we have to do in terms of visits?" Candace asked.

"Not right away. You'll need to come in once a month at the beginning of the third trimester. As I'm sure you know, premature births are more common with multiples."

"Are there any other concerns with twins?" Candace pressed.

The doctor cleared his throat and said, "There can be other complications. Often women with multiples need to go on bed rest sometime in the second trimester. Depending on whether the twins are identical or fraternal, there may be some added concerns about their development."

"But if we come in for our regular checkups and follow all of your instructions, we should be fine, right?" Lisbeth prompted.

"In theory, yes. But given your history, I'd be a little concerned that you would deliver early. We want to do everything we can to get you to your due date."

Lisbeth forced a smile. "Thanks."

"You can go ahead and get dressed. If you have any questions, please don't hesitate to call."

"Thank you."

"The nurse will be back with your pictures."

Lisbeth nodded and waited for the doctor to leave. She pulled on her underwear and pants and untied the string around the gown. She let it fall around her ankles and slipped her shirt over her head.

"Are you all right, sweetie?" Candace asked.

"Yeah. Fine. It's just a little...overwhelming. We're having twins. And this morning, I was worried we wouldn't be having any."

"He said it's not unexpected. And they said it might happen when we first started the process."

"I know. It's just taking a little time to wrap my head around it. I guess it's a good thing we didn't buy any baby furniture yet. We're going to need two of everything."

"Not everything. Come on. I'll buy you a big bowl of ice cream. It will make you feel better."

The nurse walked back in and handed them the pictures with the labels baby A and baby B tagged at the top.

"Thanks so much," Candace said and linked arms with Lisbeth.

They walked down the hall to the reception desk.

"Hi, we need to make another appointment for the middle of October," Lisbeth said.

The receptionist tapped away at her keyboard. "We've got an appointment for ten fifteen on October thirteenth."

"Do you have anything after one thirty that day?"

"No, I'm sorry. We have one on the fourteenth at two forty-five."

"I'm sure they'll understand if you miss a day," Candace said.

"I don't want to take time off early on if I don't have to. The fourteenth is fine."

The receptionist wrote down Lisbeth's name and appointment date and time on a card and handed it over. Lisbeth slipped it in her purse and pulled out her wallet. She paid for the visit, and they picked up their coats in the waiting room. Lisbeth stared at the ultrasounds and smiled. It was more than she'd been expecting by far.

"They look the same," she said.

"They are the same. At least right now."

"Well, we could get two girls. Or two boys."

"Or one of each," Candace said.

"I think it would be nice to have one of each."

"I think it's out of our hands."

"I know. How are you handling all of this?" Lisbeth asked.

"I'm still wrapping my head around it, too. I mean...we were going to be good with one baby, but two? That's a lot more responsibility."

"I know. I don't know what to think yet, either," Lisbeth agreed.

Candace slowed at a stop light, and Lisbeth looked out the passenger window. They weren't too far from the yoga studio.

"Hon, can we make a quick stop? I want to pay for a few more classes."

"Sure. Just tell me where to go."

"Take the next right, and it should be about a block up."

Lisbeth tapped the ultrasound picture against her lap as Candace pulled up in front of the studio. She stayed still for a bit longer before unbuckling her seatbelt and climbing out.

"I'll only be a minute," she said and pulled open the front door.

A blast of cool air smacked her in the face when she stepped up to the front desk. The receptionist bent over her keyboard, while another woman stood with a clipboard in hand. Lisbeth stood behind the other woman and waited.

"Here you go," the woman said and handed over the clipboard.

Lisbeth glimpsed the name Renee printed at the top.

"Let me just get your information into the computer. Now, you want to attend our Wednesday classes?"

"Yeah. Do I have to pay now?"

"We can take a check for the first two weeks of classes now, and then you can pay by class if you'd like. Or we can do monthly."

"How much is it for the whole month?"

The receptionist hit a few keys on her calculator and said, "Eighty a month. But you can pay weekly if you want."

"I'll pay the first two weeks now, I guess. Can I decide how I want to pay the rest later?"

"Sure."

Lisbeth watched while Renee fished two twenties out of her purse and handed them over. The receptionist gave her a smile and put the money in a drawer before writing out a receipt.

"You're all set. We'll see you soon."

"Thanks."

Renee took a step back, collided with Lisbeth, and knocked her purse to the floor.

"Sorry," Lisbeth said.

"No, it's my fault," Renee said and bent to pick up Lisbeth's purse.

"I'm Lisbeth."

"Renee."

"You're going to the Wednesday afternoon classes?" Lisbeth asked.

"Yeah. Looks like it. You?"

"I'll see you there, then."

"Cool." Renee handed over the purse. "Bye."

"Bye."

Lisbeth turned her attention to the receptionist, pulled out her checkbook, and made out a check for eighty dollars to cover the next month.

Chapter Eleven

September 16th

RENEE SLUMPED AGAINST THE SINK AND SWALLOWED slowly before flushing the toilet and standing up. She turned the water on and let it get cold before splashing it on her face and neck. She hated morning sickness. After all, she couldn't exactly give tours while running to the bathroom every half hour to puke her guts out. And her mom said it went away after the first trimester.

"Renee? You still in there?" Bryce called from outside.

"Yeah. I'll be out in a minute."

"Hurry up."

"Just hold on."

Renee swished some mouthwash around and spat it out. The gritty feeling still clung to her tongue and teeth, but she could hear Bryce pacing. She was surprised he was up this early. She checked herself in the mirror once more and then opened the door. Bryce darted in, and she heard the toilet seat go up. She shook her head and headed back to the bedroom to get dressed for work. Just as she finished her makeup, Bryce walked back in.

"You're not sick, are you? Because I can't get sick," he said.

She stared at him. "No."

"I heard you throwing up."

"It's morning sickness, Bryce. It's normal. Disgusting, but normal."

He pulled on a pair of jeans and a T-shirt and said, "Oh. You wouldn't have that if you'd—"

"Don't you dare," she said.

He flinched but didn't finish his sentence. She surveyed his clothing.

"Going somewhere?" she asked.

"Yeah. Meeting some of the guys for a day out."

"Oh. Are you going to be home by dinner?"

"I don't know."

"Well, call if you're not, okay?"

"Sure."

Bryce left, and Renee finished getting ready, tossing some anti-nausea meds in her pocket before heading to the kitchen. She poured a glass of milk and took her prenatal vitamins and her calcium pill. The front door slammed shut, and she could hear the elevator whir to life down the hallway.

Renee eyed the clock and jumped. *So much for making breakfast.* Without the car, she'd have to take the T in, and it was going to be mobbed. Fumbling with her T pass at the station, she had to fight through the crowd and nearly missed the train. Renee gulped down air to keep from being sick as the train trundled along the track to Government Center. Her heart pounded when she reached the platform. A train pulled out of the station as she stopped moving. *Can today get any worse?* Renee could feel tears of frustration trickle down her cheeks. Leaning against a support beam, she brushed the tears away in an effort to keep it together.

"Are you okay?" a man beside her asked.

"Yeah. Just running late this morning. One of those days, you know?"

"Yeah." He reached into his pocket pulled out some tissues. "Here."

She blushed. "Thanks."

Renee ran the back of her hand over her cheeks and blew her nose. Another train came screeching to a halt. She gave the man a smile and stepped onto the train. He waved at her through the window as the doors closed and the train left the station. She clutched the tissues all the way to the Aquarium stop.

"You're late," her boss said as she walked into the locker room.

"Sorry."

"It's been happening more often, Renee. Is something going on that I need to know about?"

Renee swallowed. "Yes. I should have mentioned it sooner, but it was all kind of unexpected. I'm pregnant."

"You are?"

"Yeah. About twelve weeks."

Her boss led her to a seat. Renee sat and waited for her boss to speak. She tried to fight the uneasy feeling in her stomach, unsure if it was nerves or more morning sickness.

"How've you been handling the morning sickness?" her boss asked.

"Um...okay, I guess. It's not pleasant. I don't think my boyfriend gets that it's part of pregnancy. He asked me this morning if I was getting sick. And he's kind of been a jerk about the whole thing."

"If you need to take shorter shifts, just let me know. We'll work around it as best we can."

"Thanks."

"Just make me one promise."

"Sure."

"You don't stay on maternity leave too long. We need you here."

"Yes, ma'am," Renee said with a smile.

"We don't have any groups scheduled for this morning. So you can take it easy."

"Thanks."

Renee spent the morning wandering the grounds. She stopped by the penguin tank, admiring the birds as they slid in and out of the water with grace and ease. It was beautiful. She got nods and waves from the trainers as they dove into the water to feed the penguins. She made the rounds to the larger outdoor animals, stopping at the sea lions for a while shortly before noon. One of the massive animals rolled onto its side and waggled its flipper at her. She couldn't help but laugh.

"It's waving at you," a little boy said.

"Yes, it is. Should we wave back?"

"Yes."

So they both waved back to the sea lion. It dove into the water in response. The boy laughed and took off running. Renee went the opposite direction down to the break room and opened her locker to get money from her purse. The ultrasound picture came into view. She ran her fingers over the tiny blob and smiled. The next day was her twelve-week checkup, which meant a new picture.

"Nee, we're heading over to grab some pizza. Want to come?" Carl said from the other side of the room.

"Sure. Let me just grab my purse."

She shut her locker and put on her jacket. The small group of five headed out of the aquarium and down the street to Pizza Palace. Renee picked at her slice of cheese pizza, wishing her stomach wouldn't protest so much about pepperoni or sausage. She missed eating meat.

"You in there?" Carl said.

"Huh?" Renee replied.

"You were zoning out."

"Sorry. I didn't sleep well last night."

Renee forced herself to eat the pizza instead of pick at it. Her stomach wasn't happy on the walk back, and she quickly left the group to head for the bathroom. She walked out and nearly collided with a woman pushing a stroller.

"I'm so sorry," Renee apologized.

"That's all right."

Renee held the door open for the woman so she could get through and then took off at a jog to meet her afternoon tour group. Thankfully, it was small, and they were young. They'd lose interest quickly, and Renee would get out of a long tour. Exhaustion consumed every inch of her body by the end of her shift. She almost missed her transfer at Government Center, her head was so in the clouds. Fifteen minutes later, she walked out of the T stop and checked her phone. No calls from Bryce. She collapsed on the couch as soon as she was in the apartment and barely had enough energy to pull a blanket over her shoulder before dozing off. When she woke, the sky was completely dark and the apartment was quiet. She sat up, and immediately her stomach rumbled. Groaning, she climbed off the couch, made some soup, and sat down at the kitchen table. There were no new messages on her phone, and Bryce was likely at work by now. *I'll see him in the morning before the doctor.*

When Renee woke up the next morning, Bryce's side of the bed was empty. She moved through the apartment, listening closely, but Bryce wasn't there. No messages on her phone. She hastily dialed his number and waited for it to ring. Five, six, seven times, and then to voicemail. After the beep, she said, "Bryce, it's me. Where the hell are you? I'm going to my appointment in an hour. Call me back."

She hung up and buttered some toast before heading out. By the time she got to the doctor's office, she was running late. She hated running late.

"Hi," Renee said and caught her breath. "Renee Blackwell."

"Have a seat."

Renee lounged in the waiting area for ten minutes before a nurse led her back to an exam room.

"Just put on the gown, and the doctor will be in to see you in a few minutes."

Renee stripped to her underwear and wrapped the paper gown around her body. It was flimsy and provided no warmth. So she sat and shivered on the exam table until the doctor came in.

"How are you doing, Renee?"

"Good. Thanks."

"Having any problems?"

"Not that I know of. I really wish the morning sickness would stop."

"How often do you find yourself getting ill?"

"A few times a day. Usually if I eat something too fast. It's usually really bad in the morning."

"That's normal. It should start to let up around the start of the second trimester."

"I can't wait."

"I'm going to have you lie back for me, and we'll take a peek at your baby."

Renee gasped when he applied the gel to her bare belly. He spread it around with the monitor and pointed to the screen beside her.

"There's your baby."

"It's bigger than the last time I was in."

"That's what we like to see. When you come back for your next checkup, we should start to see limbs forming. But that pulsing right there in the middle is the baby's heartbeat."

Renee gazed at the tiny flicker on the screen. It was strong and constant and perfect. The doctor wiped the gel from her stomach and put the scanner down.

"We'll have a picture printed up if you'd like."

"Please."

"You can get dressed now."

Renee waited until the doctor left to pull her pants and shirt back on. She sat in the calm of the room for a few minutes before going out to pay. Taking the card for her next appointment, she thanked the receptionist. The nurse walked by and handed Renee the new ultrasound picture. Renee touched the bigger gray blob in the middle with care as she left the office and hopped back on the T. At work, she walked into the locker room with a huge smile. Her boss, Pam, spotted her and jogged over.

"You look happy."

Renee brandished the picture.

"I just had a doctor's appointment."

Pam took the picture and examined it. "Can't really tell what it is."

"It's that in the middle. See how they outlined it?"

"Oh, there it is."

"They said at the next checkup, it should have arms and legs."

"I'm glad you're happy, Renee. You've been pretty glum the last few weeks."

Renee hung her head as she took the picture back. "I know. It's just been kind of a roller coaster, cheesy as that sounds."

"Well, keep up the cheerful spirit, because we've got a lot of tours today."

Renee nodded and set her purse and the picture in her locker before heading out to meet the first group of the day. Rambunctious second graders, half of which didn't seem at all interested in the marine life around them. She'd change that.

By the time the tour ended, all of the kids were chattering excitedly about what they wanted to buy from the gift shop.

By the end of the day, however, Renee was ready to go home. She took the steps at the T two at a time and managed to hop a train just as it left the station. The entire ride home, her mind raced. *Seeing the new ultrasound will change his mind about the baby.* The picture stayed safely tucked in her purse until she climbed off the train and sprinted the distance from the T to her building. Without even acknowledging the doorman, Renee hit the elevator call button repeatedly.

"Hitting it won't make it come faster," a woman said.

"I know...I'm just in a hurry."

The elevator finally arrived, and Renee stepped on before everyone else had a chance to get off. Ignoring the nasty looks, she waited for the doors to close. She had a very small window of time in which to catch Bryce before he went to work. Renee forced the keys into the lock but found the door already unlocked.

"Bryce, I'm back," she called.

No response.

She walked in and set her keys and purse in the kitchen. Carrying the ultrasound picture, she headed for the bedroom.

"Bryce, I have something to show you..." She trailed off as she walked into an empty room.

Something was off. Tentatively, she opened the closet by the door. Empty. Next, the closet they shared. All of his clothes were gone. Drawers were empty, too. Panic set in as she raced to the bathroom. Toothbrush, shaving kit, everything. Gone.

Renee tried to breathe, but no air filled her lungs. She sank to the floor, and the picture fell from her hands. The room went in and out of focus, as if she was going to pass out. It didn't make sense. He wouldn't just disappear. Finally, air pushed into her burning lungs, and her chest ached from the effort. She found enough strength to stand and return to the bedroom. Everything he owned was gone. She let her feet take her where they wanted. The kitchen. An envelope sat on the table. She picked it up with shaking hands. There was a check inside with "next month's rent" printed in the memo line. Renee tossed it back on the table and made it to the couch before collapsing and turning into a tear-soaked mess. They kept coming until she had no more tears to cry and her eyes burned. She rubbed them and only made it worse. Breaths came in ragged shallow gasps. Sitting up, she pulled out her cell and dialed his number.

It rang six times before it went to voicemail. Instead of leaving a message, she hung up and headed for the hallway. She hit the call button for the elevator and nearly stormed out into the lobby when it stopped to let her disembark. She stopped at the door to the leasing office and heard voices inside.

"We're about to close," one of the women at the front desk said when she spotted Renee.

"I need to talk to someone," Renee said, trying to keep the anger out of her voice.

"You'll have to come back tomorrow."

"It's an emergency."

The woman glanced to her left, where the manager sat. After another moment of silence, she nodded.

"You can go in."

Renee walked into the manager's office and slammed the door shut. The manager jumped.

"What can I do for you?"

"Bryce Eagan. When did he move out?"

"What unit?"

"Six fifteen."

He hastily checked his records.

"He turned in his key around two thirty today."

"What does that mean for me?"

"I'm sorry?"

"I'm still living there. But I can't pay rent on a two bedroom apartment."

"Please sit down."

Renee sank into a chair.

"Why don't you explain what's going on."

"I don't know what's going on. I got home today, and he was just gone. All of his stuff is gone, and he left me a check, but it only covers next month."

"We aren't really in a position to offer to lower your rent right now. Maybe if you renew your lease?"

"Are you deaf? I can't pay the rent now!"

"Please calm down."

"No. You know what, fuck this."

Renee stormed out of the room, her neck hot with anger. She couldn't take this. It wasn't fair, and if she wasn't careful, she was going to punch some*one* or some*thing* really hard.

She took the stairs up the six flights to her floor and ended up back on the couch, staring at the new ultrasound picture.

"You aren't going to leave me," she whispered and pressed the picture to her chest.

Chapter Twelve

September 17th

ERIKA SAT ON THE COUCH WITH HER LAPTOP ON THE table in front of her. Dane sat beside her and leaned forward to fiddle with the touchpad mouse.

"What about this one?" he asked, pointing to a glossy-looking homepage.

"No."

"Erika, this is like the tenth site we've looked at. You have to choose one."

"I don't know what I'm supposed to be looking for."

"I'm not an expert, either. And you're the one who wants to do this."

"I'm tired. Can't you just do it for me? I want to go to bed."

Not waiting for his answer, she climbed over his lap and headed into her bedroom. Crawling beneath the covers, she tried to ignore the sound of Dane still surfing the Internet in the next room. Sleep came quickly. Erika rolled over, felt a presence standing by the bed, and her heart fluttered. Dane stood there holding a Starbucks tray.

"How'd you get in?" she asked, still half-asleep.

"I stayed last night, remember?"

She shook her head.

"Here, drink this." He handed her an insulated cup.

Erika struggled to a sitting position and took a sip. Tea with about four sugars. Only way she'd drink it. Dane stood where he was, giving her an expectant look.

"Thanks."

"Come on. You have to get up."

"What for? I'm never leaving my apartment again. I'm never going near anyone ever again."

"I found a clinic and made an appointment for today."

Erika handed the tea back and buried herself under the covers. She waited for him to leave, but he stood there, watching her.

"You told me you wanted my help, Erika. So I'm helping because you obviously weren't interested. Besides, you haven't left this place in like a week."

Slowly, Erika stuck her head out from beneath the blanket. "I am interested. I don't want this thing in me. You're sure people won't know when we go?"

"Course not." He offered her a hand, and she let him pull her out of bed.

She stopped in front of the mirror and stared at herself in the semi-darkness. "God, you can see it."

"You can't. You look fine," Dane replied, guiding her toward the living room.

She shielded her gaze as the daylight struck her. Erika groaned as she pulled on sneakers and finger-combed her hair. Dane shoved the teacup back into her hands and helped her into her jacket.

"You're sure they'll do it? They'll get rid of it?"

"Erika, it's what they do."

She nodded, and they walked down to the elevator. Dane blocked her vantage point of the mirror, and she was secretly grateful. She moved almost as if she were sleep walking all the way to the clinic. Her mind was blank as Dane forced her into a chair.

"Erika." His voice was miles away.

A sharp crack echoed in her ears, and she looked at him. "Huh?"

"You have to fill this out," he said, handing her a form.

She stared at it, but none of the words made sense.

"I can't do it."

"They aren't going to take you if you don't."

"It's like it's in gibberish or something."

Dane took the clipboard back and read the questions aloud. Erika did her best to answer, but she couldn't come up with any idea of when she was due.

"Well, just guess."

Erika shrugged. "I don't know. April, maybe?"

"Okay." He looked over the rest of the form. "I think we answered everything."

Erika watched him give the clipboard back to the receptionist. She didn't even protest when he took her hand in his.

"We'll get through this."

"Why are you being so nice to me?"

"Because I care about you. And I hate seeing the people I care about in pain."

Erika felt the blush creep into her cheeks, and she turned away. "Thanks."

They sat together in the waiting room, and all Erika could do was look at Dane in profile. Maybe her head was still a little foggy, but he seemed to glow. She curled up against his shoulder and snaked her arm through his. Finally, the door at the far right opened, and a woman in a pale pink outfit walked out.

"Erika Lind?"

"That's us," Dane said, tugging her to her feet.

Erika tried to straighten her shirt and pants as they followed the woman into a chilly office. *But they don't do this in offices.*

"Please have a seat," the woman in pink said.

Erika complied and fidgeted in the chair. The air was too cold, and every inch of her skin prickled with goose bumps. Even the little hairs on her neck stood on end. The woman looked over the information Dane had filled out.

"So, tell me Erika, why do you want to have an abortion?"

Erika blinked. *Is she stupid?* "I don't want a baby. I never wanted a baby. It just happened. I can't be a parent."

"Have you considered other options?"

"Like what? There's nothing else out there."

The woman pulled a few pamphlets from her desk and passed them over. Erika took them and looked through.

Adoption.

"You think I should do this?"

"I'm not making any decisions for you, Erika. This is your baby and your choice. We're just trying to give you information about all of the available options." She stood. "I'll give you some time to think about it and check back in a few minutes."

The door thudded closed, and Erika could feel the vibrations from her feet to her ears. She tossed the pamphlets on the desk and stood up.

"Where are you going?" Dane asked.

"I can't do this. You said you were going to help me."

"I am helping you, Erika. Sit down."

"No. You lied to me. You said they would do it, and they aren't doing it."

"Damn it, Erika, sit your ass down and listen to me."

Red-faced, Dane pointed to the chair. One look at him, and Erika sat.

"I get that your life is really fucked up right now. You've got this baby you didn't ask for, and you don't know how to deal. Well, this lady is giving you an option. Have the kid, and let someone else raise it. You may not want to admit it, but your heart isn't in this abortion."

"What the fuck do you know?"

"I know you, Erika. You have a right to be scared. I'd be more worried if you weren't scared. But you can't let that control you."

"It's just a thing. A bunch of cells."

"You're just rationalizing. You know as well as I do that's the truth. Now, just consider this other option. Please."

She eyed the stack of shiny leaflets again. The people in the photographs with little babies all looked so happy and normal. As if it was the easiest thing in the world to just hand off your kid to some stranger.

"But who would want my kid?"

"I'm sure there's somebody out there that wants a baby and can't have one. This is a way out. You just have to see it."

Erika drew her knees to her chest and wrapped her arms around her legs. It was all too much to take in at once. All she'd wanted to do for weeks was forget it had happened, and after being on overload, even that was too difficult to accomplish. Before she could start coming up with reasons why it would be a bad and horrible idea to go through with adoption, the woman in pink walked back in, carrying Styrofoam cups.

"I brought you some water."

"Thanks," Erika mumbled. She took the cup and gulped the water down.

The woman sat down across from them and leaned on the desk.

"So...if I do this...I don't have to keep the baby?" Erika said and nodded toward the adoption pamphlets.

"That's right. The adoption agency will match you with a family and, depending on the agreement you come to, they may pay for doctors' visits and hospital bills, and you might be able to have some contact with the baby after birth."

Erika paled at the mention of doctors. She hadn't been to one since she found out about the pregnancy.

"Oh. You don't do that here?"

"No. But in the brochures I gave you, it lists a wonderful organization."

Erika sifted through the material until the one for Commonwealth Adoption Services stared up at her with its bright colors and happy people.

"They're here in Boston, so you can make an appointment, and they'll be happy to help you."

"What about, um…what if the baby's got problems?"

"What do you mean?"

"Like…" She couldn't make herself say it. She looked to Dane, begging him with her eyes to fill in the blanks.

"I think what she means is what if she did something that might hurt the baby…like…drinking."

Always coming through for her.

"Your doctor can test for fetal alcohol syndrome. Did you consume a lot of alcohol?"

Erika felt her face redden, and she was pretty sure she was burning like a super nova. "I really don't remember. But I did drink. I didn't even think about it."

"Have you been to see a doctor?"

"Not since August…like a month ago."

She made some notes on the clipboard and nodded her head. "You should see a doctor immediately."

"But if there is something wrong with it…doesn't that mean that no one will want it?"

"People adopt children with special needs all the time."

The woman was trying to be positive, even though her voice sounded strained. But it was nice of her to say it. The room fell silent except for the crackle of the air conditioning in the ceiling still pumping out arctic air.

"Here's my card if you have any questions," the woman said, handing over a beige card.

Charlotte Everett.

"Thanks," Erika mumbled.

"Good luck."

Erika folded up the adoption brochures and stuck them in her purse. She followed Dane out to the waiting area. After the receptionist reassured them three times that they didn't have pay if they didn't have a procedure done, they left. The air outside felt fifteen degrees warmer than it did in the office.

"God, why was it so cold in there?"

"It wasn't that cold," Dane said.

"You're a guy. You have more to keep you warm."

Dane nudged her in the shoulder as they weaved through the pedestrian traffic. They walked in silence for a minute or two before Dane looped his arm through hers.

"So, are you feeling okay?"

"You mean do I want to throw up? No."

"I mean in general. That was a lot to take in back there."

"Did you know they were going to tell me not to do it?"

"No."

She could hear the lie in his voice. He was a crappy liar.

"You did, too."

"Well okay, maybe I thought they might. But let's face it, you were pretty terrified going in there."

"I probably already screwed this kid up anyway. No one's going to want it."

"You don't know that. That lady said people take kids with problems all the time."

"She was just being nice, dummy."

"You shouldn't be so cranky."

"I'm going to be really fat, and it's your fault."

"You'll make it. Just think...With all that extra fat, you won't get cold in the winter time."

"You're stupid."

Dane pulled his arm away from hers and wrapped it around her shoulders. They made it back to her apartment and found a notice slipped under the door. Erika's heart started to beat a little faster. It was on the leasing office letterhead. She walked right past it.

"Hey, Erika, you've got something from your landlord."

"I don't want to see it."

"You should. It says you didn't pay this month's rent."

"Fuck. This day just gets better and better." Erika crawled onto the couch and pressed a pillow to her chest.

"This is serious."

"I don't have the money to pay it. I'm probably fired anyway."

Dane opened his mouth to speak, but she held up a hand.

"I'm not taking your money. I'll figure it out."

"You've got way too much going on right now to handle this. Let me give you the money. You don't even have to pay me back."

"Dane, I don't want your money."

"But you need it. They're going to kick you out if you don't pay by the beginning of October."

"Well, it's not the end of September yet, so I've got time."

Dane glared at her and pulled the brochures out of her purse. He flipped through a couple and then stopped.

"What?" Erika asked.

"This one's not about adoption."

"So?"

"It's about yoga."

"Like going to the gym and getting all sweaty?"

"Something like that, but for pregnant women. Here." He handed it to her.

She looked at the two-sided paper for Maternal Instincts Yoga in downtown Boston. She couldn't keep a snort of laughter in after seeing the pictures of really pregnant women doing hilarious poses.

"This is pretty funny."

"Maybe she put it in there for a reason."

"Maybe."

"Hey, if you need me to get you to a doctor's appointment or anything, just let me know," he said, toying with the zipper on his wallet.

"Oh, uh...okay. I'll call you."

"You really should see a doctor soon."

Erika looked at the women in the brochure again. Despite the funny poses, they looked calm and relaxed. She'd love to be calm and relaxed right now.

"I'll make one Monday."

"Okay. Just text me when and where, and I'll be there."

She got up and wrapped her arms around him. He held her close, and she remembered how good it had felt when they were together. Tilting her head up, she kissed him. Just a quick kiss, but it left a dazed, slightly dopey look on his face.

"Thanks," she said.

He let out a soft sigh and took a step away from her.

"I should go," he muttered and bolted for the door.

Erika watched him go and sank back to the couch. *Stupid. I shouldn't have kissed him. Now he's going to panic, and things are going to get all weird.* She screamed into the pillow and reached for the nearest glass. She sniffed it. Old beer. She was about to put it to her lips when she remembered how much she'd already ruined her kid's chances of being normal.

Chapter Thirteen

September 20th

SHANNON LEANED BACK, RUBBING AWAY THE SLEEPY feeling. She'd barely slept the night before. The images on the computer screen blurred, and she turned away. Work could wait until after her doctor's appointment. Even though it made Mike happy, she was beginning to regret taking on more clients. She should voice her own concerns, but she hated fighting with him. Tanner sat in the living room, watching cartoons.

"Tanner, honey, let's get your shoes on," she called.

"Where we going, Mama?"

"Mama has to go to the doctor for a baby checkup," Shannon answered, scooping him up from the floor.

He wrapped his arms around her neck and held on tight as she carried him to the front hall and slid his feet into sneakers that had Velcro straps. Shannon grabbed her purse and keys from the kitchen, and together, they headed to the car. She buckled Tanner into his car seat and slid into the driver seat.

"Why we got to go to the doctor, Mama?" Tanner asked, kicking his feet against the back of the passenger seat.

"Because we have to make sure the baby in Mama's tummy is growing big and strong."

"Why?"

"Because we do."

"When is the baby getting here?"

"Not for a long time."

The rest of the car ride to the office was quiet, aside from the occasional thump as Tanner kicked the back of the passenger seat. She pulled into the parking lot and cut the engine. Tanner kept kicking the seat as she got out and walked around the back of the car.

"Come on," she said and unbuckled him.

He didn't move.

"Tanner, get out of the car."

"No. I don't want to."

Shannon pursed her lips and kept calm. They still had a few minutes. Hopefully, it wouldn't take long to settle his stubborn mood.

"You can't stay in the car."

"Don't want to go."

Huffing, she picked him up under the armpits, hoisted him to her hip, and carried him, kicking and screaming, all the way to the office. The temper tantrum continued while Shannon checked in with the receptionist. Several women sat reading magazines, acting as if the tantrum wasn't happening. Tanner screamed as loud as he could, his cheeks red from frustration and damp with tears.

"Tanner, that's enough," Shannon scolded.

She set him in a chair and bent to his eye level.

"You are a big boy. And big boys don't throw tantrums."

"Don't want to see baby," Tanner whimpered through a hiccup and a sob.

His tiny fists pounded against her arms, each hit less forceful than the one before, until he finally slumped against the arm of the chair. She looked around, but no one seemed to notice them or say a word. Tanner sniffled beside her, and Shannon sat down in a chair. She picked up a magazine and leafed through it halfheartedly. The door to the office opened, and a young woman, maybe mid-twenties, walked in, followed by a guy about the same age. They didn't speak, only stared at each other. Finally, he urged her to the reception desk.

"Name, please," the receptionist asked.

"Erika Lind," she said.

Shannon was close enough to hear the girl answer. As she took a seat beside the young man, Shannon saw that Erika, dressed in a baggy sweat outfit despite the warm weather, was pale and had been crying.

"Mama, I'm bored," Tanner complained.

Shannon pulled out a small pad of paper and some colored pencils she always kept with her.

"You can draw."

"Okay."

She watched him for a few minutes as he scribbled on the top page. It kept him occupied for now. Erika and her friend started talking.

"I'll figure it out," Erika said.

"Like you figured out your last money problem?"

"It's not October yet."

"Can't you just let me help you? I said you don't have to pay me back."

"You don't have to help me, Dane. We went through this already."

"Fine. But what about the doctor? They're going to do tests and stuff. That costs money. How are you going to pay for it?"

"I have insurance. I'm still on my parents' insurance until the end of the year."

"Then what?"

Erika scrunched up her face and dug the heels of her hands into her eyelids. Shannon looked away, and heat crept up her neck. The room suddenly felt too small, as if she was being obtrusive, even from across the room. The pair continued to squabble until a nurse appeared and called Shannon's name.

"Tanner, come on, sweetie."

"I want to color."

"You can. We just have to follow this lady."

Tanner clutched the pencils and paper in one hand and held onto the back of her shirt with the other. They ended up in an exam room near the back of the office. Tanner finally detached from Shannon's side and sat down in the chair near the exam table. Shannon quickly settled on the bed and waited.

A knock came a few minutes later, and a woman walked in. Tanner didn't even look up from his paper.

"Hi, Shannon," Dr. DeShawn said.

"Hi."

"My goodness. This must be Tanner."

"Yeah. He's gotten quite a lot bigger since you last saw him."

"Yeah. Gosh, how long ago was that?"

"Four years," Shannon answered.

"And we're here again."

Shannon forced a smile. "Yeah."

"Well, we'll do your ultrasound and get you on your way."

That got Tanner's attention. He put down his colored pencils and paper, climbed out of the chair, and leaned against the table with his chin resting on the cushion.

"What's that, Mama?" he asked, pointing at the ultrasound monitor.

"That's where we get to see the picture of the baby," Dr. DeShawn answered.

"Picture?"

Shannon tugged Tanner by the hand so he wasn't blocking the screen. Dr. DeShawn squeezed the ultrasound gel onto Shannon's stomach, and Tanner reached out to touch it.

"Don't touch, Tanner," Shannon said, swatting away his hand.

The doctor leaned forward and positioned the ultrasound monitor on Shannon's stomach. The screen suddenly came to life in shades of gray. A sort of sucking sound echoed from the machine, which made Tanner giggle. He pressed his nose within a couple inches of the monitor.

"What's that?"

"That's the inside of Mama's tummy," Shannon said.

Tanner's gaze widened. "Inside?" He looked at his own stomach.

"You used to be inside Mama's tummy, too, before you were born."

"How did I fit?"

"You were tiny."

"Let's see if we can get a clear picture, here," Dr. DeShawn said and moved the device a little to the right. "There we are."

She pointed to a tiny pulsing shadow in the center of the monitor.

"Do you see that right there?" she asked Tanner.

"Yeah."

"That's the baby's heartbeat. That's your little brother or sister."

"It's little."

"It will get bigger," Shannon said.

"Hi, baby," Tanner shouted at his mother's stomach.

Shannon laughed, but the sensation of the monitor pressed against her skin stopped her.

"Well, everything looks good, Shannon. I'll see you back in a month."

"Great."

"I'll get that printed for you if you want."

"Sure. Thanks."

Dr. DeShawn hit a button on the machine and left the room. Tanner backed up a few steps as Shannon swung her legs over the edge of the bed.

"Tanner, can you get Mama some paper towels over there?" she asked and pointed to a low counter.

He reached for the roll, his fingers barely able to reach it. After a bit of struggling, he managed to get the roll off the counter and handed it to her. She pulled off a couple of sheets and wiped the gel from her stomach. Pulling down her shirt, she got to her feet and checked the time. Her heart skipped a beat. They'd have to hurry if she didn't want to be late dropping him at daycare.

"Come on, honey. Get your paper and pencils. We have to go."

She led him out of the exam room and back to the front of the office. Erika and her friend still sat in their corner looking sullen. Erika sat with her knees pressed to her chest. Dr. DeShawn stepped in and handed a picture to Shannon.

"Tanner, do you want to hold the picture?" she asked.

He took it and stared at it.

"Baby," he said and giggled.

Shannon quickly made her next appointment. She glanced over at Erika again and opened her checkbook.

"Um...I have a question," Shannon said and leaned closer. "Yes?"

"What is that young woman here for?" She pointed to Erika.

"I'm sorry, I can't discuss other patients. Do you know her?"

"No. I just thought she looked like she could use some help covering her appointment."

The receptionist eyed her warily.

"I'm sure she'd appreciate that, but I still can't give out any confidential patient information."

"I understand. Thank you anyway."

With that, she took Tanner by the hand, and they headed to daycare. All through the afternoon, Shannon wondered about Erika and whether she would be okay. She hadn't meant to get involved in a stranger's life, but just the sorry state she'd been in had tugged at Shannon's heartstrings. Not being able to help made it worse. At two p.m., she picked up Christian and Megan from school and made them a snack.

"Mama, can I put baby on the fridge?" Tanner asked.

"Sure."

Tanner stuck the ultrasound picture smack in the middle of the fridge with smiling flower magnets. Right in Meghan's sightline.

"What's that?" she asked and wrinkled her nose.

"Baby in Mama's tummy," Tanner answered proudly.

"That's not a baby," she told him.

"It is," Shannon said and intervened before the pair got into a shouting match.

Meghan looked at Shannon's stomach in surprise and then back to the picture.

"I thought babies were bigger. And looked like us."

"They are. They have to grow. Just like you. Come on. Did you finish your spelling homework?"

"Yes."

"Let me check it."

Meghan handed over the paper, and Shannon scrutinized her daughter's handwriting. A little shaky on some of the letters, but far more legible than Christian's handwriting at six.

"Good job."

"Can I watch TV now?" Meghan asked.

"For a half hour. And you have to share with Tanner."

Meghan dragged Tanner off toward the living room, leaving Shannon in the kitchen alone. She looked at the ultrasound picture again. Sadness and almost overwhelming guilt clinched her stomach. *Why am I not happy about this baby?* She tried to shake off the uncertainty while she made dinner. She put on a brave face for Mike through the meal and let Tanner yammer on about the appointment. Even Christian seemed interested.

Around nine thirty that night, Shannon sat reading a book on the couch, when Mike stuck his head around the corner from the dining room.

"Hon?"

"Hmm?"

"You seem a little down. Are you okay?"

Shannon put her book down and looked at him.

"It's nothing. Just a little tired."

"I know you, Shan. It's something. So come on and talk to me. Did something happen at the appointment?"

"Sort of. Nothing's wrong with the baby. There was a girl there...couldn't have been more than twenty-two or twenty-three, and she just looked so..."

"She looked what?" he pressed.

"Sad. And scared. I was going to pay for her appointment. I overheard her talking, and it sounded like she had money problems."

Mike's expression changed, and Shannon knew from past experience that an argument was brewing if she said much more. *If he'd been the one trying to help a poor soul, he'd be the hero.*

"She asked you to?" He walked into the room and sat down beside her.

"No. But it doesn't matter anyway. I couldn't help her. HIPPA and all," she answered with as much calm as she could muster. It was decidedly very little.

"Shannon, I thought we were trying to save money. Hasn't that been the concern with this pregnancy? Isn't that why you took on more work?"

Taking a deep breath and mentally counting to five, she said, "We are. But like I said, it doesn't matter because I didn't. Just forget I said anything."

She got up and headed for the stairs.

"Where are you going?"

"To bed. I'm tired."

Shannon stormed upstairs and climbed beneath the covers. She and Mike rarely fought about anything. Not that there weren't times she'd love to tell him how underappreciated she felt. Confronting conflict wasn't her style. But maybe this time, he was right. They would have to save up to have enough to buy formula and clothes and all the other accessories a baby required. She rolled over and tried not to think as she fell asleep.

Chapter Fourteen

September 29th

L ISBETH CHECKED HERSELF IN THE MIRROR IN THE women's bathroom at school. She patted her hair down with a dab of water before stepping back to get more of her figure in the reflection. Even though she was only at the end of her first trimester, she was starting to show. Resting one hand on her stomach, she couldn't fight the smile that crept onto her lips. There were concerns with having twins, but she and Candace would find a way to make it work. She was so absorbed in admiring her form that she didn't hear the door open.

"You're starting to show already," Ellen said.

"Oh, you startled me," Lisbeth replied, clutching her chest.

"Sorry, hon."

"Yeah. I guess I am. We did an ultrasound a few weeks ago. We're having twins."

"Wow. Congratulations."

"Thanks." Lisbeth grabbed her jacket and purse from the sink and eyed her watch. "Listen, I have to run. I've got yoga class in about half an hour."

"No problem. See you tomorrow."

Lisbeth raced out of the bathroom and through the hallways to the teachers' lot. She climbed into her car, and her phone rang as she buckled the seatbelt. She checked the display; Candace. Lisbeth picked up the Bluetooth attachment from the center console and slipped it into her ear.

"Hi, honey," she said.

"Hi. I hope I didn't catch you at a bad time," Candace said.

"No. I'm just getting ready to head out to yoga. What's up?"

"I wanted to let you know I'll be home early today. There's something I wanted to talk about."

"What?"

"It's a surprise."

"You know how I feel about surprises."

"I'll see you soon, sweetheart," Candace said.

Fearing she'd be late for class, Lisbeth ended the call and weaved through traffic at a manic pace. Finally, she pulled onto Boylston and spotted the studio on the left side of the road. Parking behind a now-familiar car as the driver got out, Lisbeth grabbed her change of clothes from the back seat and followed suit.

"Hey, Shannon," she greeted as the other woman headed for the front door.

"Hi. You look out of breath."

"I didn't want to be late."

Shannon gave her a smile and held the door open. Lisbeth walked in and waved to the receptionist before heading back to change. She saw Shannon duck into the stall next to her.

"You're showing already," Shannon said.

"That happens with twins."

"Oh, right. I forgot you said you were having two. Are you prepared for that?"

"Not in the least. But we'll find a way to make it work. We always do," Lisbeth answered.

They walked out at the same time and headed for the studio. A woman Lisbeth recognized as Renee walked in as they entered the lobby.

"Hi, Renee," Lisbeth said.

Renee looked distracted. "Oh, hi."

"Are you all right?" Shannon asked.

"Yeah."

Lisbeth could tell by Renee's voice that she was far from all right. She'd been fairly quiet the week before, too. Lisbeth watched Shannon guide the girl to a chair.

"What's wrong?"

"Everything just sucks," Renee answered.

Shannon wrapped Renee in her arms like a seasoned mother comforting her child. Lisbeth smiled at the gesture. A few of the other class participants skirted around them and into the studio to warm up.

"My boyfriend just left me a couple weeks ago, and I can't afford my apartment."

"Did he say anything?" Lisbeth asked.

"No. He won't take my calls. None of his friends will talk to me. He just disappeared. I know he wasn't thrilled about the baby, but we were moving past it. I mean, he wasn't happy I said no to an abortion or adoption, but I thought he'd gotten over it. I thought we were going to get through it together."

The corners of Shannon's mouth turned down as Renee explained the situation.

"Do you have family you can stay with or ask for help?"

"Yeah. But I don't want to burden them, you know?"

"Have you thought about a roommate?" Lisbeth asked.

"Who would want to room with a pregnant chick?"

Before Shannon could say more the front door opened again, and Lisbeth watched a girl who seemed younger than Renee walk to the reception desk and pick up a preliminary form.

"Why don't we find some tissues in the bathroom," Lisbeth said, and she and Shannon led Renee back to the changing area.

A short time later, after blowing her nose and splashing water on her face, Renee thanked Lisbeth and Shannon.

"He's not worth all the tears," Lisbeth said.

"Thanks, Lisbeth," Renee said.

Shannon seemed distracted by something.

Lisbeth tugged on her arm. "What's wrong?"

"Nothing. I just know that girl. Well, I don't really know her. I saw her at the doctor's office a few weeks ago."

"She looks pretty down, too," Renee said.

"Yeah, she does. Are you two going to be okay?" Shannon asked.

"Sure," Lisbeth said and watched Shannon head to the front.

Lisbeth handed Renee another tissue and let her wipe away the tear tracks. She tried to eavesdrop on Shannon's conversation without being obvious. Peering around the corner, she managed to catch part of their exchange.

"You look a little confused," Shannon said.

"Yeah...I really don't know why I'm here. I mean...I don't even have enough to pay rent, so I don't know how I'm going to pay for yoga lessons."

Shannon gave her a sad smile and said, "It's only twenty bucks. Why don't I cover it for you?"

"You don't even know me."

"Please...I can spare twenty bucks."

The girl nodded.

"I'm Erika."

"Shannon."

"Why don't you come back to the changing area? I think there are some people who'd like to meet you."

Shannon led the other girl over. Lisbeth turned around and tried to act as if she'd been tending to Renee the entire time. For her part, Renee leaned on Lisbeth's shoulder. The fourth girl looked a bit awestruck to Lisbeth as she cowered a little behind Shannon. Lisbeth could smell the faint scent of vodka on the new arrival, and it turned her stomach.

"This is Erika," Shannon said.

"Hi," Lisbeth said.

"Hi," Erika muttered and focused intently on the floor.

"You look like you need these more than I do," Renee said and handed over the unused tissues.

"Thanks."

"Your boyfriend a jerk, too?" Lisbeth asked. It seemed like the thing to say.

"No. I uh...does this stuff...yoga...really help?"

"Yeah. Once you find your balance. You can be as big as a whale and stand on one leg," Lisbeth said with a laugh.

"This is Renee and Lisbeth," Shannon said.

Erika gave a small wave and looked at Shannon as if she was scared to say anything.

"Renee's looking for a roommate," Shannon explained.

Erika's expression lit up. "You are?"

Renee twisted a strand of hair between her fingers. "Maybe. I don't know. I just...can't afford to move. And I also can't afford a two-bedroom alone."

Erika gave Renee a half-smile. "Maybe we could talk after class?"

"Sure."

The foursome headed to the studio. Carolyn had started the calming music, and the other women had their mats ready. Lisbeth took up a free spot and concentrated on pushing all thoughts out of her mind: the kids from her class learning their numbers, and Candace's surprise phone call after class. They always started with deep breathing. It surprised her how much it helped focus her thoughts on her body rather than her day or what needed to be done once she got home. The atmosphere soothed her. Definitely a feeling she longed for more often than once a week. *I should do this at home.* Carolyn's voice filled her ears, and Lisbeth focused on the acute expansion and contraction of her chest.

"Very good, ladies. Let's get in the warrior pose first today."

Carolyn demonstrated the pose, but Lisbeth had already memorized it. She let the feeling stretch from her calves up through her fingertips. All of the sound in the room, save her own heartbeat, disappeared.

They soon moved to the half moon pose, and Lisbeth looked at her toes to keep her balance while the women around her bent gracefully. She saw Erika struggling to balance and wondered if it was the exercise or the alcohol making it more difficult. Unlike her, the other women she'd started to befriend had pregnancies that weren't wanted or planned. They had hurdles to overcome. *Maybe I can help them.*

When they moved to the floor stretches, she snagged Shannon as a partner. She figured they should let Erika and Renee get to know each other.

"So do you think it will work out with Renee and Erika?" Lisbeth asked softly.

They'd managed to have little conversations during class without getting scathing looks from the other participants.

"I hope so. Erika seems desperate."

"I'd have to agree. She may also be drunk."

Shannon quirked an eyebrow. "You noticed that, too?"

"I could smell it on her in the changing area."

"Poor kid. I covered her class for today. She seemed unsure, like she's not used to accepting help from other people."

"I hope she didn't act offended or anything."

"I don't think so. She just seems in a tight spot."

Before Lisbeth could say anything, Carolyn signaled for everyone to stand up. Lisbeth allowed Shannon to pull her to a standing position. She glanced in the mirror and watched as Erika and Renee got to their feet. The class did a few new poses, which made Lisbeth ache in places she didn't even know could ache. After struggling to stand up, Lisbeth felt as if the room spun. She slowed her breathing, and the dizziness faded.

"Are you okay?" Renee asked.

"Yeah. Just came up too fast," Lisbeth answered. She picked up her towel and water bottle and headed out of the studio.

Lisbeth stepped into her stall and pulled on her regular clothes. She fanned her shirt to cool down. A nice shower was definitely in order when she got home. Erika and Renee were swapping phone numbers when she came out.

"I'll call you soon, I guess. I have to talk to my landlord about moving out," Erika said.

"That's fine. Once you figure it all that out, we can meet with my landlord and get you on the lease."

Erika smiled. "Thanks. Though I should warn you, I've got...issues."

"Trust me, so do I. Have a safe ride home."

Lisbeth watched them exchange waves and walk out. Shannon appeared next to Lisbeth, smiling.

"They looked happy."

"Yes, they did. Good thing you eavesdropped," Lisbeth said with a laugh.

Shannon joined in the laughter, and they walked to their cars.

"I hope things work out for them," Lisbeth said and leaned on the hood of her car.

"I'm sure it will. Besides, I have a feeling we'll see them next week."

"Have a good afternoon," Lisbeth said and climbed into her car.

She pulled out and drove through the one-way streets. The drive home calmed her. The air conditioning helped, too.

Twenty minutes later, Lisbeth sank into a bathtub full of foamy bubbles. The water rose to just below her chin. A clump of bubbles floated past her arm, and she settled against the edge of the tub, letting the flowery aroma fill her nose. She had plenty of time before Candace got in, even if she was coming home early.

"Hey, sleepyhead," Candace said.

Lisbeth peered through one eye to see Candace sitting on the radiator to her right. She slowly sat up in the tub, the bubbles still clinging to her wet skin.

"When did you get home?"

"A few minutes ago. I didn't want to disturb you."

"What time is it?"

"Almost quarter to three."

"I didn't realize I'd fallen asleep."

"You looked really peaceful in there."

"I was."

Candace stood and offered her a towel. Lisbeth got to her feet, letting the bath water run off her in rivulets. She wrapped the towel around her body and stepped onto the bathmat. Candace reached behind her and scooped up a handful of bubbles, dabbing them on the end of Lisbeth's nose. Lisbeth's laughter quickly turned into a sneeze, and the towel slipped.

"Oops," Candace said with a sly grin.

"Flirt," Lisbeth accused with a smile and shooed her wife out of the room.

Lisbeth emerged a few minutes later with the sound of water gurgling down the drain behind her. In the nursery, Candace reclined in the rocking chair, and Lisbeth sat in her lap.

"How was your day?" Candace asked.

"Fine. The kids were less rowdy today. I think they're finally settling into the school routine."

"And your other class?"

Lisbeth straightened up to look Candace in the face. "Met two more interesting women. Younger."

"How much younger?"

"I don't know. A few years, maybe. But they were both in pretty rough shape. Shannon kind of took them under her wing."

"You've got all these new friends. It's not fair."

"So take Wednesday off next week and come with me."

"I may just do that."

"I'd like it if you did."

"So...what did she do for them?"

"Renee was looking for a roommate, and Erika offered to move in. At least, I think that's where they left it after class."

"Shannon must be some kind of matchmaker."

"She's a *mother* who saw two people in need and did what she could to help."

Candace looked around the room and sighed.

"What are you thinking about?" Lisbeth asked and brushed a lock of hair from Candace's face.

"What I wanted to talk to you about." Her voice trembled.

She didn't sound so worried on the phone. Lisbeth stood up to face Candace. "What is it? What's wrong?"

"Let's go into the living room," Candace said and didn't wait for a response.

Lisbeth stood and stared at the empty rocking chair for a minute before pivoting and leaving the nursery. Candace sat on the couch, staring at a pile of printouts.

"Sweetheart, just tell me what's going on," Lisbeth said.

"I did some research...about twin pregnancy. I didn't like what I saw, Lisbeth."

"We know there can be risks. Dr. Ellison explained all of that at our last appointment. But he said as long as we just keep doing what he says, we have a great chance of getting pretty close to term."

"That's not what I'm talking about, Lissie. Low birth weight, developmental disabilities. These are things that we may not be able to control. Not to mention *your* health."

Lisbeth sat down and took Candace's hand in her own. Her wife flipped through some pages on the table and pulled out what look like an article.

"We will be fine. *I* will be fine," Lisbeth said.

"I really am not so sure. Even if we do everything by the book, having a multiple pregnancy is dangerous. Just...look at this article. I think it's a viable option."

Lisbeth took the papers and skimmed the first paragraph. As the words registered, her hands went numb and the pages tumbled to the floor. The numbness spread up her arms and to the pit of her stomach. Something hard and cold settled there, and she fought not to throw up.

"How...how could you think that would be an option?"

"Just hear me out. It would ensure we get to full term. We would still have one child. Nothing would change."

"Everything would change. We agreed we would take whatever we were given in this process. And if that means twins, then so be it. I can't just abandon a child."

"It's not abandoning a child, Lisbeth. We are giving ourselves better odds."

"What does Dr. Ellison say about this?" Lisbeth asked. Feeling returned to her extremities, and she moved away from the couch.

"We can make an appointment and ask. I just want you to think about it."

"I have, and I don't like it, Candace. How can you expect me to choose one of these babies to terminate?"

"You don't have to choose. The doctor makes that decision."

"Contrary to popular belief, that doesn't make me feel any better. You know, I love you, but this was underhanded and so very not like you. And I'm hurt that you'd even think it would work for us," Lisbeth said and scooped up the fallen papers on twin reduction.

"I didn't do this to hurt you. I am trying to do what is best for your health. Do you think I forgot how much pain you were in when we lost the last pregnancy? How I sat with you for days as you cried? Do you think I want you to go through that again? You know I'd take your place if I could."

"That was different, and you know it. And how the hell do you know terminating one of these fetuses wouldn't have the exact same effect?"

"Because we'll still have one baby, Lisbeth."

"You can't guarantee that. And you know, I don't think this is about me or the babies at all. This is about you. God, how selfish can you be?"

"What is that supposed to mean?" Candace retorted.

"You can't conceive so you're putting all your hope on my shoulders without any thought about what I want."

"Are you saying you don't want to do this anymore?"

Lisbeth took slow breaths and looked away from Candace. This was getting out of hand. Silence enveloped them as she tried to control her emotions.

"No. Of course I want to have children. But you're so focused on getting to term that you aren't considering that we could be perfectly fine with *two* babies."

Lisbeth headed for the front door and left Candace sitting on the couch. She needed space and time to cool down before she said something—or worse, did something—she would regret. In the cool evening air, Lisbeth paced the grounds at the front of the building as she fought back tears of anger. They burned like white-hot pinpricks against her eyes, but she refused to let them fall.

Chapter Fifteen

October 3rd

RENEE WANDERED AROUND THE APARTMENT, straightening pillows and adjusting shades. Her anxiety level rose to an all-time high as she waited. She'd already talked to her landlord with Erika. It would be fine to put her on the lease. Now all they had to do was move her in. She passed by the microwave and glanced at the time: two forty. In addition to her anxiety, Renee's patience wore thin. She hated waiting. Just then, someone rapped on the door. She jumped and pulled it open. Her brother stood on the other side.

"Max, what are you doing here?"

"Just wanted to come by. Is that a problem?"

"Uh...it's just kind of a hectic day."

He walked in and took off his coat. She hung it on the coat rack by the door and followed him into the kitchen.

"Mom told you what happened, didn't she?" Renee asked.

"Yeah. And I know you're going to hate me for this, but he never was good enough for you."

Renee smiled in spite of herself. "Thanks for that. Right now, I couldn't agree with you more."

Without warning, he pulled her into a bear hug. The best kind, where it felt like he'd never let her go. Like he'd done after Alyssa.

"If you need anything, you know you can just ask," he whispered against her hair.

"I'm not asking you to do anything."

"But you can, you know. Anything."

Renee managed to pull herself free of his arms. "Thanks. Well, you could stick around, actually."

"Cool. What are you doing today that it's so hectic?"

"I have a new roommate moving in."

"Damn. You move quick."

She jabbed him in the ribs with her elbow. He feigned injury and burst out laughing.

"It's a girl I met at yoga. She was having some problems with her apartment, and we hit it off."

"Oh."

"So be nice to her, okay?"

"You got it."

Another knock on the door interrupted their conversation. Renee gave Max a warning look as she pulled it open. Erika and a guy stood on the other side with a bunch of boxes.

"Hi," Renee said and took the boxes from Erika.

"Hey."

"Come on in."

She led them inside and down to the second bedroom. She'd cleared out all of Bryce's extra shit. Renee set the boxes on the floor and looked around.

"Oh uh...you have a bed, right?"

"Yeah. It's outside."

"Great." Max appeared in the doorway. "This is my brother, Max. He can help you bring it in."

Max and the other guy headed back outside. Erika dropped to her knees and opened the boxes.

"Do you have more to bring in?"

"Not really. I mean, you've got kitchen stuff. Seemed silly to bring mine, too. So I sold it on eBay."

"Good plan. You get a decent price for it?"

"Yeah, actually...a few hundred bucks. Enough to settle the issues with my landlord, at least."

"Good." They unpacked the boxes and got all of Erika's clothes hung up in the closet just as the guys returned with the bed. Max and Erika's friend grunted as they hefted the mattress down the hallway.

"Watch out," Max called. Renee and Erika stepped out of the way, and the guys carried in the mattress.

"We still have the rest of it," he said with a huff.

"Oh, I'm Dane, by the way," the other guy introduced himself and shook Renee's hand.

"Nice to meet you."

As soon as the guys left, Renee looked at Erika. "He's cute."

"He's just a friend."

"You sure about that?"

"We dated in college for a while, but it didn't work out. He's just been helping with all this pregnancy stuff."

"Weren't expecting it?"

"Not at all. You?"

"Nope. But I'm making it work."

"You're lucky you can actually raise a baby."

Renee looked at her. "What do you mean?"

"My life is too fucked up to take care of a baby. I've got my own problems to figure out first, you know?"

"So what are you going to do?"

"I'm looking at this adoption place. Though I don't know if they'll take the baby."

"I'm sure it will work out," Renee said, trying to be upbeat.

By half past four, they'd gotten the bed put together and the covers on it. Renee led Erika and Dane around the rest of the apartment.

"Living room area is in here. I've got a TV and stuff. Pretty standard. Kitchen, obviously, and my room's over here."

They walked in, and she flipped the light switch on.

"It's nice," Erika commented.

"Thanks. I'm going to put the crib over there," she said and pointed to the far wall.

Erika just smiled and clung to Dane's arm. They walked back to the living room, and Renee sank to the couch.

"Hey, is anyone hungry?" Max asked.

"Max, don't be rude," Renee scolded.

"I could use a bite to eat," Dane said.

"I'm kind of craving Chinese," Max said.

"That sounds good."

Erika sat down beside Renee. "Go be men and get food, then."

"Your usual, Nee?" Max asked.

"Yeah."

The guys left, and Renee pulled her legs under her. She and Erika sat in silence for a while.

"So, where do you work?" Renee said.

"I don't even know anymore. I was doing temp stuff, but I think I'm probably fired. My other boss understands, thank God. I waitress on the weekends. What about you?"

"I work at the New England Aquarium. I give tours and stuff. Lots of little kids running around everywhere."

"And you want to keep your baby?"

"Yeah. I mean, sure, it wasn't exactly what I had planned, but...it's not like I never wanted kids."

"And you're going to do it on your own?"

Renee opened her mouth but stopped. She'd been trying not to think about that. Sure, she had her family, but she couldn't always rely on them.

"It wasn't the plan to begin with. My boyfriend was going to help. It's his baby, too. But then he decided to be chicken and just disappeared off the face of the Earth."

"Bastard."

"That's what Max thinks, too."

"You two seem close."

"We are. Ever since..." Renee trailed off.

"Ever since what?" Erika asked.

"Our older sister, Alyssa. She uh, died in a drunk driving accident in 2005."

Renee willed the tears not to fall. She'd gotten over crying for her sister a long time ago. Still, her shoulders began to quiver, and a tear dribbled down her cheek. She let Erika hug her briefly.

"I'm really sorry," Erika said softly.

"Thanks. So yeah, since then, we've been really close."

"We have returned bearing food," Max called.

Renee heard him put the bags down in the kitchen and tromp into the living room. She looked at him, and his body language changed. *Damn, he noticed that I've been crying.*

"What's wrong?"

"Nothing. I just...Alyssa."

"I got it."

Renee wiped away the tears with the back of her hand, and she and Erika followed Max into the kitchen. Dane was already pulling out utensils and plates from the cabinets.

"Let's eat."

They shared a nice early dinner together before Max said goodbye. Renee hugged him longer than usual before letting him go.

"Drive safe," she said.

"Always do."

Their standard departure since Alyssa's death.

Renee turned around and nearly collided with Dane.

"Sorry. I should probably get going, too," he said.

"You can stay if you want."

"No. I have some things to do tonight." He looked at Erika. "Call me when you make that appointment. I'll go with you."

"I'm a big girl, Dane. You don't have to go. We don't both need to lose our jobs over this."

"Just call me anyway."

He grabbed his coat and left. Renee gathered up the empty cartons, tossed them in the big paper bag on the counter, and threw it in the trash.

"So, you want to do something?" Renee asked.

"Like what?"

"I don't know. We could go out or something. I haven't really been out much except for work and yoga class."

"You mean like out, out. On the town?"

"Yeah."

"I don't know."

"Come on. We may be pregnant, but that doesn't mean we can't go out and flirt. We're not tied down by guys."

Erika finally nodded, and they headed to their rooms to change. Ten minutes later, Renee was finishing her makeup. Erika appeared in the mirror.

"You look hot," Renee said.

"Thanks. You, too." She twisted the strap of her purse between her hands.

"You okay?" Renee asked as she put the lipstick down.

"I should probably tell you...I kind of have a drinking...thing."

"You drink a lot?"

"Yeah."

Renee smacked her lips together and pulled a brush through her hair.

"Okay...so we just don't drink tonight."

"It's just...really hard for me not to when I'm around it."

Renee reached out and patted Erika on the shoulder. "We'll be fine. Come on."

A short while later, they crossed the intersection of Stuart and Tremont. The bright blue glow of the W sign above the high-rise building glinted in the evening light. Renee watched the ceiling rotate through colors.

"This place is really cool," she told Erika as they walked in. She paid the cover charge for both of them and led Erika into the throng of people bumping to the heavy hip-hop music. They maneuvered through the crowd to an empty area by the bar.

"See anyone that looks interesting?" Renee asked.

"Not yet," Erika said.

"Maybe they need to see us. You do dance, right?"

Erika laughed. "Duh."

They wound their way through the nearest group of college-age looking kids and started dancing. Within seconds, a group of the guys turned around to look at them. Renee gave one of them, a blond guy, a wink. He took a step toward her, but his date dragged him away.

"Somebody's not happy," Erika called over the thrum of the music.

"And he was cute, too," Renee replied.

The music died down, and something equally loud replaced it. The bass shook the floor so much that the vibrations traveled all the way up Renee's body. Out of the corner of her eye, she spotted Erika moving through the crowd. Reminding herself that Erika was an adult and could take care of herself, Renee moved to the bar and ordered a soda. She sipped it, watching the crowd. Suddenly, she felt a presence behind her. It was Blond Guy.

"Hi," he said.

"Hi."

"Can I join you?"

She shrugged, trying to seem like she didn't care. He leaned on the bar and ordered a beer. They sipped their drinks together for a while before he leaned in.

"I'm Adam."

"Renee."

She took a sip of soda, flirting with her eyes.

"Where's your girlfriend?"

"Sulking somewhere," Adam answered, shrugging.

Renee laughed and waved to get the bartender's attention.

"Can I buy you another one?" Adam asked.

"Sure. It's just soda."

"Not much of a drinker."

"Not right now."

"Pity."

"It's kind of a health thing."

"That's cool."

The bartender set another glass in front of her. She transferred her straw and took a long draw. She and Adam chatted awhile longer until she saw Erika at the other end of the bar, surrounded by guys and holding what looked like a mixed drink in her hand.

"Hey, I'll be right back," Renee said.

"Sure." His tone bore a hint of doubt.

Renee moved down the bar until she was standing next to the guy on Erika's left.

"Hey, Erika. You doing okay?" Renee asked, having to shout above the noise.

"Hey. I'm good. This music's great."

Renee managed to snag the drink from Erika's hand. One whiff, and she could tell there was alcohol in it.

"How many of these has she had?" Renee demanded of Guy on the Left.

"I don't know. Two, maybe."

"She had anything else?"

"Why don't you fuck off? She's fine."

Renee resisted the urge to slug him in the jaw. She grabbed Erika by the wrist and started to drag her toward the other end of the bar.

"Hey, let go!"

"Those guys are losers," Renee said.

"They're cool. And really hot."

Renee didn't say anything. Instead, she plunked Erika down on the stool next to Adam.

"This is my friend Erika," she said.

"Hey."

"Could you do me a favor and keep her here for a minute? I have to make a call. And don't let her order anything to drink except water."

"Uh...okay."

"You're cute," Erika said and leaned close to Adam.

Renee tried to ignore Adam's pleading look as she shoved into the crowd and fought her way to the exit. After telling the doorman she would be right back, she stepped into the autumn air, hit speed dial number four on her phone, and listened to it ring. Twice. Three times.

"Hello?"

"Max. I need your help."

"Are you guys okay?"

"We're at the W club."

"You went clubbing with your new roommate?"

"We were both feeling kind of bummed, so we went out. Look, I need you to help get Erika home."

"She didn't do something stupid, did she?"

"Just get here."

"Where is the club?"

"It's up on Stuart Street. Just take Boylston down past Tremont. You can't miss it. There's a huge W on the overhang."

"I'm on my way."

"Thanks, Max."

Renee waited outside, shifting from foot to foot while she waited. Every time the traffic picked up again, she checked license plates as best she could. Finally, she spotted Max's car and waved wildly so he could see her.

He pulled up to the curb and left the car idling.

"Hey," he said.

"Come on. She's inside."

"You left her alone?"

"She's with someone."

After explaining that Max was only there to help escort a sick friend home, the doorman let them in without charging

Max the cover price. They weaved through the people on the dance floor and found Erika hanging all over Adam.

"Who's this?" Adam asked, giving Max a suspicious look.

"This is my brother. Thanks for watching her for me."

"Uh, yeah."

Max took Erika by the hand, pulled her close, and started to fight his way back through the crowd.

"Really. Thanks." Renee scribbled her number on a napkin and slid it to Adam.

He picked it up and tucked it in his pocket.

"I'll call you," he said.

"Sure."

She and Max finally broke free of the mob inside. Erika groaned and hung onto him for support as they made it to the car.

"You moved kind of fast, Nee," Max said.

"He had a girlfriend. He's not going to call."

"Let's get her home."

They managed to get Erika home and into her bed. They ducked out of the room and stood in the doorway of Renee's room.

"You want me to stay in case she gets sick or something?" Max asked.

"No. We'll be fine." Renee wrapped her arms around him. "What would I do without you?"

"Be very lost."

She punched him playfully in the shoulder and walked him to the front door. She locked it and crawled into bed. Sleep came as soon as her head hit the pillow.

Her alarm went off at eight thirty the next morning, and Renee smacked it to shut it up. She climbed out of bed and checked on Erika. Her roommate lay curled up beneath the blankets, so Renee retreated to the kitchen to make some breakfast.

Renee leaned against the edge of the stove, watching her eggs so they didn't get too runny. Last night's events still bothered her. She listened for any sounds that her new roommate was getting up, but the apartment remained quiet. She flipped her eggs onto a plate before pulling her phone out of her purse and sitting down at the kitchen table. She flipped through her favorites list and stopped on her mom's number. It was early, but her mom should be awake. Renee sucked on her bottom lip for a few seconds before hitting the call button and setting the phone to speaker. It rang three times before her mom picked up.

"Renee?" her mom said.

"Hi, Mom. I'm sorry if I woke you up."

"You didn't. Is everything okay? Max called and said he had to pick you up at a bar last night. You shouldn't be drinking now that you're pregnant."

Renee took a bite of egg and swallowed. "I didn't. My new roommate moved in, and we needed to get out of the apartment for a while, so we went up to the W hotel. Erika had a few drinks, and I had to call Max to help me get her home."

"Did you know she drank when you agreed to let her move in?"

"I knew she had problems drinking, yeah. I guess I didn't realize how hard it was for her not to do it. I feel bad that I wasn't there to help her. I got caught up flirting with this guy."

"Oh, honey. I know you want to be supportive. Maybe you should just talk to her. See if she wants your help?"

"I don't want to seem like a bitch."

"You won't. But don't forget that you have to take care of yourself, too."

"It seems kind of small compared to what Erika's got going on. I mean, trying to deal with an alcohol addiction while pregnant by some guy she probably doesn't even remember...that's really awful."

"You are just as important as she is, Renee."

"I will talk to her. But what if it doesn't work out? I can't throw her out. She needs a place to stay as much as I need someone to help pay the rent. I can't afford to move right now."

"Why don't you worry about just talking with her first and see what happens. You know we'll be here if you need anything."

Renee took another bite of egg. Her mother was silent for a minute or two.

"You going to be okay, honey?"

"Yeah. I'll be fine."

"All right. I'll let you go."

Renee ended the call and stared at her partially eaten breakfast. She really didn't want to accuse Erika of having a problem or try to tell her what to do about it. *She knows she's got issues.* Renee focused on forcing down the rest of her food and was standing over the sink washing her plate and fork when Erika appeared.

"Hey, how are you feeling?" Renee asked.

"I can't believe I did that last night. I'm so sorry."

"Do you want to talk about it? I feel terrible that I abandoned you. I should have been there to make sure you weren't tempted. I'm sorry, too."

Erika's smile was sullen. "You shouldn't have to keep track of me. I know I have a drinking problem. I've been afraid to face it. Hiding in a bottle just seems easier than dealing with reality."

"Is there anything I can do to help? I can look up information on AA meetings if you want."

"Maybe we could look them up together. It shouldn't be your job to keep my ass in line. But I could use the support."

Erika set the partially filled tea kettle on the front right burner and cranked the heat up to high.

"We can do it when I get home today?" Renee offered.

"Thanks. That would be great. And I promise, I'm going to get help. I've screwed this kid up enough already."

Renee set her plate and fork in the dishwasher and turned to give Erika a hug. "I'm here for you."

Chapter Sixteen

October 8th

ERIKA STOOD IN FRONT OF THE MIRROR A LITTLE before eight fifteen that morning, checking her hair and makeup for her meeting. She'd texted Dane the date and time of the meeting but said he didn't need to show up. *Maybe he'll listen for once. I need to do this on my own. He can't always save me.* Erika reapplied her eyeliner and headed for the kitchen. Five minutes later, Renee appeared, hair wrapped in a towel.

"Good luck today," she said.

"Thanks," Erika replied. A pause and then: "Do you think I look okay?"

Renee gave her a smile. "You look great."

Erika grabbed the teapot and filled it. She set it to boil on the stove and rummaged in the fridge for something edible.

"You sure you don't want me to go with you? My boss would understand," Renee called from her room.

"No. I'll be okay."

"You told Dane, right?"

"Yeah. I'm kind of wishing I hadn't."

"Why? He seems like he really cares about you. I'd love that kind of support from a guy." Renee sounded bitter.

"You can have him if you want."

"He's yours. Besides, I'm fending off Adam."

"Adam?"

"The guy I met at the club last week."

"Oh. I thought you said he wouldn't call."

"I was wrong."

They laughed as the teapot began to whistle. Erika tossed the butter on the counter and pulled out some bread.

"Well, even if Dane doesn't show up, will you call me after you're done? I want to know what happens," Renee said.

"Sure." Erika grabbed a mug from the cabinet overhead and poured the piping hot water in.

"So I had a sort of weird thought the other day," Renee said.

"Yeah?"

"Kind of a little private aquarium tour."

"For Adam?" Erika teased.

"No. I was thinking of inviting Shannon and her kids and Lisbeth."

"Like a yoga class get-together...outside of yoga class?" Erika said.

"Yeah. Why not? They're nice enough, and it'd be cool to get to know them outside of class, too. We don't exactly have a lot of time to chat while we're there."

"I guess you can bring it up next week."

"I think I will. But I have to run."

Renee waved goodbye and left Erika alone in the kitchen. Erika buttered her toast and munched on it as she paced the kitchen. She had no idea what to expect from the meeting with the adoption people today. The little voice in the back of her mind kept telling her that no one would want her baby. Oddly, it sounded like her mother. Erika shook off the nervous feeling as best she could and grabbed her coat and purse from the rack by the door. Luckily, she now lived within walking distance of the main office.

At ten after nine, she reached the building and stared at the front door sign: Commonwealth Adoption Services. She forced herself to open the door and walk in.

"Can I help you?" a woman at the front desk asked.

"I'm here for an appointment with—" she checked the note she'd scribbled "—Arlene."

"Oh, sure. Just go straight back, and it will be the second door on the left."

"Thanks."

Erika pushed the door open and walked down the hall. Before the second door on the left, she spotted her reflection in a mirror. It wasn't quite full length, but she had a decent view of her stomach. She was starting to show a little bit. Erika tugged on her shirt to cover it up and walked into the office. A handful of people, mostly women on their own, sat scattered throughout the room. A young couple sat in one corner, whispering to each other. More people than she'd expected. So she sat in a chair and waited. The clock above the reception desk showed nine twenty-five when a door on the right wall opened and a woman with dark brown hair and olive-colored skin walked out.

"Erika?" she called.

Erika looked around for a minute, half expecting someone else to stand up. When no one else did, she got to her feet and followed the woman back through the door. It led to a small office with pictures of happy families and a floor-to-ceiling bookshelf crammed with books.

"I'm Arlene," the woman said and extended her hand.

"Hi."

"Why don't you have a seat?"

Erika put her purse on the floor and sat in the chair. She felt oddly like she was back at the clinic.

"So, Erika, why don't you tell me a little about yourself."

"Um...I graduated last year from Emerson. Got my BA in theater production. I don't have any siblings...or a boyfriend. I waitress. I used to only do it on the weekends, but I had to pick up shifts during the week recently."

"Why do you think adoption is the right path for you to take?"

"I was going to get an abortion, but I kind of couldn't go through with it. This clinic said maybe adoption would be better. Well, mostly my friend did the talking and the convincing. I guess just because I don't want the baby doesn't mean someone else wouldn't."

"Well, I know we're very glad you decided to look into adoption."

Erika nodded and kept her gaze focused just below Arlene's chin.

"Now, I'm just going to ask you some questions, and we'll put your profile together," she said, and Erika's head jerked up.

"Profile?"

"The information we use to match you with a potential adoptive family."

"Oh. Okay."

"If I could get your birthday."

"February twentieth, 1988."

"Great. And can I get your current address."

Erika fished in her purse and pulled out Renee's address. She still had to get used to it. She handed it over and watched Arlene copy it.

"I just moved, so...I don't have it memorized," Erika explained.

"That's fine."

"Do you know your due date?"

"Uh...end of April."

"Great." Arlene paused to scribble something else on her form. "Do you have any health issues related to your pregnancy?"

Erika squirmed in her seat. She'd been expecting the question to come, but she hadn't really figured out how to answer it. The voice in the back of her head kept yelling that she'd be turned away. "Um..." Erika coughed and cleared her throat. "I had some tests done a couple weeks ago."

"Have you gotten those results back yet?"

"Nothing wrong like common diseases. But the doctor said that there's a really high chance the baby has FAS."

There, she'd made herself say it.

"How far into your pregnancy were you drinking?"

"Like eight or nine weeks. I stopped. And I'm getting help. In fact, I have a meeting tonight."

Arlene settled back in her chair and stared across the desk. Erika shivered under the unflinching gaze. She was going to be yelled at and thrown out. She was sure of it. That voice in the back of her head was right.

"Your doctor explained the risks to you, right?"

"Yeah. And I swear I'm not doing it anymore. I just...with finding out about the baby and everything, I just kind of reacted. It was how I used to deal with stress and well...anything."

Erika felt dampness on her cheeks and realized she'd started crying. Drying her tears with her shirtsleeve, she waited for Arlene to say something else, anything else.

"I'm not going to lie to you, Erika. Placing a special needs child is difficult. But not impossible."

"You mean you aren't going to kick me out?"

"No. We believe that every child deserves a loving home. And we strive to provide that."

"So...when do I find out if someone wants the baby?"

"We'll give you a call."

"What happens after that?"

"Once we find a family, we'll have you both come in for a meeting. You can discuss whatever you'd like with them. You can also do a home visit to see what the environment will be like for the baby. If you feel they're the right person for you, then you'll sign an agreement explaining what rights you have and what you're giving up. Traditionally, we like to foster open adoptions."

"Like I still get to see the baby and everything?"

"Pictures and letters, mostly. And usually the adoptive family will help pay for your doctor visits and your hospital stay."

Erika lit up. "Really?"

"Yes. You can negotiate that when you sign the agreement. We like to encourage our adoptive families to go to as many doctor visits as they can."

Erika leaned back in her chair. Not what she'd been expecting at all. Relief filled her to bursting. Maybe it would work out after all. It wouldn't be a bad thing to have someone else pay for her baby bills. She certainly wasn't going to complain.

"Now, are you taking prenatal vitamins?"

"Yeah. And I don't know if it matters, but I'm going to prenatal yoga once a week."

"That's wonderful. Are you enjoying it?"

"It's good. My roommate and I go together. There are some other people that go that are really nice."

"It sounds like you're starting to develop a support system. That's good."

"So do you need like my work schedule or anything?"

"No. Just the best times we can reach you, and I'll need your phone number."

"Mornings before eleven and in the evenings after six. Here's my number," Erika said and wrote it on a sticky note.

"Now, there is one thing you should be aware of," Arlene said.

"What?"

"You do have some control over the process. If, when you meet with a potential family, you don't feel comfortable, you don't have to enter into anything with them. We want you to feel completely at ease with the people who are going to be raising your baby."

"Okay."

Arlene stood. Erika followed suit.

"It was very nice to meet you, Erika. And we will be in touch, hopefully soon, with some good news."

"Thanks so much," Erika said and shook Arlene's hand.

Arlene led Erika out of her office and back to the waiting area. "Have a good day," Arlene called as Erika left.

She got to the front of the building and had to keep from shouting with happiness. The moment Erika stepped onto the sidewalk, she let out a little yelp and a jump. A couple of people on the sidewalk stared at her, but she didn't care. She pulled out her phone and rapidly started to type.

Renee—they're going to help me. Should have news soon. She hit send. She had just enough time to close her phone when it rang.

"Hi, Dane," she said after looking at the display.

"How'd it go?"

"I'm surprised you didn't show up."

"You said you wanted to do it alone."

"The one time you listen to me."

Dane laughed. "So?"

"Want to grab some lunch? I'm kind of starving."

"Yeah. I can swing by and meet you at the agency. I'm kind of nearby."

"You are such a stalker," Erika said.

"I am not," Dane said, his voice echoing on the line.

Erika turned and closed her phone. Dane gave her a half smile and offered a hug. She fixed him with a mock withering look and nudged him in the arm.

"So, come on. How'd it go? What did they say?" he asked.

"Buy me lunch first."

"You're so needy," Dane said and wrapped an arm around her shoulders.

They ended up back near Erika and Renee's apartment, eating sandwiches. Erika filled him in on the process.

"So they didn't freak with the whole...alcohol thing?" Dane asked.

"Well, they weren't exactly happy about it, but they said they could work with it."

Dane took a bite and chewed for a long time. Finally, after swallowing and downing half his soda, he asked, "What happens next?"

"Well, they try to find someone who wants the baby, and then I meet them. And if I don't like them, I don't have to give them the baby. Arlene, that's the woman I talked to, said I have to be completely at ease with the people I give the baby to."

"Well, that's a good thing, right?"

"Want to know the best part?"

"Sure."

"The family pays for my bills. Doctors and tests and when I have the baby. I don't have to pay for it."

"To you, that would be the best part."

Erika ignored his comment. For all his sweetness, he could still annoy her. A dull beep interrupted their silence.

Erika pulled her phone from her pocket and read the message. *Great! See you at home.*

"What was that?"

"Nothing. Just a text from Renee."

"Oh. So when do you think you'll hear something?"

"I don't know. I hope soon. I have another doctor's appointment soon."

"You want company?"

"You have work and stuff."

"I can get time off, Erika. You know that."

"I don't want to keep putting all this on you."

"I don't mind. It's what friends are for."

"I guess."

Erika focused on her sandwich. All day, she'd been wondering about the baby's father. The weeks where she'd most likely gotten pregnant were a definite blur, one that was probably never coming back into focus. She wanted to say something to Dane about it but couldn't prove it to be true.

"Erika."

"Hmm?"

"Did they ask you...about the father?"

Erika stopped mid-bite. *Is he a mind reader now?* All she could do was shake her head. She couldn't even form words.

"Oh. I thought maybe they would have wanted to know stuff."

Erika swallowed, nearly choking on the sandwich. "I don't know who it is."

Dane looked away and scratched his neck. "We...you know..."

"I know."

"So I could be…"

"I don't think so."

"Erika, we didn't use protection."

"Yeah, but…it doesn't work out right…the timing. Look, I have to go. I'm working the afternoon shift today, and I'm going to be late if I don't run. Thanks for lunch."

Erika grabbed her purse and jacket and left the sandwich shop, heading for the nearest T station, eager to get away from Dane. She didn't want to talk about the father of her baby. It just made everything more complicated. She made it to work and clocked in just before her shift started. She pulled on her apron and checked which tables she'd been assigned. She spotted Jessa bent over a booth, cleaning supplies on the seat.

"Hey," Erika said.

Jessa looked up. "Hey, stranger. Long time no see. Where've you been?"

"Things kind of got crazy. I uh…I'm pregnant."

"For real?"

"Yeah."

"Well, cool."

"I'm giving it up for adoption."

"Oh…well, that's good."

"Need some help?"

"Sure."

Erika took the rag from Jessa and finished wiping down the table. She laid four place settings on the table and rearranged the ketchup and mustard bottles and the napkin dispenser.

"You're being all OCD," Jessa teased.

"Doing stuff keeps my mind off everything."

"Well, that's good to know, because it looks like you've got a big group over in your section."

Erika looked over and saw Shannon sitting down with a man and three kids. Usually, Erika didn't like waiting on people with small kids, but she figured Shannon was worth it. Erika weaved through the tables to their booth.

"Hi, I'm Erika. I'll be your server today," Erika said before Shannon could say anything.

"Hi," the little girl sitting next to Shannon replied.

"Mike, this is Erika. She's in my yoga class."

"Nice to meet you," Mike said.

"You, too. So, can I start you with some drinks?"

"Sure."

"Mom, I want a Coke," the older boy said.

"One glass, Chris."

"Okay."

"I want chocolate milk," the little girl said.

"Me, too," the youngest piped up.

"One Coke, two chocolate milks. And for you guys?" Erika said, looking at the adults.

"Water's fine," Shannon said.

"I'll have the same," Mike added.

"Great. I'll be right back with those."

Erika caught Shannon smiling as she rounded the booth and walked toward the kitchen. A few minutes later, she returned with extra packs of crayons.

"I thought you guys might want some extras," she said and put the drinks on the table.

"Tanner, Meghan, what do you say?" Shannon prompted.

"Thank you."

"You're welcome."

Erika took their orders and then stopped by to hand menus to a waiting couple. By the time the first hour of her shift ended, Erika was exhausted. She stopped by Shannon's table just as the kids started to put on coats.

"I hope you guys have a great day," Erika said.

"Bye," Meghan said with a wave.

Mike took the kids up front to pay, leaving Erika and Shannon alone at the table.

"I didn't know you worked here," Shannon said.

"Yeah. I used to only on the weekends, but since I lost my other job, I had to pick up more shifts."

"How's your new apartment?"

"It's good. Renee's cool. And we hang out. I uh...I've got a lot of baby stuff going on. I decided to put the baby up for adoption."

"That's really brave," Shannon said.

"Thanks."

"Will we still see you at yoga?"

"Definitely. Renee doesn't give me any excuse not to go. So I'll see you on Wednesday."

"I look forward to it," Shannon said and slid a folded up bill across the table.

Erika picked up the bill and unfolded it. Twenty dollars. Not much in the grand scheme of things, but it meant a hell of a lot to her. Erika tucked it away in her jeans. No way was she going to share that with her coworkers. She got home that evening to find Renee curled up on the couch, reading a book.

"How was work?" Erika asked.

"Good. You?"

"Yeah. I saw Shannon. She and her family stopped in for lunch. Her kids are really cute."

Renee put her book down and scooted over so Erika could sit down.

"So everything went well with the adoption people?"

"Yeah. I should hear soon. I can't believe it. This might actually work out. It's the first good thing about this baby."

"I told you things would be good," Renee said.

"Yeah...you did."

Renee glanced at the clock on the DVR and said, "I thought you had a meeting tonight."

"I do. I just wanted to swing by and tell you."

"I'll be here when you get back. I want all the details."

"We aren't supposed to talk about what goes on," Erika said.

"About the agency," Renee said.

"Oh...right."

Half an hour later, Erika walked into a church and down a hallway to an open door. She found a few people seated already. A good-looking guy pushed metal chairs into rows at the back of the room. She hadn't seen him before. Then again, she'd only just started coming. She hadn't even shared her story yet.

"Hi," he greeted when he turned around.

"Uh...hi."

Erika fiddled with her jacket and sat down in the back. She watched the cute guy finish setting up chairs. She kept watching him as he moved to talk to a couple of people in the front row. She checked the clock every five minutes—or so it seemed—until she felt a presence beside her. She looked over to see the cute guy sitting down.

"Hey again. I don't think we've met. I'm Nate," he said and offered his hand.

"Erika. I'm...new."

"Everyone has to start somewhere."

"I guess so."

"Have you shared?"

"Oh...no. I don't think I'm ready."

A handful more people filtered in as the clock struck the hour, and Nate got up. Erika buried her hands in her pockets and waited. Nate gave a brief introduction, and then a woman named Amy stood up. Twenty minutes later, half the group was in tears and wrapping Amy in soppy hugs of support. Amy finally sat down, and Nate looked around the small group. His gaze landed on Erika, and she could feel the color simultaneously rush to the tips of her ears and drain from her cheeks. Erika shook her head, but it made no difference. Nate weaved through the metal chairs and took her by the hand.

"No. I can't. I'm not ready," she protested in a whisper.

"You are ready. I promise. I'll be sitting right in front. Just focus on me."

She moved to the front of the room, reluctant to let go of Nate's hand, even though she wanted to punch him for dragging her up there. She shot him a sideways look as he detached his hand and sat directly in front of her. Erika wet her lips and focused on Nate.

"I'm Erika, and I'm an alcoholic."

"Hi, Erika," a chorus of voices echoed.

She couldn't help thinking it was so stereotypical of what she thought AA meetings were. She paused a moment before taking a breath and plunging into her story.

"I didn't think I had a problem for a long time. I mean, I didn't always drink. Not until college. But that's kind of what everybody does. You want to fit in and stuff. I guess it started when some of my friends started going to lots of parties. I did it to hang with them. I liked it. A lot. And I guess I just started doing it because it made me feel better. When I failed a test, I drank. Even when good things happened, I drank. And I guess that's how I got here. I had one too many and ended up sleeping with some guy I don't even remember, and now I'm pregnant."

Erika paused to catch her breath and swallowed to get moisture to her parched throat. The rest of the group sat transfixed and patient. She rubbed her palms on her jeans before continuing.

"I moved in with this new roommate, and we went out, and I knew I shouldn't drink, but I did it anyway. And I realized I needed help. That's why I'm here. I need help."

Hot tears pricked the back of her eyes as she stood in front of a group of strangers, baring her soul. She wanted to hate Nate for making her talk, but she couldn't. Somehow, talking about it freed her. The burden of what she'd done and waiting for an adoptive family weighed on her shoulders. But it was made a little lighter by admitting her faults.

"I think we can all understand where you're coming from, Erika. I know I drank to be social at first. We are all here for you," Nate said.

She nodded and flashed him a watery smile before slinking to the back row. The woman beside her gave Erika a firm hand squeeze. Erika lost track of time and other people's stories. Finally, the last person had gone, and Nate said a quick blessing before the group disbanded. Erika stayed put but wasn't surprised when Nate tapped her shoulder and nodded toward the back table with coffee.

"You did it," he said.

"Guess I did. Thanks."

He turned to pour two cups of coffee, and Erika watched him in profile. He had a strong jaw and sweet eyes. *I can't think about him like that. I don't even know him.*

"I hope we can be the support you need."

"Me, too. Did you really used to drink just because other people did?"

"Absolutely. I was there with you. We all have our reasons to turn to drinking, but at the core, we're not that different."

"I really appreciate it."

Erika took the cup he offered, complete with heart-melting smile, and their conversation turned to less emotionally charged topics.

Chapter Seventeen

October 14th

SHANNON WAITED IN THE LINE OF CARS AT SCHOOL, scanning the crowd of kids as they walked out of the building. Finally, Christian and Meghan appeared. Christian ran around some younger kids and made it to the car before Meghan was even halfway up the hill.

"You're in a hurry today," Shannon said as he climbed into the front seat.

"Just happy to see you, Mom."

She smiled and reached behind him to open the back door for Meghan.

"Hi, Mama," Meghan said.

"Come on, buckle up, you two."

Once she heard two clicks, Shannon pulled out of the line and sped out of the parking lot. Instead of going straight, she took a right and headed over to get Tanner.

"Where are we going, Mom?" Christian asked.

"To pick up your brother. I have a surprise for you guys."

"What kind of surprise?" Meghan asked.

"It wouldn't be a surprise if I told you."

She stopped at the end of the driveway and got out. After telling the kids to stay in the car, she made her way to the front door and knocked. She waited for a minute before it opened.

"Hi, Mrs. Atwater."

"Hi. I know I'm a little early today, but is Tanner ready?"

"Sure. Please, come in."

Shannon crossed the threshold and waited in the front hall. Tanner appeared moments later with his shoes on the wrong feet and giggling up a storm about it.

"Mama," he called and tripped over his sneakers.

"Sit down, and Mama will put your shoes on the right feet."

He plopped to his butt and let her swap the shoes. She straightened and took him by the hand.

"See you tomorrow, Tanner," his sitter said.

"Bye."

They walked down to the car, and Shannon opened the back door beside Meghan. "Meg, scoot over to the next seat. I don't want Tanner in the road."

Meg unbuckled her seat belt and crawled to the other seat. Shannon got Tanner strapped in, and they were off.

"What's the surprise, Mama? Tell us," Meghan begged.

"We're getting a very special tour of the aquarium."

"Special?" Christian repeated.

"Just us. Nobody else."

"Fishes!" Tanner squealed.

Ten minutes later, Shannon unloaded the kids and led them inside The New England Aquarium. It was deserted except for three familiar faces. She waved to Renee and led the kids over.

"Guys, this is Renee. She works here at the aquarium."

"Hi," they replied.

"You guys have the entire place to yourselves for a whole half hour," Renee explained.

She pointed out the different areas of the indoor portion.

"You can ask anyone in a blue shirt for help. But wait for your mom before you go outside, okay?"

"Okay."

"Christian, please keep an eye on them."

"Okay, Mom."

He took his siblings by the hands and headed off toward the exotic fish display. Shannon joined the other women on the bench.

"Where's Candace?" she asked Lisbeth.

"She had to work. She said to get her a stuffed fish from the gift shop, though. And honestly, I'm a little glad she couldn't make it."

"What do you mean?" Renee asked and leaned against the wall opposite them.

"Things have been a little tense since she brought up the idea of reducing to a single fetus."

"Why would she do that?" Erika asked.

"She says she's concerned about my health. She thinks a single fetus will have a higher chance of making it to term. And less chance of having any deficiencies that are more common with twin births."

"What do you want to do?"

"I don't want to give up either of them. I mean...I don't know a whole lot about the process, but I worry that if we got rid of one, it might jeopardize the other. Plus, Candace can't have children. She was diagnosed with polycystic ovary syndrome a few years ago. So it's up to me to have these babies. But we have a meeting on the nineteenth with our doctor. We'll see how it goes."

"Good to see you again," Shannon told Erika.

"You, too. Did they grow since last week?" Erika asked and nodded toward Shannon's kids.

Shannon laughed. "I think Chris is going through a growth spurt. Or maybe he's hitting puberty early."

"How is he handling the idea having another baby in the house?" Renee asked.

"He was pretty upset at first. But he's getting used to it. Plus, I told him that for a little while anyway, Meghan will want to help take care of the baby. It's all still a little overwhelming. I took on more clients to put away some extra cash for when the baby comes. I'll admit, it's starting to take its toll."

"Did you tell your husband?" Lisbeth asked.

"No. I hate fighting with him. And I know he doesn't always respect how I feel."

"You need to talk to him," Lisbeth said.

"I'll find a way to make it work." Shannon turned her attention to Renee. "How are you doing?"

"I'm okay. I still miss him sometimes, but it's less often now. And my parents have been really supportive."

"So has her brother," Erika added.

"Max is protective."

"I hope I can make it through most of the school year," Lisbeth groaned.

"When are you due?" Erika asked.

"Beginning of April, but I think they'll probably take me earlier."

"I can't believe we're all due in April. That's going to be insane," Renee said.

"We can be hospital buddies," Lisbeth said.

Shannon looked toward the petting tank and watched Christian point to various marine life while Tanner tried to reach into the tank.

"Careful, you guys," she reminded them.

"Erika, how are things going for you? You've been kind of quiet the last few weeks," Lisbeth said.

"Oh, things are okay, I guess. I haven't heard anything yet from the adoption agency. But I'm going to AA meetings twice a week. They're helping, I think."

"That's great," Shannon said.

"It's still hard. I miss it a lot...like all the time. But I have to remember that it's not just for me."

"If you need one of us to go with you, please call," Lisbeth assured her.

"Thanks."

"Or if you need someone to talk to," Shannon said.

"That'd be nice. But Renee's great."

"Thanks, hon."

The kids raced toward them. "Mama, we want to see the penguins," Meghan said.

"Is it all right if they see the penguins?" Shannon asked Renee.

"Yeah. Come on. I think they might even be feeding them."

Tanner detached himself from his brother's grip and gravitated like a magnet to Shannon's leg. Meghan hopped to the other side.

"Tanner, you can hold Mama's hand, but you have to let go of my leg. I can't walk."

"No. Don't want to let go."

She leaned down and picked him up under the armpits. Balancing him on her right hip, she took Meghan with her free hand.

"Mom, come on," Christian called from the top of the ramp that led outside.

"We're coming."

They made their way outside and found Christian, Erika, and Lisbeth crowded around a small window near the blue penguin exhibit. Meghan ran up to stand beside her big brother, watching the tiny birds waddle down a little blue ramp and flop around in sand.

"How come they don't look like regular penguins?" Christian said.

"These are blue penguins. They come all the way from Australia," Renee explained.

"Are they babies?" Meghan asked.

"Nope. These are all grown-ups. After we finish building the new habitats for some of the other animals, the regular penguins will be back."

"Tanner, can you see them?" Shannon asked.

One of the penguins turned and looked at them. It opened its beak and let out a shrill noise.

"It talked to me," Meghan said.

"He's saying hello," Renee explained.

"How do you know it's a boy penguin?" Christian interrupted.

"Most of them are."

"Oh."

"What else can we see?" Meghan said.

"If you want, we can go around to the other side of the tank and take a look at the seals and sea lions," Renee said and looked down at Meghan.

"Can I, Mama? Please?"

"Sure."

Renee led Meghan around to an open pool of water.

"I'm hungry, Mama," Tanner said with the start of a whine in his voice.

"I know. We're almost done."

"Can we get something in the gift shop, Mom?" Christian asked.

"One thing each. And nothing over twenty-five dollars."

"Okay."

Fifteen minutes later, they stood in the gift shop, with Christian trying to supervise purchases. Unfortunately, his knowledge of money was limited.

"Mom, how much is this one?" he asked.

"That one says twenty-one dollars," Erika interpreted.

"That's less than twenty-five. Mom said we can't get anything more than twenty-five."

"You're good, then."

"What's this one?" Meghan asked, waving a stuffed penguin chick at Erika.

"Meghan, you're being a brat," Christian said.

"Am not."

Erika took the toy and read the price tag. "Sixteen dollars."

"Is that okay?"

"Yes. Why don't you go show your mom?"

Meghan took the penguin back, squishing it to her chest happily, and went in search of her mother. She found Shannon helping Tanner pick out refrigerator magnets and a postcard.

"I found this, Mama."

Shannon checked the price tag. "Okay." She turned in search of Christian. "Chris, come on. We're leaving in five minutes."

Footsteps clomped through the displays. Christian appeared and handed over a book on marine animals.

"Good choice," Renee said and stepped behind the counter.

Three minutes later, they all walked out to their cars. The kids waved goodbye to Renee and climbed into their seats.

"We'll see you on Wednesday," Shannon said and slipped into the driver seat.

"Mama," Meghan said when they were halfway home.

"Yes, sweetie?"

"How come we didn't get anything for the baby?"

"We can come back another time and get something."

"Really?"

"Maybe Daddy would like to come, too."

"Okay."

Meghan seemed content with the answer and went back to playing with her stuffed penguin. Shannon focused on the road, but in the very back of her mind, she couldn't stop thinking about the baby. She'd tried to quiet her worries. She was raising three children already and had no problems. There was no reason this pregnancy should be any different the others. *But something about this one is different.* She pushed the concerns out of her mind when they pulled into the driveway. The kids clamored from their seats and raced inside. Shannon followed and found Christian sitting down on the couch and opening his book.

"Do you have homework?" she asked.

"Mom, can't I just read a little bit? Please?"

"I don't got homework," Meghan interrupted.

Shannon just gave her daughter a small nod and turned back to Christian. "Chris, how much homework do you have?"

"Some math and reading."

"The book will be here when you finish. Come on. Upstairs, and get it done. Just think, the faster you get your work done, the sooner you can read your new book."

Christian groaned but put the book down and picked up his backpack. Shannon watched him trudge upstairs, taking every step like it pained him.

"Mama, play with me," Meghan called.

"In a little while, sweetie. Mama has to get some work done." Shannon leaned around the corner of the doorframe into the living room. "Why don't you show Tanner your new penguin."

Meghan didn't look too pleased to have to share her new toy with her little brother, but Shannon knew she'd get over it. Shannon wound her way through the kitchen to the dining room and sat down at the computer. The screen glared at her and forced her to blink to clear her vision. She was tired. She'd been pushing herself hard the last week or so to meet deadlines. *The girls were right, I need to tell Mike how I feel.* But she couldn't bring herself to disturb the status quo.

Shannon lost track of time. She hadn't heard Christian come downstairs, but he moved around the kitchen table, setting places without being asked when Mike got home.

"What's for dinner?" Mike asked.

Shannon looked around the kitchen. "I'm guessing take-out. I forgot to take something from the freezer to thaw this morning."

"What do you feel like?" Mike asked.

Two sets of footsteps thundered into the kitchen. "Pizza!" Meghan and Tanner cried in unison.

"We can do pizza," Shannon said.

Christian immediately collected the forks and knives and put them away. He didn't say anything about his homework or his new book.

"Daddy, we saw fish," Tanner said, dancing around his father.

"You did?"

"Yeah. We saw starfish and all kinds of fish," Christian added.

"And penguins," Megan said, waving her stuffed penguin in the air.

"Sounds like you had a great time," Mike replied and picked up the phone to call for dinner.

The kids rushed off to the living room to enjoy their new toys, leaving Shannon and Mike in the kitchen. After placing the call, Mike looked at her.

"What inspired the trip?"

"Renee, one of the girls from yoga, invited a group of us for a private tour of the aquarium. She works there."

"That was nice of her."

"Yeah. It was nice to see everyone outside of class." She leaned on the back of a chair. "It sounds like we all have our ups and downs."

"What do you mean?"

"Well, Renee's boyfriend ran out on her a few weeks ago. And Erika's struggling with a lot of problems. Alcohol addiction, giving her baby up for adoption."

"Does she need anyone to negotiate an agreement?"

"I think she's fine, but I can mention it on Wednesday."

"We're not having any ups and downs, are we?" he asked.

Shannon forced a smile. "No. We're fine."

"You're sure."

"Absolutely. Honey, we have three great kids. I had three great pregnancies. The doctor thinks everything is going fine."

"Okay. If you say so."

She nodded and waited for him to pick up his keys and go for dinner. He leaned over and kissed her before pulling his jacket back on.

"I'll be back."

"We'll be here."

Shannon joined the kids in the living room and played with Meghan for a little while. She couldn't remember Meghan being so excited with a stuffed animal in a long time.

"Does the penguin have a name?" Shannon asked as she leaned against the couch.

"Um...I don't know. Baby Waddles."

"That's a stupid name," Christian chimed in from the chair next to them.

"Christian, your sister can name the penguin whatever she wants."

Just then, the door opened, and Mike walked in. "Dinner's here."

Tanner and Christian abandoned their toys and raced each other to the kitchen table. Meghan smoothed the penguin's wings and tucked it protectively under her arm before following her brothers.

Long after the kids were in bed, Shannon sat in the master bedroom, watching TV with the volume turned down low. She knew Mike would be up in a few minutes, but she was enjoying the quiet. She hated lying to him, but she couldn't tell him that she wasn't exactly happy about having another child. *Please let these jitters just melt away. Let me hold this baby, and let that make everything right again.*

"You're still up," Mike said as he walked in.

"Yeah. Just watching a little TV. Don't get much of a chance these days with the kids fighting over their shows."

He crawled under the covers and rested his head on her shoulder. They lay together like that for a few minutes before

Shannon turned the TV off and wiggled down under the covers.

"Night, hon," she said and kissed his cheek.

"Night."

Chapter Eighteen

October 19th

LISBETH WATCHED AS THE CLASS FILTERED OUT TO recess. One girl, Elizabeth, stopped at the doorway and looked up. "Is something wrong, Elizabeth?"

"I got to go potty."

Lisbeth took the girl by the hand and led her down the hall to the girls' bathroom. She waited while Elizabeth took care of her business. As she stood there, Lisbeth glanced down at her growing baby bump, trying to put the looming doctor's appointment from her mind. She was perfectly happy with having twins, even the morning sickness and swollen ankles. But she was also trying to mend things with Candace, and that meant talking with the doctor about reducing to a single baby.

"I'm done," Elizabeth called.

Lisbeth stepped inside to make sure Elizabeth washed her hands before they headed out to the playground. Elizabeth took off and left Lisbeth to observe. The area was cluttered with kids from all of the morning kindergarten and first grade classes. She often wondered why they couldn't give each class their own time to play. Her musing was cut short when she spotted Jack making a beeline for her. *Great.* Lisbeth sat down on a nearby bench and waited.

"How are you doing?" he asked and joined her.

"I'm good."

"I haven't seen you around during lunch lately."

She laughed. "You really need to stop trying to flirt with me. It's kind of painful. And I told you, I only teach in the mornings during the school year."

"I didn't mean it that way. I swear. I just...I've been meaning to tell you that things with my brother are good. He's happy."

"That's great."

"What about you?"

"What about me?" she asked.

"Are you happy?"

"I'm thrilled. Even with the morning sickness. I love being pregnant."

"That's not exactly what I was talking about."

She shrugged and ignored his question. She turned and cupped her hands around her mouth. "James, you leave your sister alone. I mean it." The boy continued to fling wood chips at Margaret. "Do you want to sit in time out the rest of the morning?"

He stopped and ran off toward the slide. Lisbeth glanced around to make sure the rest of her kids were behaving. Jack cleared his throat beside her. He wasn't going away.

"I'm sorry. What was the question?"

"You're good. I asked are you happy? And don't give me you are about being pregnant, because that's not what I meant."

"Is this really an appropriate conversation to be having at work?"

"Well, seeing as you spurn my advances, yeah." He gave her a wink.

"I am happy with who I am. I love the woman I married with all my heart, and we're going to raise these two beautiful children together until we grow old."

"Twins. That's...impressive."

"We're dealing with it."

"How's yoga treating you?"

"Yoga is fun. It's diverse. And I think I've made some new friends."

"Always a good thing." He paused. "You'll have to excuse me. I've got two kids trying to kick each other off the slide."

"Good luck," Lisbeth called.

"Thanks."

"Ms. Marquez's class, time to line up," she called a few minutes later.

A collective groan crossed the playground, but her kindergarteners started to line up. Margaret was still picking wood chips out of her hair. James made faces at her behind her back.

"James, one more thing from you, and you'll be in time out."

He looked away, and Maggie smiled at his misfortune. Lisbeth led the class back inside for the rest of their lesson on colors. She picked up the giant blocks, and the class chorused the color. Some giggled when their neighbor got it wrong, but Lisbeth made sure each and every one of them knew their colors spot on before parents started to show up. Lisbeth waved goodbye to Elizabeth and grabbed her jacket and purse. Even being on her feet for a couple of hours was starting to wear her out. She knew it would only get worse.

On her way home, Lisbeth stopped by the mall and strolled through the maternity store. She looked at flowing tops and extra-sized pants. She almost laughed at some of the patterns. She couldn't imagine wearing them. One of the store attendants started for Lisbeth, who quickly backed away from the floral print pants.

"Can I help you?" The woman was about forty, with salt-and-pepper hair.

"Oh, no thanks. I'm just looking," Lisbeth answered.

"When are you due? If you don't mind me asking," the woman continued.

Lisbeth fingered a nearby paisley top and let the hem flow away from her. She didn't answer right away. "Um, April," she finally answered.

"Well, if you need anything, just let me know."

Lisbeth nodded and ducked out of the store as fast as she could. Maybe buying maternity clothes right now wasn't the best idea. Instead, she wandered the length of the mall for a while longer. She stopped in the food court and grabbed a salad. As she ate, Lisbeth watched people rush by. Some women pushed strollers and toted toddlers on their hips. She couldn't wait to show off her kids like that. By the time she'd finished eating, it was nearly one thirty. Lisbeth grabbed her bag and walked through the mall until she spotted a baby furniture store. She couldn't resist. The moment she walked in, a pair of bassinets drew her attention. They were displayed in the front window, and she sneaked around the back of the other cribs and beds to get a closer look. She ran her hand over the fabric: pale blue and pink and as soft as fleece. The tiny pillow at the head of the bassinet was soft and fluffy.

"They're nice, right?" a female voice said from behind.

Lisbeth turned to see a woman in a green blouse and a little white nametag that read Monica. "They are."

"Are you looking for anything specific?" Monica asked.

"Not really. I'm just browsing."

"That's good. To do it early."

"Do you have a lot of these in stock?" Lisbeth asked and pointed to the basinets.

"We can always order if we run out."

"Great. I may be back."

"We'll be here."

Lisbeth gave the woman a smile and headed back to the parking lot. She got into her car and headed home. She pulled into her spot and noticed Candace's car was already in her space. Lisbeth hurried through the lobby and to the elevator. When she reached the apartment, she heard Candace's voice inside.

"She's not here right now." A pause. "I don't know when she'll be back, but I'll let her know you called."

The apartment went silent, and Lisbeth nudged the door open. Candace stood in the living room with the phone in her hand.

"Who was that?" Lisbeth asked.

"Your mother. She wanted to know if you would be around this weekend."

Lisbeth flopped onto the couch. "You didn't tell her that I was available, did you?"

"I told her that you'd call her back."

"I don't think I can handle her right now."

"Honey, we can tell them together. It will be fine."

"I just...I'm scared. I think the babies would be information overload. And they still pretend like we aren't together."

Candace put down the phone and took Lisbeth's hands in her own. "I know it's a lot, but we have to tell them sometime."

Lisbeth wet her lips, squeezed Candace's hands lightly, and said, "We'll tell them. I promise."

Candace leaned in and kissed her on the lips. Despite the impending appointment, Lisbeth found she couldn't pull away from her wife's embrace. They stayed lip-locked until Lisbeth got up the courage to call her mother back. The phone rang twice.

"Hello?"

"Hi, Mom."

"Oh, honey. Where were you? I called a little while ago, but your roommate picked up."

Lisbeth cringed at the way her mother said *roommate*. "I took a trip to the mall after school. Got some lunch."

"Oh."

"What were you calling about?"

"I was hoping you were free this weekend. Your father and I were thinking of coming to visit for a while."

"Oh, sure. I think I'm free on Saturday. We could go out to lunch."

"That sounds lovely. Should we meet you somewhere?"

"We can meet at the apartment and walk from here."

"We'll see you then."

"Bye, Mom."

Lisbeth hung up and tossed the phone onto the table. Candace joined her on the couch and stroked her arm.

"You went to the mall?"

"Yeah. Just felt like the thing to do. I saw some absolutely horrible maternity clothes. God-awful floral prints. It was painful. If I ever feel the urge to buy anything like that, shoot me, okay?"

"Sure."

They laughed for a few minutes over her descriptions of the clothes.

"I stopped by the baby store, too. They had these adorable little pink and blue basinets. They would be perfect for the nursery."

"Sounds nice," Candace said and reached for her keys.

Lisbeth checked the time. They were going to be late for the appointment. Not that she was overly excited about the prospects. But maybe it would show Candace they could handle twins. The ride to the office was silent. Lisbeth kept her attention focused on the traffic out her window until they pulled into the parking lot. Her throat went dry as they walked in the front door and took seats in the waiting room.

"Lisbeth?" a nurse called.

Lisbeth stood and gripped the armrest for a moment to steady herself. They followed the nurse back to a room, and Lisbeth settled on the exam table. Candace sat opposite her and waited. An interminable time later, the doctor walked in with a clipboard. Lisbeth couldn't read his expression.

"How are you doing today?" he asked.

"Anxious," Lisbeth answered.

"I understand. This is a difficult decision and one you shouldn't rush into."

"Would it be better for her health if we reduced to one fetus?" Candace asked.

"Possibly. It would certainly increase her chances of reaching full term. But there are of course other reasons and factors that could keep her from a full-term delivery. And it is far more common to reduce multiple pregnancies in the higher level of triplets or quadruplets."

"So it's not a sure thing. And you think both babies are healthy, right?" Lisbeth interrupted.

"As far as we can tell, both babies are developing properly, and we haven't detected any problems."

"Then there's no reason to go through with it. If they're both healthy," she said.

"What about the procedure? I mean...we found some information online, but not a lot," Candace said.

"You'd come in, and we would do the procedure here. We go in via ultrasound and inject the chosen fetus and stop the heart."

"Ultrasound?" Lisbeth asked and bit back bile rising in her throat.

"Yes. And provided both fetuses are healthy as yours are, we pick one."

"But what if they're not the same gender?"

"In that instance, you would have some say. And I hope I don't need to remind you that this needs to be a decision you both agree on."

Lisbeth nodded and looked at Candace, whose face paled. Her complexion no doubt mirrored Lisbeth's own.

"Can we have a minute to talk about this?" Lisbeth asked.

"Of course. There's no need to make a final decision today if you don't want. We have a few more weeks before a final decision needs to be made."

The doctor left them to discuss the options in private. Lisbeth turned to face Candace and clasped her hands in her lap. Candace wiped her eyes, as if warding off tears.

"Did you know they did it by ultrasound?" Lisbeth asked.

"No. I knew the doctor chose which fetus, but I guess I didn't read closely about the details."

"I can't go through that. I just can't. I know it's not exactly like an abortion, but it's close enough. We can find a way to support these two children. We don't have to choose only one."

"I just want what's best for you."

"I know you do. And I want what's best for these babies, and I just don't see how terminating one is going to achieve that."

"I am sorry I didn't look further into the procedure," Candace said. "But you know I'd be here with you."

Lisbeth looked away. *Why is she still pushing the issue?*

"Why do you really think this is a doable option for us? For all we know, terminating one will cause a miscarriage."

Candace licked her lips and leaned forward in the chair. Lisbeth studied her wife's features as she waited for a response.

"You know...I was hurt when you said I was being selfish about this. And maybe I do put some pressure on you to get through this. But it's not because of my own inability to carry a baby to term. It's because I want nothing more than to spend the rest of my life with you and raise a child."

Lisbeth rested her head on the headrest of the exam table. What Candace said made sense, but it sounded like the same old argument.

"I want the same thing, but I can't get there by risking either of these children. So I'm telling you that I am not going through with it. And that's all there is to it. The doctor said we needed to agree, and clearly, we don't. But right now, and I'm sorry if this hurts, my vote counts more."

Candace exhaled through her nose and stared at her hands in silence. Lisbeth waited for something to happen. The pain and hurt flickered over her wife's features. Finally, Candace stood up and took Lisbeth by the hand.

"You're right. I should have never suggested it. I'm sorry."

Lisbeth stood up and they left the exam room. She could tell by Candace's tone that she wasn't happy about having to acquiesce the decision. They would move on from this in time.

"I love you. I hope you know that," Candace whispered as they left the doctor's office.

"I love you, too."

Saturday came too quickly for Lisbeth. She hid in the kitchen and made Candace answer the door. She could hear her parents' voices. Her mother was always polite to Candace, and Lisbeth hoped she'd stay that way after their lunch.

"Lisbeth, your parents are here," Candace called.

Lisbeth swallowed twice and smoothed her shirt before walking into the living room. She gave her parents quick hugs and pulled on her jacket before they could say much about her figure.

"Let's go," Lisbeth said and led the group out.

"Oh, I didn't know your roommate was joining us," Lisbeth's mother said.

"Mom, don't be rude. She's part of the family."

Her mother said nothing else as they walked the two blocks to a little Italian restaurant. They got a table, and Lisbeth let her parents take the booth side. She and Candace sat with their backs to the front of the restaurant and waited for menus. Lisbeth nervously flipped through hers, even after she'd decided on her meal.

"So, how is work?" her father asked.

"Good."

"You look a little...stressed out, honey. Are you sure you're okay?" her mother pressed.

"I'm not stressed out, Mom. I'm fine."

"Well, you look like you've put on a little weight."

Lisbeth's grip tightened around the plastic.

"Jeez, Mom. Thanks."

Her mother tried to apologize, but Lisbeth didn't listen. She was trying to calm down enough to get the truth out.

"Look, there's something I need to tell you," Lisbeth said.

Her parents looked at her and waited.

"I'm pregnant. With twins."

"You didn't tell us you had someone in your life. When can we meet him?" her dad asked.

"Dad, we've been over this. I'm gay. I've been gay for years. Candace and I are married."

"Honey, is this is really something we should be discussing right now?" her mother said.

"Yes, mom. We can talk about it here. You knew I got married. You just refused to come to the service."

"It's not the same," her dad said.

"Dad, actually it is. Has been since 2004. Now, in case you missed it, we're having twins."

"We heard you, Lisbeth. There's no need to get so upset. Though I'm surprised you decided to have children right now."

"Candace will be raising them with me. And if you can't find it in yourselves to accept me for who I am, then I'm not sure I want you in my children's lives."

Her parents gawked at her from across the table as the waiter came by with water and rolls. Lisbeth looked at the food, and her stomach flipped. She wasn't hungry anymore. She pushed away from the table and left the restaurant, Candace right behind her.

Chapter Nineteen

October 31st

RENEE STEPPED OUT OF THE SHOWER, WRAPPED A towel around her body, and stared at herself in the mirror. She had to wipe the mist free to see her reflection clearly. Music blared in the living room, permeating the closed bathroom door. Strange Halloween music that Erika had insisted on playing. Renee let her do it since it was Halloween. Pulling on jeans and a sweatshirt, she walked out with a towel on her hair—the costume could wait until later. Erika was doing the Thriller dance in the living room.

"What are you doing?" Renee asked. She couldn't help but laugh.

Erika stopped and blushed. "Just um...dancing."

"I see that."

"It's kind of a tradition my friends and I had in college. On Halloween, we'd dress up and do our own Thriller video."

"That sounds fun."

"Yeah. So, what are you dressing up as tonight?"

"I have a few things to choose from. You know, the old staples. Dead hooker, vampire."

Erika laughed. "I think I might dress up like one of the Pussy Cat Dolls."

"You'd look really cute. Is Dane coming over?"

"I don't know."

"You did invite him, right?"

"Yeah. I told him he could stop by. But...I haven't seen him in a while."

"You have been avoiding him."

"It's just weird. We dated in college, and I know he still likes me."

"But you don't want to lead him on. Unless you still like him."

"Exactly. But...I mean, I like him as a friend."

"Well, just tell him how things are."

Erika nodded. Renee walked by the table and grabbed a fistful of candy.

Erika made a disapproving clucking noise.

"What?" Renee asked.

"That's for the kids."

"We don't get many kids here. So we've got enough chocolate to keep us happy for a while."

When Renee came back, hair dried and makeup on, Erika sat on the floor with her legs tucked under her.

"What are you doing?"

"Yoga. I thought I'd try doing it outside of class. It's started to not hurt so much after class."

Renee sat down opposite her roommate and mirrored her position. They stretched and contorted into slightly less painful positions together for a good half hour.

"You're right, I feel less achy afterwards," Renee agreed.

Erika just smiled and stood up. "So, are we just going to hang out and gorge on candy all night?"

"Sure. We can rent movies or something, too."

"Cool. What did you usually do on Halloween?"

"I'd go out trick-or-treating. Well, in college. Kind of stopped once I graduated and got a job. When it falls on a weekday, it's really fun to see all the kids coming in dressed up."

"We used to have killer parties on campus. This is going to be the first year I haven't had one."

"Well, we're making our own traditions. Two hot mamas," Renee said with a smile.

Erika smiled and glanced down at her stomach. "Don't remind me."

"Sorry. Still no word from the agency?"

"None yet. I guess it's taking longer. I'm kind of nervous."

"Don't worry about it, Erika. You'll find the perfect people for your baby."

"Yeah. Sometimes I wonder if it's right."

Renee wrapped Erika in a hug. "You have to do what your heart tells you. No matter what it says."

"You really believe that?" Erika didn't look impressed.

"Yes. I do believe that."

"Even after Bryce? I mean, you didn't think about giving the baby up?"

The heat in Renee's cheeks deepened, and her neck warmed. She hadn't talked about Bryce in a while. She'd almost convinced herself to forget him completely.

"No. But, that's different. I mean, we talked about it. Okay, so he suggested, and I told him he was full of shit and to not tell me what to do."

"Do you think he'll ever come back?"

"I don't know. I doubt it. But that's not important. Today is supposed to be a fun day," Renee said and put on a smile.

By the afternoon, they'd decorated the apartment with lights, fake cobwebs, and spiders. The candy bowl had only taken a few hits, which were quickly replenished. Around four p.m., Renee was standing in front of the microwave, making a cup of hot chocolate, when Erika walked in. Besides the obvious baby bump, she looked like a kick-ass rock star.

"You look great," Renee exclaimed as the microwave beeped.

She pulled the mug out and blew the steam off the top of the drink.

"Thanks. I just got a text from Dane. He said he would be over around five. So you had better be in costume."

"Yes, ma'am. Oh, how are things going at meetings?"

"Um. They're okay. It's nice to know there are people who get what I'm going through. Like Nate."

Renee quirked a brow and said, "You haven't mentioned him before."

"Sure I have. He's the one that made me talk. He's really cute. But I don't know. I shouldn't be thinking about dating."

Renee shook her head, took a sip of hot chocolate, and sighed. The warmth spread through her body and invigorated her. Erika pulled a packet of cocoa mix out of the cabinet and picked up a mug.

"So did you decide what you're dressing up as?"

"It's going to be a surprise."

"Well, I can't wait."

Renee took her hot chocolate into the living room and sat down on the couch, looking around. A sudden emptiness flooded the room. Or maybe it was in her heart. Bringing up Bryce had stirred up unresolved feelings.

"Jerk," she grumbled and downed the rest of her drink. She could still hear Erika in the kitchen, making her own hot chocolate. *Might as well get dressed.*

Renee emerged from her room as a knock came on the front door. Both she and Erika reached it at the same time. Renee reached for the doorknob, and Erika snickered.

"What?" Renee asked.

"You're a waitress."

"Yeah, from that movie with Keri Russell."

"Okay."

Renee pulled open the door and stared at Shannon, her kids, and a guy she assumed was Shannon's husband.

"Hi," Renee said, confused.

"Trick or treat," the kids said.

"Oh. Let me get the candy," Erika said and raced off to the living room.

"What a surprise," Renee said.

"I thought we'd just drop by. The kids wanted to dress up early."

"Well, thanks. That's really sweet of you."

Renee examined the kids' costumes. Tanner was dressed in a red and gold suit with a mask.

"He's Iron Man," Christian said.

"I see that. Very cool. And what about you?"

"I'm a princess," Meghan interrupted and gave a twirl.

"I see. You must be an *ice* princess because you have a penguin."

"Yeah."

"I'm a werewolf," Christian answered.

"Who wants candy?" Erika asked, returning with the bowl.

The kids each took a couple of pieces. Their dad led them out into the hallway.

"Oh that's adorable," Renee said, spotting the apron Shannon was wearing. A picture of a pumpkin rested against her stomach.

"I thought it was appropriate."

"Would your pumpkin like some candy?" Erika offered.

"Maybe just a piece," Shannon said and stuck a mini Snickers into her apron pocket.

Erika balanced the bowl on her knee and rooted through it.

"So what are you doing tonight?" Shannon asked.

"Watching movies and pigging out on candy."

"Sounds like a lot of fun."

Behind them, Tanner and Meghan began to shriek and giggle.

"Sounds like the princess and Iron Man need a little help," Renee said, smiling.

"I'm sure my darling werewolf is chasing them. We also stopped by because I wanted to invite you both to Thanksgiving dinner at our place. We usually do a big family gathering, but with everyone's schedules this year, it would just be us."

"That's really sweet of you. I'll have to talk to my parents about their plans. I'll let you know," Renee said.

"Great."

"I'm in," Erika added.

"I should have more details about the time and everything in a week or so."

"Mama, Christian's trying to eat me," Tanner cried.

"That's my cue."

They watched as Shannon herded her family down the hallway toward the elevator.

"She's so nice," Erika said.

"Yeah. She is. I'm sure you'll have a great time at Thanksgiving."

"You have to come. I mean, it would be kind of weird without you," Erika said.

"You could ask Dane to go with you," Renee teased.

"Not fair. New rule. No teasing about ex-boyfriends."

"Fine. But don't blame me if you two get a little cuddly tonight," Renee said with a wink and took the bowl of candy back to the living room.

Right at five o'clock, Dane showed up, dressed as he always was. Renee showed him in and offered to get him something to drink.

"Soda, if you've got it. I'm trying not to drink around Erika anymore."

"Sure."

"How is she?"

"She's doing better. She's going to meetings twice a week. They seem to be helping. Plus, she's found a sort of sponsor."

"Good."

"What are you supposed to be?" Renee asked.

"College kid," he answered with a shrug.

"Oh. Imaginative."

Erika appeared from her bedroom and gave Dane a smile. He looked at her and laughed. Renee gave Erika a wink and handed Dane a can of soda.

"I'm going to see what movies we have," Renee said and left the two to talk.

She could hear snippets of their conversation but tried to block it out. It wasn't her business. She pulled a pile of DVDs from under the TV and started to sift through them. Renee jumped as something vibrated in her apron pocket. She fished out her phone.

"Hello?"

"Happy Halloween, honey," her mother said.

"Hi, Mom. You guys have many kids stop by?"

"Not yet. It's early. But I'm sure we'll get some. How about you?"

"Three. Shannon brought her kids over."

"Shannon?"

"One of the women in my yoga class. Speaking of, she invited me over for Thanksgiving."

"That was nice of her."

"Would you be horribly disappointed if I decided to go? There's a group of us that have gotten kind of close in the last couple months."

"You can do whatever you like, Renee. It won't be the same without you, but you have your own life."

"Thanks."

"Do you have any plans for the evening?" her mother asked.

"Just hanging out with Erika and her friend Dane and watching movies."

"Well, have fun. Don't eat too much candy."

"Yes, ma'am."

Renee hung up and was immediately accosted by Dane and Erika chasing each other into the room like little kids.

"Let's get this party started," Dane said.

Renee popped *Rocky Horror* in the DVD player, and they settled in for the night. Erika curled up against Dane's shoulder as the closing credits rolled around seven fifteen.

"Another one?" Renee asked from the chair nearby.

"What else do we have?" she asked and detached herself from the couch and Dane's arm.

Renee pushed the pile of cases across the room with her foot, and Erika sifted through them until she found *Clue*.

"It's silly, but...we need lighthearted silly after that," Erika said.

"Go for it."

Around ten o'clock, Renee stretched and turned the TV off. Erika snored lightly on the couch. Dane tried to extricate himself from her grip but appeared to be failing.

"Want some help getting her to bed?" Renee offered.

"Yeah. Thanks. It was fun tonight."

Together, they managed to get Erika to her bed. Renee walked Dane to the front door and said goodbye before heading to bed herself.

Chapter Twenty

November 16th

ERIKA BENT OVER THE TABLE, TRYING TO REACH A stray straw wrapper when she heard footsteps behind her and a voice asked, "Need some help?"

"No, I got it," Erika said and got on her knees to pick up the trash. She struggled to her feet and turned to see her boss standing there.

"I have to say, Erika, I'm surprised by you."

Erika fiddled with the crumpled up wrapper between her fingers. She didn't know what to say.

"Um, thanks."

"I just wanted to let you know, you missed a call."

Erika rooted in her apron for her phone. She'd been keeping it with her in case the adoption agency called. It wasn't there. She felt her cheeks burn with embarrassment.

"Sorry. I didn't mean for it go off."

"You've got a break now. Why don't you take the call?" Her boss handed her the phone.

Erika hastily checked her missed calls. Sure enough, Arlene had left a voicemail. She raced out of the restaurant and began pacing while the phone rang. Five, six times before someone answered.

"Commonwealth Adoption Services," a woman answered.

"Hi, um, my name is Erika Lind. I just got a voicemail from Arlene."

"One moment, please."

Erika tapped her fingers on her leg to the rhythm of the hold music. Two minutes later, the music stopped, and a familiar voice came on the line.

"Erika? It's Arlene."

"Hi. I was working, and I missed your call," Erika explained, even though Arlene probably already knew that.

"That's all right. I just wanted to tell you that we have a potential match for you."

Erika gasped. It wasn't happening. It couldn't be. She'd almost given up the hope that they'd find anyone.

"You did?" she finally got out.

"Yes. They can come in this afternoon around four o'clock. Are you available then?"

Erika ran a hand over her forehead and tried to think. She'd promised one of her co-workers she could cover her afternoon shift today. She didn't want to skip out, but this was...life changing.

"Erika, are you still there?" Arlene asked after pause of silence.

"Yeah, I'm here...I think...I'll have to check with my manager."

"Okay. Well, can you do that in the next twenty minutes so I can let the couple know whether we'll be able to meet and assess whether they're a good fit?"

"Yeah. I'll do it right now. Hang on. Don't go anywhere."

Erika bounded back inside to find her manager. She was tabulating time sheets.

"I have to leave around three thirty," Erika blurted.

"I thought you said you could do an extra shift this afternoon."

"I know. But there's this thing that just came up...the adoption agency found a family."

Her manager's face softened. "Go. Good luck."

Erika breathed a huge sigh of relief and stepped into a more secluded area. "I'll be there," she told Arlene.

"Great. We'll see you then."

Erika hung up and jumped in a little circle. She thought about calling Renee to let her know but decided to wait until after the meeting for the good news. An extra bubbly mood, broad smile included, overtook her the rest of the afternoon. At exactly three thirty, she clocked out and hopped on the T. The train trundled below the city, and Erika checked her watch repeatedly until reaching her stop. She ran up the stairs to street level and had to catch her breath as she walked into Commonwealth Adoption Services. She said hello to the receptionist and ducked down the hall to the waiting room. Arlene stuck her head out and waved Erika back before she had a chance to get comfortable in the chair.

"How are you doing?" Arlene asked as they walked to a small conference room.

"I'm okay. Been going to meetings and working a lot."

"That's great. And you've been going to your doctor's appointments?"

"Yeah. They said the baby looks good. We should know soon if it's a boy or a girl."

"Have a seat in here. Your prospective family should be here any minute. Help yourself to something to drink."

"Thanks."

Arlene left the room, and Erika poured a glass of water. She gulped it down and refilled the glass in a matter of seconds. Looking around the room with its floor-to-ceiling bookshelves stocked with a book for every shelf, Erika finally settled into one of the plush office chairs just as Arlene came back with a couple. Older, maybe in their forties. The woman was wearing a stuffy-looking high-collared dress, and the man wore a tweed suit. By their appearance, she didn't like them. Arlene sat down next to Erika and opened a portfolio.

"Well, Erika, this is Mr. and Mrs. Hilliard," Arlene introduced.

"Hi. Nice to meet you," Erika said.

Mr. Hilliard looked at her as if he was trying to look through her. She squirmed, and unease clinched her gut.

"I've explained the situation to Mr. and Mrs. Hilliard," Arlene continued, "and I think they would be a good fit."

Erika leaned on the edge of the table and looked directly at the Hilliards. "What exactly makes you a good fit?"

"We have experience with special needs children. We fostered several," Mrs. Hilliard answered.

"Oh."

"And you have money to pay for...everything?"

"Of course, young lady. We are well aware of the obligations placed upon us," Mr. Hilliard answered.

"If you had foster kids before, why didn't you adopt any of them?" Erika questioned.

"They...were returned to their parents," Mr. Hilliard said, still looking through her.

"So you want my kid because then, they can't take it back?"

Arlene interceded before they could say anything else.

"If you don't mind, I'd like to talk to Erika for a moment alone."

Erika swallowed and tried not to look guilty or freaked out as she followed Arlene into the hallway.

"You don't seem to like them."

"I don't know. They're kind of stuffy, and I don't want my kid to grow up stuffy. And I don't think he likes me. He keeps staring at me."

"They do have experience with special needs children."

"Yeah, I heard them, but I just...something about them bugs me."

Arlene held up her hands and nodded. "Okay. No problem. We'll keep looking."

"I'm sorry," Erika mumbled.

"You don't have to apologize. You need to be comfortable with this process."

They walked back into the room, and Erika watched as Arlene broke the news to the Hilliards. They didn't seem too pleased. Then again, Erika couldn't blame them. She'd be pissed if she was on their side of the table. They didn't look at her as they left the room, and she sank into her chair. Arlene patted her shoulder.

"We'll keep looking. I'm sure we'll find someone."

Erika gave a half-hearted nod. "Yeah."

"I'll be in touch," Arlene promised.

Erika left the conference room. She wandered around outside for a few minutes before getting back on the T and heading out to Brookline. She needed to think, and she knew if she wasn't at least in the general vicinity of her meeting, she'd miss it. Erika ended up sitting outside the church for nearly an hour before anyone arrived. Nate walked up and sat down beside her. Even in early November weather, he looked cute.

"You're here early," he said.

"Yeah. Just...thinking."

"About what?"

"About how life sucks sometimes. And how much I could really use a drink."

Without saying anything, he wrapped his arm around her shoulders. "We all have days like that."

"Yeah. Sure."

"Seriously. I wake up every day, and a little part of me wants a drink. But I have reasons not to now."

"You do?"

"Yeah. I'm going overseas after Christmas to do some mission work. I told myself I have to be sober to do that work."

"That's good. When will you be back?"

"It's only a couple months. So probably March."

"Cool."

A tiny voice in the back of her head told her it was *not* in fact cool that the guy who understood her was leaving for months when she probably needed him most. Sure, they were only friends, but she wasn't sure she could handle that kind of loss.

"You are coming back, though, right?" she said.

"I am."

"I'll miss you," she blurted.

"I'll miss you, too."

"Can I be honest?" Erika asked.

"Sure."

"You've kind of been what's gotten me through the last few weeks. Well, I mean, my friends have too, but...you really get it. And I'm probably being a complete idiot, but I don't know if I can handle you not being here."

Nate pulled his arm away and took her hand in his, wrapping it in warmth. He didn't say anything for a while. Just held her hand and smiled.

"You are stronger than you think. You can do this without me."

"What if I don't want to?"

"You have to."

She wanted to believe he had that much faith in her.

"So what's got you so stressed?" he said.

Erika shrugged. "Maybe I should save it for meeting."

"You can, but you've got a willing ear right now."

She smiled. In a strange way, he reminded her of Dane. "I just had this meeting today, at the adoption agency."

"I'm guessing it didn't go well?"

"Not at all. The people were stuffy and rude. I didn't like them. I didn't want them raising my baby. But...part of me

248

thinks I won't get another shot at this. Like...no one else is going to want my baby."

"Did the agency say anything about you not liking these people?"

"Just that they understand. And that I have to be comfortable, since it's going to be an open adoption so I have to stay in touch with them. But it's what they've been saying from the beginning."

"I think that is important. But you shouldn't let it stress you. You just need to have a little faith."

Erika tried not to appear annoyed. "I keep forgetting you're all about God and stuff."

"Yes, I am," he said. To her surprise, he didn't look offended by her comment.

"Come on, let's go inside."

Erika followed Nate inside the church and up to the second floor for the meeting. They were the first to arrive, so they set up chairs and settled in to wait for everyone else. Erika busied herself with her phone, playing a game and texting Renee to tell her she'd be in late. She almost texted Dane but stopped mid-message. Maybe it was better to call him.

"Hey, I'll be right back," Erika said.

"I'm not going anywhere," Nate replied.

She ducked out of the hall and dialed Dane's number. Her footsteps echoed on the polished stone floor as she paced.

"Hey," Dane said. It sounded like he was outside near traffic.

"Hi. Do you have a minute to talk?"

"Sure. I'm just meeting some of the guys for dinner. What's up? Haven't talked to you in a while."

"I know. I've been crazy busy with work and doctor appointments and stuff."

"Yeah. And you know I'm totally up for taking you if you need it."

"Maybe my next appointment. I got a call from the agency today. They had a couple who wanted the baby."

"Erika, that's great."

"I didn't like them. They creeped me out."

"That's not cool. So what happens now?"

"They keep looking for other people."

"You need me to come over?"

"No. I'll be okay. I'm at a meeting right now anyway."

"Seriously, I can come if you need me."

"Thanks. Go have fun with your friends."

She hung up as a bunch of people, Nate included, walked into the next room. She turned her phone to silent and followed them. The meeting got underway shortly, and Erika listened to everyone's stories. She felt embarrassed sometimes that her story was way more fucked up than the rest of the group. It was selfish, really. Nate cleared his throat and looked right at her.

"I think we should all take a minute and hear what Erika's been through today. She needs our support."

Erika blushed and suddenly felt a tear trickle down her cheek. She wiped it away and cleared her throat.

"I...I thought things were looking up when I got a call about a possible adoptive family. But it didn't work out. And

I'm kind of scared. And I hate that my first thought was that I wanted a drink. That I needed one."

The people on either side of her gave her gentle pats on the shoulder and a hand squeeze. She tried to keep it together, but the tears fell anyway. People gave her words of comfort and understanding. Nate even got up and gave her hug.

Half an hour later, they walked out of the meeting and to the T stop. Nate stood at her side as they waited for the same train out of the city. Just as Nate was about to step on the train, Erika leaned over and pressed her lips against his cheek. He pulled away.

"Sorry," she said and followed him onto the train.

"It's okay. I just...you know I'm leaving next month."

"That's still a long way away," she said.

Nate reached a hand out and brushed a stray piece of hair from her eyes. Even in the cool evening, his hand was warm against her skin.

"I like you, Erika. But there's kind of a rule against getting involved like that."

"You're not my sponsor. Not like officially or anything. And besides, why would we have to tell anyone?"

"Erika. I want to be there for you. Just not like that, okay?"

He leaned over and pulled her into a hug. Somehow, even his rejection didn't sting as much as it should have. They broke apart, and the train continued to trundle along.

"See you next week," she said and got off at her stop. Erika tried not to think about the stirring in her stomach. She couldn't have feelings for a guy who was going to be halfway around the world for a long period of time. He'd made that pretty clear. Still, he understood her on a level no one else did. She got home as Renee put a kettle on the stove for tea.

"How'd the meeting go?" Renee asked.

"Okay...met with the adoption people. The family wasn't right."

"I'm sorry, sweetie." Renee pulled Erika into a hug.

"And um...Nate kissed me."

"Really? He kissed you?"

"Well, okay, so *I* kissed *him*. We caught the same train after the meeting. It was nice, even though he told me that he's not really interested."

"Well, is he single?"

"I guess so. But he's leaving for this big mission trip thing next month. I won't see him until March."

"Don't be so hard on yourself. You're a great catch."

"Thanks, Mrs. Cleaver."

"Give him a chance."

"I want to. I like him. And he gets me. But...it's just weird with him leaving."

Chapter Twenty-One

November 25th

SHANNON STOOD OVER THE STOVE AND STIRRED THE pot of thick brown gravy, strengthening the scents of roasting turkey and other Thanksgiving staples. Her gaze flitted to the clock every few minutes. She'd been up cooking since six that morning and still couldn't push the worry out of her head that everything wouldn't be done when their guests arrived. Meghan wandered in, carrying her penguin from the aquarium. She never went anywhere without it these days.

"Mama, what are you doing?"

"I'm making dinner."

"Why?"

"Because it's Thanksgiving, and we're having lots of people over."

She bent over as best she could to turn on the oven light and motioned Meghan closer. She pointed to the huge turkey inside.

"The turkey has to cook for a really long time."

"That's really big. When can we eat it?"

"Soon."

"Can I help?"

Shannon looked around the kitchen at the disarray of dirty dishes and the neat stack of clean plates sitting on the kitchen table ready to be carried into the dining room.

"Sure. Can you help Mama by putting the plates on the dining room table?"

"Okay."

"Be very careful. Take one at a time."

"Where do I put them?"

"Put one plate in front of each chair."

She watched Meghan take a plate from the kitchen and set it in the dining room. She gave her daughter a nod of approval and went back to stirring the gravy. A timer went off, and Shannon opened the oven. The heady smell of stuffing wafted over her, and she pulled the dish out. She quickly set it on a cooling rack and stuck the meat thermometer in the turkey. Not quite long enough. It would have to go at least another hour. She checked the clock on the microwave: two fifteen. She would have enough time before the girls arrived.

"Mama, I'm done."

Shannon straightened up and glanced at the dishes in the sink. "Do you want to help Mama do the dishes?"

Before Meghan could answer, Tanner came tearing around the corner and slid to a stop in his socks, nearly colliding with his sister.

"Tanner, slow down," Shannon scolded.

Tanner scrambled toward Shannon and wrapped his arms around her legs. Christian appeared seconds later.

"No fair. Mom isn't base."

"Is too." Tanner stuck his tongue out at Christian.

"Guys, what are you doing?"

"Playing tag," Christian answered.

"Not in the house, okay?" Tanner didn't let go. "Tanner, you need to let go of Mama, please."

"But he'll get me."

"He won't, because you aren't going to play tag anymore."

Meghan ignored her brothers by dragging a chair to the sink and turning on the water.

"Christian, why don't you go play on the computer for a little while?"

His features brightened, and he immediately turned to the computer. Tanner stayed latched to Shannon's leg for a minute before taking off into the living room.

"Mama, I need help," Meghan said.

Shannon gave the gravy one more pass before she set the burner to low and stepped to the sink.

"Don't put so much soap in, sweetie."

Meghan giggled as the suds foamed up over the pans. "The water's really hot."

"Yes, it is."

Shannon turned on the cold water to even out the temperature. They stood together and scrubbed cookware until it sparkled.

"It smells great in here," Mike said as he walked into the room.

"I'm helping Mama," Meghan said.

"Yes, you are. You're my perfect little helper," Shannon agreed.

Mike kissed Meghan's forehead and wrapped an arm around Shannon's waist. "Are you doing all right?"

"I'm fine. Why?" she asked in confusion.

"You've been on your feet all day."

Shannon glanced down at her stomach. They'd know the sex of their baby on Monday, and she was a little nervous. Once they were sure whether it was a boy or a girl, they'd start pulling out the old crib and buying new baby clothes. And she still hadn't mustered up the courage to tell Mike how stressed she was with all the extra work.

"I'm okay. The dishes are almost done."

He smiled and went to stir the gravy a time or two before disappearing out of the kitchen. Shannon picked up a dishtowel and took the utensils and pans as Megan finished dousing them with soapy water. As soon as the dishes were dried and put away, she headed for the living room. Tanner sat on the floor, playing with his trucks and knocking down towers of Legos. He seemed content with his toys until she sat down on the couch. He abandoned his spot on the floor and scrambled to sit in her lap.

"Ooh, Tanner you're getting too big to sit in Mama's lap," Shannon said as he knocked the wind out of her.

"I'm not too big. Mama's too big."

Shannon laughed a little. "I think you're right. Mama is getting big."

"Baby takes up too much room," Tanner said and pressed his face her stomach.

Shannon scooted Tanner over so he wasn't right in her lap and cuddled him. She missed being able to rock him to sleep. He really wasn't her baby boy anymore. Sitting there listening to the vague fighting sounds on Christian's computer game, she lost track of time. Meghan finished with the dishes, and the water shut off. Only the doorbell ringing snapped her out of her daze. Shannon followed Tanner when he slid off the couch and ran for the door. They greeted Renee and Erika.

"Sorry we're a little early," Renee apologized.

"Don't be silly. Come in."

As they went into the kitchen, Mike took the turkey out of the oven to check the temperature.

"Looks really good," Erika said.

"We should be almost ready. Probably another twenty minutes," Mike answered and picked up a mixer. He finished the mashed potatoes. Surprised, Shannon gaped at him and tried to cover her shock with a faltering smile before leading their guests into the dining room. She supposed the holiday was the exception to the rule, especially since their guests were her friends.

"Chris, time to turn off the computer. We have guests," she said.

Christian gave her a pleading look but shut the game down. Erika bent down to look at the design on the plates.

"You've got such beautiful china," she said.

"It was a wedding present from my parents," Shannon replied as they moved to the living room.

They sank into chairs and watched as Meghan colored and Tanner peered over her shoulder. He tried to make suggestions, but she swatted his hand away.

"So how have you been?" Shannon asked, looking at her guests.

"Good. I'm handling the news from last week better," Erika answered.

"That's great. How many months has it been since your last drink?"

Erika blushed. "Um...two."

"That's wonderful. I know it's a constant struggle, but you've got a lot of strength in you."

"A friend of mine said that, too. What about you? How's work and stuff?"

"Oh, work is work. I've got a few extra clients right now, but I try to take it a little at a time."

Renee and Erika nodded their understanding. Thankfully, neither suggested she share her concerns with Mike.

"What about you, Renee?" Shannon asked.

"Oh, work is fine. I get a lot of comments lately. You know, some people saying how brave I am to still be working and pregnant. I try to ignore the ones who aren't so nice."

"Mom," Christian said, interrupting the conversation.

"Yes, Chris?"

"There are people at the front door."

"Invite them in, and take their coats."

"Okay."

Moments later, Lisbeth and Candace walked in and joined them. Renee scooted over on the couch so they could sit.

"Did we miss much?" Lisbeth asked.

"We were just catching up," Shannon answered.

Lisbeth gave them a sad smile. Shannon reached across the table and squeezed her hand. "How have you been?"

"Okay. We've decided we're not reducing the twins. But it's been awkward with my parents since we walked out on them at lunch," Lisbeth admitted.

From what Lisbeth had told them, her parents hadn't answered any e-mails or phone calls in nearly a month. Candace took Lisbeth's hand and ran her thumb over it affectionately. At least the pair seemed back on good terms after deciding to keep both babies.

"They'll come around. They have to," Renee said.

"Thanks."

It was obvious Lisbeth didn't believe Renee. Shannon felt bad that Lisbeth's parents couldn't be happy for their daughter. She was becoming a mother, and she had someone to share the experience with. They talked a little while longer until Mike stuck his head in from the dining room.

"Dinner's ready," he announced.

Christian, Tanner, and Meghan raced into the dining room and clambered into seats. Shannon led her friends to the table and, after shifting the chairs so everyone could fit, they all sat down. A pitcher of sparkling cider sat in the center of the table, surrounded by heaping plates of turkey, stuffing, and potatoes. Glancing around the table, Shannon was grateful for the friends she'd made. She reached out and took Meghan's hand. Everyone followed suit until their hands circled the table.

"I thought we could each go around and say something we're thankful for before we eat," Shannon said. "I'll start. I'm thankful for my wonderful husband and children and the new family I've found."

Meghan mumbled something about her penguin and the new baby. Tanner and Christian followed her lead. They got to Erika, and she had tears slipping down her cheeks.

"I'm thankful...no, grateful, for the strength you have all shown over the last few months. I don't think I could have gotten through this without you. And I'm thankful for two months of sobriety."

"Here, here," Candace said and broke the circle to raise her glass.

Moisture glistened at the corners of Lisbeth's eyes when it was her turn. "I have to echo Erika and say I'm grateful to have found such strong women at this point in my life. Knowing I can talk to any of you gives me hope that the rocky patches will smooth out soon."

They broke apart and started to pass food around the table. Shannon sipped her cider and took in the scene. Something about the group assembled made it all worthwhile, the exhaustion and sore ankles included. She watched Tanner trying to tear the turkey on his plate apart with his fork and spoon.

"Tanner, give Mama your plate, and I'll cut it for you."

Tanner picked up the plate and passed it over. She quickly cut it into bite-size pieces and handed it back. The meal finished about forty minutes later, and they retired to the living room again to let the food settle before dessert.

"Mom, can we play a game?" Christian asked.

"What do you want to play?" she asked.

"Pictionary."

She looked to Mike, and he nodded. "Sure."

"I'm with Mama," Meghan said before Tanner got the chance.

They split into two teams. Christian pulled out a painting easel from the dining room and taped a sheet of paper to it. He handed the marker to Erika, and she picked a card. She tapped her chin with the marker and started to draw. Candace, Lisbeth, and Renee started guessing, and when they got it—*windsurfer*—she broke out in a broad grin.

"Is it our turn?" Meghan asked.

"Yes. Here you go," Erika said and handed the marker over.

"Ask Daddy to help you pick something," Shannon said.

Meghan picked a card, and Mike whispered in her ear to explain what it was. She started to draw. Shannon tried to focus on the picture but found herself distracted by the baby kicking. Pressing her hand to her side, she took a deep breath, hoping no one would notice. No such luck. Candace scooted over and leaned in close.

"Are you all right?"

"Yeah, fine. The baby's just kicking."

"It must be old hat for you."

Shannon forced a smile. "Every pregnancy is a little different. But the baby's never been this active before. And on a full stomach, it's not exactly pleasant."

"How come the angel has horns?" Christian asked.

"You have to guess," Meghan answered with a huff.

"Hell's Angels?" Shannon offered.

"Mama got it!"

Shannon gave Mike a dark look. "You couldn't have picked something less adult?"

"She wanted that one."

"She's six. She doesn't know what it means."

"Next time, you can pick."

Shannon bit her tongue. It wouldn't do any good to argue about it. Besides, it was rude to argue in front of their guests. As Renee took the marker and a card, Shannon wandered into the kitchen and started washing plates. She tried to ignore the sounds in the living room, but the raucous laughter filled her ears.

"You want some help with that?" Erika asked.

"Oh, no, that's okay. I've got it."

"Can I help anyway?"

Shannon handed over a dishtowel. "Sure."

"Do you guys fight a lot?"

"Not really. It's just sometimes, he doesn't think."

"It's got to be a guy thing."

"Oh, it definitely is a guy thing. This whole pregnancy has just been...frustrating."

"I totally get that," Erika said and gave Shannon a sympathetic look.

Shannon dried her hands on her jeans. "Can you keep a secret?"

Erika nodded.

"I'm not entirely happy about this baby. It's not just having to take on extra clients to save up money. I don't think Mike's even noticed I've done that. I mean, I'm sure I'll love this baby just as much as I love Chris and Meghan and Tanner, but...we have no real place to put the baby once he or she gets older. And Mike acts like nothing has changed or will need to."

"What does he say about how you feel?"

"He doesn't know."

"You should tell him."

"I know. I just haven't found the right time." She shut off the water and started stacking dried dishes back in cabinets.

"I won't say anything. I swear."

"Thanks."

They stood in the kitchen for a while longer in silence before Shannon pulled Erika into a hug. Erika reciprocated until Shannon let go and composed herself.

"And you're really doing okay with everything?" Shannon asked.

"Well, I mean things aren't great. I'm seriously behind on paying medical bills and stuff. And I was really hoping I was going to like the people Arlene found. The longer I wait, the less I think it's going to work out. And the more I feel that way, the more I just want to crawl back in a bottle."

"You have to believe it will work out. You were put on that path for a reason. You can handle it. Erika, you have so many people around you who will keep you strong if you let them."

"You think so?"

"I do."

Erika tucked a strand of hair behind her ear and glanced at the floor. "And there are guys that are making life confusing."

"What do you mean?"

"Well, my ex-boyfriend, Dane, keeps trying to get involved with the baby. And then there's a guy at my AA meetings, Nate. And he's really cute, but he's going on some mission trip for a few months, and all I keep thinking is why am I even interested? I'm a mess. Not to mention I'm going to look like a freaking balloon in a few months. But I kissed Nate last week, and he didn't tell me he wasn't totally against it. Well, okay, so maybe a little, but it's just weird because I like him and he gets me."

"From what I've heard about Dane, he seems like a really great guy who just wants to be there for you."

"And Nate?"

"You have a common circumstance. He's trying to be supportive of you."

"Yeah, I know. I just...I wish I knew how to show him that it could work. But maybe he's worried that I won't be what he left behind when he comes back from his trip."

"Do you think Dane is trying to get involved because he thinks he's responsible?"

"Maybe. I mean we broke up a while back. We did sleep together once back during the summer, but I don't think the baby is his."

Before Shannon could ask more, Lisbeth and Candace walked in. "We don't mean to interrupt, but we're going to head out."

"It was great of you to stop by," Shannon said and gave each of them a hug.

Erika hugged them too, and the pair left arm in arm.

"They always seem so happy together," Erika said.

"Yeah. And don't worry about the guys. That will sort itself out, too."

"Thanks."

They went back into the living room. The game had devolved into hangman. Meghan carefully wrote her letters in the spaces.

"Good writing, Meg," Shannon said.

"Thanks, Mama."

"Is anyone hungry for pie?" Shannon asked.

"Pie," Tanner said and started jumping in place.

They moved back to the dining room, and Shannon brought in the apple crumb and blueberry pies with vanilla and chocolate ice cream. The rest of the evening passed quickly. Exhaustion seemed in the air by the time the dessert dishes were done and Renee and Erika had left. Tanner fell asleep as Shannon carried him upstairs to bed. She tucked him in and kissed his forehead.

"Night night, little man," she whispered before she went to check on Christian.

"Night, Mom."

"Night, Chris."

She backed out of the room and slipped into Meghan's room. She lay curled up beneath the blankets.

"Have a good sleep, sweetie," Shannon said and pulled the blanket a little closer to Meghan's chin.

Meghan sighed and buried her face in her pillow. Just as Shannon stepped out of her daughter's room, Mike came up the stairs.

"They all asleep?"

"Yes. I'm heading to bed. I'm beat."

He got to the landing, wrapped his arms around her, and pulled her close. He stared at her as if he were memorizing the contours of her face before he kissed her.

"We have to start thinking about baby shower details and when we are going get the crib and everything out of the attic," she said.

"We still have plenty of time," he said.

She pulled free of his embrace and headed for the master bedroom.

"Shan."

"Hmm?"

"Are you feeling okay? You've been distant the last few weeks."

"Everything's fine." With that, she walked into their bedroom and shut the door.

Chapter Twenty-Two

December 1st

L ISBETH PULLED HER CAR INTO A FREE SPOT ACROSS
the street from the yoga studio and cut the engine. She
was early since they'd had a snow day. Being a private
school, it was rare, but she didn't mind. Pulling her coat
tighter, she raced inside, hoping to get some time in the
studio to meditate before class. Tiny snowflakes dotted her
jacket and clung to her hair as she stepped into the warmth.

"Crazy storm," the receptionist said as Lisbeth hung up
her coat.

"Yeah. Guess the weathermen were right this time. It's
been coming down all morning."

"I'm guessing we may have a few people not show up."

"Do you think I could just sit in the studio for a bit before
class starts? Meditate?"

"Sure. Carolyn is out grabbing a bite to eat right now, so
that's fine."

"Great. Thanks so much."

Lisbeth ducked into a changing room and pulled on her
workout clothes. She'd switched to an oversized T-shirt back
in November, as the tank top she'd been wearing no longer fit.
At her next doctor's appointment, they'd find out the sex of
the twins. Lisbeth slipped out of her sneakers and headed for
the studio. She grabbed a mat and sat cross-legged as best she
could.

"Don't think," she whispered, resting her elbows on her knees.

The complete silence of the room washed over her, and she relished it. Worries about her family never reconciling along with her everyday stress dropped away. The only sensations remaining were her rhythmic breathing and the movements of the two tiny lives inside her. She let her hands rest on her belly and felt each movement with surprising clarity. Her heart began to beat in time with the babies' movements. She was so lost in her own body, she didn't hear the door open or the soft footfalls on the wood floor. The feeling of someone sitting down by her side jerked her from the relaxed moment.

Lisbeth looked up to see Shannon sitting beside her. "Thought I'd join you," Shannon said.

"Sounds good. How'd your doctor's appointment go on Monday?"

"He said my blood pressure is up a little, so I have to go back every two weeks for extra checkups."

"Do they know what's causing it?"

"They're not sure. It could just be stress, or it could be something worse. I'm hoping it's just stress."

"I'll keep my fingers crossed it was just a spike and that everything will be back to normal."

"Thanks. We found out it's a boy."

"I bet Meghan was disappointed. She told me at Thanksgiving she wanted a sister."

"She can hold her own with the boys. But yeah, she was a little bummed about it."

They sat in silence, and Lisbeth stared at herself in the mirror. Even from this distance, she could see the dark circles of exhaustion under her eyes. Before either woman could say much more, the rest of the class began to trickle in. Lisbeth struggled to her feet and made room for Erika to stand next to her.

"Thank you all for making the trek here in this crappy weather," Carolyn said. She hit play on the remote, and music filtered from the sound system as they started the breathing exercises.

Lisbeth fought to get into the triangle pose but couldn't steady herself. Her stomach impeded progress. After a few unsuccessful tries, she stood and took a drink of water. Shannon wasn't doing all of the poses, either. *Probably best to not aggravate her blood pressure.* Still, Lisbeth wished she could participate more fully. When they moved to the floor poses, she found it easier and held them longer to make up for the standing poses.

Lisbeth took her time leaving the studio once class finished. She didn't want to leave the calm and have to face her troubles out in the real world. Once she crossed the threshold, all of her family issues would tumble back at her. She expected everyone else to be gone when she got to the changing rooms but found Renee, Erika, and Shannon waiting for her.

"Am I in trouble?" she asked with a smile.

"No. We we're going to Starbucks. You want to join us?" Renee said.

"Sure. Let me get changed."

"I'm dying for some hot chocolate," Shannon said as Lisbeth stepped inside a stall.

"That sounds amazing," Lisbeth said as she pulled her sweatpants on over her workout shorts. She pulled on a hooded sweatshirt and slipped back into her sneakers.

They traipsed through the snow to their cars. Lisbeth waited for Shannon to pull out behind her, and they formed a caravan down the street that ended up at Starbucks near Chinatown. *Right near my apartment. Perfect.* They ordered drinks and took over one of the biggest tables in the corner.

Lisbeth watched people hustling along the sidewalk with umbrellas over their heads and hoods pulled, nearly covering their faces. *Good old New England weather finally delivering.*

"So is anyone else finding it harder to do yoga?" she asked.

"Yes," a chorus of voices answered.

"I can't believe some of the women can still do it right up until their due date," Renee said.

"I can barely see my toes anymore, and I'm barely twenty weeks," Lisbeth said, sipping her hot chocolate.

"Well, don't worry, your feet are still there," Shannon assured her with a smile.

They sat around the table, sipping their drinks, for a while longer. Lisbeth basked in the natural feeling around her. She felt comfortable spending time with these women. Lisbeth looked around the table just as Shannon's phone rang. She looked at it and pulled on her coat.

"Sorry to drink and run, but I have to pick up the kids from school. We should definitely do this again."

"What about Friday?" Erika suggested.

"I'm free after noon," Lisbeth answered.

"If it's more like appetizers, I'd be in," Renee said.

"Great. We'll definitely have to do it," Shannon said and ducked out of the coffee shop.

Lisbeth traced the top of her now-empty cup. *I should call Mom and Dad, make them understand who I am.* Across the table, Erika and Renee sat coordinating their TV schedules for the rest of the week. It seemed important to them, but Lisbeth wasn't interested. Finally, she stood and stretched.

"I'll see you girls later. I need to get off my feet. And maybe take a nap."

"Oh, a nap sounds amazing," Renee agreed.

Lisbeth hugged her friends and headed out the door. She pulled her coat closer and climbed into her car. Driving around the block to head in the right direction, she pulled into the lot of her building. As she stepped into the warmth of the lobby and let out her breath, she yanked keys from her purse and checked the mail.

"Hey, Lisbeth," the security guard at the front desk called as she started for the elevator.

"Yeah?"

"You've got a visitor."

"I do?"

"Yeah. I sent them up about ten minutes ago."

"No one's home."

"I told her that, but she insisted on going up. She kept complaining about the cold air coming through every time the door opened."

Lisbeth nodded and bit her lip as she pressed the up button on the elevator. She had a sinking feeling she knew who her visitor was. The doors slid open, and she stepped inside. Lisbeth counted the floors in her head until she reached her floor. Anything to keep her calm. She rounded the corner and stopped. Standing at her door was her sister, Elena.

"What are you doing here?" Lisbeth asked.

"I came to see my sister."

Lisbeth wrapped her arms around Elena before unlocking the door.

They walked in, and Lisbeth dropped her workout bag on the floor and threw her keys on the counter in the kitchen. She saw Elena out of the corner of her eye. Her sister looked a little different than she had the last time they'd seen each other back in June. Her hair was a little lighter and less curly.

"You want something to drink?" Lisbeth offered.

"No thanks. I'm fine."

"Okay."

Lisbeth walked back into the living room and lowered herself onto the couch. Elena stood in the middle of the room and looked around.

"You want to sit?"

"Uh, yeah. Sure."

"You seem distracted, Elena. What's wrong?"

Elena toyed with the zipper on her jacket before sitting down next to Lisbeth. They sat in silence for at least five minutes before Elena spoke.

"Mom is freaking out."

"I know."

"You shouldn't have left them there like that."

"She was being unreasonable. And they can't deny who I am forever, Elena."

"I...I know."

Lisbeth turned to look her sister in the eye. "Do you accept me?"

"Of course I do. You're my sister. Even if you did always steal my clothes when we were younger."

Lisbeth laughed and laid a hand on her stomach. "I'm having twins, you know."

"You'll be a great mother. And honestly, I know Mom and Dad will come around."

"No, you don't. They never forgave me for dating a white guy in high school."

"He was kind of creepy."

"Shut up," Lisbeth said and gave her sister a playful shove in the arm.

"This is just...huge," Elena said.

"Thanks. Like I don't feel like a whale already."

"Not that. I think they're happy about having grandkids. Means they can stop pestering me about it. But forcing them to accept the lesbian thing in such a public place? That was rough."

"It's not a thing, Elena."

"Sorry, wrong word. Just give them some time to cool off."

"Fine. Do you want to see the nursery?"

"Sure."

They got up and went into the second bedroom. The rocking chair sat idle by the window. A wooden changing table lined one corner, and two bassinets sat against two of the other walls.

"Do you know what you're having?"

Lisbeth smiled and nodded slowly. "A boy and a girl."

"Guess it's good you have someone to help you take care of them. I could never raise two babies on my own. Hell, I couldn't handle one."

"Yeah. I mean, ideally I'd only take a few months off and go back to work at the start of next year's school term, but we'll see. And I have a friend who is going to be a single mom. I have a lot of respect for what she's doing."

Elena pulled Lisbeth into a hug and held on tight. Lisbeth returned the gesture. They stood in the center of the room, and Lisbeth scanned every inch of the interior. They still had a lot to do before the babies were born.

"Thanks for stopping by," Lisbeth whispered.

"Six months is way too long to go without seeing my baby sister."

"You're right," Lisbeth agreed.

"When are you due? Maybe I can come down and be here to help?"

"You don't have to do that. I know you're busy."

"It's not every day your sister is having two babies at once."

"I'm due in April. Of course, there's always the chance that I'll go a little early."

"Keep me on speed dial, then."

"Do you want to stay for dinner tonight? I know Candace would love to see you."

"I don't want to crowd you."

"Don't be stupid. You're staying."

"Just give Mom and Dad time. Once they hold those beautiful babies, they'll forget all about everything they thought."

Lisbeth gave her sister a forced smile, wanting to believe. But she knew her parents held grudges. That night, they shared a nice dinner together, just the three of them. Elena and Candace talked about their respective jobs.

"I told you she would be happy to see you," Lisbeth said as Elena pulled on her coat to leave.

"You were right. I missed seeing her, too."

"Get out of here. And call me later," Lisbeth said.

"She loves you very much," Candace said as they climbed into bed that night.

"She does. I think I feel a little better about all of this. I know she's still on my side."

Candace wrapped one arm around Lisbeth's stomach and gave her a kiss.

"Have I told you how much I love you?"

"You just did," Lisbeth said and returned the kiss.

Chapter Twenty-Three

December 10th

RENEE RACED UP FROM THE T STOP AND WOUND HER way through the pedestrian traffic. Shannon and Lisbeth already knew the gender of their babies, and Renee had begun to feel left out. Groaning at the time, she bounded through the front door of the doctor's office and nearly forgot to stop at the reception desk. She hated being late for appointments, and this one had been nagging her since she'd made it.

"Renee Blackwell. I have an appointment at two fifteen," she said, gasping for breath.

"Great. Have a seat."

Renee sat down in a chair and picked up a magazine lying on the table in front of her. She started to flip through it until a nurse called her name. Nerves sparking, she followed the nurse into a room. Pulling on the gown, she settled on the exam table to wait. Seconds ticked by at a snail's pace. Every time she looked to the clock, it had barely moved. Renee tried to focus on her breathing, anything for a distraction until the doctor and nurse came. Finally, the door opened, and Dr. Kenneth walked in, smiling broadly.

"How are you doing today?" she asked.

"I'm a little nervous. I mean, the baby's healthy, but...finding out if it's a boy or a girl. It just makes my stomach do somersaults."

"That's completely normal. You've been keeping up with your diet and exercise?"

"Yeah. Yoga every week."

"Good. So we'll check the baby's heart rate and growth, and then we'll find out what we're having."

Renee settled back on the table and let the doctor set up the ultrasound machine. She glanced from the screen to her stomach and back again, hoping the butterflies in her stomach would settle.

"Let's see what we've got here."

Renee shivered as the gel hit her skin. The steady *thump-thump* of a heartbeat echoed on the screen, and Renee grinned. The image changed, and she could see her baby. She reached a hand out and touched what she now knew was the baby's head on the image.

"The baby looks good."

The image changed, and Dr. Kenneth pressed the scanner firmly against Renee's stomach. She watched the doctor squint at the screen.

"Well?" Renee asked. Her voice sounded hoarse.

"It looks like we have a girl."

Tears of joy trickled down her cheeks as she leaned closer and looked where the doctor pointed. It looked like a tiny gray blob, but she trusted Dr. Kenneth.

"I'm having a girl."

"I'll get this printed for you, and we'll see you back in a month."

"Oh...okay."

Determined not to move until she had the new ultrasound picture in her hands, Renee stayed where she was when the doctor left. *My little girl. My perfectly healthy daughter.* All the pain of the last few months melted away as Renee wrapped her head around the idea.

"You can get dressed now," the nurse said, laying the ultrasound print at the foot of the bed.

"Thanks."

Renee got dressed, one hand clamped to her belly as she went to make her next appointment.

"Guess I'll see you in the New Year," Renee said, barely able to look away from the image in her hand.

"Yep. Have a great holiday," the receptionist said.

"I will."

Renee stepped into the cold December air and exhaled, breath condensing, hanging in the air. She'd gotten the afternoon off from work and didn't want to go home and do nothing. Instead, she pulled out her phone and hit speed dial number four. The line rang on the other end a few times before someone answered.

"Hello?"

"Hi, Dad."

"Nee. How are you, honey?"

"I'm good. Really good. I just got done at the doctor."

"What did they say? Is my grandbaby healthy?"

"Yeah. She is fine."

"It's a girl?"

"Yeah. I...I can't believe it. It probably sounds stupid, but it kind of makes all the craziness of the last few months not matter."

"It's not silly or stupid at all. Listen, I hate to cut this short, but I have a meeting I have to get to."

"Okay, Dad. I'll talk to you later."

"Do you want to tell your mother, or can I?"

"You can tell her if you want."

"Okay. I love you, Nee."

"I love you, too."

Renee ended the call and started down the sidewalk, toying with the phone keypad as she walked. She thought about texting Max but didn't want to interrupt him at work, so she continued to wander until she came to the Chinatown T stop. Looking up Boylston Street to the Common, she smiled and took off up the street. Walking the Common would use up some of her nervous energy. It was fairly deserted and looked somewhat sad, with prickly brownish-yellow grass and barren trees flanking the pathways. She walked from one corner all the way to the other end at Beacon Street and back again. The wind picked up, tugging at her hair and the edges of the ultrasound picture in her hand.

"We're going be just fine," she whispered to the picture.

Renee started to shiver a short while later and ducked into the Outbound Boylston station. Unsure of where to go, she waited until an E line train to Heath Street pulled in. That made the decision easy. Getting off at Prudential, she strolled into the warm air and gazed at the sign for the Cheesecake Factory. *What I wouldn't give for a piece of cheesecake right now.* She walked up the stairs and headed for the center of the mall. She found a directory and took off for the clothing stores. She made it to the baby-clothing store and started to browse. All the fabric felt extra soft to the touch, and she couldn't help but pick up something from every rack. A sales person spotted her and met her as she moved to a table with tiny shirts and pants.

"Can I help you find anything?" he asked.

"I'm just looking. Not really sure what to get. I've never done this before."

"Well, do you know how old the child is?"

Renee smiled and pointed to her stomach. "Twenty weeks."

He smiled back and nodded. "Got it."

"It's a girl," Renee added.

"Well, if you're shopping for a newborn, I'd say your best bet is one-pieces. We've got some new designs in the back."

Renee followed him through the tables and racks to the back of the store. He pointed out a couple of pale pink and yellow one-piece outfits. She held a couple up for inspection and nodded.

"You're right. These are cute."

"I'm pretty sure they are on sale this week, too."

"Great."

She added them to her armful of items and wandered through to the baby accessories. Bottles, sippy cups, and baby utensils.

"You wouldn't happen to know where I could get a car seat or a stroller, would you?"

"We have an online catalog that has more than just clothes. I'll get the address for you."

"Thanks."

Renee examined the bottles and added two to her pile. She knew she shouldn't buy too much. After all, her mother was throwing her a baby shower soon. But she couldn't resist getting things ready for her little girl.

"Here you go," the sales guy said.

"Oh, great. I think I'm ready to check out."

"Follow me."

Renee swiped her card and watched as he artfully folded and packed the clothes into one bag.

"You're very good at that."

"Lots of practice. Besides, it's really compactable."

"Good point. Well, I might see you again in a few months."

"We'll be here. Good luck."

"Thanks. Bye."

Renee headed home. Erika sat at the kitchen table, flipping through a magazine and drinking tea.

"Hey. You're home early," Renee said.

"Oh, hey. Yeah. Slow afternoon. I thought you had a doctor's appointment today."

"I did."

"What'd they say?"

Renee pulled out the top outfit from the bag: a pink floral print one-piece. She couldn't keep from squealing in delight as Erika set her magazine down and examined it.

"A girl. You're having a girl?"

"Yeah. Can you believe it? I know I shouldn't have gone on a buying spree, but I just couldn't resist."

"Did you get an ultrasound picture?"

"Duh."

Renee pulled the picture from her purse and showed Erika.

"Supposedly, that's the vagina," Renee explained.

"If you say so," Erika said with a smirk.

"That's what I said. But yeah...my Dad was really excited about the news."

"I bet. I'm nervous about finding out what I'm having."

"The nerves go away. I promise. Besides, you'll have pictures to give the people who adopt the baby."

Erika just nodded. Arlene hadn't called in a while, and Renee knew the radio silence increased Erika's anxiety about the whole process.

"I' m going to put this stuff away and call Max."

"Okay. I was thinking of making pasta and salad for dinner. You want some?"

"Sure."

Renee headed into her bedroom and dropped the bags on the floor in the spot she'd designated for the crib. Not that she actually had one yet. She pulled out her phone and dialed Max's number. His voicemail picked up after the fourth ring.

"Hey, Max. It's your sister calling. Just wanted to tell you that in April, you'll be having a niece. Call me later."

Renee crawled onto her bed and lay on her side. She rubbed her stomach and could have sworn she felt a kick. Her first big movement.

"Every day is going to be like this, little girl," she said to the empty room. "I promise. We're only going to have good days, you and me. We don't need anyone else."

Half an hour later, Erika stuck her head in. "Dinner."

"Coming."

They shared a quiet meal and went their separate ways for the night. Renee settled into bed with a new book and fell asleep before she got more than five pages in.

Chapter Twenty-Four

December 23rd

SNOW FELL OUTSIDE THE WINDOW AS ERIKA SAT IN A cold metal chair and listened to her fellow AA goers detailing their holiday plans and resolutions for the New Year. She watched the snow absently, trying not to think about Christmas. She'd told her parents she couldn't get time off from work to go home. Not a total lie—she was working more. But going home and telling them she was pregnant and giving up the baby was unimaginable right now. She just couldn't do it yet. Maybe she never would tell them.

"Erika, what are you doing this weekend?" Amanda asked.

"Uh, I'm not really sure. Probably hanging out with my roommate and her family. They invited me for Christmas Eve."

"Sounds fun."

"Yeah."

Diane, the group leader, cleared her throat and brought them back to attention. She stood up and after a quick holiday blessing, dismissed them. Erika pulled on her coat and hat and started for the door. She got as far as the threshold, when someone flagged her down. At first, she didn't recognize him in his big puffy coat and cap.

"Hey, you," the guy said, pulling off his hat.

Nate.

"Hi," Erika said and met him halfway down the hall. "What are you doing here? Thursdays are women's meetings, remember?"

"I know that. I just wanted to see you."

The heat of a blush crept into her cheeks. She'd been avoiding him since their kiss back in November. It was safer for everyone involved if she wasn't tempted to start something.

"I thought we talked about this," she said, leaning against the wall.

"I didn't mean like that. I just...I'm leaving on the twenty-eighth, and we aren't going to have any meetings next week, so I wouldn't get to say goodbye."

"Oh. Right."

He joined her against the wall. She squirmed under his gaze and started to melt when he gave her his little half-smile.

"You're a mystery. You know that?" he said.

"Yeah, because it's so normal to just go halfway around the world for four months."

"You don't let people get close to you."

"That's not true. We were pretty close that one time."

He took her hand in his. It was warm and a little sweaty, but she didn't pull away. Her stomach did a little flip at the touch—not an unpleasant sensation. Erika let him hold her hand while the rest of her group filed out of the room. None of them seemed to notice what was happening, and Erika was glad for it.

"So, what are you doing for Christmas?" he asked.

"Just hanging out with Renee and her brother probably."

"That sounds fun."

"Yeah. What about you?"

"Packing mostly. Hey, do you want to go grab some coffee?"

"I don't know...I really shouldn't drink coffee."

Another half-smile. "Hot chocolate, then."

After a minute of waffling, Erika nodded. "Sure."

They headed out into the cold and snow. Flakes stuck to Erika's nose and hair as they raced along the sidewalk and into the nearest Starbucks. They ordered and took a seat at a table near the back of the shop, letting the heat warm them. For a Thursday night, it wasn't crowded. Erika and Nate sat in silence, enjoying their drinks for a bit.

"So...you really think I'm not likable?" Erika blurted.

Nate's brow knit together. "I didn't say that at all. I said you don't let people get close to you. There's a difference. I think you're scared right now, and that's completely okay."

"I guess I'm going through a lot of life-changing shit lately."

"You're twenty-three. That's okay."

"Oh yeah, because you're so old," she teased.

"You don't have to have your life all figured out right now. Trust me. I didn't know where my life was going when I was your age."

"Doesn't feel that way."

"So you had some bad luck the last few months. It will turn around," he said, sipping from his drink.

"I was such a mess in college; I'm trying to fix it now. With this baby and everything."

"Can I ask what happened to the last guy you were with?"

"Um...that's a little personal."

"I'm just trying to help. Knowing why you made the decisions you did in the past can help you make different ones going forward."

Erika set her cup down on the table and shrugged.

"Dane's a good guy. I'm pretty sure he's still in love with me. It just...ended. I'm not really sure why."

"Is he still around?"

"Yeah. He's been great about all of the pregnancy stuff. He was kind of overprotective at first."

"Maybe you should give him another chance."

Erika looked Nate in the eye. "Seriously? I don't know what I want. And I know you said you're not interested, but I like you, Nate. A lot."

"Right now, you need a friend who gets what you're going through with your addiction. I can be that. Sure, I'll be gone for a little while, but think about all the stuff we'll have to catch up on when I get back."

"I'll be as big as a house," Erika said with a laugh.

"And you will look amazing. And you will be getting your life back."

"You're sweet."

"Do you know if it's a boy or a girl yet?"

"It's a boy."

"Does that make it harder?"

"Make what harder?"

"Giving him up."

"No."

Before Nate could ask any more questions, Erika's phone rang. She pulled it out of her purse and looked at the display.

"I have to take this."

"Sure."

She hit send and answered the call. "Hi."

"Hey. What are you doing?" Dane replied.

"Just at Starbucks with a friend. Why?"

"No reason. Just wanted to see what you were doing. Been thinking about you lately."

"You have?"

"Yeah, I have. I miss you."

"You can come over tomorrow if you want."

"I'd like that. Anything new with the baby?"

"No. Arlene hasn't called since the last time you asked."

"Give him a kiss goodnight for me."

Erika felt the blood drain from her face. "What?"

"The baby. Give him a kiss for me tonight."

"Oh, yeah."

"You're with a guy, aren't you?"

"What's that matter?"

"Is he cute?"

"Dane, shut up."

"Oh come on."

"A little. I have to go. I'll see you tomorrow."

"Bye."

Erika ended the call and gave Nate an apologetic look. "Sorry."

"No problem. I'm guessing that was the ex?"

"Yeah. I told you. He's kind of overprotective."

"It's getting late, and I have some errands to run in the morning. So, can I walk you to the T, strictly as a friend?"

"I'd like that."

They walked arm-in-arm out of the coffee shop and across the street to the T. They huddled together waiting for the train. Before Erika stepped onto her train, she gave Nate a quick kiss on the lips. His body tensed against hers, and she fought not to deepen the gesture. His hand pressed against the small of her back, making it more difficult not to shove her tongue down his throat. When they finally pulled apart, her cheeks burned.

"Be safe, okay?" she said.

"You bet. You promise me something."

"Okay."

"Give him a chance. He might surprise you. Hell, you might even surprise yourself."

"What?"

"Your ex-boyfriend. I want you to promise me that you'll give him a chance. You said you don't know why you broke up. Maybe there's a reason he's come back into your life."

"I...okay. I promise I'll give him a chance."

Erika twisted a strand of hair between her fingers through the whole ride home. She could feel butterflies in her stomach at Nate's words. Maybe he was right and she should give Dane another chance. It wasn't like she didn't like spending time with him. And he'd been so supportive of the pregnancy and everything.

The next morning, Erika climbed out of bed and answered the front door, still in her pajamas. She fumbled with the lock and pulled the door open to see Dane.

"What are you doing here?" she asked.

"You invited me, remember?"

"It's like seven in the morning. I didn't mean at the ass-crack of dawn."

Dane gave her a smirk and walked inside. "I'll just make some coffee and hang until you're awake."

"No. I'm up now," Erika grumbled and led him into the kitchen.

She rummaged in a cabinet for a coffee filter and beans. Dane plugged the coffee machine in and filled the pot. Erika set the kettle on the stove.

"Not drinking coffee sucks," she said.

"Only four more months."

"Yeah. So you're not spending Christmas with your parents?" she asked.

"Not this year. You're doing stuff with Renee tonight, right?"

"Yeah. I think so. I'm sure they wouldn't mind it if you came along. It's just dinner."

"Thanks."

The coffee percolated, and shortly, the teakettle whistled. Erika pulled it off the stove just in time for Renee to appear, looking bleary-eyed.

"Oh, I didn't know we'd have people over this early," Renee said.

"Me, either. Tea?"

"No, thanks. I'm going back to bed. Just heard voices and stuff."

"See you later, then."

Erika poured the hot water in a mug with a tea bag and settled at the kitchen table. Dane sat across from her, and she ran a hand through her hair. *Ugh. Bed head. I bet I look like a wreck.*

"We should go out somewhere today," Dane said.

"What do you mean? Like Christmas shopping?"

"No. Just get out of the house."

"I thought that's what we were doing tonight."

"That's tonight. And with a lot more people."

"You mean like a date," Erika said, trying to quell the sarcastic tone.

"If you want it to be."

Erika spun her teacup in a circle and tried to collect her thoughts. She wasn't sure she could say yes. A part of her wanted to, but what about Nate? *I can't say yes just because he told me to give Dane a second chance. Am I ready for it to be a date?*

"I don't know. Maybe just see where it goes?"

"Okay. Come on. Get dressed."

"Why don't we just hang here for a little while? Until it's not such a crappy time of day."

"Sure."

They headed into the living room and sat together on the couch. Christmas music played on the TV. Erika rested her head on Dane's shoulder and settled in. He wouldn't mind if she fell asleep.

The next thing she knew, Erika's entire body shook. She peered out of one eye. Dane stood over her, one hand on her shoulder. He gave her a smile, and she slowly sat up.

"How long was I out?"

"Only about an hour."

"Oh. Why do I get the feeling you aren't going to let me just sit here?"

"Probably because I'm not. Come on. There's something we have to do."

Erika groaned but got to her feet. "I have to get dressed first."

"Dress warm. It's cold out there."

"Thanks for the warning."

She ducked into her bedroom and pulled on jeans and a sweater. Five minutes later, she emerged and nearly collided with Renee.

"You guys going out for a while?" Renee asked.

"Yeah. I hope it's okay...I kind of invited him to dinner."

"Yeah, that's fine. The more the merrier. It's Christmas, after all."

"Great. Thanks."

Erika took a couple of steps, but Renee caught her by the arm. "You didn't tell him about Nate, did you?"

Erika blushed. She'd told Renee about Nate's request while he was gone. And the second kiss. "No. I didn't."

"Good."

"But I'm going to give it a try."

Renee squeezed Erika's arm and let go. "Have fun. And just, you know...try not to imagine kissing Nate."

"Thanks."

Dane was waiting for her by the front door. She slipped into her coat and followed him out into the crisp air. Wispy clouds dotted the sky overheard, and the air invigorated Erika as she held Dane's hand and let him lead her down the street.

"Where are we going?" she asked.

"You'll see."

"We better not be going far. Unless you want me to waddle."

"Would you stop? You look beautiful. And you don't waddle."

She didn't say anything but couldn't keep from thinking about how different it felt to be with him. For the first time, their relationship wasn't about drinking or sex. And she was surprised how happy that made her.

Ten minutes later, they arrived at the end of the Common on the corner of Beacon and Charles. Erika looked through the iron gates to the snow-covered ground.

"What's going on?"

Dane pulled her along one of the paths to a large open area. He took two steps into the snow and bent down. When he straightened, he held a firmly packed snowball.

"If you throw that thing at me, I swear I'm going to kill you."

"I can live with that," he said and then tossed it at her.

She squealed as it hit her jacket and fell to the ground in a powdery mess. She scooped up snow and flung it back. Before she realized it, they were ankle deep in snow, flinging chunks back and forth at each other. Erika bent double to catch her breath. She'd forgotten how much fun they could have just goofing off. Just as she stood up, something wet and frozen dripped down her neck.

"You bastard," she shrieked and spun to see Dane holding snow in his hand.

She wiped her neck and shoved him. He landed on his butt in the snow. Instead of getting angry or throwing more snow at her, he laughed. And it was damn infectious. Soon, Erika was in the snow with him, laughing. They ended up on their backs, holding hands.

"This was fun," Erika said.

"Glad you liked it. It reminds me of the first date we had."

Erika smiled. "Yeah. Except I'm pretty sure this one was more memorable."

Snow crunched as Dane moved an inch closer. He leaned over, and she didn't stop him when he kissed her. It was barely a touch, but it sent electricity through her body.

"How about we go find dry clothes and hot chocolate? I'm freezing," she said, struggling to her feet.

"Okay. Hey...I didn't mean to rush things."

She dusted off her jeans. "You didn't. I'm just really cold."

Erika took his hand in hers and started out of the Common. They got back to the apartment to find Renee bent over the oven.

"What are you up to?" Erika asked.

"Oh, just making some cookies. I told my mom I'd bring a batch."

"They smell great. Gingerbread?" Dane asked.

"Yeah. They're her favorite. Max's, too."

"I'm going to go change. Maybe take a shower," Erika announced.

She hung her coat by the door and stepped out of her boots. A short time later, she let the warm water cover every inch of her. In the back of her mind, she wondered why Nate believed in her so much. She felt a smile creep onto her lips at the simple thought of him. A friend who said he wanted to see her with someone else. What a guy. By the time she climbed out of the shower and got dressed in clean clothes, it was close to noon.

"So what time are we heading over?" she asked Renee in the living room.

"Mom said dinner is at three."

"Guess I won't eat lunch, then." Erika looked around. "Where's Dane?"

"He went home to find dry pants."

Erika nodded and joined her friend on the couch. "We went over to the Common and had a snowball fight."

"That's sweet."

"It was our first date back in college."

"He's got it bad for you."

"So everyone keeps saying. It's different, though. We used to just drink and have sex."

"Is that why you broke up?"

"I guess. I mean, I don't even really remember why we did. There was probably some other guy I wanted to sleep with and Dane wouldn't accept that. He's a one-relationship kind of guy."

"Those tend to be the ones you keep around."

"I get that now. I never realized just how sweet Dane is. I always thought he was kind of clingy and overprotective. But...I wouldn't have gotten through the last four months without him."

"Consider it your ultimate Christmas present."

Erika smiled and pulled Renee into a hug. "Thanks. What about you?"

"What do you mean?"

"Your love life. Where do you think it stands?"

Renee shifted and moved a step away from Erika. "I don't know. I haven't really thought about it much. I've just been trying to focus on the baby. And Adam stopped calling a while ago."

"Oh." Erika watched Renee's expression change. "I didn't mean to upset you."

Renee rubbed the tears away and shook her head. "You didn't. I just...I try not to think about him. It's better that way."

"He really is a douche bag for running out on you," Erika said.

"Thanks."

"What are friends for?"

Renee laughed and stood up. "I think the cookies are cool enough to pack. Besides, I think we need to try them."

Erika grinned back, and they raced to the kitchen. Erika nearly dropped her cookie as she took a bite.

"Hot. Really hot still."

Renee blew on hers before taking a bite. "But so good."

The front door opened, and Dane waltzed back in. "Cookie tasting without me? I'm offended."

"He's right. We need a third opinion," Renee said and gave Erika a wink.

Dane picked up a cookie and ate it in one bite. "Pretty good." He turned to Erika and said, "Can we talk for a minute?"

"Um, sure."

They walked into her bedroom, and Dane closed the door partway. Erika watched him as he shoved his hands in his pockets. Her stomach did a somersault as worst case scenarios played in her head, even as she tried to block them out.

"What's up?" she finally asked.

"I wanted to give you this before we left."

He held out a tiny box. Erika swallowed and took it from him. She stared at it for a minute before sliding her finger under the bit of tape on the bottom. The wrapping paper fell away, and she held a velvet box. Too big to be a ring box, so at least he wasn't going to blindside her with a ring. Her hands shook as she opened it to find a gold necklace nestled against the white interior.

"It's beautiful," she said.

The bed shifted as Dane sat down beside her. Erika pulled the chain out and held it up for closer inspection. Clearly, the image of a mother and child with an empty place where the baby's body should be. The mother's torso held a tiny purple stone. Amethyst. Her birth stone.

"What is this?"

"It's a mother and child pendant. You put the baby's birthstone there."

"But…I'm not keeping the baby, Dane."

"I know. But you can't just forget about him. You'll still be in his life. And he'll still be in yours."

Erika fingered the pendant in silence. He had a point. And she couldn't just reject his gift. He'd clearly spent a lot on it. She undid the clasp and put it on. She touched the empty spot with the tip of her index finger.

"It's going to be an emerald," she said.

"Let's wait and see. I mean, he could come early, right?"

"Oh, don't even joke about that."

He wrapped an arm around her shoulders and kissed her cheek. "Merry Christmas."

"Merry Christmas." She paused. "I didn't get you anything."

"Just seeing you happy is enough."

"It's not fair, though."

"Who gives a shit about fair?"

Erika leaned over and planted a kiss firmly on his lips. She could feel his surprise as he laced his fingers through hers. As she pulled away, she gave him a flirty smile.

"That's a good Christmas present, too," he murmured.

Erika couldn't help but laugh as he squeezed her hand and brushed his lips against her cheek. "You are such a flirt," she teased.

"Can't help it when I'm with a beautiful woman."

Before she could say anything, Renee knocked and stuck her head in. "We're going to leave in like ten minutes. Max just got here."

Erika untangled herself from Dane's embrace and straightened her sweater. She walked arm-in-arm with him out of the room and into the kitchen. Max eyed the wrapped plate of cookies.

"They're really good," Erika said.

She got a glare in response. Then Max smiled and hugged her.

"Merry Christmas."

"Merry Christmas."

"We ready to go?" Renee interrupted.

"Would you relax, Nee? They're not going to start eating without us."

Ten minutes later, they piled into Max's car and headed out. Erika watched the people racing along the sidewalks. They all looked so determined, as if they knew exactly where they were going and what they were doing. She wanted to feel that way, too. But it wouldn't happen until she knew there was someone who would take her baby. She was so lost in her thoughts that she didn't register the car coming to a halt in a driveway.

"We're here," Dane prompted and nudged her in the shoulder.

Erika unbuckled her seatbelt and followed the others into a one-story house decorated with multicolored lights. An inflatable snowman waved in the wind on the front lawn. Renee's mother greeted them.

"So good to have you," she told Erika.

"Thanks for inviting me. This is my friend Dane," Erika said.

"The more the merrier at Christmas. Please, come in. Would you like anything to drink?"

"No thank you," Erika answered.

The inside of the house was as decorated as the outside. Strands of prickly green garland lined every windowsill and doorway. Erika wandered into the living room and stared in awe at the enormous tree. It sparkled with tinsel and lights. A blinking star adorned the very top.

"That's huge," she said.

"It was a pain getting it into the house," Max said as he came up behind her. "Want the rest of the tour?"

"Sure."

Max led her through the living room and into the dining room. The table sat prepared for six with two pristine white candles situated in the center. Rounding the corner to the kitchen, they walked into the smell of roasting meat and boiling potatoes.

"Mom loves making Christmas dinner," Max confided as he eyed the huge bowl of salad on the counter.

"Well, it smells really good," Erika said.

Max led her up the stairs to the second floor. As they passed a closed door, she wondered where Renee and Dane had disappeared to. She didn't have to wonder long. Apparently, Renee had gotten the same idea and was showing Dane around.

"There you are," Renee said as they met in the hallway.

"Just giving her the tour," Max said.

"Why don't we switch? I don't really want to know what your room looks like," Renee replied.

Erika giggled but followed Renee back down the hall into a spacious room with a yellow and green floral print on the wall. A queen-size bed stood pushed to one side.

"I'm guessing this was your room."

"Yeah. Mom and Dad redid the wallpaper last year, but it's basically the same as when I was little."

Renee flopped onto the bed and stared at the ceiling. Erika stayed quiet and looked around the room. Noting the old framed pictures on a shelf, she reached over to examine them. Three kids in swimsuits on the beach.

"Is this you?" Erika asked.

Renee sat up and held out her hand for the photo. Erika handed it over. Almost instantly, Renee's face clouded with sadness and tears spilled, dripping off the end of her nose and chin.

"Yeah, it's me, Max, and Alyssa."

Erika wracked her brain for the reference. She knew that it meant something. Then it clicked.

"Your sister." Renee nodded, and Erika sat beside her. "How old were you here?"

"I was fourteen. Alyssa was ten, and Max was nine." Renee's breath hitched, and she rubbed her eyes. "She was only nineteen when she died. She never finished school or got married or..."

Renee broke down sobbing, and Erika held her. She hadn't meant to bring up such painful memories, but she'd been curious about the girl in the photo. They sat together in Renee's old room until she stopped crying.

"Christmas time must be really hard on everyone," Erika said.

"Mom and Dad try to act normal, but I know it kills them. Her birthday is pretty bad, too. But every year, it hurts a little less. We light the candles on the table at dinner, one for her and one for Christ."

"I like that."

"Knock, knock," Max called and walked in.

"Hi. Dinner ready?" Renee asked.

"Yeah. You all right?"

"Yeah. Just...talking about Alyssa. You remember that summer?" Renee answered, showing him the picture.

"Yeah. I remember you dumped sand down my bathing suit every day. And Alyssa buried me just when the tide was coming in."

"She thought it was pretty funny."

"Of course she did. She loved picking on me."

"We both did. I still do. Now, come on. Let's eat."

They headed back to the dining room. There was barely enough room on the table for the plates. Erika sat next to Dane. He took her hand under the table, and she could feel her cheeks flush. Renee and Max squeezed in opposite them. After a quick grace, Mr. Blackwell lit the two candles. Erika said a little prayer for Alyssa.

"So, how are you doing, honey?" Mrs. Blackwell asked Renee.

"Fine, Mom."

"Our little granddaughter is healthy?"

"Yes, Mom. She's just fine. In fact, she's perfect."

"You think of a name yet?" Max prodded.

"Maybe. But I want to keep it to myself for now."

"You're going to name her something like Pumpkin or Carrot, aren't you?" he said.

Max grimaced, and Erika guessed Renee had kicked him in the shin. She smiled behind a spoonful of mashed potatoes.

"How about you, Erika? How are things with you?"

"They're going. No news lately from the adoption agency. I just have to be patient."

As if on cue, Erika's phone rang in her purse. She blushed in embarrassment but darted to the kitchen to answer it. She pulled it out and nearly dropped the phone. Arlene's name flashed on the Caller ID.

"Hello?"

"Erika, it's Arlene."

"Hi."

"I hope this isn't a bad time."

"No. It's not. Not at all."

"Good. I have some news."

Erika grabbed the countertop for support. "Yeah?"

"We've found another couple who wants to meet you. They're going to have to do it after the New Year."

"Are they nice?"

"Yes. They asked me to pass along their e-mail address so you can contact them before you meet. They're traveling right now, so that's the best way to reach them."

"I can stop by the office tomorrow."

"I've already e-mailed you their contact information."

"Oh, great."

"We'll talk more in January about setting up a meeting."

"Okay. Thank you so much. Merry Christmas."

"Merry Christmas. Have a good night."

Erika hung up and failed to contain a yelp of excitement. She turned, and everyone at the table stared at her.

"They found another couple who wants to adopt the baby. They want to get in touch with me before we meet."

Dane leapt to his feet and threw his arms around her. She let him squeeze all the air out of her. It helped bring her down off her high.

"That's wonderful," Mrs. Blackwell said.

"Erika, that's amazing. It's like...the ultimate Christmas present," Renee said.

"More like a miracle."

Erika took several breaths to calm her nerves. She sat down and finished the rest of her meal. She spent the remainder of the night walking around on cloud nine. Something about this couple just felt different. They wanted to talk to her first. Deep down, she knew they were going to be the right people to raise her baby. That night, she curled up in bed and drifted off to sleep, Dane's arms wrapped around her. Everything was falling into place.

Chapter Twenty-Five

January 8th

SHANNON PACED HER BEDROOM. SHE COULD HEAR THE voices downstairs filtering up from the living room. Her closest friends gathered for her baby shower, and she was terrified. It wasn't that she hadn't been expecting one. Of course she had. It's what one does when expecting. But the thought of facing all of her friends and accepting their gifts had increased her stress level since Christmas. They still hadn't gotten the old crib down from the attic or the changing table. She couldn't do it on her own, so not waiting for Mike wasn't an option. Mike still had no clue how much the pregnancy skyrocketed her stress level. Not to mention her blood pressure.

"Honey? You still up here?" Mike called and appeared in the doorway.

"I'll be down in a minute," she answered without looking at him.

She stopped pacing and stood in front of the mirror. Their little boy was growing every day and with it, her anxiety over how they were going to take care of him.

"Everyone's waiting, Shan."

"I know. I said I'd be right down."

A shadow of hurt fell over his face, and she tried to give him an apologetic look. It didn't help. He stormed off, and each footfall on the stairs echoed his annoyance. Shannon took one last look at her reflection before making her way downstairs. Ten women sat in the living room, each with a brightly wrapped gift. She gave each of them a smile and a fast hug before sitting in the center.

"Here, Mama," Meghan said, handing her a cup of juice.

"Thank you, sweetie."

Meghan raced off into the dining room, where Christian and Tanner were coloring and doing homework.

"You look amazing, Shannon," Eleanor, an old college friend, said.

"Thanks. How are your kids doing?" Shannon asked.

"Oh, they're fine. Have you decided on a name yet?"

"No, not yet."

To cut off the conversation, Shannon took the first present and made a show of shaking it. Her friends laughed as she carefully removed the paper. Diapers with little blue rattles on the front.

"They're reusable," one of the women said.

"That's great. Thanks so much."

Halfway through the gathering, Shannon sat surrounded by new bottles, two more packages of reusable diapers, and some clothes. She was about to take Eleanor's gift, when she felt a firm kick to her kidney. Shannon grimaced and pressed her hand against her side.

"Baby moving?" Mike asked from behind her.

"Kidney shot." She winced again. "He's never been this active before."

"I bet he's excited for all the presents," Eleanor replied.

Shannon forced a smile, took several deep breaths, and massaged her stomach. Once the feeling subsided, she unwrapped Eleanor's gift: two sets of baby utensils.

"Thanks so much," Shannon said and showed the gift off.

Her friends grinned back at her, and Shannon forced herself to get through the rest of the presents before she couldn't stand it anymore. She went the long way to the kitchen and poured herself a glass of water. She sucked it down in two big gulps and refilled it. Throbbing pulsations on her optic nerve blurred Shannon's vision, but it dissipated as quickly as it had come. She sank into a chair and held her head in her hands. Everyone was expecting her to be thrilled about this major change in her life, and here she was, sobbing in the kitchen.

"Are you okay, Mom?" Christian asked.

Shannon looked up and gave her son a watery smile.

"I'm just a little tired, honey. And the baby's moving a lot."

Christian pulled a chair up next to her and sat down. "You're crying."

Shannon wiped the dampness away with a quick brush of her fingertips. "I have a headache."

He held her hand while she tried to regain her composure. "Mom?"

"Yes?"

"Does the baby make you sad sometimes?"

"What do you mean?"

"He makes me sad sometimes."

"Why's that?"

"I don't know. But it's okay. I won't tell Daddy."

"Won't tell me what?" Mike asked.

"It's nothing, Mike."

"Are you sure you're okay?"

Shannon bit her tongue. She couldn't keep lying to him...or herself. "No, I'm not. I'm exhausted, and I think everyone needs to leave right now."

"What? They're our guests, Shannon." He looked to Christian and said, "Go watch your brother and sister, please."

"What aren't you telling me?" he demanded once Christian was out of the room.

"We aren't prepared for this, Mike. Where are we going to put the baby?"

"I know the other kids had their own nursery, but he can sleep in our room."

"That's fine while he's young, but once he starts sleeping in a crib, he'll need his own room. We don't have the space for that."

"We'll figure something out."

"Mike, when have you ever known me not to have a plan in place."

"We shouldn't be talking about this now. You should go back in there and spend time with your friends."

"I can't, Mike. I've kept this to myself for too long. This is something we need to talk about now, not later."

Shannon got to her feet and left Mike standing in the kitchen. She returned to her guests and took a deep breath.

"I'm sorry to do this, but I need to cut this short. I'm not feeling very well."

Most of the group gave her sympathetic looks and wished her well. Eleanor stayed after everyone else had left.

"What's really wrong, Shannon?"

"I'll be fine. I just have to rest for a while."

"I think I know you better than that."

Shannon bit her lip. "We have some things to take care of as a family. Things that we've been putting off for a while."

"Okay. Well, you call me if you need anything. And I mean anything."

"Thanks. I will."

Shannon walked Eleanor to the door and said her goodbyes. She could hear Mike telling the kids to go play in their rooms because Mama and Daddy had to talk about grown-up things. Shannon waited until she heard footsteps on the stairs before she let go of the doorknob and walked back into the living room. She gathered up the bits of wrapping paper and threw them out. Mike stood motionless in the dining room, his fingers drumming on a plastic cup.

"Well?" he said once she stopped stalling.

Shannon sat down at the table and stared at her hands. "I want you to understand something," she said.

"I'm listening."

"I don't want you to think I don't want this baby."

"Why the hell would I think that?"

"Because I know you, and you probably thought about it early on. But let's be honest. I don't know how we're going to support him, Mike. We aren't going to have enough room for long. He's going to need his own space. And we can't put him in with Tanner or Christian. And there's no way he can share a room with Meghan."

"Shannon, we'll figure it out."

"Okay. So let's figure it out. Right now. Do we have the money to buy a new house? Hire a moving company? What about your commute to the office? Are you willing to extend it if we can't find something nearby?"

"Who said we have to move?"

"We have four bedrooms in this house. And we need five. There isn't enough room."

"So we put on an addition. We can get a loan from the bank."

Shannon gritted her teeth and tried to calm down, taking slow, meditative breaths that did little to loosen her nerves. "It's really that easy for you, isn't it?"

"What's that supposed to mean?"

"What if an addition isn't feasible? What if we have no choice but to move? That's going to screw up the kids' school. It wouldn't be fair to them."

"Kids move all the time," he said.

"What about my job?"

"What about it, Shannon? You work from home as it is. You can still work with the baby. The other kids will be in school full-time."

"I took on more clients because I knew you wouldn't. I did it because I knew someone had to get more income. But why couldn't you have taken on more clients? Why can't you take time off work to be with the baby? I've had to take time off with all the kids. You didn't."

"You want me to take time off? Fine, I will," he said.

Shannon stood up and turned away. This wasn't going well at all. She was expected to sacrifice her time for this child. And she knew his offer to stay home was merely to appease her. This time, it wasn't going to work. Storming out of the room, she grabbed her car keys, slipped on a coat, and yanked the front door open.

"Where are you going?" Mike shouted.

"Out."

Shannon drove around for what felt like hours with no idea where she was going. It didn't matter. She just needed to get out and away for a while. Finally, she fished her phone from her purse and hit number eight on her speed dial. It rang three times before someone answered.

"Hello?"

"Candace? It's Shannon Atwater."

"Oh, hi. Lisbeth's in the shower right now."

"I was kind of hoping I could stop by if you two weren't busy."

"Sure."

"Great. Thanks."

"Do you need directions?"

"No, I think I can find it."

Shannon hung up and pulled into the right lane. Weaving through traffic until she spotted the far edge of the Common, she knew she was close. At the corner of Tremont and Boylston, she spotted a sign for parking up past the UPS store and turned left. After handing over a twenty for parking, Shannon climbed out of her car and walked half a block to

Lisbeth's building. She stopped at the front desk, and they let her go up. Candace opened the door before Shannon could knock.

"Come on in."

"Thanks."

Shannon crossed the threshold, and Lisbeth met her with a cup of tea. "Candace said you sounded like you needed it."

Shannon sank to the couch and clutched the cup of tea to warm herself. "Things just sort of blew up at home."

"What happened?" Lisbeth asked, joining her.

"It was my baby shower. I really didn't want one. And Mike and I ended up arguing. I sent everyone home early."

"Oh no."

"I'd been bottling it up for a while. We aren't prepared to have another baby. Sure, we have the space right now, but in a year, what then? He says we can build an addition, but I don't know if that's feasible."

"It's good that you brought it up now. Though you've been feeling this way for a while," Candace said.

"And it's probably not helping my blood pressure."

"Did they ever figure out what was causing the spikes?" Lisbeth asked.

Shannon shook her head. "They think it might be some effects of advanced maternal age. It seems to have settled down now. Though they want me to go in for a three-hour glucose tolerance test to check for gestational diabetes and a few other things. Just what I want."

She ran her hands over her face and exhaled a long breath.

"I hate fighting with him. But I just couldn't keep it to myself anymore. And I know he expects me to just stay home with the baby because I work from home as it is. Not that he really sees what I do as a job."

"He doesn't want to take leave?"

"He's got a solo practice. His clients are more important than his family. It's nothing new. I guess this time, it just was too much."

"You'll work it out, I'm sure," Candace said.

Shannon shook her head. They were trying to reassure her, but it felt like they were siding with Mike.

Lisbeth squeezed Shannon's hand. "You can stay here if you want. We can make the couch up."

"That's sweet, but the kids will start to wonder. And Tanner won't go to bed without me kissing him good night."

"Well, we'd love for you to stay for the afternoon."

"I think I'll take you up on that offer. You wouldn't by chance have some chocolate? I'm in the mood for something absolutely horrible."

Lisbeth gave her a wry grin and went into the kitchen. Candace took her spot on the couch and set her mug on the table. They sat in silence for a minute or two before either said anything.

"You think he has a point?" Shannon blurted.

"Oh, I don't know. I mean, it seems rather unfair that he's putting all the childcare responsibilities on you simply because you already stay home. To be honest, I didn't think there were many people out there who still had such...traditional views of gender roles."

"I guess that's really my big issue. Though feeding another mouth is going to be more than we're used to."

Just then, Lisbeth returned with a bowl of chips, salsa, and chocolate. "I grabbed all the bad stuff I could find."

"Oh, that looks amazing," Shannon said and took the box of chocolate.

They squeezed together to let Lisbeth sit down and began to eat. Shannon couldn't help but smile to herself. This felt more like the kind of gathering she would have preferred for a baby shower: her current friends who knew exactly what she was going through.

"So have you heard from Erika lately?" Shannon asked.

"I haven't. I know she was feeling a little under the weather last week and that's why she didn't come to class."

"I hope it's not something with the baby," Candace said.

"I think she may have just gotten a cold at work. But I'm sure Renee is taking good care of her," Lisbeth said.

"Well, I think Dane might be staying over. They seem to be back together," Shannon said.

"He sounds like such a sweet guy," Candace added.

"I hope we see her next week. I want to hear what's happening with the adoption."

"From what Erika said at New Year's, they were exchanging e-mails through January. I think they're supposed to meet at the end of the month," Lisbeth said.

"What about you two? How are you holding up?" Shannon asked.

She watched as Candace and Lisbeth exchanged glances. They both smiled, and Lisbeth fidgeted with the chip in her hand.

"We're good. We've been working on the nursery. Want to see?"

"Sure."

She followed them into the nursery. Both cribs now had pads and blankets draped over the edge. The changing table was full of newborn-size diapers, and rattles and balls were stenciled around the room.

"We just have to paint next weekend, and we'll be ready."

"Well, we need clothes, but that's part of next weekend. The big shopping extravaganza," Lisbeth explained.

"Sounds like you've got it all planned out."

"And I'll be on maternity leave until October. I've already worked it out with school."

"Have you thought about names yet?" Shannon asked.

"We've been thinking of a few, but we haven't really nailed any down for sure."

"Well, I thought we decided on one," Candace corrected.

"Oh, right."

"We've decided on Rachel Maria."

"Oh, that's pretty. Are you hyphenating their last names?"

"Yeah. Sherman-Marquez. Has a nice ring to it," Lisbeth replied.

"It does. So you're having trouble with the boy?"

"Yeah. We can't quite decide. What about you? Or have you not talked about it?"

"I've been thinking about Carter or Aiden. I'm personally leaning toward Aiden. I guess we'll see what Mike says. Once he's speaking to me again."

"He will. He'll come to his senses and stop being a jerk."

"Here's hoping."

They went back to the living room and finished off the chips and salsa. By the time Shannon looked at the clock, it read nearly five thirty.

"Are you doing okay?" Lisbeth asked.

"Yeah. The kids are probably wondering where I am."

"I'll walk you downstairs."

"Thanks."

Shannon got up and gave Candace a quick hug. "I'll see you later."

"You bet."

Shannon and Lisbeth headed out and waited for the elevator. "You're lucky you've got someone so supportive."

"I am pretty lucky, aren't I?"

"Have your parents come around?"

"Not yet. I think they're more accepting of the fact they're going to have grandchildren in a few months. But me being a lesbian...they might never be okay with that. But my sister is on my side, so I can't complain too much."

The elevator arrived, and they stepped in. A minute later, they stepped off in the lobby, and Shannon said goodbye. She thanked the parking attendant when she got back to her car and pulled out into traffic. She drove around the block a few times just to clear her head before heading home. Shannon pulled into the driveway, and the clock on the dash displayed ten after six. She climbed out of the car and reached for the front door. She could hear voices inside, and something beeped. The microwave. *So much for cooking dinner.* She opened the door and walked in. Christian reached into the microwave and pulled out a bowl of macaroni. Tanner danced around the kitchen with the packet of cheese.

"Give me the cheese," Christian said.

"Mac and cheese."

"Where's your sister?" Shannon asked once Tanner handed over the packet.

"Mama, where'd you go?" Tanner squealed and nearly knocked her over in his haste to hug her.

"Mama just needed to go out for a little bit."

"Meghan's upstairs playing in her room," Christian answered.

"Did you offer to make her something to eat?"

"Yeah. She said she wanted to wait until you came home."

"Okay. Where's Dad?"

"Upstairs."

"Make sure you wait until it cools down," she said and gave Tanner a stern look.

Shannon set her purse down and headed upstairs. She went to Meghan's room and found her daughter playing with her dolls.

"Honey, are you hungry?"

"Mama, where were you? Daddy was really mad. Why did you leave?"

"I just went to see some friends. I'm sorry you got upset." She pulled Meghan into a hug and said, "Come on, I'll make you some dinner."

"Okay."

They headed downstairs, and Shannon barely glanced at the closed bedroom door at the end of the hall. Christian and Tanner sat at the table, sharing macaroni and cheese.

"Christian makes good mac and cheese," Tanner proclaimed.

"Did you say thank you?"

"Yes."

"Good. Meg, what do you want?"

"Hot dog. And mac and cheese."

"You got it."

Meghan sat down at the table and tried to sneak a bite of Tanner's dinner. He whined and smacked her hand.

"Meg, don't do that. You'll have dinner in a few minutes."

"Sorry, Mama."

Shannon made two more packets of macaroni and cheese and two hotdogs. She put them on the table and poured each of the kids a glass of milk.

"Mama?"

"Yes, Meghan."

"Why did everyone leave?"

"Because Mama wasn't feeling well."

"Why?"

"Eat your dinner."

Shannon watched her kids eat and wondered what their new addition would be like in a few years. Would they still be here, or would they have to move? She tried to push the thoughts out of her mind, unable to handle thinking about them anymore. Not today. Twenty minutes later, she stood over the sink, washing dishes. She could hear the kids arguing in the living room over the TV remote.

"You have to share," she shouted over her shoulder.

Footsteps echoed in the front hall, and Shannon braced herself. But Mike didn't yell. He just walked in and leaned against the stove. Shannon focused on her task and waited for him to speak. That's how their fights worked.

"Where did you go?" he finally asked.

"To see a friend."

"The kids were worried."

"I know. I'm sorry I upset them."

"You should have told me you were upset before."

"I knew you'd react like you did."

"Here we go."

"Mike, look. I don't want to fight. Not tonight. I'm tired. We can worry about living arrangements down the line. But you can't just expect me to take time off from my career because we're having another baby. Just because I work from home doesn't mean I can devote ample time to both."

"I told you I'd take time off."

"You said it to make me feel better."

"I will take time off, Shannon. I don't think it can be six months, but a couple. I can talk to some friends and see if they'll take on some of my cases."

Shannon shut the water off and turned to face him. "Fine. But honestly, do you even understand how you belittle what I do just by making it such a big deal to take time off?"

"What's that supposed to mean?"

"I feel like your clients are more important to you than your family."

"That's not true."

"Couldn't prove it by me."

"Where is this coming from?"

Shannon gripped the dishtowel between her fingers and took a breath.

"I never said anything because I hate fighting with you. But I think this baby has made me realize that there are things we need to address. I...I want to see a counselor."

"You're serious?" he said.

"Yes. It's the only way we're going to get through this."

Mike didn't look pleased. But he didn't say no, either. She hoped that getting a third party's perspective on the situation would help them learn to communicate. She couldn't bear the thought of what would happen if they couldn't work their problems out before the baby was born.

Chapter Twenty-Six

January 16th

LISBETH STOOD AT THE CHALKBOARD AND WROTE THE numbers ten through fifty big enough for the kids in the back to see. The chalk squeaked on the board as she finished the last zero. She dusted her hands off and turned back to the class.

"Okay, everyone. Let's see how far we can get today."

She received a few whines from the back of the room, but the class started reciting the numbers as she pointed. They'd get to one hundred by the time she took maternity leave. She was determined to get them ready for first grade. She hit thirty, and the unison recitation broke in scattered answers. She smiled at the kids.

"Thirty," she told them, and they parroted it back to her.

They repeated it a few times before moving on. They made it to forty before the bell rang and class ended.

"That's great, everyone. We'll pick up here on Monday. You can put your books in your desks and get your coats."

Chairs skittered over linoleum and books clunked into desks while Lisbeth erased the numbers from the board. James and Margaret were the first to line up at the door. She was pleasantly surprised when they stood side by side and didn't argue or pick on each other. Once the rest of the kids fell into line, she walked them out to the bus. Most of her kids were now riding the afternoon bus. She saw Ellen and waved.

"You're not running off today, are you?" Ellen asked.

"I don't really have plans until tonight. Why?"

"We're having a grade meeting."

"I didn't know about that."

"They just decided it last minute."

"Teacher's lounge?" Lisbeth asked.

"Yes."

"I'll see you there in a few minutes."

Lisbeth headed back inside and tidied up the classroom. Fridays were always the worst mess-wise. In the back of her mind, she knew there really wasn't a staff meeting. She'd heard rumblings of a baby shower, but she'd feign surprise for her colleagues. She picked up her coat and purse and headed down the hall to the faculty lounge and was about to walk in, when Ellen grabbed her wrist.

"I don't think everyone's finished getting their kids to gym and arts."

"That's okay. We can get settled."

"I think we should wait."

Lisbeth didn't argue. "Actually, I'll be right back."

Ellen nodded, and Lisbeth headed for the bathroom. Rachel had been pressing on her bladder all week, and it made avoiding the bathroom nearly impossible. They still hadn't settled on a name for their little boy, and she hated not being able to say his name at night before going to bed. Five minutes later, Lisbeth emerged from the bathroom, and Ellen stood waiting.

"Can we go in now?" Lisbeth asked.

"Yeah."

They walked in. The lights were off, and the chairs were placed at odd intervals around the table. She could make out the top of someone's head behind the couch. Behind her, Ellen flipped the lights, and everyone popped up.

"Surprise!" half of the staff shouted.

Lisbeth laughed and felt color flood her cheeks. Even though she'd known about it, it still caught her off guard. She made her way to a chair and doubled over with laughter.

"Careful, don't want to go into labor too soon," Jack said.

Lisbeth looked at him and shook her head. "This is great. Thank you so much. I hope it doesn't interfere with your afternoon classes."

Some of the third grade teachers brought out a giant cake and set it on the table. Pink and blue bottles and rattles surrounded the edges with *Congratulations* scrawled across the middle in big letters.

"It looks amazing."

Jack handed her the knife. "You can do the honors."

"Is it like birthday cake, where I get the first slice?"

"Take two. You've got growing babies in there."

"Just for that, you're getting the tiniest piece," Lisbeth joked.

She cut into the C of Congratulations and handed it over. She made short work of the rest of the cake, and soon, people settled in for presents. Lisbeth eyed the small stack, and Jack sidled up beside her.

"You're like a kid on their birthday," Jack said.

"You're just full of funny today."

"I try. But it's Friday, and I'm allowed be a little crass."

"There are children in the room."

"Oh, they can't hear me."

"Don't be so sure about that."

"Lisbeth, smile," Ellen called and snapped a picture.

Lisbeth put her cake down and stood up. "Sitting too long makes my ankles hurt."

"So do they have names yet?"

"One of them does." She put her hand on her left side. "This is Rachel."

"Her brother doesn't have a name yet?"

"We keep trying to find one that fits, but no luck yet."

"You could always call him Baby B."

"Yeah, I don't think he'd ever talk to us again."

"Okay, everyone. Time for presents," Ellen announced.

By the time Lisbeth got through them all, she had six pairs of clothes, a dozen bottles, and bibs. The lunch period was nearly over, and the higher-grade teachers needed to head back to their students.

"Thank you, everyone. I really appreciate all of this. I'm going to miss not seeing your smiling faces until October."

"You're not going anywhere for a while," one of the other kindergarten teachers said.

"That's not really up to me," Lisbeth replied and patted her stomach.

"Just keep them in there as long as you can."

Lisbeth grinned and started to gather the presents. Jack waved goodbye and left the staff lounge. She managed to fit everything into two bags and headed for the parking lot. With everything in the back seat, she checked her phone for the time. Enough time to drop off everything before meeting the girls for appetizers. She was about to get into the car, when Ellen ran toward her.

"Did I forget something?" Lisbeth asked.

"No, sweetie. Just wanted to say we're going to miss you while you're gone."

"I'll be back. I'm not due until the middle of April. So I'll probably be here at least through February."

"Have a good weekend."

"Bye."

By three thirty that afternoon, Lisbeth pulled into the parking lot of a little diner in Cambridge. She spotted Shannon's van a few spots over and hoped she wasn't too late. She walked in and spotted her friends in a nearby booth. Pointing to them, she smiled and nodded to the hostess before walking over.

"Sorry I'm late," she apologized, squeezing into the booth beside Erika.

"Don't worry. We haven't ordered yet," Erika said.

"You look flushed," Renee said.

"I was rushing around after work. They had a surprise shower for me."

"Lucky. All I got at work was a whiny two-year-old who threw French fries at me," Erika said.

"See what you're giving up?" Shannon teased.

"I'll pass on the tantrums, thanks."

"How are you doing?" Lisbeth asked Shannon.

"Things aren't exactly great. But we've started going to a counselor. We're working on our communication, and we've managed to decide on a name for the baby. Aiden. What about you? Does Rachel's brother have a name yet?"

"No. I feel so bad."

"What if we all write down a random name and see what sounds best?" Renee suggested.

"This from the girl who has her daughter's name but is keeping it under lock and key, like it's a national secret," Erika said.

"I like that idea," Shannon said. She pulled a bunch of napkins out of the dispenser and passed them around.

Lisbeth watched her friends scribble names down and pass them to her. She looked through them, smiling and laughing as she read the suggested names. She was sure some of the other people sitting around them gave her dirty looks.

"What?" Shannon asked.

"Which one of you wrote down Evan-Michael-Jamal."

Erika raised her hand.

"He's got two last names as it is. Can't make his life hell by giving him three first names."

"He'd be unforgettable though."

Lisbeth shook her head and flipped to the next one. "Patrick wouldn't be too bad. I'll keep that one."

The last one. "Nicholas isn't too bad, either."

"Sure, pick the traditional names," Erika said with a wink.

Before Lisbeth could tease her back, their waiter arrived with four waters and two chocolate milkshakes.

"Oh, that looks good. I'll have one of those," Lisbeth said.

"Sure. Are we ready to order?" the waiter asked.

"We still need a few minutes," Lisbeth said.

He nodded and disappeared in the direction of the kitchen. Lisbeth turned to the menu in front of her and flipped through it.

"You guys have any preferences?"

"Something big and greasy," Renee answered.

"Aren't we the poster child for health," Shannon said.

"I have a craving. Onion rings."

"Oh that sounds good. Let's order two," Erika agreed.

"What would Carolyn say?" Lisbeth asked with a smirk.

"She'd say to steady our breathing."

"I'm so glad I met you all. You've made the last six months amazing," Lisbeth said as the waiter came back with her milkshake.

"We're going to order two of the onion ring platters," Renee said.

"And one chicken quesadilla," Lisbeth said.

"And for you?" the waiter asked, looking at Shannon.

"Oh, no. I'm splitting with them."

"I'll have those out for you ladies shortly."

Lisbeth leaned back against the seat and felt Rachel kick. No one said anything when she winced. *They'll have a kick line going soon enough.* She took a few sips of her drink to give her something else to focus on: brain freeze.

"So, Erika. What's the latest?" she asked.

Erika spun her glass between her fingers before answering. "They seem really nice. Michelle and Andrew. They're a few years older than me, and they're traveling around Europe until the end of the month. They're really excited and can't wait to meet me."

"I know you haven't met them face to face, but what's your impression of them?" Shannon asked.

"They sound really fun, and they say they can handle a special needs kid. We've been sending pictures back and forth. They were in Spain last week. And I sent them my latest ultrasound."

"Wonderful," Lisbeth said, patting Erika's hand.

"They've already started calling him Peter. I like it."

"That's sweet. It sounds like it's all going to work out," Lisbeth said.

"Yeah. And Dane likes them, too."

"So things are going well with him?"

Erika blushed. "Yeah. He's good. Hangs around the apartment a lot."

"Yeah, he does. But hey, he cooks, so you aren't going to hear any complaints from me," Renee said.

"And he's handy. He helped us put together the crib last weekend."

Lisbeth smiled. "It really looks like everything is turning out right for all of us."

"Well, we'll have to keep doing this even after the babies are born," Shannon said.

"We could have our own little yoga class," Renee suggested.

"I like that idea," Erika said just as the waiter returned with their appetizers.

They split the appetizers between them and chatted for the next hour. They talked about the new movies they wanted to see and the latest TV gossip.

"We should have a *Bones* marathon sometime," Lisbeth said, looking at Shannon.

"It's my one guilty pleasure show. We'll definitely have to make a night of it," Shannon agreed.

Lisbeth sucked down the last few dregs of her milkshake and was about to get up to go to the bathroom, when her phone rang.

"I'll be right back."

She walked a few paces toward the bathroom and answered. "Hi, honey."

"You girls having a good time?"

"Yeah. I should be home in a little while."

"Okay. Did you go shopping?"

"Oh, no. The school had a surprise baby shower for me today."

"Lucky you."

"I'll see you soon."

"Love you."

"Love you, too," Lisbeth said and hung up.

When she walked out of the bathroom stall, Erika stood in front of the mirror, fixing her hair.

"That's really pretty. I don't think I've seen you wear it before," Lisbeth said, pointing to Erika's necklace.

"Oh, I've worn it a couple times. Dane gave it to me for Christmas. We haven't bought the other stone yet. We're waiting until Peter is born."

"It feels kind of weird to call him by his name, doesn't it?" Lisbeth asked.

"Yeah. I'm trying to do it only every now and then. Sometimes when I think about it too much, I get all weepy."

Lisbeth dried her hands and placed one on Erika's shoulder. "You're doing the right thing. And besides, they seem like really good people, and they want you to stay in Peter's life."

"I know. And I know there's a chance I can keep him, but...I'm still not all together yet. I need to be sober longer and figure out my life. So, yeah. It sucks sometimes when I think about it, but I really can't raise a baby." She patted down her hair. "Besides, I've got a built-in surrogate."

"She's never going to tell us that baby's name," Lisbeth said with a laugh.

Erika smiled and said, "I know. It's insane."

"You sure you're going to be okay once the babies are born?"

"What do you mean?"

"You're giving up your baby, but Renee is keeping hers. It just might be a little hard."

"I didn't even think of that."

"Just something to consider so you're ready," Lisbeth said.

They walked back to the table and split the bill. Lisbeth walked arm-in-arm with Erika out to Shannon's car.

"You all carpooled?"

"Yeah. It was fun. You can just drop us near the T," Renee answered.

"Don't be silly. I can drive you home," Shannon said and unlocked the car.

Lisbeth waved goodbye and headed for her own car.

She had the napkins with the names on them tucked in her pocket, anxious to show Candace, while she rode the elevator up. She felt like they had an actual chance to finally give their little boy a name. Candace was putting the baby shower presents away.

"You didn't have to do that," Lisbeth said.

"Just trying to stay organized."

Lisbeth shed her coat and purse and wrapped her arms around Candace's waist. Candace turned around, and they shared a chaste kiss.

"Have I told you lately how amazing you are?" Lisbeth asked and let Candace go.

"Nope," Candace answered.

"You're amazing, and I am so damn lucky I married you."

"Yes, you are. Some of these outfits are adorable," Candace said.

"Aren't they? We'll have to pick what they're going to wear home from the hospital," Lisbeth said and patted a pale blue one-piece.

"I think we have some time unless there's something I don't know."

"Oh, no. Well, I did have some chicken quesadillas and onion rings with the girls."

"Aren't you a rebel?" Candace teased.

"We also talked about baby names. I have some input that I think might work."

Candace put the last sleeper in the drawer and followed Lisbeth to the kitchen. Lisbeth laid out the napkins on the counter.

"Okay, I'm guessing Erika came up with this one," Candace said and pointed to the one with three names.

"Yes. I have to say, I like Patrick. And Nicholas."

"I think I have to veto Nicholas. Though, Michael doesn't sound too bad with Patrick," Candace said.

"Would you object to using the Spanish equivalent?"

"Miguel? Not at all."

"Patrick Miguel," Lisbeth said and looked at her swollen belly. "There you go, little man. You finally have a name."

She got a kidney shot in response. "I'm going to take that as he likes the name and not a protest about my food choices today."

Candace laughed and laced her fingers through Lisbeth's. "Come on. Let's relax."

"You don't have to tell me twice. My feet are screaming at me to sit down."

"Then they'll be begging you for circulation," Candace said.

"I wish they'd make up their minds."

They settled on the couch for the rest of the night, flipping through channels and finally settling on one of the *Bourne* movies. Lisbeth halfway paid attention as she dozed off. It felt good to be home with her three favorite people. As the sound of a car chase filled her ears, Lisbeth wondered what her twins would be like. If they'd be healthy when they finally arrived, or if they would have to spend some time in the hospital. She knew the chance of twins making it to full-term was rare. She was ready to go early but hoped it wasn't too early.

"Babe, do you want to go to bed?" Candace asked, rousing Lisbeth from her stupor.

"Hmm? What?"

"You look beat. I asked if you wanted to go to bed."

Lisbeth looked at the clock. "It's barely nine. But bed sounds like a good idea."

Candace offered a hand and pulled Lisbeth up. Together, they walked to the bedroom and crawled into bed with their clothes still on. Lisbeth curled up as best she could against Candace's shoulder and drifted off to sleep.

Chapter Twenty-Seven

January 19th

"THANKS FOR TAKING THE DAY OFF TO HELP," RENEE said as Erika bent over a stack of drawers.

"No problem. Honestly, waiting tables kind of sucks when you have to pee all the time."

"Tell me about it. Giving tours when the baby is extra active is not fun, either."

"So are you ever going to tell me what you're naming her?" Erika asked.

"Maybe," Renee said with a wink.

Erika shook her head and went back to fitting drawers into the chest in front of her. Renee sat folding baby blankets and stacking them on top of the changing table. Her room would be crowded, but she was okay with that. The baby wouldn't take up that much room.

"Are you and Dane going out tonight?"

"No. He has to work an extra shift today. Or else he probably would have stopped by to help with this stuff."

"We don't need his help. We're tough chicks. We can put things together."

Erika laughed. "You got that right. What else do we have to do today?"

"I think we have to hit the mall, and I was going to make a little name plate for her crib."

"See, you'll have to tell me now."

Before Renee could respond, a sound echoed from the front of the apartment. Someone was trying to open the door.

"Are you sure Dane wasn't coming over?"

"Positive. I'll go see," Erika said.

"No, that's okay. I got it," Renee said.

She got up and walked to the front door, undoing the lock and pulling the door open a few inches. Breath caught in her lungs as she stared at the person standing across from her.

"Can I come in?" Bryce asked.

"Who is it?" Erika called.

Renee tried to form words, but her voice caught in her throat. She heard Erika moving from the bedroom, and Renee tried to say something. Erika appeared and looked at Bryce.

"What is *he* doing here?" she asked.

Renee had shown Erika pictures of them together on Facebook. Renee just shook her head and swallowed over a lump in her throat.

"I don't know."

"Who is she?" Bryce asked.

"What are you doing here, Bryce?"

"I wanted to see you."

"Don't give me that bullshit."

"Okay, I get it. You're like hormonal or something."

"She's not hormonal, douche bag," Erika said, her tone hostile.

It almost made Renee smile. But the fact that her ex was standing in the doorway kept her from feeling anything happy. Still, she should at least give him a chance to explain.

"I got this, Erika."

"Are you sure?"

"Yeah."

"I'll be down the hall if you need me," she said.

Renee smirked as Erika turned around and left her and Bryce standing by the front door. In silence, Renee watched Bryce lean against the doorway, gaze fixed intently on her swollen belly.

"So, you got big," he said.

Renee glared at him and walked into the kitchen. He shut the door and followed her. Leaning against the counter by the sink, she glared at him and tapped her foot absently. It didn't help control her nerves. It had never been this awkward between them.

"Aren't you going to say you're happy to see me?"

She stopped moving and looked Bryce in the eye. "Happy to see you? You took off without a word or warning. Did you think I could just cover your half of the rent?"

"I left you money."

"For one month."

"It worked out."

"I got lucky. You were really selfish."

"I never said I wanted to be a dad. Or did you forget I asked you to consider other options?"

"You didn't ask me to consider them. You shoved them down my throat. Do you think I was ready to be a mom? It takes two to make a baby. I've had to handle it. I'm going to raise this baby on my own. Did you even think about that before your ran?"

"I came back. That counts."

"You could have talked to me about this. We could have figured it out together."

"You wouldn't have listened," he said. His hands balled into fists.

"How do you know that? You didn't even try. All you said was get an abortion or give the baby up. There was no discussion of how we could raise this baby together," she accused.

"You were so happy about the baby, you wouldn't have listened. It was all you cared about."

Fire roiled in her gut and the tips of her ears burned with fury when he referred to her daughter as "it."

"Well, I am the one caring for *her*, Bryce. Of course she was my focus," she said.

"It's a girl?"

"Don't change the subject. The point is, you left me alone and pregnant. You can't just show up six months later, wanting back into my life. Because believe it or not, there isn't room for you."

"I did some stupid shit, I get that. But I'm trying to fix that."

"What exactly are you trying to fix? Are you going to help raise our daughter? Pay child support? Watch her when I have to work?"

"I don't know. I have stuff to do with the guys a lot."

"See, that's why I don't need you. You can't put your precious friends on hold for your child."

"You won't let me. I could be a good father."

Renee shook her head and turned her back to him. She wasn't going to have this conversation with him. Not when he kept flip-flopping his agenda. She was going to raise her daughter on her own. She could do it without him. Besides, not two seconds earlier, he'd claimed he wasn't ready to be a father.

"She's my kid, too, Renee. Even if you don't want me around, she deserves to see her dad."

"I don't need your help, Bryce. You made it clear you weren't willing to give it when I needed you."

"I already said I was sorry."

"This time, sorry doesn't cut it. You made a conscious choice to walk out on us. On our relationship *and* our baby. You don't get to just show up and kiss it and make it better."

"You are such a bitch," he shouted.

"Get the fuck out of my apartment before I call security," Renee replied.

Bryce's anger was obvious as he stomped out of the kitchen and slammed the door hard enough that the entire apartment shook. Renee stayed rooted to the spot until she heard footsteps coming from the bedroom.

"Everything okay?" Erika asked.

"No. He wants back into my life. I told him to leave. I don't need his sorry ass in my life. I don't care if he wants to apologize."

Erika hugged her. "We can tell security to not let him in the building anymore."

"Maybe."

Renee glanced over her shoulder at the clock on the microwave.

"We should head out. Class starts in an hour."

"You sure you want to go?" Erika asked.

"I need all the meditation I can get right now. Before I put a hole through something."

They changed into their workout clothes and headed for the T. They arrived at the yoga studio just as Lisbeth lumbered out of her car. She shut the driver door and moved as quickly as she could across the street.

"How are you doing?" Erika asked, holding the door open.

"Oh, you know. It's getting harder to do things. Luckily, the nursery is done. The doctor said the twins are growing nicely, though. She did suggest I probably shouldn't be driving, but I don't really have a choice today."

Renee tried to look interested in her friend's news. But she couldn't get Bryce out of her head. She didn't even hear the receptionist tell them to wait a few extra minutes because Carolyn was going to be late.

"Renee," Lisbeth said, snapping her fingers to get her attention.

"Huh?"

"Did you hear what I said?"

"No. Sorry."

"I asked when we're going to know what to write on the congratulations card for when the baby is born."

"Oh, um, soon. I'm really sorry. It was just a really stressful morning."

"You look kind of distracted."

"Bryce showed up."

Lisbeth gave her a sad look and dragged her toward the changing area, where Erika and Shannon were filling their water bottles.

"Were you there when it happened?" Lisbeth asked, looking at Erika.

"Yeah. What a jerk."

"What happened?" Shannon asked.

"Bryce showed up this morning," Erika said.

"Oh, Renee. Honey, is everything okay?"

"I don't know. He said he wants back in my life. And he wants to see the baby."

"Did he give any sort of explanation for why he left?"

"No."

She couldn't admit that she hadn't really given him a chance to explain.

"What did you tell him?" Lisbeth asked.

"Mostly, I told him he was a jackass and to get out."

"So nothing is settled. That's a difficult situation," Shannon said.

"He just makes me so angry."

"I know you don't want to deal with him, but you have to think about the baby. Would her life be better with her father in it?"

"Not if his prior actions are any indication. I mean, say I let him see her. What do I tell her when he doesn't show up because he's off hanging out with his friends?"

"You could give it a try, and if he bails too many times, then you change the arrangement or end it," Lisbeth interjected.

"You think that would actually work?"

"It gives him a chance to grow up and be a mature adult. Besides, you don't want him to take you to court," Shannon said as they headed for the studio.

"I'll think about it," Renee said, setting her mat on the floor.

Renee focused all of her energy on her breathing and pushed all thoughts of the world outside the studio from her mind. Her heartbeat slowed so each beat was in harmony with an exhalation. She looked to her right and noticed how much Lisbeth struggled. Their gazes met, and Renee flashed a supportive smile. In a few short weeks, Renee would probably be too big to do most of the exercises, too. But until then, she would enjoy the community of women around her. If it hadn't been for them, she wouldn't have gotten through the last few months. Not with her sanity intact.

Class ended, and Renee wiped the sweat from her forehead and the nape of her neck. She felt more relaxed, even if she was in need of a shower. Despite the feelings of anger swirling below the surface, tension no longer tugged on her neck and shoulder muscles. She walked out of the studio, and the cool air from outside filtered in as someone opened the door. She let the air cool her for a moment before continuing to the changing area.

"Anyone want to go for coffee?" Lisbeth asked.

"I can't. I've got to pick the kids up early from school today," Shannon said.

"What about you two?" Lisbeth looked at Renee and Erika.

"We still have some of the nursery to put together. Plus, I have to deal with Bryce."

"No problem. Good luck."

"You all right to drive home?" Shannon asked.

"Yeah, I'll be fine. I can still reach the pedals," Lisbeth said and patted her stomach.

They grabbed their jackets and all walked out together. Renee and Erika waved goodbye as they headed for the T. They took the stairs down, and Renee groaned.

"What's wrong?"

"Oh, it's just I'm all sweaty, and the air down here is kind of gross."

Erika laughed. "You're calling dibs on the shower, aren't you?"

"Kind of, yeah."

"Okay. I have to check my e-mail anyway. Michelle and Andrew said they'd send some new pictures today."

"They are so the perfect people for you," Renee said as a train came screeching to a halt beside them.

"And we haven't even met face to face."

"When is that meeting?"

"The twenty-fifth."

"Oh, I didn't realize it was next week."

"Yeah. I think I'm going to ask Dane to go with me. I've been telling him so much about them. He'd probably ignore me for a month if I didn't take him."

"You haven't talked about Nate since Christmas," Renee said.

"He's halfway around the world."

"You aren't telling him all about this?"

"No way of contacting him. Kind of annoyed he didn't give me an e-mail address so I could."

They climbed onto the train and rode it back to their apartment. Renee stopped at the front desk and asked if Bryce had come back. The doorman shook his head, and Renee thanked him. *So much for working things out now.* She rode the elevator and hopped in the shower. Half an hour later, she was dressed, refreshed, and significantly less gross. Renee stared at the haphazard appearance of her bedroom. She scooted the chest of drawers against one corner and tried to drag the changing table next to it.

"Hey, Erika?" she called.

"Yeah?"

"Can you give me a hand?"

"One second."

Renee stuck some of the blankets in the crib and clothes in the dresser. Erika appeared in the doorway moments later.

"What's up?"

"I can't move the changing table by myself."

Together, they situated the changing table to Renee's liking. Renee took a step back and examined the room. *Almost ready for my little girl.*

"It looks good," Erika said.

"Yeah. I think I just need diapers and bottles."

"Well, a stroller, too."

"Oh, shit. I completely forgot about a stroller and car seat."

"But you don't drive."

"Still, some of the strollers come with a car seat in them. And if my parents ever want to take her, I'd need one."

"Do you want to go now?"

"No. We don't have to do it right now. Right now, I just want to relax and not do anything. I'm going to enjoy my day off, damn it."

She and Erika left the bedroom and ended up in the living room, seated side by side on the couch. Renee flipped through channels.

"So did you get pictures?" Renee asked.

"A few. They're excited to come back to the U.S. They can't wait to see me."

"I bet. Have you talked to Dane today?"

"Not yet. I'll call him later. He said he might stop by tonight."

"Okay."

Renee turned her attention to the cheesy daytime soaps and couldn't contain a bout of gut-wrenching laughter at the overdramatic nature of the scenarios and characters. It was nice to find someone else's messed-up life entertaining. Definitely cathartic. In the back of her mind, she wondered where Bryce had gone and if he'd be back. A part of her hoped he would give up and leave her alone. But the bigger part knew he'd be back. He could be persistent when he wanted. And the thought she might have to face a judge to keep him at bay scared her.

Chapter Twenty-Eight

January 25th

Erika paced frantically at the front door to the apartment. Renee had left for work half an hour earlier, and Dane was late. He was never late, and she started to worry. She reached for her phone and nearly hit send, when a knock stopped her. Yanking open the door, she nearly threw herself at Dane.

"Sorry I'm late. Traffic was crazy today."

"Let's go. Come on."

She didn't give him time to catch his breath before she dragged him back to the elevator.

"Would you calm down?"

"But today's the day. I've been waiting for this since Christmas."

"I know, Erika. But you're going to pull my arm off. Just slow down. We have plenty of time to get there. We aren't going to miss them."

Erika huffed and slowed her pace. Dane laced his fingers through hers, and they walked out of the building and to the T. As the heat within the station pressed against Erika's face, she couldn't stand still, and the baby kept punting her bladder like a football, making the wait unbearable.

"I think you're both nervous," Dane commented as they stepped onto a train and found seats.

"Can you blame us?"

"No. You know, I'm really glad you let me come with you."

"I figured you wouldn't talk to me for months if I didn't. Besides, I've told them about you, too."

Erika counted the stops in her head as the train whizzed along the tracks. Dane's hand wrapped in hers calmed her frayed nerves. Her thoughts drifted to Nate, and she wondered where he was, what he'd think of her news. *He'd say he was proud of me.* The train stopped, and they stood. Just as they started to make their way to the doors, Erika felt a firm kick to her kidney and doubled over.

"What's wrong? Is it the baby?"

"He just kicked really hard," Erika gasped, trying to suck down air.

She let Dane guide her off the train so they wouldn't miss their stop. She leaned against a support beam until she didn't feel so winded.

"I'm okay. Let's go."

"Take it slow."

She flashed a smile and walked through the turnstile and up the stairs to the street level. The sun peaked out from behind thick clouds as they crossed the street and walked the two blocks to the adoption agency. Erika walked in and headed for the back office. She darted around the corner to the bathroom and ducked into a stall. Her stomach cramped as she sat doubled over on the toilet. After heaving for a few minutes, the pain subsided. Erika rose on shaking legs, hobbled out to the sink, and splashed cold water on her face. Examining herself in the mirror, she watched as the color slowly returned to her cheeks. Hopefully, no one would know anything was wrong.

"Where'd you go?" Dane asked when Erika sat down beside him.

"Just had to stop at the bathroom. You know my bladder is the size of a pea these days," Erika lied.

"I talked to the receptionist. She said they'll take us in about ten minutes."

"Have you seen them yet?" Erika asked, settling into the chair beside him.

"I don't think so. But then again, I wasn't really paying attention. They could already be back there."

Erika nodded and turned her attention to the outer door, staring intently until Arlene appeared in her peripheral vision.

"Erika, you can come back."

Erika blinked a time or two but stood up and followed the woman back to the room with the high bookshelves and the large conference table. Michelle and Andrew sat in the same seats the Hilliards had occupied on her last visit. She recognized them instantly and, despite the stomach discomfort, gave them a broad smile. As soon as Erika walked into the room, Michelle stood up and hugged her.

"It's so good to finally meet you," Michelle said.

"You, too. I hope your flight back was good."

Andrew walked around the table and joined in the hug. "Yeah, no problems. How about you? How are you feeling today?"

"I'm fine. Peter's moving a lot today."

"You look fantastic," Michelle doted.

Erika blushed. "You think so?"

"Absolutely."

"I hate to interrupt, but we need to get the logistics worked out," Arlene said.

Erika let Michelle and Andrew sit down and then took the seat beside Dane.

Arlene started explaining what would happen next. "I know you three have been sending e-mails back and forth for the last month, so you seem to fit quite well."

Erika nodded, and Michelle and Andrew smiled.

"I'm going to take that to mean we'll be moving forward with the adoption."

"Yes," Erika said.

"I've drawn up the paperwork." Arlene passed out two copies of a typed document. "We have a few things to stipulate before you both sign."

"Didn't you say something about a home visit?" Erika interrupted.

"I did. We can certainly work that into the agreement."

"Why don't you just swing by tonight after the meeting? I mean, we haven't exactly unpacked yet, but that stuff is only in our bedroom," Michelle said.

"I'd be okay with that," Erika said.

"All right. Let me get that down. We'll amend the agreement before you both sign."

"What else do we have to discuss?" Erika asked.

"You need to come to an agreement about what communication you will retain with the child after birth."

"I think we can handle that," Andrew said.

"You'll also need to turn over any bills for medical procedures and set up a payment plan for fees already incurred."

"Is that it?" Erika asked.

"There will be a few things to sign after the baby is born, but for now, that's all. I'll leave you to figure these details out. Someone can get me when you've decided."

Arlene stood up and left the room. Erika stared at the doorway for a moment.

"Um...I don't have bills or anything on me right now," she said.

"Well, do you have them at home?"

"Yeah. I've paid a few of them, but I don't really make all that much to cover them all."

"That's what we're here for," Andrew said.

"Do you want me to run back and get them for you?" Dane offered.

"We can always drive you home after you stop by our place and pick them up then," Michelle said.

"Okay. We can stop by after we figure this out."

They flipped back to the first page of the agreement. "Andrew and I were talking about this on the flight home, and we definitely want you to be a part of Peter's life. We'll send you photos and letters at birthdays and Christmas."

"Okay. Can I...send him cards?"

"Absolutely," Andrew said.

"What about like...phone calls when he gets bigger? Just on Christmas and his birthday."

"We can talk about that when he gets older. I think for now, letters and photographs and cards will be enough to keep you in each other's lives."

Erika licked her lips and thought about their offer. It sounded reasonable. After all, if she wanted more interaction with her son, she wouldn't be giving him up.

"I know we don't have the bills right now, but what about upcoming appointments and the stay at the hospital when I have him? I mean...I'm guessing you want to be there."

"We'll need to talk to your OBGYN about billing us instead of you for the appointments and the stay. We can go with you to your next appointment to sort that out, if you want."

"That would be great. It's actually this afternoon."

"You didn't tell me that," Dane interrupted.

"You didn't ask." Erika stood up. "I'll let Arlene know we're ready."

Erika crossed the hallway and knocked on Arlene's door.

"Come in."

"We're done figuring everything out."

"Great."

They walked back into the conference room, and Erika, Michelle, and Andrew shared the arrangement they'd come up with. Arlene dutifully took notes and disappeared again. She returned five minutes later with freshly printed copies of the agreement for each of them to sign. Erika slid her copy across the table and waited while Arlene witnessed both copies and stuck them in a folder.

"We're done. We aren't going to have any other meetings unless something comes up that you can't work out amongst yourselves."

"Great."

Michelle and Andrew shook hands with Arlene and they, along with Erika and Dane, left the room. Once they had coats and hats on, they headed outside.

"So what time is your appointment?" Michelle asked.

"Not until two. We have time to stop by your place and then swing back and get those bills if you want."

"Sure," Michelle said.

Erika followed them down to their car and slipped into the back seat. Dane slid in beside her, and Andrew pulled into late morning traffic. Erika watched the other cars fall into the stilted stop-and-go pattern in the middle of the city. Before long, they'd merged onto the highway and pulled off at one of the Cambridge exits. Another ten minutes elapsed before Andrew eased the car to a halt in front of a two-story brownstone. Erika unbuckled her seatbelt and followed the couple inside.

"Well, let's give you the tour," Michelle said, taking Erika by the wrist.

"Or we can just see the nursery. That's okay."

"Don't be silly."

Erika allowed Michelle to drag her through the kitchen, dining room, living room with plasma TV, and up to the second floor. She heard Dane and Andrew downstairs discussing sports or HD channels. Typical guy talk.

"So this is Peter's room," Michelle said and opened the door to a spacious room with pale blue wallpaper and airy beige curtains. A large crib sat against the far wall, and a matching changing table and dresser lined the wall opposite the window.

"It's beautiful," Erika said, and breath caught in her throat.

"We've got a stroller down in the garage and a baby seat in my car," Michelle said and ran a hand over the blanket lining the crib.

"He's going to be so happy here," Erika said, willing the tears not to fall. Too late.

"We sure hope so," Michelle said and wrapped her arms around Erika's shoulders.

"Thank you for doing this. You have no idea how much it means to me," Erika whispered.

They stood there in the nursery, crying into each other's arms for a solid five minutes before the guys appeared.

"We should head out if we're going to make the appointment on time," Dane said.

"Way to break up a girls-only moment," Erika said with a watery smile but untangled herself from Michelle and followed the guys back to the driveway.

They headed back to the city and parked on the street.

"It shouldn't take too long. The car should be okay," Erika said, leading them into the lobby.

The security guard at the front desk flagged them over.

"Hi," Erika said. "They're coming up with me for a minute. They're friends."

"That's fine. Just wanted to let you know Bryce is here looking for Renee."

"She's at work."

"I don't want to bother you, but could you tell him that?"

Erika grimaced but nodded. "Where is he?"

"Waiting upstairs, I think. I tried to tell him to wait while I got in touch with one of you, but he wouldn't listen."

"Okay. I'll deal with it."

She led her guests to the elevator.

"Who is Bryce?" Andrew asked.

"My roommate's ex-boyfriend. He's kind of a jerk."

"You want me to handle it for you?" Dane offered.

"Please."

They stepped into the elevator and ascended. Erika, Michelle, and Andrew hung back as Erika handed Dane her key. Bryce was pacing in front of the door.

"He looks a little...sketchy," Michelle whispered.

"He left Renee when she was like three months pregnant. He showed up last week, wanting back in her life. Real charmer."

Erika listened as Dane confronted Bryce. She only heard snippets of their conversation. Bryce demanded to know where Renee was. Dane said work and she'd be back later. Bryce's voice carried out into the hall.

"I have to see her."

"Well, you'll have to come back later," Dane said.

Erika took a deep breath and stepped a little closer. "She said she wanted to call you last week but didn't have any way to get in touch with you. So um...if you leave your cell number, she'll call you."

"You sure?"

"Yeah. I'll tell her. I promise."

Bryce seemed to calm down a little and rooted through his pockets. He pulled out a wadded-up receipt, scribbled his number down, and handed it over.

"She'll call," Erika said again as Bryce headed for the elevator.

Once the elevator dinged, Erika led her guests into the apartment. She threw her coat on the hook by the door and flicked on the light in the kitchen.

"Want the tour?"

"Sure," Andrew answered.

She led them quickly through the kitchen, living room, and her bedroom. They stopped for a minute to peer into Renee's room.

"She's having a little girl in April," Erika explained.

"So you'll have a chance to help raise a baby anyway," Andrew said.

"Yeah. I guess."

Erika stopped back in her room, searched through the bottom drawer of her dresser, and pulled out all of her doctor bills. Michelle and Andrew were in the living room.

"Where'd Dane go?" she asked.

"He had to take a phone call."

"Oh. Here are the bills."

"So, I'm assuming he's more than a friend?" Michelle asked.

"Yeah. He's my boyfriend. At least, I think he is. It's complicated. There's this other guy...Nate. We kissed a couple of times, but he's on this mission trip on the other side of the world. But Dane's been really good about all of this."

"Is he the baby's father?"

"No. I don't know who the father is. Dane and I weren't together before. I mean, we dated in college, but we'd been broken up for a while."

"Oh. Well, it's good that you're back together. Major life changes often have that effect on people."

"I had no clue that would happen. But Nate sort of challenged me to give him a second chance."

"The one who kissed you?"

"Well, I kissed him, really. And then he fled the country. He's sort of my unofficial AA sponsor, so I don't think we're supposed to be more than just friends."

"Still, he sounds like a good friend," Michelle said.

"Yeah. He's cool. Been great with the alcohol thing. You're really okay with taking a baby with health problems?"

"We believe every child deserves a loving home," Andrew answered.

"He's going to have great parents," Erika said.

An hour and a half later, Erika laid on the exam table, waiting for her doctor to arrive. Dane stood on one side, Andrew and Michelle on the other. Erika craned her neck when the door opened.

"We've got a full house today," the doctor said.

"This is Michelle and Andrew. They're adopting the baby," Erika said.

"Well, it's great to meet you."

"We're excited to be here. We've seen the earlier ultrasounds, but this is a new experience," Andrew said.

"Well, let's get down to it. How've you been feeling?" he asked Erika.

"I'm okay. He's kicking more. That's good, right?"

"Fetal movement is a good thing. Definitely."

"He kicked really hard today, and I was kind of winded."

"That's normal." He turned on the ultrasound monitor and began the scan. He stopped so everyone could see Peter's heartbeat, strong and steady. "He looks good. A little smaller than we generally like to see at this stage of development, but that's most likely due to the FAS."

"But he's still going to be okay, right? I mean...as okay as he can be?" Erika asked.

"Yes. He'll be as healthy as a baby with FAS can be. You have to go on bed rest for a few weeks near the end, but for now, you're good."

"Thank you. Oh, who do we talk to about billing? Michelle and Andrew are going to be paying for my appointments from now on."

"Talk to Alana at the reception desk. She'll get you all sorted out."

"Okay. Thanks."

He left, and Erika pulled on her clothes. They stopped by reception and got the billing figured out. Erika grinned the entire way back to the T stop. Everything was perfect. She was going to have wonderful people to raise her baby, and he was as healthy as he could be.

"We'll see you later. We have some errands to run. Feel free to call us," Michelle said, and they went their separate ways.

"Today was a good day," Erika said as she and Dane walked through the turnstiles a little while later.

"I haven't seen you this happy since Christmas," he said and kissed her cheek.

They got back to the apartment, and Erika settled on the couch. Dane disappeared in the direction of the kitchen and returned moments later with a bottle of water in each hand. She took the one he offered and unscrewed the cap.

"Can I ask you something?" he said.

"Hmm?" She sucked down a gulp of water.

"Are you going to be okay here once the baby is born?"

Erika turned to look at Dane. What was he getting at? She let the question sink in for a minute or two before answering. "Yeah. Why?"

"Well...think about it for a minute. You're giving your baby up, but your roommate is going to have a baby living here. Don't you think that might be a little hard for you?"

"I guess I didn't think about it. It hasn't happened yet...still seems far away."

"I know it seems far away, but it's not. You need to figure out if you're going to be okay with this set up."

"Okay."

"And you know I'm here for you. If you need to talk about it."

"I know. Right now, I just want to enjoy the fact that things don't suck."

Chapter Twenty-Nine

February 10th

SHANNON SAT BEHIND CHRISTIAN IN THE BATHROOM while he vomited. She rubbed his back and patted his neck until he stopped convulsing.

"Do you feel better?" she asked, handing him a glass of water.

He swished it around in his mouth and then spat into the toilet. "A little bit."

"I'm going to change your bed. You just stay here."

Shannon got to her feet, a rather difficult feat considering her current size, and walked into her son's bedroom. She quickly stripped Christian's bed. She heard footsteps in the hallway, and Meghan stuck her head into the room.

"Mama, is Christian sick?"

"Yeah, Meg. You need to go downstairs, please. We don't need you getting sick, too."

"Can I stay home from school?"

"No."

"I don't want to go."

Shannon balled up the sheets and started toward the bathroom.

"You're going to school. You aren't sick."

Meghan coughed. "Yes I am."

"Nice try. Go downstairs and eat breakfast. Tell Daddy to make you waffles. And take your brother with you."

Meghan pouted but headed for the stairs. Shannon heard Tanner follow her down. Christian stood in front of the sink and brushed his teeth.

"I'll be right back."

Shannon headed down to the basement, tossed the sheets in the washer, and hit the power button. She stopped in the kitchen. Mike was sitting at the table with the newspaper. Meghan and Tanner stood next to him.

"Can you please make them some breakfast?" she asked.

Mike looked up, "What's wrong?"

"Chris is sick. I would really appreciate it if you could make them breakfast and get them to school and daycare. You can drop Tanner off early. We'll pay for it, but it's just one day. I don't want him around Christian."

"Shannon, I have to go to work."

"You can't take a little time out of your day to help your children? I thought we were working on this," Shannon said, trying to keep her tone even and calm.

Mike set the paper down and looked at Tanner and Meghan. "Can you guys go into the living room for a minute so Mommy and I can talk?"

"But I want waffles," Meghan said.

"Just give us a minute, Meg," Shannon said.

Reluctantly, Meghan dragged Tanner by the hand out of the kitchen. Shannon rested a hand on her stomach and took steady breaths.

"I am trying to communicate what I need from you, Mike. But it's not going to work if you don't at least try."

"How sick is Chris?"

"He's throwing up. I need to finish changing his sheets."

"I guess I can take Meghan to school."

"Thank you."

He went back to his paper, and Shannon walked the three steps to the freezer to pull out frozen waffles. She had hoped he would have handled breakfast, too. Apparently that was too much to ask at this point. Ten minutes later, she set plates down on the table, and Tanner and Meghan reappeared.

"I'm going up to check on Christian. Put your plates in the sink when you're done."

Christian sat on the floor in his room, staring at his bare bed.

"Give me a minute to change the bed, sweetie," she said.

Christian scooted out of the way to change his pajamas while she quickly put the fresh sheets and pillowcases on the bed. She kissed his forehead and tucked him in.

"You get some more sleep. I'll be downstairs if you need me."

Shannon made her way downstairs to find Tanner and Meghan each placing their plates in the sink. She stepped up to the sink and ran the water over the plates and utensils.

"Do you think you'll be able to pick them up this afternoon?" Mike asked from the table.

"I don't feel comfortable leaving Chris home alone, even if it's just for a half hour," she answered.

Mike didn't look pleased as he folded up the paper and stuck it in his briefcase. She watched him while he pulled on his suit jacket.

"He's ten, Shannon. He'll be asleep. He won't even know you're gone."

"I'm not comfortable leaving him alone, Mike."

"Fine. I guess I can pick them up this afternoon and bring them to the office."

Shannon could see he wasn't entirely pleased with the arrangement, but she wasn't all that concerned. He would have to get used to taking the kids places once the baby was born.

A short while later, Mike and the kids left, and Shannon sat in front of the computer. She tried to get a little work done, but her thoughts kept drifting to Christian upstairs. After a few more fruitless minutes, she pushed away from the desk and headed up to check on him. Christian was fast asleep. She crept back downstairs and forced herself to get a little work done until about eleven o'clock.

"Mom?" Christian called.

"I'm on my way, Chris."

He stood at the top of the stairs.

"Is everything okay?" she asked.

"I'm hungry."

"Okay. Go back to bed. I'll make you some broth."

"I want crackers."

"You need to keep down liquid before we move to crackers, hon."

He grumbled as he turned around and headed back to his room. Shannon pulled out some chicken broth and heated it on the stove before she sidestepped up to his room. She balanced the tray in her arms and let Chris pull it down into his lap.

"Take small sips," she said, sitting on the floor beside his bed.

"Thanks for staying with me, Mom," he said.

"Of course, sweetie. Hopefully you'll feel better tomorrow."

"I'm done," Christian said a short time later and pushed the half-empty bowl away.

"Okay. You just rest. Do you want me to bring up one of your video games?"

"No, thanks."

"All right."

Shannon used the edge of the bed to hoist herself to her feet and took the tray from Christian's lap. She carried it to the stairs and was about to head down when she heard movement behind her. She had enough time to turn around to see Christian run into the bathroom. Shannon put the tray on the floor and rushed in behind him. He hugged the toilet bowl, and the broth spewed back up. She could see frustration etched around his eyes. She grabbed a washcloth, ran it under cold water, and rubbed his neck.

"I think the broth was a little too soon," she said as he sat back.

"I hate being sick," Christian said with a sniffle.

"I know you do. I'm going to call Daddy and tell him to pick up some Pepto-Bismol for you. That might help."

She helped him back to bed and left the washcloth with him while she went to call Mike. She sat down at the computer and watched the screen wink out of focus. *Not a good sign.* She dialed Mike's cell number and listened to it ring.

"I'm about to head into a meeting. Can I call you back?"

"I need you to pick up some Pepto-Bismol on your way home. Chris is still throwing up."

"Can't you run down to the store?"

"Just pick up the medicine and bring it home."

Shannon hung up and watched the screen blur again. Her stomach churned. *Definitely not a good sign.* She raced as quickly as she could to the downstairs bathroom and cringed as her breakfast came up. Thankfully, it quickly moved to dry heaves. *Perfect. Now I've got his bug.* She flushed the toilet and headed upstairs to lie down.

The next thing she knew, the bed shifted beside her. She rolled over to see Meghan looking at her.

"Mama, you look sick."

"I think I got Christian's stomach bug. When did you get home?"

"Just now. It's dinner time."

"Did Daddy give Christian his medicine?"

"I don't know."

"Can you go ask him for me?"

"Okay."

"Daddy," Meghan shouted as she ran out of the room.

A minute later, Mike appeared. "You caught the bug?"

"I think so. What does the label say about taking Pepto-Bismol while you're pregnant?"

"I don't know."

"Look, please."

He scanned the pink bottle for an answer. "It says here it's a class C drug and you should consult your doctor before taking it."

"Can you get my phone from the dining room? I'll call and ask."

Twenty minutes later, Shannon hung up the phone and told Mike to pour her a dose.

"You're sure the doctor said you can take it?"

"Yes. Does Chris look any better?"

"He seems to. I'll make him some soup in a little while and see if he keeps it down this time."

"All right. I'm going to stay up here."

"I'll make you some soup, too," he offered.

She blinked in surprise. He seemed more agreeable, and he even offered to help with the kids. That was new.

"Thanks."

Shannon managed to keep the soup down and went in around seven that evening to check on Christian. His soup bowl sat on the floor beside his bed, and he was curled up on his side with the blankets pulled up to his chin.

"How are you feeling, Chris?"

"Tired. And cold."

"Try to get some more sleep."

Shannon started for the door.

"Mom?"

"Yes?"

"Sorry I got you and the baby sick."

"That's okay, honey. We'll be just fine."

She slowly made her way downstairs, where Meghan and Tanner were watching cartoons. "You guys need to not bother Christian tonight, okay? He's still not feeling well."

"What about you, Mama?" Megan asked.

"Mama's not feeling very well, either."

"I want a kiss night night," Tanner said and tugged on Shannon's sleeve.

"Daddy will give you extra kisses tonight, okay?"

Tanner seemed disappointed but turned back to the TV. By nine o'clock, all the kids were in bed, and Shannon was pulling the covers up to her chin. She rolled to her side and got comfortable. The Pepto-Bismol seemed to be working, and she'd just taken another dose.

Mike walked in and sat down on the edge of the bed. "You need anything?"

"Just a good night's sleep," she answered.

"Okay."

He started to leave, when Shannon reached out a hand toward him. He stopped and looked at her.

"Tell me something," she said.

"What?"

"Why is it so hard for you to do things like take the kids to school?"

Mike cleared his throat, stared at her for a minute, and said, "I guess...my father taught me growing up that it was a man's place to provide for his family, and taking care of the family was the woman's job."

"We live in the twenty-first century, Mike. Roles have changed a lot since then."

"I know. I'm trying, Shan. I know it doesn't look like it, but I am. Some habits are just hard to break."

He kissed her forehead and shut the light off as he left. Shannon sighed and settled in for a long night with one hand pressed against her stomach. She hoped Aiden's immune system was strong enough to fight off the bug. She wasn't sure she could handle having him sick before he was even born.

Chapter Thirty

February 16th

LISBETH CROSSED THE STREET AND HEADED INTO THE yoga studio just as her phone showed noon. She hated being late, but getting anywhere quickly these days was an amazing feat. Luckily, she wasn't the only one straggling into the studio. She dumped her clothes and bag in the changing area and waddled in. She took up a spot beside Renee and tried to focus on her breathing. She could feel her heart thundering in her chest as she tried to relax. It slowed a little bit, but she could still barely catch her breath. The moment she tried to move into the warrior pose, a sharp pain shot across her stomach from left to right. She tried not to cry out as she massaged her side.

"You don't look so good," Renee whispered.

"I'm okay. Don't worry about it," Lisbeth lied.

The pain was still there every few seconds, shooting across her belly. Instead of slowing, her heart quickened as the pain came more frequently in sharp strikes and slashes against muscle. In a matter of minutes, she was doubled over in agony. She felt hands supporting her as she sank to the floor. She looked up at her friends.

"Let's get her outside," Shannon said.

Lisbeth let them lift her to her feet and guide her out to the lobby area. She sat down and gasped for breath.

"What's wrong?" Shannon asked.

"I don't know. I've never felt anything like this. I think something's wrong."

"Where does it hurt? What does it feel like?"

"Sharp, shooting pain in my stomach. From left to right. And I can't catch my breath."

Before any of them could say another word, she doubled over again. This time, it felt like her stomach was being torn in half.

"Oh God, I think I'm having contractions."

"But you're too early. I mean even with twins...you can't be going into labor now," Erika said.

"Everyone, stay calm," Shannon said. She disappeared and then returned with her purse.

"We're going to go the hospital. Erika, I want you to call Candace and let her know where we're going. Renee, I want you to ride with Lisbeth."

"She can't drive in this condition," Renee said.

"My keys are in my bag," Lisbeth said.

Lisbeth waited for Renee to come back. The pain seemed to have subsided now, and she got to her feet. She leaned on Renee's shoulder while they walked to her car.

"Can you send me Candace's number?" Erika called from behind them.

"Yeah. Let me get in the car, and I'll text it to you."

"We'll be right behind you," Shannon said as Lisbeth climbed into the passenger seat.

She texted Candace's work number to Erika, hoping that Candace wasn't with a patient. She tried to keep her breathing even as Renee pulled out of the parking spot and sped off into traffic.

"How are you feeling?" Renee asked when she stopped at a light.

"The pain seems to have stopped for now. But that doesn't mean it won't come back."

"Do you think something specific triggered it?"

"I have no idea. All I did was try to do the warrior pose, and the next thing I know, my stomach's on fire. I don't feel like the babies are in distress or anything."

"Hopefully someone at the hospital can help."

"Yeah. I'm not sure we're ready for this."

"I thought you had everything all ready."

"I mean, to have them this soon. They'll have to be in the intensive care unit for a while. Who knows how long that will last?"

Renee gave her a sympathetic look through the rearview mirror, pulled into the left lane, and signaled into the parking lot of New England Medical.

"Try to stay calm."

Renee killed the engine, pulled the keys from the ignition, and climbed out of the driver seat. Lisbeth unbuckled her seatbelt and opened the door. Just as Renee rounded the front of the car, the pain returned.

"I don't think I can walk," Lisbeth gasped.

She watched as Renee flagged someone down. Lisbeth heard a car pull up on the other side, and two car doors slammed.

"How is she?" Erika asked.

"Not good," Renee answered as someone approached. "We need a wheelchair," she said.

A voice crackled on a radio, and the person Renee was talking to stepped around the passenger side door.

"Ma'am, can you tell me what's wrong?" he asked.

"I think I'm having contractions. I'm thirty weeks."

"We have a wheelchair coming."

"I got Candace. She's on her way," Erika said.

A second attendant arrived with a wheelchair.

Lisbeth managed to get into the wheelchair without a problem, and they raced into the hospital. They pushed her into an elevator and went up two floors to the labor and delivery floor. By the time they reached a room, she was gripping her stomach with both hands and breathing hard.

"Let's get you on the bed," the first nurse said.

Ten minutes later, she laid situated in the bed with monitors hooked up. The pain had dissipated again, and Shannon, Erika, and Renee were allowed into the room.

"Hey, how are you?" Shannon asked, reaching for Lisbeth's free hand.

"Okay. They're monitoring what's happening before they do anything. They think it's probably false labor, but they want to be sure."

The door opened, and Candace came in. "Are you okay, honey?"

"Yeah. I think we're all okay. Yoga today just wasn't the right thing to do."

"What did the doctor say?"

"Not much. They're monitoring the babies. They seem okay."

"Excuse me," a female nurse said, approaching with a bag of clear liquid.

"What is that?" Lisbeth asked.

"Magnesium sulfate to stop the contractions."

"It won't hurt the babies, will it?" Candace asked.

"There are some possible side effects, but we'll be monitoring them closely. The doctor will be in shortly to talk to you."

Lisbeth grabbed Candace's hand and squeezed tight. The pulse-ox made her grip awkward, but Candace didn't seem to mind.

"We knew there could be problems with multiples," Lisbeth said to Candace, though it was more to reassure herself.

"I know."

For the first time in months, Lisbeth's thoughts turned to the reduction. *Would we be here right now if we only had one baby to worry about?* A knock drew her attention, and a doctor with shoulder-length blond hair walked in. The doctor's entrance banished all thoughts of singletons from her mind.

"Lisbeth?" she asked.

"Yes?"

"I'm Doctor Melissa. It seems you had some preterm contractions this afternoon. We've got the magnesium sulfate to slow those down and hopefully stop them."

"The nurse said there are some possible side effects for the babies?"

"Muscle tone weakness, slowed heart rate, but we'll be monitoring the babies the whole time. We'll also be giving you some steroids to help their lungs mature."

"We aren't having them now, are we?" Candace asked.

"No. We'll keep them in there a little longer. We would like to keep you on bed rest until you deliver, though."

"That's going to be a long time," Lisbeth sighed.

"It's what's best for the babies," Candace told her.

"I know. You'll have to call the school and tell them. I hadn't been planning to leave until March."

"Well, we will keep you as happy and comfortable as we can until you have your babies," Doctor Melissa said. She turned to the rest of the group. "She'll be fine. But visiting hours end in a few hours. We don't want to overdo it."

"We'll be heading out shortly," Shannon assured her.

With that, Doctor Melissa left the room. Shannon walked over to the bed and gave Lisbeth's hand a pat.

"We'll be by when we can. You just relax and try not to get too bored in here."

"I'll do my best," Lisbeth said, waving goodbye to her friends.

"You want me to stop at home and pick up some clothes?" Candace asked.

"Yeah. But you don't have to go right now."

"I'm not going anywhere," Candace promised, sitting down beside her.

"I hope you didn't have to cancel too many patients," Lisbeth said.

"They all understand. I can take some time off now if you need me to."

"No, I'll be okay. Just visit me every day."

"You won't be able to get rid of me," Candace teased.

Lisbeth smiled and settled against the pillow. Despite the early hour, the urge to sleep tugged at her conscious thoughts.

"I think I'm going to crash for a little bit," she said.

"Okay. I'll stay awhile longer before I head home and get your things."

"This is going to be a long two months," Lisbeth muttered and tried to sleep.

Chapter Thirty-One

February 28th

RENEE SAT DOWN IN THE LOCKER ROOM, EXHAUSTED. Every inch of her screamed in agony. Even her hands hurt. She bent down and rubbed her ankles. Standing and walking around even for a half hour took its toll on her. But she'd do it for as long as she could. She needed the money.

"Do you want someone to cover your next tour?" Pam asked from the doorway.

"How long do I have?"

"Half an hour. Forty minutes, maybe."

"No. I'll be fine. I just need to take a little breather."

"How are things at home, Renee?"

Renee shrugged. "Okay. We're ready for the baby when she comes. But it won't be for another couple months."

"What about...Bryce?" Pam asked.

Renee groaned and shook her head. "I tried to call him, but it just went to voicemail, and he didn't call back. I don't know what's up with him. He's like ADD or something."

Her boss walked into the room and sat down on the bench beside her.

"You'll figure it out. You're a smart girl."

"I just wish he would make up his mind. He's driving me crazy. What if he's like this after the baby comes? I can't rely on him if I can't even get in touch with him."

"Just see how things go. Keep trying to reach out to him."

"It doesn't seem fair that I have to do all the work when he was the one who up and left."

"Not everything in life is fair. You just have to take the good with the bad and make the best of it."

"I guess so," Renee muttered, standing up.

She dug her knuckles into her lower back, trying to loosen the muscles. After pacing around, she headed back out to the aquarium. At least the winter tours were shorter. Usually smaller groups, too. Renee strolled past the tanks with all the tropical fish.

"You have the easy life," she said.

Twenty minutes later, she met her mid-morning group and led them through the indoor area. A few of the kids begged her to take them outside, but their parents scolded them.

"Most of the animals are sleeping right now," Renee explained.

"I want to see bears," a little boy, about five years old, said.

"Please?" a chorus of tiny voices begged along with him.

"We don't have bears here, guys. I'm sorry," Renee said.

A few of the kids groaned in disappointment, but they brightened when she dropped them at the gift shop.

"Thank you," a little girl said.

"You're very welcome."

Renee checked her watch and sighed. Lunch time. She headed into the locker room to pick up her purse and jacket, and one of her coworkers raced in.

"There you are," he said.

"What's up?"

"Someone's looking for you."

Renee's mind immediately flew to Lisbeth in the hospital. *She couldn't have had the twins yet.* Her heart pounded a little faster as she looked at him.

"Who is it? Did you get a name?"

"A guy. Just said he needs to see you."

Momentary relief flooded her body. At least she didn't have to rush to the hospital. But she had a feeling she knew who was waiting for her, and her emotions quickly ebbed to anger.

"Thanks."

"Sure."

Renee walked to the front of the aquarium, and sure enough, Bryce stood there waiting. She walked past the entrance and stopped a few feet from him.

"Hey," he said.

"It's my lunch break. So we're going to have to talk while I eat."

"Okay. I can drive."

They walked to his car and headed for a diner a few miles away. Renee looked out the window as they passed over a bridge. The car stopped, and she got out without looking at him. He didn't seem bothered by it until they were seated.

"I tried to call you," she said.

"I know."

"You said you wanted to be in my life, Bryce. In our daughter's life. But when I reach out to you, you aren't there."

"I'm sorry, Renee. I mean it. I should have called back. I guess...well, I showed up, and your roommate was there with a bunch of people, and this guy basically told me to fuck off."

Renee smiled a little. "That's Dane. Erika's boyfriend."

"Oh. Well, he's kind of intense."

"Yeah. So...what's it going to be?" Renee asked.

"What do you mean?"

"Are you in, or are you out? You have to make up your mind. I don't want excuses for why you weren't there before. I need to know you're really going to be committed to this going forward."

"I'm trying."

"Not from where I'm sitting."

"So, maybe we just...start fresh from here. Today."

"I guess we can do that. Look...you can see her. But not all the time. Not whenever you want."

"What? Like weekends or something?"

"And holidays. Like Christmas and birthdays."

Bryce scratched the back of his head as he thought about her proposal. Their waitress came back with drinks and took their orders.

"Okay. That...that's good. But like...every weekend?"

"Are you still working the same schedule?"

"Yeah."

"Every other weekend. Does that work for you?"

"Yeah. When um...does this all start?"

"She's not due until April. And I'm not sure I want her sleeping in different places until she actually sleeps through the night. Besides, she'll need to be fed every few hours."

"I can do that. Like a bottle and stuff. Just give me a chance, Nee. I can do this. I'll prove it to you."

"Let's take it one step at a time, okay? See where we go."

"Sure. Do you want me there? For the birth?"

"I...hadn't really thought about it. I don't know how many people they allow in the room. And I already told my mom she could be there."

The waitress returned with their meals and, after making sure they had everything, darted back toward the kitchen. Renee focused on her sandwich, hoping that Bryce would be occupied by his food and not talk more about the baby.

"What's her name?" Bryce blurted.

"What?"

"Well...does she have a name yet?"

"Yeah. She does."

"Are you going to tell me?"

"I haven't really told anyone yet."

"Why not?"

"Because I just haven't."

"I want to know."

"You and everyone else."

"She's my daughter, too. Renee. I deserve to know. And I want to be there when she's born."

Renee chewed on the crust of her sandwich, thinking. She had been waiting to share her baby's name until she was born. But it couldn't hurt to tell Bryce now. It's not like she would let him convince her to change it.

"Alyssa."

"You're naming her after your sister?"

"Yes."

She could tell he wanted to say something, mostly likely protest her choice. He opened his mouth to speak, but she cut him off.

"It's not up for debate, Bryce. I'm naming her Alyssa, and that's all there is to it. Look, I have to get going. I have a tour in fifteen minutes," she said.

It wasn't really a lie. She did have an afternoon tour, but it wasn't for another forty minutes. Still, he seemed to buy it and flagged down the waitress for the bill. To her surprise, he paid.

"So I guess just call me when you go into labor," Bryce said a short while later as they pulled into the aquarium parking lot.

"Okay."

"Do you need anything...like baby stuff?"

"No. I'm fine. Thanks."

She climbed out of the car and headed back through the entrance. She got past the tropical fish before she spotted a familiar face.

"Hi," Meghan Atwater greeted, breaking away from her group.

"Hi, Meghan. Are you here with school?"

"Yes. I like the fish. They look brighter today."

"They do, you're right. Why don't we go find your teacher so they don't think you got lost?"

"When does your baby come out?" Meghan asked as they walked upstairs to the second level.

"Pretty close to when Aiden does."

"I wanted a little sister, but Mama said we don't get to pick."

Renee laughed. "Want to know a secret?"

Meghan leaned in close and nodded. "Yeah."

"I wanted a little sister, too. But I got a brother instead."

"I got all brothers."

"Well, that means you're Mama's little princess and you're extra special."

"That's what Mama says."

"Meghan. There you are," a frazzled-looking woman said and hurried to meet them.

"I'm sorry. I didn't mean to distract her. Meghan's mom and I are friends," Renee explained.

"Oh. Okay. You have to stay with the class," her teacher said.

"Tell your mom I said hello," Renee called.

"Okay. Bye."

Renee watched Meghan run after her teacher and couldn't help smiling. In a few short years, she'd be watching Alyssa go off on field trips with school. It suddenly made her worries about Bryce dissipate. She'd wanted to marry him once. She couldn't let one bad experience sour everything, and her friends were right: he was trying to do the right thing now. She had to give him credit for that.

Chapter Thirty-Two

March 8th

ERIKA PACED BACK AND FORTH IN THE BAGGAGE CLAIM of Terminal E at Logan. She'd gotten a short e-mail from Nate the day before saying he'd be back today. Wanting to surprise him, she hadn't responded. It had been shocking that he had e-mail access. His plane was taxiing to the gate, and he'd be off soon. Sitting in one of the tiny seats by the window, Erika watched the escalator. To get his luggage, he'd have to walk past her, and she could easily ambush him. Finally, people started to appear at the top of the escalator. Though she felt hugely pregnant, they walked by her, as if she was invisible, and out the doors to taxis or the Silver Line or to the baggage carousels. Erika heaved herself to a standing position as a break in the flow of people revealed Nate coming from the other direction.

"Where'd he come from?" she grumbled, moving through the horde of people to meet him. "Hey," she called.

"Erika?" Nate asked as he spun around.

She grabbed his arm to keep him from spinning around again and threw her arms about him. "I thought I'd surprise you," she said.

He pulled her close and held on tight for what seemed like ages, but Erika didn't mind. It was good to see him again. She'd been lonely in her AA meetings.

"I'm so glad you're back," she said into his shoulder.

"Me, too. I missed you," he replied and stepped back. He looked her up and down. "And look at how big you are."

"I've got amazing news," she said.

"You found a family?" he asked.

"Yeah. We started e-mailing back in December. I got the call on Christmas Eve, actually. We met in January to figure out the paperwork and stuff. So now they're paying for my bills and everything. They named the baby Peter."

"Peter is a good, strong name. And I told you things had a way of working out."

"I hope so."

They walked the length of the baggage claim area until they reached the farthest one.

"I should have expected you to show up when I e-mailed you yesterday," Nate said.

"Yeah, well, I wanted to give you a proper homecoming. Everyone at group misses you. Though I don't know why you couldn't e-mail more often."

"I missed them, too. But we did a lot of good work. I'm really pleased with what we accomplished. And it wasn't like we had Internet everywhere we went. So how are things with you and Dane?"

"Good. Really, good. We're back together."

"I'm glad."

She reached out, took his hand in hers, and gave it a squeeze. A siren blared, and the machine began to spit luggage out, sending it around the big track. Nate reached out and grabbed his bags. By the time he finished, he had four large suitcases sitting at his feet.

"Did you bring back people as souvenirs?" Erika asked as she pulled out the handle on a roller suitcase.

"Very funny. I had to get some extra souvenirs for some family members."

"Sure you did," she teased as they headed out to the shuttle. They climbed on and took up three seats.

"Oh, I got you something, too."

"You didn't have to," she said.

"I know. But I thought it'd be special. But you have to promise me something."

"Okay. You're just full of promises."

"Don't open it until September."

"September? Why?"

"You'll know why when it's time."

"You just like to see me squirm."

"Not true. So how long have you and Dane been back together?"

Erika blushed. "Officially since New Year's. And I've been going to meetings every week. Though I may have to take some time off when the baby is born next month."

"Understandable. It's all about taking care of yourself."

"Yeah. I am. Believe me. I'm in a much better place now than when you left."

"I'm so glad. And I really have missed you, Erika. There's one more thing I think you should consider doing before April."

"What?"

"I know you haven't wanted to tell your parents about everything, but maybe you should."

"But I'm giving Peter up. They aren't even going to meet him."

"I don't think that matters. You are going through a healing process right now, and that means making amends to those you've hurt. Don't you think keeping this a secret has been just a little unfair to them?"

Erika shoved her hands into the pockets of her pants and looked at her feet. Or as much of her feet as she could still see.

"I don't know what I'd say to them."

"You'll figure it out. I have faith in you."

"Thanks."

They got off at South Station and walked to his platform. "I'm going the other way," she said.

"Okay. I'll see you tonight."

"I'm counting on it. You'd better not forget my present."

He laughed as a train to Braintree arrived and he got on. She headed over to the platform and waited for a train heading toward Alewife. That was the one thing she hated about the red line. She had to wait longer for trains. Living on the green line spoiled her. By the time she got back to her apartment, she had just enough time to change and head out to work. She tapped her foot impatiently as the elevator rose to her floor. When she reached the door, it was open. Her brow creased with worry as she pushed it open.

"Hello?" she called.

No answer.

"Dane? Renee?"

Erika moved into the apartment and quickly checked the living room. No one. She walked into her bedroom and noticed the door to Renee's room was shut. She didn't remember Renee leaving it closed that morning. She pushed it open and saw Renee curled up under the covers.

"Renee?" Erika said softly.

"Hmm?"

"Are you okay? I thought you went to work."

"I'm not feeling very well. I came home."

"Oh. Can I get you anything?"

"No thanks. How was the airport?"

"Good. He got me something, but he didn't tell me what it was. He said I couldn't open it until September."

"Sounds exciting." Renee didn't sound very enthused.

"I have to go to work. I'll be back later. Do you want me to call Dane? Or Max?" Erika offered.

"No. I'll be fine. I'm just kind of dizzy. I'll sleep it off."

"Okay."

Erika went into her room and got ready for work and then hit the second speed dial on her phone and waited for Dane to pick up.

"Hey. What's up?" he answered.

"Are you coming over tonight?"

"Yeah. I was planning on it. Should I not?"

"No, you can. Renee just isn't feeling well. So we should probably do something low key."

"We can do that. Besides, you've been all over the place lately. You should slow down. Don't want to stress Peter out."

"Yes, sir."

"I'll see you later."

"Bye."

Nate's words repeated in her head. *You should call your parents and tell them what's been going on.* The thought made her stomach turn. *Maybe Peter is getting comfy for the night?* She smoothed her hair and reached for her cell phone, scrolled through to her parents' number, and hit send. It rang twice.

"Hello?"

"Hey, Mom," Erika said. Her voice faltered.

"Honey, this is a surprise. Is everything okay? You sound upset."

She sank to her bed. "I have to tell you something. Is Dad around?"

"Yeah."

"Can you get him? I need to tell him something, too."

"Give me a second."

Erika listened. Footsteps echoed and distorted voices crackled until her dad's voice became distinguishable.

"Erika. What's going on?" he said.

"I...have been going through some things lately."

"What kind of things?" her mom interrupted.

"I need to just tell you. So just let me talk." She got to her feet and paced. "I found out I was pregnant back in August. And I was having some trouble dealing. I didn't want to admit it in college, but I had a drinking problem. I still do. I...I've been getting help, though. I go to meetings twice a week. And I've been sober since September."

The other end of the line was silent. Holding her breath, she waited for her parents to say something. Anything. Her heart pounded an erratic rhythm that danced lower and lower, threatening to drop into the pit of her stomach.

"Mom? Dad? Are you still there?" she asked.

"We're here. You...you're sure you're pregnant?"

Erika looked down at her swollen stomach. "Yeah. I'm sure. I'm due in April."

"Are you...keeping the baby?" her dad asked.

"No. I'm giving it up for adoption."

"That's a big decision. Are you absolutely sure you thought it through?" he asked.

"Yes, Dad. It's the right thing for me to do. I can't raise a baby with where I am in my life. I need to clean up and get my head on straight. He's going to be raised by a great couple."

"Why didn't you tell us sooner?" her mom pressed.

"I was scared. I didn't know how you'd handle it. I thought...maybe you'd be angry at me."

"Of course we aren't angry, honey. Are you happy with your decision, sweetheart?" her mom said.

"Yes."

"Then we're happy for you. And if you need anything, just tell us."

"I will, Mom. Thanks. I have to head to work. I love you, and I'll call you soon. Promise."

She hung up and headed to the kitchen to grab her keys and purse before heading out. That night, after her meeting, Erika curled up on the couch with Dane at her side and watched the end of a marathon on USA Network. She couldn't tell if it was original programming or something in syndication, but she thought maybe the *Law and Order* credits scrolled at the end. She kept spinning the tiny box from Nate between her fingers. It had a note attached to not open it until September.

"You want me to hold onto it for you?" Dane asked.

"Nope. I'll be fine. I just...it's going to drive me crazy until September."

"Just what we need. You going crazy."

"Shut up."

"You're really happy he's back, aren't you?"

"Yeah. It's nice to have someone I can talk to that really gets what's going on. I mean, it's not that you and Renee don't. It's just different with Nate."

"I get it. I'm glad he's back. He makes you happy, and I love seeing you happy."

"You're such a big dork."

He leaned over and kissed her cheek. "But I'm your big dork."

"I talked to my parents today. Told them everything."

"How'd that go?"

"They were surprised. But...I think they're happy I'm getting things figured out."

"I'm glad they're being supportive."

She patted his knee. "Let's go to bed. I'm exhausted."

Chapter Thirty-Three

April 1st

LISBETH WOKE UP TO FIND HER HOSPITAL ROOM DARK. A blurry figure, who her sleepy brain interpreted as Candace, sat slumped in a chair beside the bed. She looked around for the clock, and her gaze finally landed on the timepiece. Only four in the morning. *Why am I awake right now?* Lisbeth tried to roll over but found the movement sent ripples of pain through her stomach. It didn't help that the bed sheets tangled with the mass of wires from the monitors attached to keep track of Rachel and Patrick's vital signs. She gasped in pain, and it was enough to rouse Candace. Lisbeth felt a hand wrap around hers.

"What's wrong?"

"I don't know."

Candace moved to turn on the light, and Lisbeth tried to move to a sitting position. Something was wrong. The bed felt wet.

"Candace."

"What?"

"Get a nurse. I think my water broke."

She watched Candace run from the room and heard the soles of her shoes smacking against the floor as her voice echoed in the empty corridor. *Don't wake the whole floor.* Lisbeth took slow, even breaths as she waited for a nurse to come. The pressure in her lower abdomen, below her belly button, was probably contractions. *This time for real.* At least they were less painful than the last time. After what seemed an eternity, Candace came back with a nurse.

"Do you know what time your water broke?" the nurse asked.

"No. I just realized it a minute or two ago. I can feel pressure and movement. I think they're contractions."

"I'm just going to check your cervix, okay?"

"Yeah."

Lisbeth settled onto the bed and watched as the nurse lifted up the blankets. She squirmed in discomfort as the nurse's fingers searched uncomfortably between her legs while her other hand pressed above her uterus.

"It looks like you're about one centimeter dilated. I'll let a doctor know, and we'll check you again in an hour to see how you're doing."

"I'm still three weeks from my due date," Lisbeth said.

"You're doing just fine. Just relax. Three weeks early with twins is very good. You can use the call button to reach someone if the contractions get too much. You're still too early to get an epidural."

All Lisbeth could do was nod. It was out of her hands now. She'd progress as quick or slow as her body wanted. Being a first-time mom led her to believe labor would be long and slow. For a split second, she envied Shannon. She'd probably have a smooth, short delivery. Lisbeth rubbed her face and looked over at Candace.

"What day is it?" Lisbeth asked.

"What?"

"What day is it?"

"April first."

"Some April Fool's joke this is," Lisbeth said with a hiccup of laughter.

"Our kids think they're funny, that's all."

"They're hilarious."

Candace remained standing.

"Get comfy. I think we're in for a long one," Lisbeth said.

She did her best to stay calm and comfortable as the contractions continued over the next several hours. Around eight that morning, Doctor Melissa came in, followed by a nurse.

"How are we doing?" Melissa asked.

"Okay. I don't think the contractions have changed much. I don't think they're getting closer together."

"Are they still the same level of pain?"

"Yeah. But it's not as bad as when I came in the first time."

"Okay. Let's see where we are."

Melissa bent down and lifted up the sheet. "You were about two and half centimeters last we checked. It looks like you haven't changed in the last hour."

Lisbeth moaned. "I know they say labor the first time takes forever, but it doesn't make it any less stressful."

"We'll wait another hour, and if nothing changes, we'll give you some Pitocin to help speed things along."

Lisbeth nodded and let out a slow breath. Candace gripped her hand, and they both watched Doctor Melissa leave them to wait out the monotony.

"I guess we just have to hope that things progress in the next hour," Candace said.

"That's all we can do," Lisbeth said.

Three hours and a Pitocin drip later, Lisbeth's hope of having a vaginal delivery plummeted. Her labor stalled at three centimeters dilation, and she was pretty sure she could feel some distress with the twins. She kept her gaze locked on the fetal heart monitors as they beeped away at high speeds.

"I think we need a nurse," she said, reaching for the call button.

"What is it? What's wrong?" Candace asked.

"I'm not sure, but something feels wrong."

She hit the button, and a minute later, a nurse and Doctor Melissa came rushing in.

"I think something's wrong," Lisbeth said.

"Lay back," the nurse instructed.

Lisbeth did as she was told and grimaced as another contraction sent a ripple of discomfort through her lower back and stomach. The monitors beside her started to beep erratically.

"We have some fetal distress," the nurse said, looking at Melissa.

Melissa pursed her lips and took a couple of steps closer to the head of the bed. "We have two options at this point."

"I'm listening."

"We can see if the babies calm down on their own and wait for you to dilate so you can deliver them vaginally, or we can do a C-section and get them out in the next hour."

Lisbeth looked at Candace, and an understanding passed between them. "C-section. I don't want to put any more stress on them than we have to."

"All right. We'll get you prepped, and we'll be having these babies in about an hour."

"Great."

The nurse came back in with an anesthesiologist, and they gave her an epidural. She also signed off on the consent form for the C-section.

"It should start to work in a few minutes," the anesthesiologist told her.

"I can stay awake for the procedure, right?" Lisbeth asked.

"Absolutely."

"Good. Thank you."

Forty minutes later, a group of nurses rolled Lisbeth into the operating room. She gripped Candace's hand as they set up a curtain right above her belly button.

"How are you feeling?" Melissa asked.

"Nervous."

"Don't worry. We'll have these babies out in no time. You just relax and let us do the rest."

Lisbeth tried not to listen to the voices beyond the curtain talking about cutting and scalpels. All she wanted to hear was the sound of her babies' first cries. As long as they cried, she would be the happiest mom in the world.

"Lisbeth, look," Candace whispered.

Lisbeth blinked, and one of the nurses showed her a squirming baby girl. Exactly twenty-one seconds later, a little boy appeared above the curtain, wailing just as loudly as his sister.

"We did it," Lisbeth gasped as tears streamed down her cheeks.

All worries about whether it would have been right to reduce to a single baby disappeared when the nurses walked over and presented them with their newborn bundles.

"Can we hold them?" Lisbeth asked.

"Sure. They look pretty good for thirty-seven weeks. We may need to keep them for observation, but you should be able to take them home in a few days."

Chapter Thirty-Four

April 10th

SHANNON STOOD BESIDE HER BED, FOLDING LAUNDRY. Tanner sat on the floor next to her, playing with trucks.

"I want to help," he said, casting his toys aside.

"Okay. Come here. You can be Mama's sock sorter."

"What's that mean?"

"Climb up here, and I'll show you."

He jumped onto the bed and sat in a pile of unfolded clothes.

"Find all of the socks and match them up."

"Okay."

He rooted around until he had a pile of socks in his lap. Shannon smiled as she continued to fold shirts and pants. Every few minutes, she felt a twinge in her stomach. It'd been there all morning, but she'd done her best to ignore it. *Aiden is being overactive.* She was due any day now, but still, she couldn't be having contractions now. A very familiar sensation knocked her out of lying to herself.

"Tanner, stay here. Mama will be right back."

"Okay, Mama."

Shannon made her way to the bathroom and sat down on the toilet. She felt a pop and a gush. Clear fluid filled the toilet bowl.

"Damn," she swore.

After sitting for a few more minutes, she got up and went back to the bedroom. She pulled a bag from her closet.

"Tanner, come on. We have to go."

"Where are we going?"

"The hospital. Mama's going to have the baby."

Tanner leapt off the bed and thundered downstairs, Shannon right behind him. She grabbed her purse, keys, and a jacket.

"Mama, I need help," Tanner said as he struggled with his shoes.

Shannon did her best to help, but bending triggered another contraction.

"You can put your shoes on in the car."

Five minutes later, they were on the road, and Shannon dialed Mike's work number. It rang three times.

"Hon, I'm about to go into court. Can this wait?"

"No. It can't. My water broke about ten minutes ago. I've been having contractions all morning. I'm on my way to the hospital with Tanner. I need you to meet us there."

"Are you sure you can drive?"

"I'm sure. Just get there."

Shannon ended the call and focused on driving.

"Mama?" Tanner asked as they pulled into a parking spot at the hospital.

"Yes, Tanner?"

"Can I play with the baby?"

"Not right now. He has to come out first. And he's going to sleep a lot when he first gets home. Remember how we talked about that?"

"Yeah. When is he coming?"

"Soon, buddy. Very soon."

Shannon pulled into the parking lot and parked the car. She took Tanner by the hand and walked through the front entrance. She stopped at the front desk and explained her situation. A nurse marched over with a wheelchair, and Shannon sat down.

"I want to do it," Tanner said.

"Be careful, and don't push too fast. And you go where this nice lady tells you," Shannon said.

Going slow and doing exactly as the nurse instructed, he did a good job getting her to her room. She was grateful for his good behavior as another contraction winded her. This one felt stronger than ones before. The nurse gave her a gown to put on and Shannon changed. The contractions were closer together. Maybe five or six minutes at most. Definitely the fastest labor she'd had. She hoped that Mike would make it before it was over. Breathing through a contraction, Shannon relaxed just as her doctor came in.

"Well, it seems we're right on time," he said.

"Seems so."

"I'm going to check you to see how dilated you are." He lifted the sheet, and Shannon felt pressure. "How long have you been having contractions?"

"I think all morning. But my water broke only maybe forty minutes ago."

"You're already five centimeters. We're going to have this baby really soon."

"The benefit of being a mother," Shannon mused.

Mike raced in. "You made it," he said.

"Of course I did. I told you I'd be fine. I hope the judge understood you having to rush off."

"Don't worry about that now, honey. How are you doing?"

"Five centimeters. If I keep progressing this fast, we may have our little boy within an hour and half," Shannon said.

"Wonderful."

They'd come far since January. Shannon was happy that, at least right now, he was being so supportive and understanding. The doctor ducked out of the room, and Mike leaned over the bed. He kissed Shannon on the lips and rested his forehead against hers.

"Can I do anything?" he asked.

"Make sure someone picks the kids up from school."

"Yes, ma'am."

"I helped," Tanner said proudly.

"You did?"

"He pushed me from the lobby all the way here like a big boy."

"I am a big boy."

"Yes, you are."

Around noon, Shannon started pushing. One of the nurses took Tanner to the kid's wing to play with some of the toys since he was too young to be in the room for the birth. Shannon gripped Mike's hand, pressed her chin to her chest, and exhaled slowly, counting to ten in her head.

"You're doing great, Shan."

She heard suction and knew that at least Aiden's head had made it through the birth canal. She felt another contraction and pushed.

"Good, keep going. We're almost there," the doctor said.

Shannon whimpered as she felt the pressure dissipate between her legs. A moment later, the nurse deposited a healthy-looking baby boy on her stomach. She toweled him off, and he began to cry loudly and vigorously. His tiny arms and legs flailed in time to his cries.

"Happy birthday, Aiden," Mike said and then followed the nurses to the scale with his phone.

Shannon lay back to catch her breath before the afterbirth, listening as Mike babbled to the baby and snapped pictures on his phone.

"Healthy boy. Twenty inches and seven pounds, two ounces," the nurse said, handing him over.

Shannon grinned, kissed the top of his head, and ran a finger over his cheek.

"Hi, little man."

He squeaked at her, and she couldn't keep from crying. "He's perfect," she said.

The door opened, and Tanner burst in. He climbed up the bed rail and into his mother's lap.

"Oomph," she said at the added weight.

"Why's he wrinkly?"

"That's the way babies look. But you have to be quiet and gentle, Tanner."

Tanner leaned over and kissed his baby brother's forehead. "Hi, Aiden. I'm your big brother."

"Yes, you are."

"Shan, I'm going to run home and get a few things."

"Okay. Why don't you pull the kids out early?"

"I'll be back."

An hour later, the door opened again, and Christian and Meghan walked in. Tanner sat by the window, watching the ambulances and other cars whiz by outside.

"He's little," Meghan said, kissing Aiden's cheek.

"You were that small once, too," Shannon said.

"Can I hold him?" Christian asked.

"Sure. Sit down first."

Christian pulled a chair over, and Shannon handed Aiden to him. He held his little brother like a pro.

"I want to hold him, too," Meghan said.

"In a minute, Meg."

Shannon looked over at the door, and Mike walked in with a balloon bouquet. She laughed as he set it by the bed.

"See, it all turned out fine," Mike said in her ear.

"You're right. It did."

Chapter Thirty-Five
April 12th

RENEE STEPPED OUT OF THE ELEVATOR AND STARTED down the hallway, scanning each name she passed until reaching the one she was looking for. She knocked and walked in to find Shannon sitting up in bed, nursing Aiden.

"Hey," Renee said.

"Hi. I didn't think anyone was going to stop by."

"I heard that you delivered, and I wanted to see the little guy. Lisbeth said she and Candace just brought the twins home yesterday."

"I did see them in the nursery for a few minutes the other day. They're beautiful babies."

"So is this little guy. Hey there, Aiden," Renee cooed.

"He's been pretty good about nursing, and he's a good sleeper. Thank God for small favors. How about you?"

Renee pulled a chair over and leaned on the edge of the bed. "I'm okay. Just waiting for things to get moving. How are you feeling?"

"I'm all right. Tired still, but I'm starting to get my energy back. You should be ready to go anytime now, right?" Shannon answered.

"Don't remind me."

"You'll be happy to hold her when it's all over."

"I am excited. I just want everything to be perfect."

Shannon placed a hand on Renee's arm. "I hate to tell you this, but giving birth is rarely perfect. Take it from someone who's been there four times."

"I guess I'm a little scared about the whole thing. I know they drug you up and stuff, but...I'm probably being silly."

"You're not. It's a very profound experience. But you'll have people who care about you there to help you through it and to share it with you."

Renee nodded and leaned back in the chair. Aiden made soft sucking noises as he continued to nurse, and Renee couldn't help but smile at him. She couldn't wait to see her little girl for the first time.

"Can I use your bathroom?"

"Of course."

Renee got up and headed to the bathroom on the other side of the room. She sat down, and her muscles tightened across her midsection. Like a cramp, but twenty times worse. The pain didn't go away when she bent double. Inhaling through her nose as deeply as she could, she held it for a count of five and then exhaled just as slowly. By the time she hit five, the pain subsided, and she tried to stand, but the room spun.

"Oh shit."

Once the feeling passed, she stepped back into the room.

"Do you think you could call a doctor?" she asked Shannon.

"Oh no. Did your water break?"

Renee paled. "I don't know. But I think I just had a contraction."

"Just sit down and stay calm. Take deep breaths and try to focus through the contractions."

"Okay."

Renee watched Shannon reach over and hit the call button beside the bed. They waited until a nurse stuck her head in.

"Can I help you?"

"Yeah. I think I'm going into labor," Renee said.

"Oh, my. Wait right here, and I'll get a wheelchair."

"So much for some time to get over panicking," Renee muttered.

"You'll be fine. They'll admit you and call your mom."

"Right. And she can stop by the apartment and get my bag. At least I was all packed."

"See, being worried beforehand can have its advantages," Shannon said.

The nurse returned and wheeled Renee down the hall to a nurses' station, where they admitted her and let her call her mother.

"Mom. It's me. The baby's coming. I need you to get here as soon as you can."

"I'll be there as soon as I can, honey. Just try to stay calm."

"I have to call one more person," Renee said.

"You need to get into a bed, hon," the nurse said, starting to roll her away from the desk.

"But...the baby's father needs to know. It will only take a minute. Please."

"Make it fast."

Renee dialed Bryce's number but got his voicemail.

"Bryce, it's Renee. It's about noon on the twelfth. I'm at New England Medical, and I'm in labor."

She hung up and let the nurse wheel her down the hall to the labor and delivery ward. By the time her mother arrived, Renee was almost two centimeters dilated and gripping the bed rail in pain.

"I'm here, sweetheart," her mother said.

"Make the pain stop," Renee begged.

"I don't think they can give you an epidural yet. But you're doing great."

"It hurts so much."

"Squeeze my hand. It will make it hurt less."

"No, it won't."

"It will. Trust me."

Renee took her mother's hand and on the next contraction, squeezed as if her life depended on it. To Renee's surprise, it actually made the pain lessen. She lay back a few minutes later and looked at her mother.

"How'd you do that?"

"It makes you focus on something else."

"Thanks."

"Do you want anything? Some water?"

"No. I think if I drink anything, I'll just throw up."

"Let me get a cloth to wipe your face."

Renee didn't object as her mother wet a cloth from the bathroom and dabbed her forehead and cheeks.

"I hope I didn't interrupt work," Renee said.

"Honey, don't be silly. You know I'd be here no matter what time of day. Your dad and brother will stop by later tonight."

"Okay. I called Bryce, but he didn't pick up. I don't know if he'll get here in time or not."

"He'll be here. I know he's trying."

"He says he's trying. I guess the real test will be once she's here."

"You're going to tell me what to call my grandbaby, aren't you?"

"Yeah, Mom. I'm naming her Alyssa."

Tears welled in her mother's eyes. "Your sister would be so proud of you right now."

"I hope so. She's going to grow up knowing her aunt loves her very much, even if she's not around to say it."

By four o'clock that afternoon, Renee was seven centimeters and doped up on an epidural. Bryce had yet to show up. There was a knock at the door, and Shannon appeared, walking slowly, as if stiff joints plagued every inch of her.

"How are you doing?" Shannon asked.

"Better now that I have drugs. This is my mom. Mom, this is Shannon. One of my friends from yoga. She had her little boy two days ago."

"It's nice to meet you," Shannon said, shaking Renee's mom's hand.

"Your first?" Renee's mom asked.

"Fourth. If you need anything, I'm right down the hall," Shannon said.

"You haven't seen Bryce have you?"

"No. I haven't. I did let Erika know where you were. She says she'll stop by later tonight if she can."

"Okay. Thanks."

"You're doing amazing," Shannon said and gave Renee a quick hug.

Six fifteen p.m. rolled around, and Renee started pushing. Just as she bore down for the first time, footsteps thundered in the hallway. She tried to block them out, figuring they were just an orderly or a nurse, but gasped when Bryce appeared.

"I'm here. I made it," he gasped.

"Sir, you can't be in here," the nurse said.

"It's okay. I'm the father," he said.

The nurse looked at Renee, and she nodded.

"Stand over there."

Bryce moved to stand by the window and watched as Renee pushed. Her mother counted to ten beside her, and she relaxed. Three more pushes, and Alyssa's head crowned.

"How many more?" Renee complained.

"That's up to you. Give us some really strong pushes, and we'll have this baby," the nurse answered.

Renee sucked in a big breath and blew out slowly as she pressed her chin to her chest. She heard her mother squeal happily as the baby slid out. Renee' listened intently for the telltale cry, and she laughed as Alyssa wailed loudly in the doctor's arms.

"Happy birthday, little lady," the doctor said, placing her on Renee's stomach.

Renee reached down and took her daughter by the hand. "She's perfect."

"Do you want to cut the cord?" the doctor asked Bryce.

"No."

Renee wasn't surprised. He'd been hands off the whole pregnancy; why should now be any different. Still, he did ask to hold her. As he handed the baby over, he leaned close to Renee's ear.

"You did good, Renee."

"Thanks. I'm glad you were here."

"I'm sorry I was late."

"You were here for the important part."

"How is it you just went through six hours of labor and you still look beautiful?" he asked.

"Don't push it," she warned.

He smiled and backed off. Renee looked down at the baby in her arms and let the rest of the world melt away. It didn't matter what was going on around her; she finally had her little girl.

Chapter Thirty-Six

April 19th

ERIKA SAT IN HER AA MEETING BUT COULDN'T FOCUS. She'd been to see Renee in the hospital and was starting to feel nervous about delivering her own baby. It didn't help that Shannon and Lisbeth had delivered already. She knew she wasn't supposed to have the baby until the end of the month, but she kept thinking that they might take Peter early because of the FAS.

"Hey, are you all right?" Nate asked, tugging on her shirtsleeve.

"Just...thinking. I'm kind of worried about the baby. Renee had Alyssa kind of unexpectedly. And Lisbeth had to have a C-section to deliver the twins. I guess I'm just...I'm not ready for this."

"Come on, let's go for a walk," he said.

"But the meeting isn't over."

"That's okay. You look like you need some air."

They walked out of the church and into the crisp night air. The sky darkened on the horizon while they walked up and down the sidewalk.

"You're worried something could happen during delivery?" he asked.

"I don't know. I just don't know what to expect. I mean, I know he's going to have some problems, but what if that means he can't come out...normally?"

"Have you talked to Michelle and Andrew about it? Did they have an opinion?"

"They said to do whatever I was most comfortable with and what was best for Peter. But how am I supposed to know what that is if I've never done this before?"

"That's okay. You've got time."

"It doesn't feel like I do. I feel kind of sick. And my stomach hurts. Has been for the last couple of hours."

"Hurts how?"

"Like cramps. But I mean...I can't actually be having the baby now. It's not like my water broke or anything."

"Maybe we should go to the hospital, just to be sure?"

"I don't want to make Andrew and Michelle pay for a visit if they don't have to."

"This is your baby we're talking about, Erika. I don't think you should worry about the money right now."

She bit her lip. "I...okay."

They headed for the T, and Erika pulled out her phone. She dialed Michelle's cell number first. She answered on the first ring.

"Hi, Erika."

"My friend is taking me to the hospital. I think I might be having contractions."

"Which hospital? We'll meet you there."

"New England Medical. I don't know if it's anything, but...I don't want to do something that could hurt the baby."

"I understand. We'll see you there, honey. Do you need me to call anyone?"

"Do you have Dane's number? I want him there if anything happens."

"I think we have it, yeah. I'll call and let him know."

"Thanks."

A short while later, Erika lay in a hospital bed with monitors hooked up to her and the baby. Michelle, Andrew, Nate, and Dane surrounded her while she tried not to burst into tears from the pain.

"Don't they have drugs to make the pain go away?" she begged.

"We'll see if we can find a doctor," Dane said and led Nate out of the room.

Erika gripped the bed rail as another contraction ripped through her. She couldn't take much more of this. Feeling a hand on top of hers, she looked to see Michelle leaning over.

"You are doing so well. You can get through this."

"I can't. I can't do it. It's too hard."

"Just keep trying. I promise, you'll make it."

The fetal heart monitor went haywire just as Dane and Nate walked back in. It spiked and then nosedived.

"What's happening?" Erika asked. Her voice was barely audible over the beeping machines.

A team of nurses pushed through and checked the monitors and her progress with labor.

"What's wrong?" Erika demanded.

"We're not sure. The baby's heart rate is decreasing," the head nurse said. She turned to one of her colleagues and said, "Get an ultrasound tech down here now."

"That's bad. Tell me what's going on."

"You need to try to stay calm. Just take slow breaths and relax."

"Don't tell me to relax! What's wrong with my baby?"

"Ma'am, you're not helping the baby right now. You need to lie down and try to take deep breaths."

Dane wrapped his hand around Erika's and squeezed it hard. "We're right here."

It eased her worry the tiniest bit and lasted long enough for the ultrasound technician to come in and scan. Grim worry was etched in every line of his face.

"What?" Erika gasped.

"It appears the cord is wrapped around the baby's neck and is cutting off oxygen."

"What does that mean?"

"It means in order to get your baby out safely, we're going to need to perform a C-section."

"Won't that hurt him?"

"No. It will be less stressful than trying to make it through the birth canal."

"Does she have to sign anything?" Nate asked.

"A consent form. We'll get it right now."

Fifteen minutes later, Erika and her entourage hustled into the OR. Erika watched as doctors scrubbed down and wheeled in a tray of sharp instruments. She held onto Dane's hand the entire time. The epidural dulled the pressure below her belly button. She strained to hear some semblance of a cry. It was almost an eternity before she heard it.

"He cried," she said.

"He did," Michelle agreed.

"Can I hold him? Just for a minute?" Erika asked.

Michelle and Andrew exchanged a look before Michelle nodded. After the nurse cleaned him up, they brought Peter over.

"You can hold him for a minute, but he has to get checked out in the intensive care unit."

Erika stared at the baby in her arms. He seemed so small and perfect. His cheeks were puffy, and his skin was tinted purple, but he was regaining normal color. That was more to do with the cord being wrapped around his neck than the FAS.

"Happy birthday, Peter."

She kissed the top of his head, and he squirmed in her arms. She gasped as he surveyed the world for the first time and looked right at her. In that moment, she could feel her resolve falter. For just an instant, she thought she could raise him on her own. Then she looked at Michelle and Andrew, waiting in expectation of holding their son, and Erika knew she couldn't keep him. He would be well looked after with his adoptive parents. She handed him to Michelle.

Epilogue

September 20th

SHANNON PUSHED THE STROLLER UP THE PATH ON THE Common, and sun shone through the trees, dappling the grass with patches of light. She spotted a small group with blankets and baby carriers and stopped. "Sorry I'm late/" She unbuckled Aiden from the stroller and laid him on the blanket beside the other babies.

"No worries. God, he's getting so big," Lisbeth said, leaning over to tickle Aiden's stomach.

He kicked and gurgled in response.

"They all are. I can't believe it's been six months already," Renee said and stuck a pacifier in Alyssa's mouth.

"I miss seeing you all at yoga," Erika added from beside Renee.

"I think we should start our own little class. Just the four of us. We can do it over at my place. We have the room now," Shannon offered.

"So the addition is finished?" Lisbeth asked.

"Yeah. They finished at the end of August. I was actually surprised how fast they worked. And I only lost my mind a couple of times. The kids were really good about staying out of the way. And things are good between Mike and me. I think we just needed an outside observer to help us work through our issues."

Everyone laughed and watched the four babies squirming around on the blanket.

"Are you ready to go back to work?" Renee asked Lisbeth.

"Yeah. Candace is working a shorter schedule, and since the twins are pretty good about their naptimes, she can bring them to work with her. I'm going to miss them. The school is actually letting me start back earlier than I expected."

"I'm sure they'll miss you, too."

"You still think you made the right choice?" Erika asked.

Lisbeth smiled and said, "Yes. I knew the minute I held them for the first time that we'd made the right choice. It wouldn't have been right to only have one of them."

"How are things with your family?" Shannon asked, smoothing the blanket by Aiden's head.

Lisbeth shrugged. "They've seen the twins a bunch of times. Mom adores them. They babysat a couple weekends ago when we went out to dinner. Our first real date since we brought them home in April."

"Have they said anything about...?" Renee trailed off.

"They are civil to Candace and have even called her my partner, so I think I should be happy with that. They're back in my life, and they'll get to know their grandchildren. That's all I can ask for. Besides, Elena's been great."

"That's great. I knew they couldn't stay away once Rachel and Patrick came along," Shannon said.

"So, It's September, and a certain somebody hasn't opened their *other* boyfriend's present yet," Renee said, prodding Erika.

"He's not my *other* boyfriend."

"Just your super-hot friend who you still think about kissing sometimes. If you don't want him, can I have him?" Renee asked.

"He is pretty cute," Shannon agreed.

Erika spun the small box between her fingers and laughed at her friends. "I guess you can have him. Just be gentle with him."

"Come on. I want to know what he got you," Lisbeth said.

"Okay, okay."

Erika unwrapped the package and pulled the top from the box. A golden coin with her name etched in one side sat nestled against a little red velvet pillow. She picked it up and turned it over. The other side simply said one year.

"There's a note in there," Shannon said.

Erika didn't bother with the note, so Shannon reached over and picked it up. She unfolded it and read it aloud.

"It says, 'Erika I had this made for you while I was away. You deserve something special on your first anniversary of sobriety.'"

"That's so sweet," Renee said.

"He had it made for me. I...I can't believe he did that."

"I can," Lisbeth said. "He's a good guy, and he really wants to see you succeed."

"How am I supposed to say thank you?"

"With your mouth," Renee teased.

Erika blushed and snatched the note back from Shannon. She tucked it back in the box and stuck it in her purse for safekeeping.

"How have things been with the two of you?" Lisbeth asked, nodding her head at Erika and Renee.

"It was hard at first when Renee brought Alyssa home. I broke down a few times, but I'm good now. It was just harder than I thought it would be."

"What about you and Bryce?" Shannon asked.

"It's going okay. I mean, he's forgotten a couple of times, but so far, he hasn't done anything stupid while he's had her. So I guess I can't complain."

Shannon nodded and watched Erika fish something out of her purse. "Michelle and Andrew sent this to me the other day."

She passed around the photograph of Peter, and everyone said how cute he was and how big he was getting.

"They say he's doing really well. Not really delayed that much. Though I guess it doesn't show up until he gets older."

"That's great. Are you still happy you gave him up?" Lisbeth asked.

"Yeah. I am. I wasn't ready for all of this. Next time—and there will be one—I'll be ready."

"Maybe we all will," Renee mused.

"Oh no. Four is my limit," Shannon said.

"And I think we used all of our good luck with Rachel and Patrick," Lisbeth agreed.

Beside them, Rachel rolled over and landed partially atop her brother. Alyssa half-crawled, half-wormed her way closer to the other babies and reached out her hand toward Aiden's arm. He cried out as she pinched it. From his position beneath his sister, Patrick kicked out a leg, and Alyssa released her grip.

"She's never done that before," Renee said, giving Shannon an apologetic look.

"She's probably never had anyone her size around that she can play with."

"Well, that's going to change. They can't very well go through all of their milestones alone," Renee said.

"You're right. We'll just have to bring them along when we get together so they have each other to play with," Erika said.

Acknowledgements

First and foremost, I need to thank my parents for believing in me and encouraging me to follow my dreams. Without them, I don't think this book would have come about. A big thanks goes out to the team at Musa Publishing for taking a chance on me back in 2012. They allowed me to share Shannon, Lisbeth, Renee and Erika's journey with the world for the first time. I'd be remiss if I didn't also mention Sharon, my lovely editor, without whom I couldn't have combated all of that repetitive phrasing and exclamation point overuse. You were a joy to work with.

I have to give a shout out to Lori and Nena for muddling through those early drafts and imparting their invaluable advice and suggestions which made this book so much stronger and the characters so much deeper. In an odd way, I also need to say thank you to Professor Greenberg, who taught my Torts class my first semester of law school. If it hadn't been for her, I'm not sure this story would have even taken shape.

About the Author

Sarah lives in Massachusetts with her boyfriend. She is a licensed attorney and spends her days combatting employment discrimination as an Investigator with the Massachusetts Commission Against Discrimination.

Unplanned is her debut novel and quite appropriately, was inspired by a course during her first year of law school. Sarah is a self-professed TV junkie and in her spare time (what's that?), she runs a TV recap blog with her best friend (and sorority sister), Jen.

You can connect with Sarah at her website: www.sarah-biglow.com and follow her on Twitter @SBiglowWrites.

For those TV-obsessed souls, you can head on over to the recap blog: www.more-tv-please.com. You can also follow the blog on Twitter @MoreTVPlease and check it out on Facebook: https://www.facebook.com/MoreTVPlease.

Made in the USA
Middletown, DE
29 December 2017